GW01086921

To Sue

Best wishes and thanks

- Craig

Remnant Tales of Stilly:
Passion and Benevolence

By Craig J Stanford

Remnant Tales of Stilly:
Passion and Benevolence

Author's Note and Acknowledgements

This book has been a long time coming. I started writing a draft in 2007 in my spare time, usually in the evenings and after work. Unhappy with my job, I decided to distract myself with writing. I had a handful of characters with different personalities and a simple idea for a story, but developing that story has proven difficult and has taken years to put together. For a long while, and as my mood became low, I lacked the will to get on with the story, and what I did write, I disliked. As a result, I effectively gave up.

In 2009, I was made redundant. I returned to the story and rewrote everything, changing ideas, character traits, and writing style. In 2012, I came to know a company named Brentwood Community Print (BCP), a local interest group that specialised in helping adults who, at some point, have suffered mental health difficulties. A printing shop, BCP aimed to help such people rebuild their confidence and get them back into paid work.

Owing to the patience and support of those at BCP, and in between helping in the shop, I could work on this book and finally complete it. With that in mind, I have many people to thank.

I am grateful to all who worked at BCP for showing an interest in my novel, especially Tim Warncken and Tony Merritt, who had more confidence than I did in publishing it. Additionally, thanks to Tony for being my mentor and support.

My parents have been an enormous benefit to me. Their endless support and patience allowed me to see this project through.

Thank you, Tony Clarke, for introducing me to BCP.

Thank you, Mrs Warncken, among others, for proofreading the story. A fresh pair of eyes helps when it comes to reading a manuscript.

A special thank you to my family and friends for your interest in my work, and last but not least, my gratitude to those who have picked up my book. I hope that you enjoy the story.

Remnant Tales of Stilly:
Passion and Benevolence

**For Brentwood Community Print,
2012 - 2020.**

Remnant Tales of Stilly:
Passion and Benevolence

Places.

Pronunciations are bracketed.

Adelaide: (ah-dee-layd) Southwest province of Stilly.

Drieloca: (dree-low-ser) Northwest province of Stilly.

Neffaloom: (neff-i-loom) A highly dense region in northwest Drieloca. Seèrt residents fear it.

Pothaven: (pot-hay-vn) Village on the western border of Thane.

Seèrt: (see-ert) Drieloca village.

Stilly: (still-ee) A former kingdom that contains four main regions.

Thane: (thay-n) Eastern province of Stilly.

Wilheard: (will-erd) The capital of Stilly and centremost province; location of Castle Stilly and home of past monarchs.

People.

Abraham Gibenn: (ay-brer-ham gi-bn) Middle-aged father of Ebony Gibenn. A retired carpenter and architect.

Albert Comyns: (al-bert com-inns) Elderly owner of Wilheard's library: Bookish Charm.

Alim Larring: (ah-lim) A scholar from Thane who assumes his grandfather's role.

Basil Wolleb: (ba-zl wor-leb) Mayor of Wilheard.

Remnant Tales of Stilly:
Passion and Benevolence

Benjamin Oswin: (ben-ja-mn oz-win) Assistant of Mayor Wolleb.

Caleb Psoui: (Kah-leb soo-ee) Naitsir ordaiest of Sanct Everard sancture.

Charmion Sanine: (shaar-me-n say-neen) Queen to Doran Sanine and father of Godfrey and Clover Sanine.

Clement Suavlant: (kleh-mnt swar-vlnt) Older brother to Maynard and one of the sovereign knights.

Clover Sanine: (klow-ver say-neen) Younger sister of Godfrey Sanine; daughter of Doran and Charmion Sanine.

Cordelia Lawford: (kor-dee-lee-er lor-fd) Lieutenant to Oliath Burley; female double to Nolan Shakeston.

Darwin Loydon: (dar-win loy-dn) One of the sovereign knights; has a dark past

Dexter Theryle: (dex-ter theh-ry-all) Member of *Other Four*.

Doran Sanine: (dor-rn) King to Charmion Sanine and father of Godfrey and Clover Sanine.

Drah Leets: (dray lee-ts) Wilheard's blacksmith.

Ebony Gibenn: (eh-bo-nee gi-bn) Bookish young woman who lives with her father.

Elgin Hosp: (el-jin ho-sp) One of the sovereign knights.

Remnant Tales of Stilly:
Passion and Benevolence

Emmanuel Grellic: (ee-man-yoo-all greh-lik) Minach of Sanct Everard; good friend and most trusted confidant to Godfrey Sanine; mentor of Evelyn Sanine; author of original Passion and Benevolence.

Evelyn Sanine: (eh-ver-lin say-neen) Daughter of Godfrey and Verity Sanine. Last queen of Stilly.

Fordon Latnemirt: (for-dn lat-ni-mer-t) An aged royal retainer-turned-renegade.

Ghennitteemn Noitanitsa: (gen-i-teem noy-tan-eet-sah) Elderly resident of Seèrt. Ghen Noit for short.

Godfrey Sanine: (god-free say-neen) Last king of Stilly; king to Verity Sanine and father of Evelyn Sanine; older brother to Clover Sanine; son of Doran and Charmion Sanine.

Harold Dolb: (hah-rol-d dol-b) Myrah Dolb's husband and Hazel Dolb's father.

Hazel Dolb: (hay-zl dol-b) A farmer who is childhood friends with Ebony Gibenn. She is the owner of Colossus and the daughter of Harold and Myrah Dolb.

Ithel Olvewhort: (ih-thl ol-vwort) King to Teri [Olvewhort] Sanine and father to Olann Olvewhort.

Lilac Firs: (ly-lak fers) Joint owner of the gunpowder shop Blow Your Mind!, which she runs with albino twin brother Whitaker Firs.

Luanna Gibenn: (loo-an-er gi-bn) Late wife to Abraham Gibenn and mother to Ebony Gibenn.

Remnant Tales of Stilly:
Passion and Benevolence

Malcolm Psoui is (mal-com soo-ee) The husband of Rose Psoui and father of Caleb Psoui.

Maynard Suavlant: (may-nerd swar-vlnt) One of the sovereign knights; younger brother to Clement Suavlant.

Meddia Penrose: (meh-dee-er pen-ro-z) A member of *Other Four*. Despite the shared name, Wiley is not directly related to her.

Mikki Sanine: (mih-kee say-neen) Queen to Theodore and mother of Teri [Olvewhort] Sanine.

Mrs Whickett: (wih-ket) Sauce specialist from Thane.

Myrah Dolb: (my-reh dol-b) Wife of Harold Dolb and mother of Hazel Dolb.

Nolan Shakeston: (no-ln sh-ayk-ston) Lieutenant to Oliath; male double to Cordelia Lawford.

Olann Olvewhort: (o-ln ol-vwort) Prince and son of Teri [Olvewhort] Sanine and Ithel Olvewhort.

Oliath Burley: (or-ly-erth ber-lee) Captain of the Guard; personal boss to Nolan, Cordelia and *Other Four*.

Paul Sanine: (po-l say-neen) Prince and younger brother of Teri [Olvewhort] Sanine and father of Doran Sanine.

Mr Relles: (reh-lih-ss) Merchant from Thane.

Rida Priory: (ree-der pry-er-ee) A member of *Other Four*.

Rose Psoui: (ro-z soo-ee) Wife of Malcom Psoui and mother of Caleb Psoui.

Sombie: (som-bee) Ninapaige's given nickname for the mysterious vigilante.

[The] Snake: (snay-k) A career criminal living in Wilheard.

Sylvia Enpee: (sill-vee-er en-pee) Doctor from Pothaven.

Ted Larring: (ted lah-ring) Grandfather to Alim Larring; rewriter of Emmanuel Grellic's Passion and Benevolence.

Teri [Olvewhort] Sanine: (teh-ree ol-vwart say-neen) Queen to Ithel Olvewhort and mother to Olann Olvewhort. Sister to Paul Sanine.

Theodore Sanine: (th-ee-o-dor say-neen) Earliest recorded king of Stilly; king to Mikki Sanine and father of Teri [Olvewhort] Sanine.

Verity Sanine: (veh-rih-tee say-neen) Queen to Godfrey Sanine and mother of Evelyn Sanine.

Vincent Sawney: (vin-snt sor-nee) Retired captain of the guard who is now Wilheard's butcher.

Whitaker Firs: (wih-tih-ker fers) Joint owner of the gunpowder shop Blow Your Mind!, which he runs with albino twin sister Lilac Firs.

Wiley Penrose: (wy-lee pen-ro-z) A member of *Other Four*. Despite the shared name, Meddia is not directly related to him.

Creatures, nonhumans & Deities.

Anjyl: (ahn-jell) Naitsir angel.

Colossus Dolb: (coe-lo-sus dol-b) Great Dane owned by Hazel Dolb.

Daloug: (day-low-g) Long-bodied dragons that come in different sizes; created by Fordon Latnemirt.

Lithe: (ly-th) Shire horse belonging to Maynard.

Livnam: (liv-nam) Plural of livnom.

Livnom: (liv-nom) Naitsir demon.

Livomic: (liv-or-mik) Resembling livnom.

Ninapaige: (nee-na-pay-j) Two-foot female jester with a liking for masks; Creation of Rosaleen.

Redifass: (reh-dee-fass) Humanoid creature created by Fordon Latnemirt. There are three types: Skirmisher, Warrior and Brute.

Rosaleen: (roz-a-leen) Banished ytied; creator of Ninapaige and Omnipotent.

Suoidi: (soo-ee-dye) Plural of suoido.

Suoido: (soo-ee-doe) Beast created by Fordon Latnemirt.

Traeh: (tray) Naitsir God.

Ytied: (yee-ty-d). An ancient and mysterious race believed by some to be gods due to their apparent creationism. The word Ytied is singular and plural.

Ytiedinity: (yee-ty-din-itee) Ytied as a species, as how *humanity* relates to *humans*.

Miscellaneous.

AS: Initials of Afore Stilly.

Ardruism: (aar-droo-ih-zm) Gold and silver greatsword.

Ascendancy: (ah-sen-dn-see) Sapphire crafted by Fordon Latnemirt.

Fair Eve: Formal greeting: good evening.

Fair Morn: Formal greeting: good morning.

Fair Noon: Formal greeting: good afternoon.

Gransanture: (gran-sang-turr) A large sancture akin to a cathedral. It is shortened to Gransanct before a name.

Lunsser: (lun-ser) A flintlock pistol.

Minach: (min-aark) High-ranking ordaiest; similar to a minister.

Naitsir: (nayt-ser) Most recognised religion in Stilly.

Omnipotent: (om-nih-poh-tnt) Orb created by Rosaleen.

Ordaiest: (or-day-ist) A naitsir clergyman/clergywoman.

[The] Other Four: Group working specifically for Oliath Burley. Members: Dexter, Wiley, Meddia and Rida.

Pentominto: (pen-too-min-toh) Written language of ytied and foundation of magic.

Phyeroc: (fy-rok) Pentominto word meaning prophecy.

Sancture: (sang-turr) Religious building. Akin to a church. It is shortened to Sanct when in a name.

Sanct Everard: (sang-kt ev-raard) Sancture of Wilheard.

SN: Initials of Stilly Naissance.

Sovereign Knights: (so-vrin ny-ts) Four warriors who served the monarch and realm during King Godfrey Sanine's reign. Members: Maynard and Clement Suavlant, Darwin Loydon and Elgin Hosp.

Stillian: (still-ee-n) Name given to the peoples or objects of Stilly. The spoken language of Stilly.

Castle Stilly: (still-ee car-sl/ca-sl) Castle residing in Wilheard.

Stinnep/Stinneps: (stin-ip) Stilly's form of currency.

Tender spirits: Denotes surprise, bother or anger.

Traehen: (tray-n) That of, or pertaining to, Traeh.

Ytyism: (yee-tiz-m) A complex and ancient magical art associated with ytied.

Remnant Tales of Stilly:
Passion and Benevolence

Stillian Flag

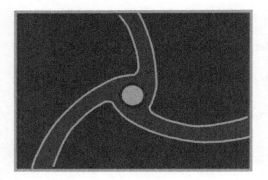

Prologue

Spring 1784SN

Trotting against the harsh wind whistling through the trees of eastern Wilheard, two stallions towing a simple wooden cart made a sharp stop, snorting as their master tugged on their reins.

Sitting at the front of the cart, the merchant in control of the beasts peered round to the four people sitting under the canopy that sheltered his cargo. 'I believe this is your stop, Ms.'

Shifting her feet towards the cart's rear, a woman wearing a dark cloak jumped clumsily to the soaked ground below, splashing mud up her legs. Pulling back the hood of her cloak and releasing her hair, she looked round at the darkness surrounding her. Shuddering, she pulled her jacket tight as a wind blew over her dampened body. She bit gently down on her bottom lip. She was nervous, perhaps unsurprising, considering the circumstances: it had been almost ten years since she was last here. Had it *really* been that long?

'Are you sure you'll be all right,' the merchant said with a hint of concern. 'I hate to leave a lady alone in such a place.'

The woman brushed her blonde hair behind her ears and regarded the merchant with a meek smile. She placed a silver stinnep coin on the wooden plank that made his seat.

Picking up the coin, the merchant rubbed his thumb over its surface and held it under the lantern hooked up next to him. The coin glinted in the dull light. 'Wilheard is in that direction', he pointed before prompting the horses onwards. 'Take care, Ms.'

The woman watched the cart disappear into the darkness, taking with it the yellow light of the lantern. She looked once more through the dense woodland and sighed. Although the past decade had taught her to avoid isolation in such places, it was for the best. Even as she sat in the cart, she could feel their glower: the invisible livnam eyes that intruded into her life all those years ago. She did not want those innocent travellers to get hurt because of her.

The eyes spied her from within the treetops, scanning her face with confusion. Was she the one they wanted? The scent suggested as much, even if her appearance did not. Time has altered her in more ways than she cared to consider. The cynic in her insisted that the adverse changes far outweighed the positive, but at least she was more ready for the dangers that might lie ahead. Whatever the case, she was unwilling to stand and let the eyes burn into her soul a moment longer. Now was the time to go—and to go quickly.

Remnant Tales of Stilly:
Passion and Benevolence

She ran as fast as her cold legs would allow, darting between the many trees while jumping over puddles and other pitfalls as she headed in what she hoped was the right direction. The eyes grew weaker, but she knew she must not stop yet. They were losing her, but she would not look back; she must not look back. Thankfully, the merchant had led her true. Clawing lank hair from her sight, the woman could finally see tiny dots of light. A smile creased her face, her tear-reddened eyes stinging as she forced them to stay open. She had done it. She had finally reached Wilheard after all these years.

Out of the forest, the woman was now safe from the dangers that lurked within. However, one pair of eyes had retained their target.

Hiding within the leaves, a yellow-and-grey-clad figure wearing a mischievous grin peered over the sleeping town. 'Oh, Sylvia. Did you honestly believe you could escape my notice? Foolish girl.'

The being giggled and placed a mask with a cheerful design over her face. Her gaze shifted towards Stilly's castle. 'Not to worry, my child, for it seems the time of your return has come. Spring is a time of bloom, and soon, the fruits of your exertions will truly blossom'.

Remnant Tales of Stilly:
Passion and Benevolence

Chapter One
Summer 1784SN

The morning sun rose over Wilheard, bathing the town with warm colours.
Typically, during this time of year the early sun does not receive much notice
from most, but a minority always appreciates the extra light at such hours.
Wilheard, the smallest province of Stilly, was no different.

Farmers awakened early to sort dairy produce, ready for delivery; bakers
made haste to their ovens to prepare their high-in-demand variety of bread;
and drowsy night soldiers surrendered their posts for freshly awakened
comrades. However, one individual was also awake that summer morning.

A cottage sat near the south of Wilheard, following a foot-trodden path
that led up a hill. In the house, Ebony Gibenn, a woman of twenty-eight
years, lay wide awake in bed, thinking of the busy day ahead. Unlike others
throughout town, work was not on her mind.

Ebony turned on her side and stared out the window of her bedroom. The
house was almost silent: the chirping birds outside and the ticking of the old
clock hanging at the farthest end of the upstairs landing were the most
audible sounds. That was, save for the word *change* echoing in her head.
Jaded by her routine life, Ebony had been thinking of change for the past
week, but now she decided it was time for action.

Snapping from her daydream, she tugged at her bedcover and swung her
legs out. The wooden floor, squeaking with a low creak as she stood on it,
was pleasantly warm under her bare feet. Walking towards the window, she
stretched her sleep-stiffened body before leaning on the open window frame
to inhale the morning air; with the sun not yet over the horizon, its light cast
rays of lengthy shadows across the misty landscape. It was quite a sight.

It's beautiful but not unique, Ebony thought. She murmured the
word *change*, turned from the window and moved towards her wardrobe.

Standing in front of the wardrobe, Ebony stifled a yawn. She had not slept
well the past few days, which was becoming more evident as the week
passed. Although able to fall asleep quickly, she could not maintain her
slumber, frequently awakening throughout the night. Despite being a nightly
occurrence, this recent insomnia did not strike her as unusual. After all, the
cause was merely a result of bad dreams, which eventually pass, even if these
nightmares are also recent.

Ebony opened her wardrobe, the door hinges whining as she did so. She
fingered through her selection of clothing, counting them as she did so.
Taking a step backwards, she sighed. The content was pitiful. Overlooking

trousers and shirts mainly for labouring work (that amassed unloved to one side) and numerous pieces of winter attire, the wardrobe contained just five dresses: one brown, one yellow and three blue. The footwear also failed to inspire much enthusiasm: consisting of two pairs of outdoor slippers, one black and the other brown; a pair of formal shoes with slightly-raised heels; ill-fitting work boots designed for men; and a pair of boots that looked a little too risqué. Even though Ebony did not like them much, the lattermost boots were at least functional in winter and hardly noticeable under a long coat.

Ebony pulled out the sleeveless yellow dress and laid it on the bed. A thin smile played on her lips as she stared at the clothing. It had been a while since she had worn this one, something its dusty smell confirmed. Ebony wore the dress and gazed at the mirror leaning against her bedroom wall. It measured tightly but comfortably over her slim figure. She was pleased to see it still fit after all this time.

Brushing her fringe behind her ear, Ebony looked at her face, her deep-brown eyes staring back. *Mother had never been keen on this one*, she thought. Ebony's mother Luanna had always said it did not contrast well with her eyes. Ebony had considered the comment odd; she had never seen someone with yellow eyes. The remark was Luanna's way of saying that she did not think yellow suited her daughter, and although Ebony disagreed at the time, she could now see why her mother may have felt that way. The dress was bright, and it had not faded at all over the years.

Luanna had died ten years ago. Before her death, she had given Ebony a small, heart-shaped crystal, stating that the stone was generations old. Luanna told Ebony to take care of the jewel, telling her it would bring good luck. Although the idea of the crystal being a good luck charm was childish, Ebony had appreciated the appeal. It served as little more than a memento now, but at least that was something.

Ebony woke from her reverie, her attention disturbed by a loud snort from the room next door. Her father Abraham was snoring. She forced a smile. Thinking about her mother had naturally surfaced emotions, but she was determined not to spend the day sulking.

'Change,' she muttered to her reflection one last time, stepping into the brown shoes she had also pulled from the wardrobe and exiting the room.

Remnant Tales of Stilly:
Passion and Benevolence

Desperate not to disturb her father, Ebony gently closed the cottage's front door before pulling a timepiece from her hand basket: 6.30am.

Closing her eyes and inhaling deeply through her nose, Ebony once again took in the morning scent of her hometown. Rainfall had been sparse lately, leaving the air dry and greenery parched. Still, the summer sun would provide an improved mood for what she hoped to achieve and give her the enthusiasm to go through with it. Whatever the weather, today would be fun, and that was something about which she could be glad.

Ebony made her way down the well-trodden path that led from her home and walked in the direction of the town market. Rabbits hopping at the edge of the eastern woodland pricked their ears, disturbed by the sounds of her footsteps. She pursed her lips and made kissing sounds at the creatures, causing them to wiggle their noses and bound away. Ebony smirked and continued her walk down the trail, humming a tune as she went.

Wilheard certainly had a lot of charisma, and from Ebony's current view, its charm was easy to see. Buildings of many shapes and sizes formed modest market squares and winding streets. Over the crooked roofs of these buildings, older structures towered above, noticeably that of Clock Tower. This tower compensated for the lack of a clock on Sanct Everard, the sancture, which sat several blocks away and north of town. Sanct Everard, although just over half the size of Clock Tower, rose above most of the other buildings in Wilheard, exerting itself as the third tallest building in the town. The most prominent architecture was the tallest, beyond the sancture and on a steep hill away from the other structures: Castle Stilly.

As she reached the town market, Ebony paused to examine the long street of New Market Square. The thoroughfare, lined with stalls, was already coming to life with people going about their business. Mingling with crowds was not one of her favourite events, so she would spend only a little time dallying, therefore avoiding the inevitable bustling that would come later. Besides, she needed to do some errands, and the sooner she completed them, the sooner she could get on with the things she wanted.

As she passed the various merchants shouting out what they had to offer, Ebony stopped at a stall selling an assortment of clothing. The elderly stall owner smiled at Ebony, revealing a mouth full of crooked teeth. 'Fair morn,' the old woman said hoarsely. 'Would the pretty young lady be interested in a new pretty dress?'

Ebony smiled back and browsed through the dresses on offer, pausing upon noticing a cream dress.

'Ah, yes,' the old woman crooned, 'a pretty dress that complements your lovely complexion. It will surely bring out those eyes.'

Ebony cringed inwardly at the intended flattery. 'Thank you. Perhaps another time.'

Money was not something Ebony had in abundance, so purchasing new clothing was not a luxury in which she could indulge. That was a pity, considering the dismal assortment in her wardrobe, and it would have helped with the whole focus on *change*. Ebony's ideals, especially when they involved money, often came second, and she decided that her father's welfare should come first.

After Luanna's disappearance, Abraham never recovered. Her father's despondency left Ebony thinking of ways to lift her father's mood, and perhaps today, cooking his favourite meal would be a good start. Although not particularly finicky when it came to anything cooked, Abraham had a soft spot for chicken, and adding some vegetables and a sauce dressing would complement it. To make this possible, however, Ebony would need to buy the ingredients.

The first stall she visited was one of fruit and vegetables. The stand belonged to a portly man named Harold Dolb, a friend of Abraham and father of Ebony's best friend Hazel. Harold sat on a barrel to one side of his stall, his attention away from his stock. A mischievous boy in dishevelled clothing, playing with another boy and a girl, noticed Harold's lack of awareness. The boy's two friends pointed at Harold's stall before whispering to each other. In what seemed to Ebony as a dare, the boy sneaked up to the stall, his eyes drawn to a shiny red apple. Licking his lips and keeping one eye on Harold, the boy took the fruit from its pile before wheeling round to escape. Unluckily for the child, he had not heard Ebony approach the stand, resulting in him bumping into her.

'Oomph!' the boy grunted as he crashed into Ebony. The other two children gasped.

Harold turned back to his stall. The boy's lips trembled as the moustachioed owner glowered at him. 'What's *this*?' Harold said, snatching the apple from the child's hand. 'Have you enough stinneps to pay for this, boy?'

'I-I'm really s-sorry, mister,' the boy stuttered. 'It was just a little bit of fun.'

'Fun?' Harold bellowed back.

Ebony rolled her eyes upon noticing the child's unease (who must have thought his life would end). Placing a coin on the stand, Ebony forced a stern expression. 'I'll pay for the apple this time, young man'—she put another apple in his hand—'but if I catch you trying to steal again, then I will have no choice but to inform the guards. Understood?'

'Yes, Miss—thank you, Miss,' the boy replied, running away with his friends.

Harold gently shook his head and turned to face Ebony, his anger disappearing as quickly as it had come. 'Generous as ever,' the stall owner said, smiling and handing the coin for the apple back to her. 'Fair morn, dear. I hope you are well.'

'Fair morn to you too, Mister Dolb. I am well, thank you. How are you?

'Toiling along. I'm all the better now that I have seen you.'

'That's good. What about Myrah? I haven't seen her in what seems like ages.'

'The wife is sticking her nose where it don't belong, as usual, bless her. Come to think of it, she has made a new friend—a doctor at the surgery or something—and keeps insisting that she wants to introduce your old man to her.'

'Does she now? Well, I am not sure how Father will react to that. He doesn't care much for surprises.'

'That's what I keep telling her, but she's having none of it. I have to keep my eye on that woman.'

Ebony smiled and looked behind Harold. 'What was holding your attention a moment ago?'

Harold turned and made a low groan. 'I was just spying that crowd over there,' he said, gesturing with his thumb.

Remnant Tales of Stilly:
Passion and Benevolence

Ebony peered over to the small gathering that was surrounding a vacant house. The crowd mainly consisted of townspeople, but Ebony noticed several reporters questioning a man who stood at the centre of the commotion. This man was Oliath Burley, Captain of the Guard.

Oliath, a tall and muscular man, stood fists-on-hips as he watched two guards lead a suspect away. By the looks of things, he had impeded a robbery with the help of his most loyal soldiers. This was not unusual; the captain was expected to perform such duties as a highly trained warrior who held a distinguishable position in Wilheard's armed forces. That fact did not stop the news reporters present from their fawning.

A man wearing an undersized top hat and a woman with long, pretty hair alternately questioned Oliath. In an attempt to get answers, the pair used words that they believed would bolster the captain's ego but instead came across as superficial and condescending.

'What a tough guy!' Top Hat said. 'Fair morn, Captain Burley—I'm from The Wilheard Chronicles. Would you care to elaborate on what happened last night? Is there a new recruit in Wilheard's army, or are you being replaced? Rumours suggest it is the latter.'

'Nothing too serious,' Oliath replied, not acknowledging the reporter's gibe. He continued to watch the troops lead the perpetrator away. 'More or less the same as what you lot have been writing about for the past ten or so days.'

'Nothing serious? You're such a confident hero, even in the face of competition.' Pretty Hair said, joining the conversation. 'I'm from Village Express. I'm sure most of Wilheard is not as blasé as you. Please, Captain Burley, put the people's minds at ease by telling us more.'

'Look,' Oliath said. 'There is word of a vigilante about town, but that does not mean that he—whoever he is—is competition. All you need to know is that the suspect was apprehended quickly and without struggle. As you know, this building is unoccupied; therefore, nothing valuable will have been taken. An investigation will follow shortly, and there is no threat to Wilheard's people.'

Top Hat and Pretty Hair exchanged confused looks.

'The suspect… was arrested without struggle?' Top Hat said.

'That's what I said, yes,' Oliath answered.

'Really?' Pretty Hair said.

Oliath frowned. 'Tender spirits—yes! What's the problem?'

At the front of the crowd, a bystander snorted his distaste at the captain. Oliath and the reporters looked at the man, who was now shaking his head and tutting. 'The *problem* the young lady has might be something to do with that rather sizable hole.' The man made a vague gesture towards the hollow before exhaling an overstressed breath. 'Considering the apparent ease of the apprehension, it is a shame that you could not prevent damage being caused to the building.'

Oliath glowered at the man and turned to look at the house. Positioned at the lower-left corner was an opening that appeared large enough for a carthorse to pass through. Caressing his chin, Oliath hummed pensively. 'Yes, it is strange, but the man who made it was even stranger... he did not look like someone in his usual state of mind.'

'What was that, Captain Burley?' said Top Hat. 'We didn't quite catch what you said there.'

Oliath snapped out of his daydream and faced the crowd once more. 'Never mind—forget that I said anything. As I mentioned, an investigation will take place soon. You can find out more when that has concluded.'

'Is that a new dress?' Harold asked Ebony.

'Pardon,' Ebony replied, looking towards Harold Dolb once again. 'Sorry, I was distracted.'

'I was just asking if that's a new dress. I could swear you usually favour less vibrant colours?'

Ebony brushed her hands down her dress, clearing away several aphids attracted to its yellow. 'No. I have had it a long time, in fact.'

'Either way, it looks nice on you, dear.'

'Thank you. I think the greenflies share your sentiment.' Ebony selected a small variety of vegetables. 'What's going on over there, anyway?' She said, nodding towards the damaged house.

'I know nothing about that, dear. Only what I've read in yesterday's news. Harold patted a newspaper that lay on the edge of the stand.

Remnant Tales of Stilly:
Passion and Benevolence

The Wilheard Chronicles

Vandalism is on the rise in Wilheard. Some people from out of town, The Wilheard Chronicles can report, have caused most of these damages, but a few locals are also involved.

Yesterday, two windows belonging to one of the back rooms of Wilheard Hall suffered damages.

Captain of the Guard Oliath Burley had attended the crime scene some 15 minutes after the alarm was raised. Although reacting relatively slowly to the signal, Captain Burley, with his team, prevented any significant robbery, and only a gem (said to be counterfeit and low in cost) had been taken. Peculiarly, soldiers could not find the item on the unconscious suspect, leading to the possibility of there being further suspects.

The Wilheard Chronicles spoke to Captain Burley about the Wilheard Hall incident. When questioned about what happened, he stated, "As with similar incidents, nothing of value has been taken, and the suspect will be interrogated when conscious."

When asked about his response time to the crime scene, Captain Burley did not comment.

After reading the front page, Ebony looked back at Harold. He was holding out wrapped paper containing Ebony's goods. 'We are living in troubling times, dear,' he groaned, shaking his head. 'Stay away from trouble and look after yourself, you hear me?'

Ebony gave a slow nod as she placed the package in her basket. 'You know me, Mister Dolb,' she said, leaving some coins on the stall for the vegetables.

'I do, my dear, and in that respect, you're just like my daughter. Give my regards to your father.'

Remnant Tales of Stilly:
Passion and Benevolence

A small bell chimed as Ebony opened the door belonging to a butcher shop.

Vincent Sawney, a man nearly seven feet tall, stood behind the counter with his back turned to any potential customers. Holding a cleaver that seemed too large to be ordinary, the butcher brought the blade down on a piece of meat, cutting it in two with one chop. Ebony grimaced as she watched Vincent at work. It took a second chime as the door closed for him to stop what he was doing.

Twisting his head, Vincent saw Ebony's slim figure come into view. He put down his knife, grabbed a cloth and turned properly to greet his customer. 'Well... if it ain't young Ebony,' Vincent said, wiping his hands. 'And 'ow are you on this fine morning?'

'I am very well, thank you, Mister Sawney. I trust that you are as well?

'Aye, lass, I can't complain.' Vincent replied, splaying his hands on the meat display. They looked three times the size of Ebony's hands. 'So what can I do for ya?'

Ebony stepped closer to the counter and glanced at the produce on offer. Vincent peered down at her. Along with his rugged face and coarse voice, his size often frightened people, even more so when noticing the battle scar to the side of his left eye. Having known him from a young age, Ebony did not share other people's unease. As a girl, she had once asked Vincent about the (as she put it then) ugly scar. He had simply smiled at the comment. As a man who enjoyed storytelling, he had been happy to explain. Yet, because of Ebony's age at the time, he had left out the more macabre details and stated that he got it in an unfortunate disagreement while guard captain.

'I will have a chicken, please. A small one like that.' Ebony pointed to her choice.

'Comin' right up. Jus' for you, I'll get an even fresher one.'

Vincent went to his storage room to retrieve a chicken similar to the one on display. Ducking under the doorway on his return, he placed the poultry on a pile of kraft paper. 'So... what's this all about, love?' Vincent said as he prepared the meat. 'Chicken ain't *your* usual dish.'

Ebony nodded in agreement. Chickens were one of the dearer items on offer. 'It's for Father. I thought I would cook him something different for dinner.'

'I see. A treat?'

Ebony nodded again.

'That's nice of ya, lass. It'll make a nice change, to be sure.'

Ebony looked down at her dress. 'Yes, and as it happens, I am very much in the mood for change.'

'Oh, right,' Vincent said, finally noticing the dress. 'I thought there were something different 'bout ya. For some reason, I couldn't put my finger on it. You look nice, lass.'

Ebony responded with a smile. 'Thank you.'

Vincent finished preparing his sale and gently pushed it across the counter. 'There we are—one chicken. Will there be anythin' else?'

'I don't suppose you sell any sauces suitable for marinating chicken, do you?'

Vincent raised his eyebrows in pretend hurt feelings. 'Of course I do! What kind of shoddy business do you think I run 'ere?' Vincent moved to a cupboard in a corner of the room. He ran his finger along a collection of bottles. 'What do you 'ave in mind, lass? I've Mint, Chutney, Malt and Balsamic vinegar, even Sherry vinegar—if you're into that kind of thing.'

'Actually, I was thinking more like a cream tomato sauce.'

'Ah right, I get-cha.' Vincent scratched his head as he looked at the bottles. 'I'll just look round back.'

As she waited for Vincent to return, Ebony looked out the shop window and watched the people outside. Peering past the increasing crowd, the vandalised building behind Harold's stand again grabbed her attention. The immediate area was almost empty except for half a dozen guards to deter looters and a few newspaper sketch artists.

Short of a minute after leaving the shop floor, Vincent re-entered with something in hand. 'Is this similar to somethin' you wanted?'

Ebony jolted.

'Sorry, lass. I didn't mean to make you jump,' the butcher said, putting a glass jar on the serving counter for Ebony to see.

'I was miles away.' Ebony picked up the cubic jar and rotated it between her palms to find a label.

Mrs Whickett's Recipes
Creamy Tomato Sauce
Contains garlic and traces of salt & pepper.
Made in Thane, Stilly.

'This is exactly what I am looking for. Thank you.'

'As always, it is my pleasure, lass,' Vincent said as he priced the sale. 'That'll be five coppers if you'd be so kind.'

Ebony picked out five bronze stinnep coins and stacked them neatly on the counter.

'Cheers, Love,' said Vincent, scooping up the money. 'Do you want me to 'old on to these to save you carryin' them about, or are you going straight 'ome today?'

Ebony took a moment to think. She had planned on going to a few other places before returning home. 'Now that you mention it, that sounds like a good idea,' she said as she left the shop. 'Thanks again, Mister Sawney.'

8.02am.

Time was passing by quickly, more so than Ebony had initially realised. Now was the time for most of the townspeople to be out of bed, ready to take what the new day would throw at them. That, it seemed, involved adding oneself to the daily rush of pedestrians and cart-pulling horses.

Continuing her errands about Wilheard, Ebony entered the northwest of the town and away from the crowd. After a short walk, she stopped to rest her arms on a wooden fence enclosing a sheep pasture. The sheep and other animals belonged to Wilheard's farm, which also owned a windmill and a small body of water. It was a lot quieter, the calm bleating of sheep replacing the activity of New Market Square.

Ebony gazed blurry-eyed into the middle distance. *Ho-hum—peaceful but dull,* she thought. *What I wouldn't do for a bit more excitement.*

25

Remnant Tales of Stilly:
Passion and Benevolence

Ebony turned her attention to the barn upon hearing a high-pitched whistle. Hazel, a well-toned, slim woman and one of the farm's owners, was walking towards Ebony with a raised eyebrow and a twisted smile. 'I had a feeling I would see you today.'

Hazel stood on the other side of the fence, placing her hands on her hips. Her golden hair, braided into a single ponytail, shined under the sunlight.

'Yikes!' Hazel said as she reached Ebony. 'Are you trying to blind people with that dress?'

Ebony grinned. 'It is a bit garish, I suppose.'

'Just a bit. How are ya anyway, Ebs?'

'I am well, thank you. Yourself?'

'Busy as always, m'dear—but what's new?' Hazel leant back against the fence and breathed deeply. 'At any rate, what are you doing loitering near my territory?'

'I'm admiring the scenery while enjoying the weather.'

'Is that so?' Hazel snorted. 'You might get sunstroke if you stand there too long.'

'You're not envious, are you?'

Hazel turned her head to face Ebony and once again cocked a brow. 'Perhaps,' she said with a languid smile. 'But perhaps not. Despite my love for the sun, it does make my work that much harder. If you are wanting something from me, we should go into the windmill first. I could do with getting some shade.'

'All right,' Ebony said, brushing her hands down her dress for what seemed like the fiftieth time. 'Maybe the greenflies will leave me alone then.'

In the farmhouse, Ebony sat beside a desk amassed with paper and books scattered over its surface. Like the desk, the flooring was messy; animal fur and dust coated the whole area. Indeed, cleanliness was not something Ebony and Hazel had in common.

Hazel dashed between the living room and kitchen of the windmill as she prepared several orders, one of which was Ebony's request for eggs and cow's milk. The building was small for a two-storey house, excluding that of the windmill, but Hazel was content with what she had. She lived with her parents, Harold and Myrah Dolb, and dog Colossus, a beige Great Dane with a large brown patch on its left side. Watching Hazel rushing about made Ebony tired. She yawned and gently scratched behind Colossus's ears. The dog groaned with gratification and rested his chin on Ebony's lap.

'Did you hear about what happened this morning?' Ebony said, hoping a bit of talking would keep her from yawning further.

Hazel continued to rush about the windmill. 'Are you talking about that old house near the market stalls?'

Ebony nodded.

'Yes. After dropping Mum's harvest off to my pop, I rode past Oliath Burley and his crew. Before that, I had heard some banging and crashing coming from what sounded like that direction, but…'

Hazel paused, her pace slowing. This hesitation piqued Ebony's interest. 'But *what*?'

Hazel frowned and stopped her movement completely. 'Well…' She looked at Ebony. 'This will sound weird, but when I looked to find out what all the noise was about, I'm sure I saw bright light shoot from the windows— light too strong to be confused with a candle or the like.'

Ebony did not answer. She peered down at Colossus, whose head was still resting on her legs. The dog shifted its gaze to meet Ebony's eyes.

'Anyway, Ebs,' Hazel continued. 'I'd appreciate it if that was kept between you, me and Colossus… I don't want people gawping at me like I've lost it.'

Ebony said nothing, her expression deadpan.

'You believe me, though, right?' Hazel asked.

'Of course,' Ebony said and looked back at Colossus, who had lifted his head to look at his owner after hearing his name. He panted, causing drool to add more mess to the floor. Ebony wrinkled her nose. 'Changing subject, would you like my help round the farm or house. To be candid, I would be grateful, as I am running dry financially. I could start with cleaning this place.'

'Any time you want, Ebs.' Hazel said, passing her friend six eggs. 'Anyway, the windmill is all outta milk. Come with me to the barn.'

Remnant Tales of Stilly:
Passion and Benevolence

Ebony stood in the centre of the barn where three cows and four goats were sheltered in stables. An acrid smell filled the space, typical of the animals, but the summer heat made it all the more pungent.

Following the pair out of the farmhouse, Colossus panted into the barn. The dog plodded behind Ebony and pressed his wet nose against her leg. Ebony grinned at Colossus and leant towards the hound. She rubbed both sides of his neck and looked at Hazel. 'About those unfamiliar bursts of light you mentioned...' Ebony said. Hazel, who was milking a cow, tilted her head to show she was listening. 'I saw Oliath Burley when buying some vegetables from your father. I heard him speaking to news reporters. He seemed somewhat flummoxed, especially as two soldiers led a man away. I got a glimpse of the arrested man, and I have to admit he looked unusual. He seemed to be in a trance-like state.'

Hazel screwed lids onto several jars of milk. 'Flummoxed, eh? That's an unusual word. Anyway, what you said all sounds interesting enough.'

'I'd say,' Ebony uttered, turning back to the Great Dane. 'Wouldn't you agree, Colossus?'

Colossus stopped panting, pricked his ears and tilted his head to one side.

'I can see by your mug, Ebs, that you find it interesting. I don't know what to make of it all myself. Anyway, here's your milk. Sorry it's a bit warm, but it's as fresh as can be.'

'Thank you, Hazel.'

'You're welcome, m'dear. What have you got planned for the rest of the day?' Hazel spoke on, leading her friend out of the barn. 'I dare say, maybe it involves seeing what happened in that vacant house.'

Ebony curled her lips. 'Maybe... I could do with pursuing something more exciting. For now, though, I am going to the library.'

'Suit yourself,' Hazel replied, continuing to face Ebony. 'I'm getting back to work, but if you find out anything exciting, keep me in the know... and make sure you stay out of trouble, ya hear me?'

Ebony chuckled. 'You sound just like your father.'

Remnant Tales of Stilly:
Passion and Benevolence

Far west of Wilheard existed Old Market Square, a boulevard of cobblestones outlined by trees and buildings. As with its neighbouring streets, this open area bore a dreary silence that seemed unjust to its pleasant and old-fashioned quality. According to Ebony's parents, the emptiness owed itself to all the popular shops relocating to New Market Square before her birth. Some old shops were converted into homes, while others simply closed and were left to fall into disrepair.

The main attraction of Old Market Square was arguably the government building Wilheard Hall. Easily the largest of the structures, it housed the office of Basil Wolleb, Mayor of Wilheard, and most other political matters. It was an impressive part of the area, to be sure, but the water fountain with a female statue at the square's centre always stole Ebony's interest first.

Atop a plinth in the middle of the fountain was a weatherworn statue of a woman. The sculpture resembled Evelyn Sanine, the last Queen of Stilly, in a kneeling position. With her gaze skywards and right arm outstretched, she seemed to be offering something above. This, at least, was what Ebony presumed; the right hand was missing, so she could only guess. Having been in the square for several generations, what had actually happened to the statue had become a muddling of folklore. Vincent Sawney, the butcher, for example, claimed that the hand had been inadvertently broken off during the statue's relocation from the castle grounds. Other people believe that the sculpture had never been within the castle and that the hand had secretly held something treasurable, something that, when discovered, was removed to avoid thievery. This resulted in the accidental breaking of the whole hand. It was all speculation, but the inscription on the plinth gave such theories credence.

For Traeh, with gratitude, I verily entrust to you. Watch over us.

Ebony's knowledge of Stilly's history was sparse, but this was not due to a lack of interest. It need not stay that way, however. After all, she was off to the library, and studying local history might be a subject that sparked her imagination.

Remnant Tales of Stilly:
Passion and Benevolence

The library, Bookish Charm, resided east of Old Market Square and next door to what used to be a music shop. The library windows were foggy and aged over time. Ebony peered through the glass before making her way inside.

Ebony scanned the walls and shelves. The room was tight, had a low ceiling and was to the point of bursting, yet the space seemed well used, and she loved its charisma.

Ebony crept about the customer floor and peered round the cases to see if Albert Comyns, the library's owner, was there. Looking down the farthest aisle from the entrance, Ebony spied a girl in her mid-teens. The girl, thumbing through a children's book, regarded Ebony with a glance as she came into view, only to return her attention to the book moments later. Ebony left her alone and walked to the doorway on the other end of the room.

'Mister Comyns…' Ebony called as softly as possible. 'Are you there?'

After a delay, an elderly voice called back, followed by plodding footsteps and a walking cane tapping on the floorboards. 'Who's that calling my name?' the 94-year-old man said in a curmudgeonly tone, squinting as he stepped onto the shop floor. His eyes focusing, the librarian saw Ebony smiling at him, causing him to relax his bushy eyebrows. 'Oh… oh, it's you, young Ebony. Forgive me if I came across as grumpy.'

'That's all right, Albert. Sorry if I am troubling you; I just wanted to let you know I'm here.'

'You are never a bother, girl. Are you after another book so soon?'

'Yes, please. One that should keep me entertained for a while.'

'At the speed you read, I expect that will not be a *long* while,' Albert chuckled. He walked short steps over to a stool beside a table and sat down with a puff. 'So… what will it be today?'

Ebony once again looked round at the many books. 'Well, I think I might deviate a little bit'.

'I see. I suppose everyone needs a change every once in a while,' the elderly man said hoarsely. He caressed his pointed chin and raised his eyebrows once more. Ebony had always wondered if Albert's eyebrows impaired his vision. He always seemed to be lifting them when he looked at people. 'Well, I will not stop you. Look until your heart is content.'

Remnant Tales of Stilly:
Passion and Benevolence

Ebony ran her fingers along the spines of the shelved book. She typically favoured romantic stories, and as she continued to peer across the lines of books, she found an old favourite. Ebony pulled the novel from its place and looked at the front cover. It had been a while since she had read this particular book, but borrowing it would merely go against her desire for *change*, and her yellow dress reminded her of this.

Ebony wrinkled her nose and put the book back where it belonged. Taking a step backwards, she peered up to the top of the shelves and looked from side to side, inspecting all the different categories of fiction. She linked her fingers behind her back. There must be something a little less familiar.

After browsing for a while, Ebony spotted the worn spine of a hardback. She had noticed the book on past visits but had never bothered to look at it. Unfortunately, there was a good reason for this: the book was out of her reach. She turned her head to find Albert. He was still sitting on the same stool but had since fallen asleep. Ebony pursed her lips and looked back to the book. She did not particularly want to climb to reach it, yet she wished to disturb Albert even less. The thought of the infirm man climbing ladders, particularly on her behalf and for the sake of a single book, was ludicrous. She looked about the room for an object sturdy enough to take her weight. The ladder used to reach books rested against the wall behind where Albert was sitting. He would surely stir and insist on fetching the book if she attempted to get it.

Ebony pulled up a wooden chair and took a moment to look back at the book. *Be brave, Ebony,* she told herself. *It isn't that high.* By now, she had again gained the attention of the girl, who was staring at her with child-like curiosity. Ebony touched her lips and made a hushing sound before slipping off her shoes and stepping on the seat. Holding onto the shelf as tightly as possible, Ebony stretched for the book, successfully removing it and a coating of dust.

Ebony stepped back off the chair and blew a sigh of relief. *That wasn't so bad,* she thought, smirking and proud of herself. *As long as you don't look down, you will be fine.* She put her shoes back on and returned the chair to its rightful place.

Ebony looked over the simple cover design. Dull-gold lettering filled the book's centre.

Passion and Benevolence

Written in 1468SN by
Minach Emmanuel Grellic

— ◆ —

Revised in 1737SN by
Ted Larring

Ebony jolted as Albert snored, breaking the room's silence. Drolly, the snort woke him.

'Sorry,' Albert said as he cleared his throat. 'I'm prone to nod off if you don't keep an eye on me. Did you find anything of interest?

Ebony walked towards the librarian. 'I think I have.'

'Good… and what about you, young Meddia? Are you still there, girl?' The teenager poked her head into view at the call of her name. 'Have you chosen a book yet?' Albert asked.

The girl shook her head rapidly

'All right. Don't worry—there's no rush.' Albert turned back to Ebony and whispered. 'Awfully timid that one.'

Ebony placed her chosen book on the desk for Albert to see. The elderly man adjusted his glasses. 'I see,' he murmured, curling his upper lip as he lifted the front cover. 'I haven't seen this one for a long time. Phew! And what musty pages it has.'

When she was young, Ebony had asked Albert if he had read all the books in Bookish Charm. Albert had chuckled at the question and replied that he had read most of them. As Ebony got older, she realised he had not been exaggerating and could give his opinion on everything she showed.

'What is this book like?' Ebony asked.

There was a moment's silence before Albert answered as he concentrated on noting the book's imminent departure. 'From what I remember, it is a peculiar one. Imaginative, but certainly peculiar.' Albert closed the book and pushed it towards Ebony. 'You will definitely like it. The story is even set in Wilheard, and many of the characters—if my memory serves—are based on actual historical figures.'

Historical figures? Ebony thought. *That's a coincidence.* She placed the book under her arm. 'Picturing the story will seem all the more realistic, I suppose,' Ebony said as she stepped sideways to the library's exit. 'I won't bother you anymore. Thank you for lending me the book.'

Albert raised his cane and nodded. 'Any time, girl—any time.

Remnant Tales of Stilly:
Passion and Benevolence

Chapter Two

Wiping his forehead with the cuff of his shirtsleeve, Abraham Gibenn leant against a wall of his cottage and blew an exhausted sigh. The sun pelted down on him as he laboured the morning away. It would not be long until the heat forced him to take some shade, but he did not mind so much, so long as he had least tried to keep himself occupied.

Abraham shielded his eyes from the glare and squinted over Wilheard. Light gleamed off the ceramic slates of rooftops and various other objects about the town, including the well-polished armour worn by Wilheard guards on patrol.

Tender spirits, he thought. Though he was suffering, they would be sweltering under all that metal.

The corners of his whiskered lips lifted as contentment spread through him. It made a change to feel sorry for someone other than himself. The town's simple but charming landscape never failed to please him, and the view from Wilheard's southern highland was incredibly satisfying. In fact, his home stood there for that reason.

Before his wife's disappearance, Wilheard's community had revered Abraham as a talented architect, carpenter and even somewhat of an inventor. Despite this artisanship, Abraham rarely had the opportunity to use his expertise on more significant developments. One of his bigger projects had been his own cottage, which he built with little help from others in the trade. Although modest, the house was two storeys tall, and the extra floor allowed for additional room. Not that space was a problem those days.

Abraham sighed again and used his sleeve to wipe his face a second time. He took a sip of water from a wooden beaker, grimacing as he pulled it away from his mouth. The water was warm. He tossed the rest of the drink away and returned to work. He had spent most of the morning chopping wood, and this labouring was for no reason other than to keep busy. Recent inactivity only allowed him to brood, and he had become more fed up with his own company as the weeks passed. This needed to stop, and he was willing to do almost anything if it kept his mind occupied.

Remnant Tales of Stilly:
Passion and Benevolence

Abraham looked at a rounded piece of wood in the centre of a tree stump. Without looking away from the target, he tightened his grip on the sweat-dampened handle, licked his lips with the tip of his tongue and lifted the axe above his head, halting when somebody entered his periphery. He lowered the axe.

Cradling a heavy wicker basket in both arms, Ebony walked towards her father while looking at the chunk of wood, switching her gaze upwards when she got close. Abraham gazed back at his daughter, stony-faced and saying nothing.

'Fair morn, Father. Been busy, have you?' Ebony said.

'Yes,' Abraham replied. 'Just thought I'd get the ol' heart pumping.'

'I see. Are you thinking of building something?'

Abraham shook his head.

'What is the wood for, then?'

Abraham shrugged and embedded the axe in the tree stump. 'Nothing in particular—we can use it as firewood, I guess.'

'During summer?'

'Of course not.' Abraham breathed out slowly, trying not to sigh. 'Besides, freshly cut firewood tends not to burn well because of its water content. It is best to let it season so it can dry out.'

'I guess that makes sense,' Ebony said. 'I learn something new every day.'

A moment of silence passed.

'Besides,' Abraham continued, 'I haven't been doing this all morning. I went to the water mill earlier.'

'That's good—the water tank was almost empty.'

'Yeah, I filled it up.'

'Really?' Ebony said, somewhat surprised. 'That must have taken several trips back and forth.'

'Quite a few, I guess. I fancied the walk.'

More silence passed.

Abraham shrugged again and walked towards the cottage, dusting his hands together. Ebony smiled and followed behind him.

Once inside, Ebony placed her wicker basket on the kitchen table and emptied the contents. Sitting opposite his daughter, Abraham rested on his forearms and watched her put each item next to the basket. Having not eaten that morning, he wondered what food his daughter had bought. The milk was his first victim of scrutiny, the jar of which he turned to find a label.

Dolb's Farm of Wilheard
Cow's Milk

Abraham swallowed in anticipation and reached for the bottle's lid.

'I hope you're not planning on drinking from that bottle,' Ebony said, peering at her father sideways.

Abraham grumbled something incoherent and put the glass down.

Next, Ebony pulled out the chicken she retrieved from Vincent after visiting Bookish Charm. Abraham's eyes lit up, and he extended his arm to reach for the poultry, retracting after receiving a slap to the back of his hand.

'With those dirty things?' said Ebony, her expression stern. 'Honestly, Father!'

Abraham turned his hands over. Wood particles and various bits of dirt covered his palms. 'Oh... sorry,' he said as he wiped his hands on his trousers.

'Don't do that, either!' Ebony scolded.

Keeping his head down, he shifted his eyes towards his daughter, pulling a pitiful look. 'Sorry, mater.'

Stifling a grin, Ebony rolled her eyes and walked to the pantry, placing the milk on the cool stone floor. 'I can see that you are hungry. If you like, I can cook some eggs—and after you have *thoroughly* cleaned your hands with *water*, perhaps you can slice and butter some bread.'

Abraham got to his feet. 'All right.'

Ebony ignited the stove. Using a small saucepan and wooden spoon, she stirred the eggs with milk, whipping the eggs with a slow, dreamy motion as she hummed aloud.

Abraham looked at his daughter as he cut the bread. She seemed in a good mood. 'That's a tuneful song.'

Ebony stopped humming and blushed. She had been too busy daydreaming to notice what she was doing. 'I did not realise I was humming so loudly.

'Where did you hear it?'

'It's one Mother taught me years ago on the Piano. Don't you remember? It's called Ballad of the Deity.'

'All right,' Abraham said. 'It does sound familiar. I heard it somewhere else recently.'

Ebony frowned. 'You heard it somewhere else?'

'I think so. I heard something similar, anyway.'

'That's strange. It is a family song, but I suppose others might know it.'

There was a moment of silence, which Abraham broke. 'Actually, I haven't heard it recently, and I might be mistaking it for another tune.'

'Such as?'

'I don't know exactly—you know I'm not the musical type... It was just guitar sounds.'

'Now that you mention it, I have heard a guitar recently.' Ebony paused to think. 'No one was playing Ballad of the Deity, but something has made me remember it lately.'

Abraham once again interrupted his daughter's musing. 'Anyway, the bread is buttered and the plates and cutlery out. How're the eggs doing?'

Ebony looked down at the sizzling eggs. They were on the verge of burning. She moved the pan from the stove. 'Sorry. I hope it is not too overdone for you,' she said, scooping some egg onto her father's plate.

Abraham thanked his daughter and waited for her to sit down opposite him.

As she ate, Ebony looked at her father intermittently. He poked and shifted his food about the plate before eventually eating a fork-full.

'Have you eaten already today?' Ebony asked before putting a forkful of egg in her mouth.

Abraham looked up at his daughter. 'Pardon?'

Ebony swallowed. 'I thought you were hungry. You are playing with that food more than you are eating it.' Ebony finished her breakfast and placed her cutlery neatly on the empty plate. 'Have you eaten this morning, or are you feeling unwell?'

Abraham looked down at the scattered food. He groaned then. 'You must think I'm going mad.'

Ebony furrowed her brow. 'No... What makes you say that?'

Abraham did not answer. He rested his chin on his clasped hands. 'I saw the look you gave me outside by the tree stump—you must think I'm stupid. I am clearly a burden on you.

'What has got into you, Father?' Ebony stood up, walked behind Abraham, and wrapped her arms round his neck. 'No, I do not think you are a burden. I never have, and I never will.'

Abraham placed one hand over his daughter's and forced a smile, which quickly faded. Sighing, he released himself from her embrace and stood up. 'Thank you, Ebony... but *I* think that I am.'

Ebony shifted back to the other side of the table, keeping her gaze on her father. 'Are you feeling unwell? Perhaps have a lie-down--'

'No, I'll be all right,' Abraham interjected. 'Honestly. I think I just need to leave the cottage for a bit.'

Ebony simply nodded in response.

'Thanks again for breakfast,' Abraham said, then left the kitchen.

The poor girl, Abraham thought. *She tries so hard for me.*

Indeed, if things stayed as they were, his low mood would bring his daughter down. Was he just paranoid? Perhaps, but it did not matter anyway. This feeling made him hate himself.

Oliath Burley tilted back in his seat and watched a fly circling the ceiling. He was sitting cross-legged, his feet on the table before him and his arms folded. Drumming his fingers on his enormous biceps, Oliath rocked the chair back and forth on its hind legs and reflected upon the morning's incident. This was the first time that day he had managed to get away from the churlish reporters and public, yet he could not get their barbs out of his head.

Remnant Tales of Stilly:
Passion and Benevolence

He loosened his scowl and glanced round the elongated room, formally known as The Repose. Although part of the guards' quarters, the room was not particularly popular among the soldiers. Because of this, Oliath favoured the area. Then again, it was a good chance that the captain was keeping troops away; his ferocious temper on occasion could put more than just local children on edge. Whatever the truth, this was the least of his concerns.

Two of Oliath's personal lieutenants were in The Repose with him: Cordelia Lawford, sitting by a round table just to the left of the captain of the guard, and Nolen Shakeston, who was standing opposite him.

Oliath tilted his head to glance at Cordelia. His finest female soldier held a solemn expression as she read an article from Village Express. Although her look made clear what to expect from the article, he needed to know how flawed his efforts were this time.

'How does the news fare today, Lawford?' Oliath asked, gazing back at the ceiling.

Cordelia kept her eyes on the paper, not bothering to look up. 'It is hardly flattering, sir.'

'The thankless…!' Oliath hissed, stopping short of swearing. 'What have we done now?'

'Apparently, it has more to do with what we have *not* done.' There was a moment of silence as Oliath looked at Cordelia. She continued. 'To get to the point, sir, the paper accuses us of tardiness before going on to complain about—and I quote—"Either a tight-lipped attitude to the investigation or an incompetence to properly understand recent crimes about Wilheard."'

Oliath closed his eyes and rubbed his temples; he was getting a headache. 'And to top it off, there are the rumours of a vigilante making our work harder.

'You would do well to ignore that tripe, sir,' said Nolen, placing a glass of water on the table before his boss, 'the Vultures would rue the day if your services were to suddenly cease.'

Vultures was a name often given to local reporters, aptly so as far as Oliath was concerned. He drank a mouthful of the water and stared forward. 'Indeed. Some people don't know how lucky they are or how hard we work.' He downed the rest of the liquid and sneered. 'Still, they have a point.'

Nolen and Cordelia stopped what they were doing and looked at their boss, surprised by his sudden acceptance of the criticism.

Oliath ran his fingers through his greased-back hair and stood up. 'These recent attacks have me puzzled. You two know as well as me how odd the last few *criminals* seemed—if we can call them that.' Oliath looked out the window at the passing people and groaned. 'The ones in custody may not be from Wilheard, and outsiders may act differently than you or I do, but even a child could see something abnormal about these individuals. They are clearly not your average delinquent.'

Nolan agreed. 'That is true. They look almost innocent… as if unaware of their actions.'

'Precisely, Shakeston,' Oliath replied, pointing at the other man with a flick of his wrist.

Cordelia folded the newspaper and slapped it on the table. 'What is our next move, sir?'

Oliath rubbed his chin and turned back to look out the window. He knew the other two would not like what he was about to say. 'Summon the *Other Four.*'

As Oliath expected, Nolen and Cordelia grimaced in disapproval.

'But' sir,' Nolen blared, 'I am sure their involvement will only hinder the investigation.'

Cordelia was quick to support her comrade. 'Shakeston is right. Those buffoons are better off out of the way. We can do this much better without them. Leave it to us, sir.'

Oliath dismissed the disapproval. 'For now, I don't intend to let them do anything substantial—I trust the pair of you with the most important tasks. Nevertheless, no one can deny what the four have to offer, and their expertise may be exactly what we need right now.'

The lieutenants reluctantly agreed.

'Get the four to snoop about town. If anyone in Wilheard knows what is happening, I want to hear about it. Perhaps they will find out more about this vigilante. Meanwhile, I will pay the mayor a visit—with his permission, I may be able to interrogate the prisoners.'

'Yes, sir,' Cordelia and Nolen replied simultaneously and left The Repose.

Oliath sat down again and watched the fly buzzing about a moment ago scurry across the table ahead of him. He slammed his palm onto the surface, missing the insect by an inch. Oliath grunted; he despised anything escaping his grasp.

He was not about to give up on this investigation, nor would he let news reporters get the better of him. He would find out what was going on in Wilheard, and as always, he would see it through, no matter how long that might take.

The time was mid-afternoon, and the heat would now begin to subside. At least, that was Ebony's hope.

She sat down under the shadow of a tree and dabbed a handkerchief over her face. On her lap rested the newly borrowed book. The tree's location, part of the countryside spanning hundreds of acres south of Wilheard, would ensure she got some peace and quiet to read, away from playing children and popular walking routes.

Lying on her back, Ebony gazed at the blue sky through the tree leaves. She closed her eyes for a moment and listened to the wildlife. Perched on the tree branches, birds twittered and sang while bumblebees zigzagged from flower to flower, going about their busy existence. Ebony breathed contently. The smaller the creature, the less it seemed to rest. It was as if they did not know how to take it easy, and this only relaxed her further. That was until a fly landed on her nose. She shooed it away, sat up, and leant against the tree.

The hardback Ebony had borrowed from Bookish Charm laid face-up. She reread the words on the cover, flicked through the pages and then turned back to the front to read the introduction.

Remnant Tales of Stilly:
Passion and Benevolence

Thou art heartily welcome.
(Translated from Old Stillian.)

"One man's hope is another man's bane. To protect loved ones is to deceive them. Misperception eventually begets understanding. One is **not** traitorous. One is **not** misbegotten."

This dialect, which I realise will seem cryptic to many, alleviates much of the strain on my heart. It took almost a lifetime for me to appreciate its implications. In principle, these words guide those who question their worth or perhaps those who believe their actions are immoral. As a rule, however, this phrase is not one to take lightly.

I sit here writing these very words and think of the past: to my service as a Minach to King Godfrey Sanine. It has been nearly three years since his passing, and I can confidently say that we were true friends. However, is it possible that I betrayed this friendship?

The king held spirituality close to his heart, and his heart was definitely of a noble kind. Equally, his ethics were sometimes stubborn, impractical and even discriminative. Although a patient ruler, his tolerance had limits. There were things that he despised, hate born from fear and a lack of understanding.

It is perhaps unfortunate, then, that one of those distastes was something I avidly practised, something people like me were forced to do clandestinely. It is only natural for people to misunderstand what life has to offer; ignorance is a part of me as much as any man, and not one of us can ever obtain the knowledge of everything. However, is it arrogant to assume that if one does not open the mind, then one is obtuse? Can any one man genuinely claim that his actions are right for humanity? Some in the world are brazen enough to claim as much, and if there was one man to whom I can bind such audacity, it would be another old friend.

As is sometimes the case, this friend took a wrong turn in life. Be it his own will or because something led him down that path, the matter falls into irrelevance. I may never know the truth and thus have no right to judge.

Remnant Tales of Stilly:
Passion and Benevolence

As the years pass and fade from existence, so do my memories, yet I still have my journals.

Take heed. What I failed to grasp is now for you to learn.

Minach Immanuel Grellic. Sanct Everard, sancture of Wilheard.

Passion and Benevolence.
Return of an unfamiliar friend.

The sudden return of Lord Fordon Latnemirt was, not to put it lightly, unexpected. After two years of nary a word or sighting, it was widely presumed that the man had long departed from this physical sphere. Yet, there he was: flesh and bone. Nevertheless, although alive, I cannot say he was well.

Upon hearing that two Royal Sentinels had found Fordon collapsed outside the castle, I joined King Godfrey Sanine in the courtyard, where the two guards brought the man through the portcullis. The guards were to either side of the skeletal Fordon, his arms hung over their shoulders as they effortlessly carried him into the castle grounds.

Mutterings filled the halls, as did questions. What had happened to the man? Why had he returned after all this time?

Godfrey must have been asking himself similar questions but would have put such things aside for the time being, instructing the Royal Sentinels to seek immediate medical attention for Fordon. However, much to the astonishment of everyone, the lord requested he be taken to his chambers (the isolated south-eastern tower), asking he be left alone to rest. Fordon assured King Godfrey that he would treat his own discomforts, his only wish being that servants bring him food and water.

I can only presume the king was as perplexed as I was by Fordon's request. However, he agreed to it, perhaps pessimistic that the man would survive the night and should be left alone to pass away how he wanted.

Death did not occur, however.

During the week of his return, Fordon recovered with surprising speed, his state returning to the one I remember before his disappearance.

Yet, as his strength continued to improve, his desire to be alone only seemed to increase, and his willingness to explain what he had suffered failed to surface. I not once visited Fordon during this time, but tales stated that, when questioned, his reaction would range from complete silence to belligerence.

After a time, King Godfrey decided that he had been patient enough with Fordon's withdrawn conduct and summoned a meeting with the man, which took place in the throne room. Situated in the centre of the throne room was an ornate table, its top circular edge decorated with lavish carvings of spiritual beings, holy and unholy alike. This reflected the king's religious tastes: the sacred anjyls banishing the damned livnam back to the horrors below. As lavish as it was, the table seemed to cause ambivalence for whoever sat round it. Fordon had never been keen on the table's design. I remember him telling me once that it caused him perpetual disquiet in the pit of his stomach, and as I watched him pinching the head of one of the etchings, a frown creasing his brow, I gathered his opinion of it had not changed.

Sitting opposite Fordon was King Godfrey, his queen Verity and their daughter Princess Evelyn, staring silently at the haggard man in black and waiting for him to speak. I sat halfway between, parchment and quill in hand, ready to document the meeting. Two other men were also present at the time, although not at the table: Clement and Maynard Suavlant, brothers who made two of the four sovereign knights. The pair had asked for my consent to watch over the meeting. Intrigue must have got the better of the two, and I had no objections. In truth, I was curious about their opinion.

Throughout the discussion, the brothers would remain silent.

Fordon eventually broke the hush. 'My thoughts have been troubling,' he uttered. He apologised for his discourtesy, stating that he never meant to cause any disquiet on his return.

The king had given a languid nod. Two years ago, he had ratified Fordon's decision to travel to Drieloca. According to Fordon, it was a journey that would last six months. Yet, not only did that time stretch four-fold, but Fordon had returned alone despite taking a dozen men and horses as a company. The reasons for the journey were inconsequential, be it adventure, discovery, or simply to travel; King Godfrey had never hidden his distaste for Drieloca. The province (according to His Majesty) is an unnatural, heathen place with false gods. He had once confessed to me: "I dreamt that I removed that malignance from Stilly. I do not know how, but it was gone."

Fordon's return perhaps fortified the king's contempt for the province, but he was at least thankful to Traeh that it was a safe return. Perchance, Godfrey would have been tempted to put the matter to the back of his mind then, but he deemed it necessary to know more.

Lord Fordon had not once looked King Godfrey in the eyes. From what I could tell, the man had been staring vacantly at the surroundings as if he had heard nary a word. On the contrary, he answered the king's every question.

Fordon explained that the journey to Drieloca went smoothly and without trouble. Arriving in the region after many weeks of travelling through weather vicissitudes provided relief amongst his party despite its dark and unwelcoming façade. Finding human life had been slower than expected, taking days, and even then, Fordon explained that the village population they found was slight.

'We eventually came across a simple hamlet called Seèrt. The village dwellers were notably introverted,' Fordon told the royals. On his account, the populace got few visitors and was, to a degree, oblivious to the world outside Drieloca. Upon seeing Fordon Latnemirt and the accompanying soldiers, the residents instinctively assumed trouble. 'There is no law enforcement in Drieloca—at least nothing akin to the rest of Stilly.'

King Godfrey snorted his disgust, referring to them as savages.

Fordon shook his head. Although they did not own an elected authority, the people still had morals. He mentioned that, although highly secretive (he only saw what they allowed), they had a creed, one that is unorthodox to that of Wilheard.

The king continued to voice his distaste, now labelling them as heretics.

Remnant Tales of Stilly:
Passion and Benevolence

I remember Queen Verity being less curt as she listened to Fordon. 'If not a leader, as such, did the peoples have a person of influence?' she had asked.

Fordon had smiled wanly. An elderly man of 112 years was an idol; his age and life experience made him a natural father figure.

I recall feeling awe at the age, even if King Godfrey remained unimpressed.

'His name is Ghennitteemn Noitanitsa—or Ghen Noit to those with foreign tongues.' Fordon said (he wrote the name on parchment for me). Ghen introduced Fordon to Seért's practises and was mainly welcoming, albeit sometimes foreboding. On Fordon's explanation, Ghen claimed to have anticipated visitors from afar, claiming he had dreamt it. Ghen also mentioned he knew Fordon Latnemirt's dreams and his desire to find The Neffaloom (a dense part of Drieloca that the natives feared). 'He tried to dissuade me from following these dreams further than I already had. Regrettably, I did not heed this advice.'

At last, Godfrey took a serious interest in what Fordon was saying.

Near two weeks after arriving in Seèrt, Fordon and the soldiers set off for Neffaloom, leaving the horses in the village due to the density of what would lie ahead. The journey took another three days, each one darker than the last to the point where the sheer amount of trees almost entirely blocked natural light.

Fordon spoke on. 'The wildlife, abundant for most of the journey, became thinner and less noticeable. This was when the shadows came.'

Fordon began to sob at this point, stirring sympathy from Queen Verity. King Godfrey's temperament had also softened.

Fordon claimed not to know what happened to the soldiers; as he and the party reached a certain point, they disappeared one after the other.

Princess Evelyn spoke then, repeating the word shadows. Assuming Fordon had suffered an ambush, she asked what he had seen.

'Monsters' was Fordon's simple answer. He described shadow beings in human form, but more livomic than man.

'You know not what happened?' King Godfrey asked.

Fordon shook his head, his upset vanishing within seconds. This sudden change in demeanour struck me as peculiar and caused me to doubt the following statement.

'It is almost as if I have missed the past two years of my life. I remember very little of any of it.'

By then, King Godfrey had appeared satisfied with what he had heard, and the meeting ended.

Later that day, I approached Clement and Maynard to ask their thoughts. It turned out that the two men shared my apprehension despite not disbelieving Lord Fordon's claim. Clement, in particular, commented on Fordon's unforthcoming appearance, stating that the lord had said only what he needed.

Maynard nodded his agreement.

Whatever the case, I decided to put it all to one side for now.

The day had passed more quickly than expected by the time Ebony's eyelids began flicking. She put the book down, yawned and rolled her head from side to side while rubbing the back of her neck. She had read only a few chapters but felt ready to rest her eyes for a little while. The time was edging late afternoon, and she would head home soon, but she saw nothing wrong with a rest.

Ebony lay on the grass and resumed listening to the surrounding sounds. It was quieter than before; bees had moved on, and the distant calls of playing children were all but gone. She drifted into a light sleep.

Although the story is enthralling enough, Emmanuel Grellic was a sombre man. Ebony wondered how true some of it was; it was all somewhat mysterious. Even if exaggerated, Emmanuel's life had been exciting, especially since Ebony now had an idea of what was within the walls of Castle Stilly. She had never been in the castle before, as it had been sealed from the public for over a hundred years. She and Hazel had spent a lot of time as children searching for a secret entrance into the grounds to no avail; the murky water of the moat fronting the architecture had been a noteworthy hindrance to such explorations.

Remnant Tales of Stilly:
Passion and Benevolence

Ebony jolted awake from her thought, feeling a sudden and continual discomfort in her right hip. She opened her eyes and sat up sharply. The prodding sensation stopped, followed by gasps. She looked to her right and jolted again as she noticed a group of three children standing a metre away. At a glance, they were aged between eight and eleven and appeared to be siblings. The younger two children, both girls (one with red hair, the other blonde), hid behind the older and chubbier boy, grasping at his shirt. Both girls had gaps where their milk teeth used to be. This resulted in slurred speech, where *TH* replaced most *S* sounds.

The boy was holding a stick.

'*Th*ee,' the redheaded girl lisped in what was a poor attempt at whispering, 'I told ya she weren't dead!'

'She *th*ure looked it,' the other girl said back. 'Better *th*afe than *th*orry—that'*th* what Dad always *th*ays!'

Although tickled by the children's apparent concern, Ebony avoided smiling. She folded her arms and looked sternly at the three.

'She's looking at u*th*,' the redheaded girl continued.

The blonde girl moved behind the boy more. 'She look*th* mean—like she wan*th* to eat u*th*. Maybe she is one of those zombies from the book*th* Daddy reads. Or maybe she's a witch.'

'I can assure you I am not a zombie, little girl,' Ebony said. 'A witch, however…'

The girls squeaked in surprise and disappeared almost entirely behind their older brother. The boy cleared his throat. 'Sorry, lady. We thought you was dead, is all.

'Yes, so I heard. And you thought jabbing me with the sharp end of a twig'—Ebony nodded towards the stick—'was the best way to certify this?'

The three looked at each other with puzzled expressions. They were not sure what *certify* meant.

'I think you should put it down, young man, before you poke somebody's eye out.'

The boy glanced down at his hand and dropped the stick by his feet. He looked back at Ebony. 'Mummy said we shouldn't talk to strangers.'

'And she is absolutely right!' Ebony exclaimed. 'Also, you may want to remember that you should not *poke* strangers either, especially with sharp objects. Do you understand?

The three nodded rapidly.

'Good. Now run along; I am getting hungry. We witches find that children make for tasty meals.'

The children's eyes widened. Without saying another word, they ran off home, not once looking back.

With the children gone, Ebony finally allowed herself a chuckle. She dabbed her forehead with a handkerchief and reached into the wicker basket with her other hand. Fumbling through the various items, she came across the circular object she was after. Enveloping the small, silver-rimmed pocket watch in her fist, Ebony pulled it from her basket. She squinted through the glass, tilting it away from the sun's glare.

The time was 3.54pm.

Ebony placed Passion and Benevolence to one side and reclined again. She did not need to return home yet, so she relaxed a while longer. With some luck, the sleep would not be interrupted this time.

Abraham Gibenn left the cottage not long after his daughter that afternoon. The nice weather was always something of which to take advantage, and while Ebony went off to read her new book, he gathered that some more sun might help remedy his mood. He was not entirely sold by the idea, but it was at least a favourable substitute to moping about the house.

Abraham closed the cottage's front door and locked it, giving the doorknob a tug to ensure it was secure. The latch rattled; it had loosened after years of extensive use and would eventually need fixing. Perhaps he would use some of that wood he chopped earlier. A good idea, maybe, but he was damned if he could be bothered with that right now.

After several minutes of ambling, Abraham reached nearer the heart of Wilheard. He strolled down the market streets, meandering by fellow pedestrians and glancing at the stalls and shops surrounding him. Abraham spent roughly ten minutes poking and fondling different items stocked, going as far as picking some up for a closer look. He found one particular object so curious that he squeezed it, shook it, and even smelt it to establish what on earth its use could be. This behaviour irritated some of the merchants, resulting in one pointing to a hand-written sign:

PARENTS—DO NOT LET CHILDREN TAMPER WITH THE GOODS.

After a while of increased hostility, Abraham moved on, eventually passing the stand of his old friend Harold Dolb.

Being afternoon, Harold's business had slowed. This was typical for the time, and the stall owner would soon retire for the day. Still, the less produce he had to cart back to the farm, the better, and the heat-exposed fruit and vegetables were not something he would keep for resale the following day. If Harold could sell more in the next hour or so, his disappointment with any waste would subside. In the meantime, he would continue to read his newspaper, shoo away insects and take periodic glimpses for potential customers.

Harold turned the page of his newspaper and briefly shifted his eyes upwards. As he looked up, the vague shape of someone approaching entered his sight.

'My, my,' Harold said. 'It has been a while since I last saw you wandering about.'

Abraham forced a smile that looked more like a grimace. He did not say anything in return. Upon reaching the stall, he slouched as he glanced at the piles of vegetation, habitually putting his hands in his trouser pockets, only to pull them out again when they became clammy.

Harold continued talking. 'I would ask if you wanted anything on offer… but I'm sure you know your Ebony came by this morning.' Harold paused as he spoke, clarifying whether he had seen Ebony that day. It could have been yesterday; he was constantly losing track of time. In the end, the newspaper's articles confirmed the truth.

'Nah, I'm fine, thanks, mate,' Abraham said, 'I'm just out for a walk.'

Harold nodded, squinting at Abraham in the bright sunlight. 'Either way, it is good to see you. How have you been, my good man?'

'I have my moments,' Abraham sighed, looking about as he spoke. 'All in all, I guess I can't complain. I've got to fix the front door of my cottage.'

'Trouble?'

'No, just a loose doorknob.'

'I see. Well, as long as you're all right.'

Abraham grimaced again, intending another smile. 'How are things on your end?'

'Full of activity. Like you, I can't complain.'

'Good... How's the family?'

'I'm sure Hazel is working her fingers to the bone while Myrah manages the shop and is her usual busybody self. You know what those two are like.'

'Some things don't change,' Abraham replied, rubbing the sweat from the top of his balding head, transferring the moisture to his trouser leg.

'You look in need of a bit of shade, my friend,' Harold said. 'And I suppose you didn't think to bring a hip flask of water out with you.'

Abraham shook his head.

Harold chuckled. 'Same old Abraham. Perhaps you can pop into one of those new places down the road. I believe they call 'em tearooms.'

'I'll think about it.'

Moments later, an elderly woman sneaked up next to Abraham. 'Have you got any strawberries, young man?'

'I'm sure I can find some for you, my darling,' Harold responded with a cheery grin.

'I best leave you to your customer, then. See you round, Harold,' Abraham said, walking away with a wave.

'See you later, Abe. Take it steady.'

Abraham continued to plod about Wilheard, walking almost randomly along different streets, roads and narrow passageways as he kept to the shadows. After a few minutes, he eventually came to a boulevard lined with tearooms, restaurants and a pub. The street, named Efflorescence Way, was popular among the more adult in Wilheard and connected to the ancient arches belonging to Castle Way: an incline that led to Sanct Everard and

eventually Wilheard Castle itself. The route up to the castle was one of
Ebony's favourites when strolling, but the fifty-five-year-old Abraham was
not as enthusiastic about such treks. Besides, all he wanted to do now was sit
in the shade with a drink.

Abraham looked through the window of the first shop he saw and curled
his top lip. He was not keen on coffee and tea, and how these places fancied
up the beverages made it all the worse. Furthermore, a hot drink of any kind
on a summer day did not appeal to him, and if he did not have anything hot to
drink, a cool glass of water seemed the best choice.

Then again…

He shifted his gaze across the street to the public house. The Wooden
Duck: a place for one to drink too much and party hard, and the leading cause
of aching heads the following morning. Morning consequence
notwithstanding, entering the pub sounded most agreeable, and a pint of ale,
at the very least, would alleviate his dehydration.

To heck with it! Abraham thought as he pulled up his trousers, ready to
march to the building. Inside would be plenty of shade and enough cool
beverages to go round. Indeed, that sounded like the best idea he had had in
ages, and there was nothing to put him off taking advantage of it all… except
the woman with rosy cheeks sitting outside a tearoom ten yards away, who
was staring at him with a disconcerting gawp.

Abraham looked at Rosy Cheeks for a moment, peered behind himself for
anything unusual and then looked back. He remained straight-faced as he
eyed the woman, wondering if she was even looking at him at all. She
appeared to be, and although Abraham was not showing it, her stare made
him feel nervous. It took a moment for Rosy Cheeks to realise what she was
doing, and she averted her gaze to the drinks menu on a nearby sandwich
board. Her face reddened further. Once again, she lifted her head and saw
Abraham still gazing back. She raised the corners of her lips to smile, a smile
that grew after Abraham returned an ungainly grin.

Rosy Cheeks beckoned Abraham over and signalled to the empty seat by
her table. His belly jumped, and he once again looked behind himself. Could
this gorgeous woman really be gesturing to him?

Remnant Tales of Stilly:
Passion and Benevolence

'No guts, no glory,' Abraham muttered as he took a deep breath and approached the stranger.

Abraham walked towards the woman, searching his mind for something to say. Whilst she did not stand out from the crowd, Rosy Cheeks was undeniably attractive. Her pale complexion, long, wavy blonde hair and sapphire eyes stole Abraham's attention.

The woman sat straight, one leg folded over the other as she waited for him to come closer. Her scarlet bodice and skirt complemented her slender physique and matched her reddened face. Then, there was that alluring smile.

Abraham sat down on the opposite side of the table to the Rosy Cheeks, awkward silence passing before he spoke. 'Fair noon. It's a nice day to be out and about.'

Abraham felt silly. That was hardly the best way to start a conversation, even if he had had little time to think of something else.

'Sorry—that was terrible. I've never been put in this position,' Abraham added.

Fortunately, the woman appreciated that he was in an unexpected position.

'Don't worry about it, Abe,' Rosy Cheeks said. 'For many, talking to a stranger is never easy.'

Abraham frowned and reclined in his seat. '*Stranger?*' he repeated. 'You know me?'

The woman gazed at Abraham momentarily in confusion but quickly realised what she had said. 'Oh... sorry... yes. That would have sounded odd. You see, a friend of mine spoke about you—indirectly, that is—she wanted to introduce us at some point and... uh...' Rosy Cheeks paused and sighed. Embarrassment filled her face. 'Forgive me. You must think I'm a complete fool.'

'No, not at all,' Abraham said. 'You just surprised me. Who is this friend of yours?'

'Myrah Dolb. She seems to know a lot of people.'

'Myrah, huh?' Abraham muttered, thinking back to a little while ago. 'I guess that makes sense. I saw her husband not long ago.'

'In any case, it is a pleasure to finally meet you. I've seen you about town a few times. I hear you're quite the architect.'

'Well… I'm more of a carpenter, actually. Mind you, I'm not so much anything these days.' Abraham rubbed the back of his head. Perhaps he should have kept that to himself. 'Anyway, my name is Abraham Gibenn, but as you already know, my friends sometimes call me Abe.'

'My name is Sylvia Enpee,' the woman said, holding her hand out. 'I am a doctor.'

Abraham relaxed and shook Sylvia's hand. 'I see. That's a coincidence because my…' Abraham paused. He shifted the conversation. 'Sylvia is a pretty name.'

'Thank you.'

'So… I presume that when you say doctor, you mean that you work at Wilheard's surgery?'

'That's right.'

'That's good. Helping people and all that,' Abraham said. 'You must be really busy most of the time. I can't say I have seen you about before.'

'Well, I only moved to Wilheard last season.'

Abraham nodded. 'Where from?'

'Pothaven.'

'Pothaven? Is that a village in Thane?'

'It is on the outskirt of Thane, yes.'

Thane, the largest province of Stilly, was a city that differed considerably from that of Wilheard. Known for its gothic gransanture and other large, stone buildings, many saw the city as the modern capital, where all the action and all the newest and greatest activities took place. Abraham had never visited, but its mention made him shiver inwardly.

'It was nice talking to you, Sylvia,' he said plaintively. He pushed himself up from the chair. 'I'll leave you to order your drink.'

Sylvia grabbed the carpenter's hand before he could take it off the table. 'Please don't go. I hope I haven't offended you. I really would like to get to know you better.'

Abraham looked down at his shoes, unspeaking.

'If it helps, you can tell me what is troubling you.' Sylvia tittered. 'Trust me... I'm a doctor.'

Abraham remained quiet.

'Or... if you want, tell me to get lost! I really hope you don't, though.'

Abraham chuckled at last, causing Sylvia's cheeks to glow once more. 'That is very thoughtful of you, Sylvia. I would be lying if I said I didn't want to get to know you, too. What did you have in mind?

Sylvia looked round. 'I noticed you eyeing up The Wooden Duck moments ago.'

'The Wooden Duck? A bit grubby for one such as yourself, surely? No offence.'

'Well, once you get to know me,' Sylvia winked, 'you'll realise that I'm hardier than I look. A grubby tavern is the least of my worries.'

Sylvia took Abraham by the hand and led him towards the building.

Ebony consulted her watch one last time as she reached within view of the cottage.

6.03pm—that is not too bad, she thought.

She had fallen asleep under the tree, more deeply than she had intended, and now she was late home. Quickening her pace, Ebony reached the cottage a minute later and leant her back against the front door to catch her breath. As her breathing steadied, she inhaled through her nose, smelling a pleasing aroma coming from inside. Was her father cooking? If true, that was certainly unexpected. Ebony made her way into the cottage.

Startled by the sounds of footsteps from the kitchen doorway, Abraham turned to see who was there. 'Oh! Fair eve, sweetheart. You're late home today,' he said, giving his daughter what appeared to be a genuine smile.

Ebony took a moment to study her father. He had been drinking; she could tell as much just by looking at him. Still, his movements were steady enough. 'Fair eve, Father. Sorry about being late; I lost track of time.'

Remnant Tales of Stilly:
Passion and Benevolence

Ebony sat at the kitchen table and watched Abraham move about. Before asking him what was going on, she decided to have a guess of it. Before parting ways earlier, she remembered that her father had been in a low frame of mind. Generally, he avoided drinking ales and the like as it typically exacerbated any low mood. What could have been different today? Abraham (as far as Ebony could remember) did not care much for parties and friendly gatherings these days, especially when unplanned.

'This is a nice surprise,' Ebony said. 'Your hands are clean, aren't they?'

Abraham wheeled round to his daughter and showed her both sides of his hands. As he leaned closer, the smell of alcohol on his breath confirmed what he had been doing. Regardless, Ebony remained silent over the matter.

Ebony walked over to her father and took hold of some of the nearby kitchen utensils he had been using. 'Do you need any help?' She asked, almost rhetorically, reaching for the boiling saucepan before him. 'I'll just--'

Ebony quickly withdrew her hand after getting a gentle pat on her wrist.

'Sit down, you. You do enough as it is, and it is my turn to do something for a change.'

Ebony took a step back and placed her hands on her hips. 'You sure have surprised me,' she said, her curiosity now at its limit. 'Not to sound suspicious, but what have you been up to today?'

Abraham concentrated on the cooking, not bothering to look at his daughter. 'I know what I'm doing. Having watched you cook for years, I am sure I have learned a thing or two.'

'Fair enough. As for what I asked?'

Unperturbed by his daughter's questioning, Abraham continued cooking, his smile remaining. Do you really need to know? Does it not just make a change to see me happier?

Ebony relaxed her stance. 'Not at all—I am relieved that you are, but--'

'Marvellous!' Abraham blurted.

'But,' Ebony repeated, 'that does not mean I don't have an interest in what you get up to.'

Abraham shrugged. 'I am just happy. Sit down and let me finish preparing dinner.'

Ebony readied herself to argue further, but her father once interrupted.

'Do as you are told, young lady,' he chirped. 'All you need to know is that all is well. Please just sit down for me. Actually, go and sit on the bench outside. I will call you when I'm finished.'

Taken aback by her father's sternness, Ebony closed her mouth and did as instructed, using the cottage's back door to go outside.

With dusk looming, natural light began diminishing as the sun descended, taking the day's heat. Still, it would not get dark for a while yet.

Ebony closed her eyes and listened to Abraham from inside the kitchen. Tapping her fingers on her folded leg, she chuckled as she thought of her father. It delighted her to see him smiling at long last. However, she was still curious to learn the reason for the sudden shift in his mood. One does not rise from depression for no reason.

Ebony reopened her eyes and peered at the landscape, sighing from the corner of her mouth as she waited to be let back into the cottage. Fortunately, she did not have to wait much longer, as Abraham called her five minutes after sending her out. She jumped to her feet in anticipation, wondering what her father had prepared.

Ebony and Abraham sat in silence as they ate. Considering she could not remember the last time her father had cooked, the meal turned out well, even if he had overdone the chicken a little. Abraham found everything Ebony had bought that morning, including the creamy tomato sauce; he used that to reduce the dryness.

'That was a tasty meal, Father. Thank you.'

Abraham wiped the short hairs that formed his beard with his sleeve. 'Glad you liked it.'

'So,' Ebony continued, dabbing her mouth with a cloth, 'are you going to tell me why you are happy?'

'If you tell me why you are wearing a bright yellow dress,' Abraham replied, his tone snide.

Ebony stared at her father and placed her elbows on the table, resting her chin on her clasped hands. 'I felt like a change.'

Abraham grunted in response, suggesting his answer was the same.

'Come on, Father—this attitude is uncalled for. I would genuinely like to know.'

Abraham hung his head in shame. It was one thing being defensive and quite another being rude. All the same, he remained quiet.

Ebony adjusted her approach. 'What did you get up to today? It must have been fun.'

Abraham tittered and downed the glass of water in front of him. 'I suppose it was.'

Ebony waited for her father to go on.

'Well, aside from fixing the handle on the front door, I made some new friends... in The Wooden Duck.'

Ebony beamed. 'That's fantastic—both about the front door and your new friends. They must have been nice to make you want to cook dinner.'

Abraham did not answer. That last part made him uncomfortable, even if that had been unintentional. 'Be honest with me, Ebony,' he said, pushing the glass away. 'Do you see me as a liability?'

Ebony frowned, instantly forgetting the conversation. 'This again? As I said this morning, Father—*no*. Has someone been putting ideas in your head?'

'No, it's just...' Abraham paused. 'Since your mother disappeared, you have taken over her role in many ways and more—you have become a carer for me. It is as if I have just noticed I am taking advantage of you. I feel useless.'

Ebony grimaced and took hold of her father's hands. 'I love you, Father, and that is why I care for you. As your daughter, I know more than anyone else that you are a kind-hearted, loving and persistent man when it comes to life—and this may surprise you—but I admire you for those things. I like to think that is where I get my qualities, and I have never considered that you are taking advantage of me. These are achievements alone, not including all your architectural work. You are far from useless.'

A fleeting smile played on Abraham's lips.

Ebony continued. 'What you must remember, though, is that everyone has weaknesses. No one is perfect.'

Abraham nodded feebly. 'I know, and I want you to understand that I appreciate everything you have done for me over the years.' He took his hands from his daughter's and stood, taking the empty plates from the table. 'However, there are going to be changes.'

Ebony pushed herself up. 'There is nothing wrong with change if that is what you want. I am always here to support you. I'll fetch a bucket of water from the tank, and then I can help you clean. Cooking me dinner is more than enough today.'

Between themselves, the pair washed and dried the plates, cutlery and other dishes in silence. Abraham, rubbing the moisture from a plate with a towel, stared pensively out the kitchen window as the sun continued to sink further towards the horizon.

Ebony looked periodically at her father, noticing his pace had slowed and the wet crockery was piling. She peered out the window for a moment to see what was holding his attention, but upon looking at him again, it seemed that this was nothing in particular.

'A stinnep for your thoughts,' Ebony said.

'Sorry?' Abraham uttered as he awoke from his musing.

'You were miles away there. Is something on your mind?'

'Nothing that hasn't already been said.'

'Are you still thinking about what we spoke about at the table? About being a liability?'

Abraham blew an audible sigh. 'A little, but don't worry about that—I haven't forgotten what you said. I guess I will be thinking about my problems for a while longer. That is until I can figure out what I really want.'

Abraham looked down at the pile of cleaned crockery in front of him and quickened his pace.

Ebony watched her father. 'Have I ever done anything to make you question your self-worth?'

'Never on purpose—but don't think you have done me wrong, sweetheart,' Abraham added before Ebony could feel guilt. 'How you looked at me this morning while I chopped that wood made me wonder if I was losing my sanity. You seem baffled with many things I do these days.'

'I am sorry…'

'Don't be,' he said as he finished drying. 'I cannot blame you, and I am not. Honestly, I have started to question myself, and when that happens, I must be doing something wrong. Now, if we are finished here, I'm going outside for a bit.'

Abraham went outside through the rear cottage door and sat on the bench. Ebony followed and sat next to him. 'That wood you chopped… would you be able to use it for anything creative?'

The wooden bench on which the pair sat was something Abraham had put together years ago, and although it was showing its age, the bench was still as sturdy as it had always been, which exemplified his craft.

Abraham looked at the top edge of the bench's backrest, where his daughter was brushing her fingers. 'Maybe,' he said. 'The pieces might be too small for anything worthwhile, but I guess I can have a look.'

Ebony nodded and stared forward to admire the landscape. After a moment of silence, she broke it by humming a tune.

Listening to his daughter's crooning, Abraham tugged at the bristles on his chin. The tune was the same one that she had hummed earlier. Where had he heard that music before?

Without warning, he clapped his hands together, making Ebony jump. 'I know where I've heard that tune! That one you were humming earlier today… or was it yesterday? Well, whenever it was, I remember where else heard it now.'

'You mean Ballad of the Deity?'

'Yeah, that's the one,' Abraham continued. He paused and plucked at his chin once again.

'Well? From where did you hear it?' Ebony pushed.

'From the east, I think. I've even seen the musician—played on a guitar, he did.'

Ebony looked towards Wilheard's eastern forest. 'What did he look like?'

'Well, it was a while ago, so my memory's sketchy, but from what I remember, it was a man… pretty scruffy—probably a traveller. He had longish hair and untidy clothes. He was not exactly standing nearby. In truth, I didn't pay him much mind at the time.'

'I see,' Ebony said, not looking away from the forestry. Despite his apathy on the subject, Abraham had managed to captivate his daughter's imagination. 'What colour was his clothing?'

Remnant Tales of Stilly:
Passion and Benevolence

Abraham frowned at the question. 'What kind of a thing to ask is that?' he said, snorting a laugh. 'I can't remember. Why do you care anyway?'

Ebony shifted her gaze away from the woodland and back towards her farther. She had a vacant look in her eyes that suggested she had not heard her father's reply.

Abraham groaned. 'You're not thinking of doing anything silly, are you?'

Ebony blinked. 'Pardon?'

'I recognise that look on your face, and I know what you're like. Your decisions can be quite wild when you have something on your mind. You were like that even as a child.'

'Yes, well... I am not a little girl anymore, Father. In case you forgot, I am twenty-eight.'

'Twenty-eight, forty-eight, or even ninety-eight—you are still my daughter. I understand your curiosity with mysterious things, but that man is a stranger—one that skulks in the woods—it would be--'

'Skulking?' Ebony interrupted her father. 'He cannot be hiding that much if he was playing the guitar in plain view. Assuming that you saw him under such circumstances?'

Abraham groaned again.

Ebony went on. 'Anyway, you needn't worry. I have no plans to chase after mysterious men.'

'You have no plans? You mean, as of yet?'

'I mean, I have no reason to want to.'

'You have no reason *yet*, or...?

'Let's just leave it at that, Father, all right.

'Yeah, well, if you start getting stupid ideas, just think that this bloke might not be a people person. Like I said'—Abraham peered back to the landscape—'when I saw the man, he didn't *seem* to want much attention. Besides, you probably won't find anyone. Like I said, I saw him a while ago, and he was probably a vagabond.'

The pair sat in silence; a short time later, Ebony pulled out her pocket watch. The time was approaching 8.30pm, and the sky had darkened to a deep mauve-red. She kissed her father fair night and headed for bed.

Remnant Tales of Stilly:
Passion and Benevolence

An oil lamp stood on the dresser behind the headrest of Ebony's bed. The dull light produced by the flame flickered restlessly, causing the shadows in the room to waver. Ebony sat cross-legged on her bed and opened to the last page she had reached in Passion and Benevolence. Tired, she would not be up for much longer, but since she had already changed into her nightwear, it was just a matter of extinguishing the oil lamp and slipping under her quilt.

Passion and Benevolence.
Malevolent Eyes.

Near 60 days had passed since the return of Lord Fordon Latnemirt, and although I remember him as a private man before his two-year absence, he brought back a colder and darker mindset.

Although growing calmer as days passed, Fordon's mood remained disparaging, showing disinterest in social situations, responding monosyllabically and oft displaying a wan expression. Even after the meeting in the throne room, I felt none the wiser about what cruelty had befallen him. Whatever the cause of this desolation, it was apparent he did not intend to share his thoughts, even with those who had before been close friends, and he spent most of his time shut away in his tower. Indeed, only a handful of times did Fordon emerge from this solitude. Perhaps one can forgive my surprise that such an appearance came during the annual Summer Festival, when the castle saw its heaviest activity, owing to King Godfrey permitting unrestricted entry to the castle gardens.

It was partway through the seven-day-long festivity when I spied Fordon. At first (however unlikely it may have been), I wondered if he was watching over the flowerbeds. He had always been an avid gardener and might have been making sure damage was minimal. He circulated the gardens, keeping to the shade of archways, foliage and other tall objects. He had no interest in mingling with the crowds, content to watch from a distance, and the joyous ambience did nothing to alleviate his sour expression.

Jugglers, dancers, buffoons and other such performers entertained the masses of people that had flooded the grounds, most of whom making merry as they danced and swilled casks of mead and wine, all the while growing ever more flirtatious with the opposite sex. Being a man who shouldered a certain social standing, I did not indulge in such behaviour. Regardless of my position, I held little desire to spend my time in such a way, and I could only assume Fordon was of a similar mind. Even though I had no reason to suspect him of anything sinister then, his loitering afforded me enough suspicion to see what he was up to, which I did by merging with the jamboree. If Fordon's intentions were as baleful as his stare, I cannot imagine that I would have been capable of doing anything to stop him.

However, it turned out that I was not the only man interested in his movements.

'You seem troubled, my lord,' the soft voice of another man said.

Fordon calmly looked to his left. Cross-legged on a stone step, Darwin Loydon, a man with ragged clothes and exceptionally long red hair, gazed back at him with squinting eyes. Fordon gave the younger man a searching look, perhaps surprised he had not spotted him sooner. In most instances, Darwin did not blend well in crowds, but with the current flamboyance of surrounding performers, he did just that.

I sneaked closer and listened in on the conversation.

Fordon showed no agitation or interest in Darwin's presence and resumed his wistful stare into the masses.

Darwin looked down at the tin flute he had been playing moments ago. Twisting the instrument between his fingers, he peered up again, the faint smile he always wore not leaving his lips. 'Although you speak no words, your eyes reveal all.'

'What do you want of me?' Fordon sighed, his tone as hostile as it was impatient.

Darwin stood up with a gracious twist, keeping his eyes on Fordon. 'A smile would suffice.'

Fordon pulled a mocking grin before turning his attention away again. This made Darwin chuckle.

Remnant Tales of Stilly:
Passion and Benevolence

'At least you retain some form of humour,' Darwin said. He tooted on his whistle. 'Alas, you don't look like you are enjoying yourself. Such an atmosphere is meant for--'

'Is there a reason for your provocation?' Fordon interrupted.

Darwin chuckled again, his lips expanding. 'I mean not to provoke anyone. It is such a lovely day. Such times bring needed joy to my heart.'

Fordon sneered. 'Spoken like a true fool. I feel no such joy.'

Darwin gave Fordon a cheery slap on the back, causing the older man to jerk. 'Then I'm glad you have not truly lost your ability to *feel*, my lord. I had feared you had lost more than your vigour for life. This calls for a song!'

Darwin danced, blowing his whistle again and hopping about from one foot to the other as he turned circles round the older man.

Fordon glowered. 'What would you know of what I have lost?'

Latnemirt wheeled round, sending his robe into motion. He walked away then and to a quieter part of the garden. Darwin stopped prancing and followed, as did I.

Walking a pace behind Fordon, Darwin continued talking. 'Admittedly, I know not as much about you as I once did, but whisperings carry rumours.'

'So that is why you and your three associates spy on me—idle talk?' Fordon smirked when Darwin failed to answer. 'Let me be frank, Sovereign Knight. I cannot abide this scrutiny—by you or anyone else. If we are to stay out of each other's way, I am positive that relationships will not turn bitter.'

Darwin tilted his head forward. 'I agree, it would be unfortunate for any sentiments to turn bitter, but yours already have. Negative emotions can lead down undesirable paths. Metaphorically speaking, I hear rumours that you are lost... and might be treading the wrong path.'

Fordon stopped walking and turned his attention back to Darwin. 'I suspect you hear many claims. Be what may, I do hope you are astute enough for the prattle within the castle not to influence your judgment.'

Darwin bobbed his head. 'In any case, why do you believe we are watching you?'

Remnant Tales of Stilly:
Passion and Benevolence

Fordon sneered. 'It might be true that I have changed during my absence from Wilheard, but my eyesight is not among those changes, I can assure you.'

'I am not questioning your ability to see, my lord,' Darwin insisted, his long hair rippling as he shook his head. 'I was simply wondering if you know why we might be watching you. You understand, surely, that the task of maintaining balance is a tricky one. I do not imagine anyone wants the scales to be tipped, especially on the whims of any one man.'

Fordon laughed humourlessly. 'Do not play with me, Sovereign Knight. If you mean to make threats, then come out with it. That you can stand there and lecture me on my practices is an insult. My actions are not harming anyone, as you would doubtless know if you are indeed watching me.'

Fordon moved closer to Darwin then. 'Speaking of which, and before you reply with some sardonic remark, perhaps you should reflect on your forgotten privileges before talking down to others. You cannot boast about your past, and the evidence is etched forever onto your body. Thanks to Emmanuel Grellic, you can enjoy these privileges. Incidentally, my studies are essentially parallel to the minach's own. Perhaps you should divert your attention to him.'

I remember clearly: the mention of my name caused my heart to skip a beat. Still, neither man seemed aware of my presence.

Darwin remained unperturbed by the reproach, his simper lingering. He spoke one last time before Fordon left; the following words made me shudder.

'I have clearly struck a nerve, my lord, and for that, I apologise. I fear my company will only aggravate you further, so rest assured that I will be out of your sight presently. Before I do, however, allow me to clarify one particular detail. My comrades and I have closely watched Emmanuel over the years, as we do everyone. It is our duty as the Sovereign Knights, and we hold no prejudice.

'As you say, what you and Emmanuel research is something I owe my life. Yet, I argue that what the good minach practises differs from what occurs in your chambers. After all, your purpose—your ambitions—are not shared with Emmanuel. The world is not in black and white, my lord, and like anything in life, what your work achieves can be positive but also harmful. This is why you are so secretive, no? You were a true friend to the realm before your fateful disappearance. These days... well, I am not sure what you are.

'In any case, if you change your mind about sharing your thoughts, do not hesitate to reach out to me. I am still very interested in what you get up to, and people say I am a good listener. In the meantime, my *associates* and I would rather keep all doors upright.'

Fordon turned his back on Darwin and made a start towards the castle. 'I'll bear that in mind, although one will find that my door is of a sturdy kind.'

9.30pm.

Sitting in front of a table and mirror while looking out the open window of her rented room, Sylvia gazed at the dull-coloured sky as the sun-deprived the town of its remaining light. Contentment playing on her lips, the view made a pleasant end to an all-round pleasant day.

Wringing a flannel over a water bowl, the doctor wiped the rose-red makeup from her cheeks and lips. She was thinking about Abraham. Since arriving in Wilheard in spring, and despite Myrah Dolb's promise of an introduction, Sylvia had only seen him in passing. Yet, today had been the day: Sylvia and Abraham had finally met.

Sylvia gazed at her reflection in the oval mirror as she rubbed the flannel round her eyes. Partway through wiping, she paused upon feeling the presence of the *little woman*.

'I was wondering when you would reappear,' Sylvia said. 'Come out where I can see you, Ninapaige.'

'I already am out where you can see me, young one.'

Sylvia shifted on her chair and looked behind herself. Ninapaige, a two-foot-tall imp clad in a flamboyant yellow and black jester outfit, was sitting on the end of Sylvia's bed. She watched the doctor through the eyes of an earthen mask with a huge and creepy smile.

'Take that thing off,' Sylvia sighed, returning to the mirror. 'You know I don't like them.'

Looking at Ninapaige in the mirror, Sylvia noticed that the happy mask had changed to a sad-faced one, with blue lining underneath the eyeholes to represent tears. Ninapaige continued to stare at Sylvia with her large, violet eyes. Despite the sad expression of the mask, Sylvia could tell that the being was smiling underneath.

'And I hate how you do that even more,' Sylvia complained. 'Changing those things round in the blink of an eye… It gives me chills.'

Ninapaige shrilled a laugh. 'I have always lamented over your distaste for my masks. It is such a shame.'

Sylvia turned to face Ninapaige directly once again. The mask was now gone, revealing the previously hidden face. With her child-like body and slightly oversized head, Ninapaige was an oddity, but her otherwise human similarities prevented her from being particularly frightening. Despite her form, Ninapaige was no child, and Sylvia had known her long enough to see past this harmless façade.

Sylvia looked deep into Ninapaige's eyes. 'How long have you been in Wilheard?'

'For as long as you.'

Sylvia parted her lips to ask if she had followed her from Thane but considered the question needless. 'Why now? Why have you not come to me sooner?'

'I thought it would be fun to see what you would get up to from a distance and give you more space. Do not think, however, that I have not been watching you closely. I notice you have been very busy the last few months. A place to live, a position at the surgery'—Ninapaige smiled mischievously—'Making new friends. Indeed, you are doing very well for yourself. You have my felicitations.'

Sylvia closed her eyes and took a deep breath, shaking her head as she exhaled. 'Please don't get in my way. I know you mean well, but I have long waited to return to Wilheard…'

'I can see what you have been up to, girl. I am not stupid, nor am I blind.'
Ninapaige pulled a patronising expression. 'Do you really think you can
waltz into the town and everyone will accept you with open arms? Ten years
is quite a long time for you humans, or so I have heard, but in those years,
you have changed significantly no matter how much you fail to see that.'

'I *am* aware of my circumstance, but do you really need to make it seem
so bleak?' Sylvia said, opening her eyes to find Ninapaige again.

'Let's not play games, girl,' the imp said, making Sylvia jump. She had
somehow moved herself to the table in front of the doctor without making a
sound. 'We both know what you have been through, and all I mean to say is
there is no need to be so headstrong. Slow down a bit.'

'Please don't interfere. I beg you.'

'*Interfere*?' Ninapaige repeated with a scornful cackle. 'Is that really how
you see me? As an interference. Have you ever noticed that you have not
once thanked me for what I have done for you? Ungrateful, *foolish* child.'

Sylvia ignored Ninapaige's raised tones and remained calm. Defiance
shone in her blue eyes. 'I am *not* a child, and I resent you treating me like
one.'

Sylvia looked back into the mirror and wiped the flannel over her face,
pretending she could no longer see Ninapaige. The imp chuckled and flicked
her silver hair back, causing it to glitter in the dimming sunlight. 'Well, you
oft act as peevish as one. It is difficult to tell, sometimes, whether you have
changed at all. It is as if you are still that same girl I met all those years ago.'

'Let's not go there again,' Sylvia sighed, suspecting she was about to be
given the tired lecture of how they met. 'Not now.'

'Yes, I remember it as if it were yesterday,' Ninapaige continued,
disregarding Sylvia's request. 'How far would you have got if I had not
found you? After that unfortunate incident with that suoido. Stuck in that
perilous situation after fleeing, who was there to help you? Who ensured that
beast did not live to hunt you down any further? My *interfering* played a part
in all of that!'

Sylvia dropped the red-stained flannel into the bowl of water. 'I
remember it as well as you. It is not something that I can forget.'

'In any case, never mind that for now. I am not here to argue, nor am I here to *interfere*. I come with advice.'

Sylvia met Ninapaige's eyes.

'Actually, it is more of a reminder,' Ninapaige continued. 'That suoido may be long gone, but that does not mean you should abandon your senses. Troubles still lurk in the shadows.

'Then what must I do?'

Ninapaige smirked. 'You need just be careful, especially when getting close to other people. As always, I will help you where I can.'

Sylvia bit gently on her bottom lip. 'I appreciate what you do to help me, but I know what I am doing. I will take care of things myself if need be.'

Ninapaige shrugged and jumped from the table. Moving to the open window, she peered at the twilight sky. 'Do not do anything hasty, young human. I realise how capable you are, but you are not invulnerable.'

As Ninapaige jumped onto the sill, Sylvia called to her, causing the imp to halt. 'I have never doubted you, Ninapaige, and...' She paused, her lips pursed, ready to say something else, but nothing came.'

Ninapaige nodded, her grin changing to something more self-satisfied. 'I will continue to watch over you, Sylvia, whether you like it or not.'

With that, Ninapaige was gone.

The hour was early, and silence filled the darkened streets of Wilheard.

Exhausted from their hours of patrolling, night guards yawned uncontrollably as they stared towards Clock Tower, counting the minutes until the morning unit would relieve them. As far as evenings went in Wilheard, everything seemed in order, including the periodic squabbling of cats, barking canines and even the rattling of a wooden cart from the edge of the town.

Pulled by two mares, a merchant sat upon his consignment and groaned as his cart entered Wilheard. It had been a long night of travelling, and the man (and his horses) was looking forward to a well-deserved rest, not least because he was feeling unwell. By the time he had reached a mile from the town, the merchant's head and chest had begun to hurt. At first, the discomfort had been mild, but the closer he got to Wilheard's border, the more agonising it became.

The merchant wiped the sweat from his face as the pain in his chest became more intolerable. The headache had developed into a migraine, thumping inside his skull and causing blurred vision. Was he having a heart attack? Whatever the problem, he had little time to dwell on it. Clutching the centre of his chest, the merchant's face contorted into an expression of extreme pain. With his eyes rolled back, the man slanted to his left and fell off the cart, crashing to the grass below.

Startled by the man's abrupt dismount, the horses halted. Letting out a whinny, the horse to the front left of the cart turned its head to find its master. Sure enough, the merchant was lying close by, his body violently twisted into an unusual position. The mare shook its mane and peered forward once more. Although it did not understand what was happening, the animal could sense the merchant was still alive and simply waited for him to get up again. The merchant's fingers twitched a minute later, followed by other body parts as his distorted form unravelled with an unpleasant crunch. His body returned to its original shape, the merchant got to his feet at a speed that defied his portly figure.

The merchant wavered past the horses, accidentally bumping into the left mare and agitating both animals. Showing no concern for anything around him, the man stopped walking when he reached the top edge of a mound. He looked over Wilheard, the rising sun shining on his pallid face as he stared with vacant eyes at what lay ahead. He could hear whispering: an undistinguishable voice giving him orders.

Meandering onwards, the merchant obeyed.

Remnant Tales of Stilly:
Passion and Benevolence

Chapter Three

Ebony was not sleeping well again. Waking half a dozen times during the early hours, she twisted and turned, falling back to sleep only to suffer the same dream.

She walked through a dense forest, dark from the lack of natural light. As she crept through the dusky surroundings, she eventually came to an open area with a lone tree stump at its centre. Ebony looked from side to side and then skywards, finally bringing her attention back down to the stump on which a man now sat, his light-brown hair obscuring his face. On his knee rested a guitar, his fingers on both ends of the strings and in the playing position. He made nary a sound, his posture seemingly frozen in time.

Ebony stood, observing the man, until she heard an unnerving laugh shrill from her left. Turning her head, she noticed a woman hanging from a muddy ledge. The mud was soaked in liquid of a putrid colour that seeped from round the unknown figure's hands. The collapse of the ledge was imminent, and she would eventually lose her hold and fall into the abyss below.

Instinctively, Ebony tried to move to the woman but found something restricting her movements. Tree roots and wildflowers bound her ankles, anchoring her to the ground. Clawing at her restraints, Ebony turned to the man. 'Help!' she called. 'There must be something you can do…'

The man, seemingly unaware of Ebony's pleas, remained on the stump. To no avail, Ebony continued her struggle with the roots, watching as the hanging woman, who not once turned round to look, slid closer to her doom. Despite her peril, the dangling figure made no sign of panic; she did not scream or call for help. Ebony did not understand what was happening.

It did not take long for the inevitable to happen. The mysterious woman lost her hold, falling backwards into the void below, cascades of the disgusting fluid that weakened the ledge following her.

Trembling with frustration, Ebony called to the insensible man once again. 'W-why? Can you not see what just happened? You did nothing!'

As expected, he did not respond, and his position remained unchanged. Yet, something about him was different. The guitar previously on his lap was gone, replaced by a sword. Behind the man, beast-like shadows emerged from the trees, growling with belligerent intent. As if suddenly unfrozen, the man took the blade by the hilt and rose to his feet, his attention facing forward.

Was he looking at Ebony? She could not tell; shadow darkened his face.

She watched as the beasts behind the man shifted ever closer, yet he did not move. Closer and closer—so close they were now directly behind him… then next to him… now in front of him. The shadows were not after the man at all; they were after her.

Ebony could not move; this time, fear, not roots, held her still. She wanted to scream, but her lungs betrayed her.

The same laugh from before shrieked behind Ebony, followed by a whisper. 'Time to awaken, girl!'

Ebony woke in a cold sweat.

Captain of the Guard Oliath Burley paced up and down the lobby of Wilheard Hall, outside from the mayor's Office. Although not particularly nervous, the muscular man had a lot that he wished to discuss with his employer and did not feel relaxed enough where he could sit down comfortably.

Nolen and Cordelia were nearby. The lieutenants stood and looked about the well-decorated hallway, reading various notices as they waited for their boss's invitation into the office.

Oliath stopped pacing at the office entrance and read the bold lettering on the door's frosted glass.

Basil Wolleb, Mayor of Wilheard.

Oliath grumbled and folded his arms. Speaking to neither Nolan nor Cordelia in particular, he asked how the investigations into the recent events were going.

'Cordelia and I have relayed the orders to the *Other Four*, sir,' Nolan answered.

'To be more specific, sir,' Cordelia continued, 'we conveyed your instructions to Dexter Theryle. However, we have yet to hear back from him.'

'Understood,' Oliath said, rubbing his chin. 'I suppose it is too early to expect decent results.'

Oliath chuckled to himself, thinking about what Cordelia said. He knew why the pair had decided to talk to Dexter over the other three. Theryle, however boorish, was the easiest to deal with, and whatever the given task, he would relay it to the other three. This, Oliath gathered, saved for a lot of vexation.

'I presume all is well, anyway,' Oliath said. Although not actually asking, the way he looked at the pair suggested otherwise.

Nolan nodded in response.

The door to Mayor Wolleb's office opened with a click. Standing at the entrance to the room was a well-dressed man with a moustache that looked much like a broomhead. This facial hair, along with his receding hairline, suggested he was older than the forty years he claimed to be. Although his face displayed that of a tired, old man, he possessed stamina more akin to someone half his age, which was a blessing when it came to his busy work life. His name was Benjamin Oswin, and he was the mayor's assistant.

'Fair morn,' Oswin said to Oliath before glancing at Cordelia and Nolan. 'Mayor Wolleb will see you now, but might I suggest that your lieutenants remain--'

Oliath, in no mood for the assistant's pernickety behaviour, ignored what Benjamin had to say and effectively barged past him, followed closely by the other two. All Oliath wanted was to get his meeting with the mayor underway.

Although ruffled by Oliath's arrogance, Benjamin controlled any annoyance by jutting his chin forward and rolling his neck. He straightened his bow tie and walked back into the office.

Oliath stood a metre from the front of a sizable desk and waited for its owner to notice him. Clutter filled its surface, revealing the true nature of

Basil Wolleb, who was sitting on the opposite side; a troubling sight, considering it belonged to the man who governed the town.

Oliath shifted his eyes about the office and groaned inwardly. Not much in life worried him. Indeed, he tackled daunting tasks all the time with not so much as a bat of the eyelids, but something about this office bothered him, something that made his gut turn. Upon entering the office, an acrid, dusty smell assaulted anyone who dared breathe. This was a shame, as the office was an otherwise pleasant room; spacious and practically empty, Oliath reckoned over twenty fully-grown people could squeeze inside if attempted, which made Oswin's desire to keep Cordelia and Nolan outside unjustified. On opposite ends of the room stood bookcases that completely covered the walls. Both cases were filled with politically themed books, ranging from the history of law to various dogmatic ideals. Near the farthest bookcase was a trophy cabinet and a desk belonging to Oswin. This desk also reflected the owner's personality, which was well-kept and orderly.

A Stillian flag hung on the wall above Oswin's desk: three red bands on a dark blue backdrop spiralled from a gold circle centring. Gold accented the stems and flag borders. From what Oliath remembered from his school years, the circle represented Wilheard, the heart of Stilly, and the arms signified the three other regions of the kingdom: Adelaide, Drieloca and Thane.

'I have had easier days, I must admit,' the ageing mayor droned. He had his head down as he finished reading over a document with the heading *Public Diplomacy*, the quill pen in his hand disrupting the silence as it scratched across the paper.

Oliath's eyes snapped forward. Wolleb gazed at the piece of paper before him, picking it up and balancing it on his fingers. Oliath looked at Basil in silence, keenly noticing a frown on the older man despite a grey beard covering a proportion of his face.

Dropping his quill on the desk and removing a broken pair of reading glasses, Wolleb sat back in his chair and looked up at the captain. 'Sit down, man, sit down,' he said, gesturing to the seat on the other side of the desk. 'I promise I won't charge you for the pleasure.'

Remnant Tales of Stilly:
Passion and Benevolence

Oliath stepped in front of a high-backed leather chair and sat to face Basil. He folded his legs. 'Is something troubling you, Mayor? Anything I can help with?'

Wolleb gave a thin smile. 'Much obliged, my good man, but I was only thinking about this very meeting and what we will discuss.'

Oliath acknowledged with a nod.

Oswin offered everyone a hot drink; none accepted.

'Thank you, Benjamin, but this shouldn't take long,' Wolleb answered, getting the meeting underway. 'So, Oliath, do you have anything to add to what I already know?'

'Only the recent offender's identity, and that I have dispatched my personal team to investigate matters further.'

'I see.' Wolleb shifted forward in his chair. 'And what is the location of the offender?'

'He is in custodial detention. It didn't seem necessary to put him in a cell like the other felons.'

Wolleb nodded. 'Agreed—the poor fellow did not sound like your average wrongdoer.' He held his spectacles to his eyes and looked down at a poorly written note beside a pile of paper. 'And you say the man is a traveller, like the previous detainee?'

'Yes, sir—a merchant, to be specific. As with the one before, he has an unusual air about him and appears to be suffering from memory lapses.' Oliath unfolded his legs and sat forward. 'With that said, I haven't found out all I can about the merchant. With your permission, I would like to interrogate him.'

Wolleb reclined again and picked up a nearby paperweight. He bit down on his bottom lip as he toyed with the spherical object.

Oswin entered the conversation. 'With all due respect, Captain Burley, your interrogation methods tend to be... well... a little coarse.'

Oliath gave the assistant a sideward glance. 'I suppose I can be a little heavy-handed at times, but it will only be an interrogation. I see no reason why it should go any differently from how we are talking now.'

Oswin folded his arms. 'Nevertheless, perhaps I should undertake the questioning myself. I have a way with these things.'

Oliath snorted. Never in his life had he seen that little twerp do anything even close to questioning a suspect, let alone be any good at it. 'I appreciate the offer, but that will not be needed.'

'In fairness, Oliath, he has a point.' Wolleb put the paperweight down. 'I think it would be a good idea for Benjamin to talk with the merchant. In the meantime, there are other things more suited to your time, I'm sure you will agree. In fact, you are welcome to do whatever else you feel necessary.'

Oliath prepared to argue against the decision but changed his mind. Instead, he gave a single nod and pushed himself up from the seat. He ran his fingers through his hair, as he often did, and suppressed any irritation. 'Very well. Is there anything else you wish to--?'

'Can I make a suggestion?' Wolleb said before Oliath could finish speaking.

'Of course, Mayor.'

'The place the merchant had his sights on...' Basil again sought the scrawled note, 'Blow Your Mind!... Was that the place?'

'Yes,' Oliath replied monotonously. Regardless of how fitting, the shop's name sounded ridiculous when said aloud, especially when uttered by one such as the mayor. Specialising in gunpowder and other flammables, the twin owners had an acquired sense of humour.

Wolleb continued. 'What is the damage to the place?'

'The back door was blown inwards,' Oliath said.

'Ironic—to have their own gunpowder used against them.' The mayor grumbled. 'Perhaps it will serve as a lesson not to sell such substances to everyone.'

Oliath hummed, thinking back to the crime scene. He had seen no evidence of gunpowder use.

'What do you think the connection is?' Wolleb asked, interrupting Oliath's musing.

Oliath did not answer, assuming the question was rhetorical. He was still waiting for Basil's suggestion.

'Weaponry, Captain Burley—weaponry,' Oswin answered, filling the silence. 'Don't worry, I'm not missing the bigger picture, but it would be foolish not to at least consider the simpler details. You should be careful—overlooking such details can stall progress.'

Oliath bristled, giving the shorter man a withering stare. The condescending twerp has become not only a proficient interviewer but a detective as well. Years of training and experience attained in mere minutes. Exchanging insults with Oswin would be easy, but he was in no mood. Besides, Oliath had already considered weaponry.

'Forgive me for saying, Mayor,' Oliath said, 'but wasn't the last attack on a vacant building?'

Wolleb nodded and answered quickly. 'I understand the two latest attacks are not exactly comparable, and the attack on the house could have been a simple mistake.'

Oliath regarded the mayor dubiously, but it seemed Wolleb had predicted such a reaction. 'In any case, my good man, I trust you haven't forgotten the attacks a few months back—the oil refinery, for example. Even that unusual chemical and powder shop. I reckon such things can be used for something harmful.'

Oliath grunted in acknowledgement and moved towards the office exit. 'I will re-examine the recent scenes and inform you of any news.'

Benjamin Oswin watched Oliath Burley and his lieutenants walk down the lobby and out of sight. 'Ignorant fool!' he said, stepping back into the office and closing the door.

'Now, now, Benjamin,' Basil said, looking down at his desk to resume his paperwork. 'Didn't you promise you would show some restraint when Oliath is present? He was exercising self-control if you hadn't noticed.'

'I know, Mister Wolleb. Besides, I like to think that I was restrained during the meeting. Now that he is gone, however... well, I'm sure we both say all kinds of things behind each other's back.' Benjamin paused and gritted his teeth. 'I'm sorry, Mayor... it's just the man is an infuriating idiot.'

Remnant Tales of Stilly:
Passion and Benevolence

'No, Benjamin, he is not an idiot. Perhaps arrogant, rash, short-tempered and—like you—stubborn, but he is certainly no fool. In any case, I cannot see why you wind yourself up—just look at yourself, man! It really does your demeanour an injustice.'

Benjamin jutted out his chin and straightened his already tidy bow tie. He looked at his reflection on one of the well-polished silver dishes in the trophy cabinet and twitched his lips, causing his broom-like moustache to dance from side to side. He ran his index finger down the bristles and pulled an exaggerated expression of shame.

'Just remember you are a grown man,' Basil chortled. 'Anyway, lectures aside, I trust you are prepared to go through with the interrogations and that you did not say such things simply to annoy Oliath.'

'Come now, Mister Wolleb. As it happens, I have been doing my own research into these recent episodes since the beginning. I'm offended you had not noticed.'

'I do beg your pardon, Benjamin. You know that I struggle to keep up with your multitasking. I am not surprised, however, that you have an eye on these things. With that said, I hope you have finished your work before sticking your nose into Oliath's.'

'Of course,' the assistant replied, already preparing to leave the office.

'And what about the organisation of the upcoming festival?'

'All prepared for, as too are my assessments written. I put the work on your desk last night.'

Basil looked at the piles of paper on his desk. He groaned and stroked his beard. 'If only I had ten per cent of your orderliness.'

'Thank goodness you don't,' Benjamin countered. 'I would be out of a job.'

'By obtaining a measly ten per cent?'

Benjamin winked at the mayor.

Basil laughed aloud. 'Such conceit!'

Benjamin opened the office door once again and looked at Basil. 'Seriously, though. With the upcoming festival, and if these attacks continue, Oliath will have a lot on his plate. We may not see eye-to-eye on everything, but I would hate to see him be overwhelmed with his duties.'

Basil relaxed his face and looked his assistant in the eyes. 'I recognise that look... you've got a bad feeling about something.'

'I'm sure everything will be fine, Mayor, but, like Oliath, I just want to know more about these travellers.'

Abraham had awakened early that morning, leaving the cottage to meet his mysterious new friends.

Ebony had given some thought as to what these people were like. If, indeed, there was more than one. Ebony had suspicions about that; judging from her father's coyness, it was likely only one person and someone of the opposite sex. The thought intrigued Ebony, but she did not plan to spy on her parent. Besides, something else was occupying her mind.

With the library book underarm, Ebony yawned as she made her way down a foot-trodden path and away from home. She pulled out her pocket watch. The hands read 8.36am. She was later than usual, thanks to her restless night. Her dream had been as strange as it had been frightening. Ebony could not remember the nightmare entirely but vividly recalled the man with the guitar. This figure likely came about because of what she and her father spoke of the night before.

Whatever the dream meant, if anything at all, Ebony was not worried about it. Nightmares, no matter how scary, were still only nightmares, and now that she was awake, the thoughts no longer had such an effect.

Ebony pulled Passion and Benevolence from under her arm and read while walking.

Passion and Benevolence.
Troubled Princess.

An entire season had passed since my old friend Lord Fordon Latnemirt's return, and even though the trees were changing, his seclusion was not. In truth, however, Fordon was not the only one isolating himself.

King Godfrey, increasingly aware of his daughter's solitude, had asked me to visit her. Being a minach and the (then) princess's mentor, His Majesty was convinced I was the one she trusted the most with any concerns. I like to think that Evelyn and I shared a positive bond, and I did not argue the matter. Godfrey, at the very least, hoped we would share a prayer.

Princess Evelyn's bedchamber was situated in the second of the three western towers of the castle. Holding a copy of Scripture of Naitsir: Traeh Blessings to my chest as I made my way up the winding stairs, I paused a moment at the top, as I often did, to catch my breath and think what to say; nothing particular came to mind. I felt that this recent wish to distance herself was due to Fordon, though I did not know what exactly was on her mind.

I rapped on the arched chamber door and stated my name.

'Minach Emmanuel?' Evelyn's muffled voice called from the other side of the door, a hint of surprise in her voice. 'Please... come in.'

The chamber door creaked as I pushed it open. Evelyn knelt upon her bed, gazing dreamily out the single window of her chamber. Judging by the unmade bed and the nightgown hanging from her shoulders, the princess had not long awakened.

'You look flushed, Your Highness,' I commented, looking at her across the circular room. 'Are you with fever? You ought to get dressed and warm yourself.'

Evelyn shook her head. 'I am well, Minach. Truth be told, I likely appear flushed because I am warm.'

The princess could tell just by looking at me that I was unconvinced. Shifting from the unkempt bed, she padded barefoot towards me, taking my fingers in her hands. She pressed my palm against her forehead. 'Truthfully... I am well.'

I nodded. 'If Your Highness insists. What about your mood? I hope that is well, too.'

Remnant Tales of Stilly:
Passion and Benevolence

Evelyn shut her eyes and exhaled softly. Turning on her heels, she returned to the open window, bidding me to close her chamber door. I sat on a stool by the foot of the bedstead, keeping the Scripture close to my chest, which I now had under my folded arms. I remember how Evelyn's auburn hair flowed behind her back that morning, fluttering as a breeze blew into the chamber. She rested her forearms upon the stone sill and returned to gazing outside.

I glanced out the window and at the sky. 'It is a curious thing…'

Evelyn gave me a sideways glance.

'The sun always hides when you are feeling down.'

Evelyn looked upwards. Large white clouds passed across the deep blue sky and snatched the sun's brilliance, blocking its direct warmth. She chuckled. 'Is that so? Then I should endeavour to smile more often.'

I looked towards the sky once more. The cloud unveiled the light as soon as the princess showed the slightest hint of a smile. 'You see?' I said. 'The sun is shy for you.'

Evelyn hummed and rested her chin in her arms. 'Indeed. I cannot hide my feelings from any, it seems.'

'What ails you, child? Is it that you worry for Lord Latnemirt?'

'He is indeed on my mind, but I do not worry for him.'

At the time, I knew little of Evelyn's feelings regarding Fordon's return to Wilheard. Despite this, it did not surprise me that something was troubling her.

'Do you worry for those around him?' I asked after Evelyn failed to elaborate.

'I worry for everyone in Stilly. In the two years Lord Latnemirt has been gone, I can see he has experienced and learned much. Perhaps more than one should have in such a time.' Evelyn straightened her back and looked at me. 'I do not know exactly what this amounts to, but judging from the interloper we have received in his return…'

'An interloper, Your Highness? I have never known you to use such harsh wording.'

Evelyn closed her eyes and lulled her head to one side. 'The Lord has certainly lost what he used to be. His emotional integrity—indeed, his very being—has been taken from him. You see this too, Minach Emmanuel, do you not?'

I averted my gaze from the princess and looked down at the scriptures, now resting upon my lap. I could not argue with such truths.

Evelyn continued. 'A more spiritual side of the man has awakened, but it does not concern what is in your hands.'

I groaned at the thought.

'Minach, you know as well as I do why the lord hides away in his chamber, and even if my dear father were a more tolerant man, I have reservations that the lord would be so forthright.'

'Lord Latnemirt undeniably confines himself to his chamber, but you are scarcely seen either. With respect, Your Highness, how is it you know this?'

'The lord has a distinctive aura about him... one I have never felt before. I have seen Latnemirt in passing several times, but I do not need to be near him to feel this force. Even now, I feel this aura, as if he is standing next to me.'

'What do you feel needs to be done?'

'Take action where action needs taking. You have been watching Lord Latnemirt, have you not? I ask that you continue this scrutiny, Minach, and share your discoveries with me. In the meantime, I will be fine. Please tell my father as much.'

I stood from the stool and bowed my head. 'I will do as you wish, Your Highness.'

I pulled on the chamber door's ringed handle and yanked it open. Stepping from the room, I paused momentarily and turned back to Evelyn. She smiled weakly at me, speaking one last time before I departed.

'Lord Latnemirt is not the only one privy to the otherworldly. My trust in you is boundless, Minach, and our combined strengths can repel what may come.'

Sauntering amongst Wilheard's crowds, Ebony made her way through town and headed towards Efflorescence Way.

Remnant Tales of Stilly:
Passion and Benevolence

Passing the tearooms and walking under a set of arched ruins, Ebony climbed the steep route of Castle Way, her eyes focused on the charismatic edifice of Sanct Everard. Standing outside the sancture was Naitsir Ordaiest Caleb Psoui, greeting those walking by.

Caleb loved conversing with anyone and everyone and seemed like a man who shone with perpetual happiness. Ebony enjoyed the company of the ordaiest immensely, who (in her opinion) seemed young for such a position: a man in his forties with nary a grey hair.

Noticing Ebony approaching, Caleb waved to her.

'Fair morn, Ordaiest Psoui,' Ebony called from the lowest step of the sancture. 'Another hot day today, isn't it?'

Caleb smiled and waited for Ebony to reach him. 'Indeed it is. On days such as this, I do enjoy being outside, my surroundings hushed and my thoughts to myself... a wonderful thing indeed.'

Ebony replied only with a polite nod. She could not help but disagree with the ordaiest's statement; she grew tired of her thoughts when left to ponder for too long. It seemed to Ebony that Caleb did not want much in life, and this brought to mind an old saying that she had once read. *Profound aspiration may be born from simple sow.* In essence, the world is what one makes of it.

'And what, young lady, brings you to me on this fine day? I hope you are staying out of trouble.'

'I don't get into trouble, Ordaiest Psoui,' Ebony replied. 'You must have me confused with someone else.'

'On the contrary, I remember the curious girl I saw when I first came to Wilheard, a child who—with the companionship of a certain other girl—got into all sorts of mischief.' Caleb looked to one side and exaggerated his thinking. 'Yes... I seem to remember the other girl having fair-coloured hair. I say! Doesn't she keep the local farm?'

Ebony tittered with embarrassment. 'Fair enough, Ordaiest, fair enough. However, Hazel and I fulfilled our fair share of climbing walls and tormenting the town residents years ago.'

'I will take your word for that, but I recall fondly you two playing about the sancture and the castle.'

'Yes,' Ebony muttered, her expression suddenly sinking.

Neither Ebony nor Hazel, as children, had been ones to shy away from risk-taking. Be it climbing trees, tiptoeing along the top of an uneven wall, or even, as they had once dared each other, jumping into the castle moat from its drawbridge, which must have been about six metres from the water. That stunt put the pair in a lot of trouble with their respective parents, and even though scoldings usually followed such foolhardiness, it had nevertheless been great fun.

That was until the pair decided to climb the side of a rundown building.

Although she had not wanted to do it initially, Ebony followed Hazel up the wall after persuading herself that she would be treated to a pretty view if she reached its top. Unfortunately, she had lost her grip on one of the crevices as it crumbled underhand, sending the child crashing down to the paving below.

Ebony woke from the memory and placed her fingers on the top of her head, feeling where she had injured herself. Whilst she had not sustained any long-term pain, the damage to her head had been severe enough to leave a scar on her crown. It was a rueful reminder, even if her hair hid the mark. Climbing stopped for both children that day, neither daring to scale anything taller than a small fence after the incident.

'Anyway,' Ebony continued, removing her hand from her head. 'To answer your question, I am passing by—I'm off to the castle for a little read. It will be quiet up there.'

'I see,' Caleb said, a frown creasing the bridge of his nose as he looked to the ground.

'Is something the matter?' Ebony asked, noticing Psoui's demeanour suddenly change.

Caleb shook his head and went back to smiling. 'Not really. You just reminded me of something from a few days ago. So, what book are you reading?'

Ebony pulled the book from under her arm and showed Caleb the front cover. He took the hardback from her.

'Passion and Benevolence,' the ordaiest read aloud. 'Is it a romance?'

Ebony paused before answering. She was still wondering what Caleb had been thinking about moments ago. 'Umm... no. It's more historical, I suppose, albeit with a twist.'

Caleb continued to scan the book and read aloud what he saw. 'Written in 1468 by Minach Emmanuel Grellic. Tender spirits, that is interesting.'

'Do you recognise that name?' Ebony asked.

'I cannot say I do, young Ebony, but'—the ordaiest opened the book and read the foot of the introduction—'if this Emmanuel is a past cleric from Wilheard's sancture, I might be able to find some kind of record. Traeh bless me, I'm getting excited just thinking about it!'

'That *is* exciting. You will have to let me know if you find anything.'

Feeling the sun's heat on her skin, Ebony brushed her fingers over her nape. If she stood there much longer, she would start to burn. She took the novel back from Caleb. 'In any case, Ordaiest Psoui, I will be on my way. I think I will need to find some shade.'

Caleb walked with Ebony as she started for the left side of the sancture, where a set of steps led to the castle.

'Before you go,' Caleb said, 'there is something I wanted to tell you.'

Ebony stopped walking and looked at the ordaiest. He placed his hands behind his back and looked up the stairway. 'Far be it my intention to worry you, but,' Caleb hesitated a moment and frowned again.

'Whatever is the matter?' Ebony asked.

'It is probably nothing—perhaps just my imagination—but I am certain I heard some banging and crashing coming up there the other evening. Like distant thunder, it was.'

'Inside the castle?'

'I know that sounds silly. The castle is under a tight lock, after all.'

Ebony nodded. 'Did you ask any night guards if they heard anything?'

'Yes, and a group even went up to investigate. Apparently, nothing out of the ordinary. Mind you, I neglected to mention the "inside the castle" part.'

Ebony looked to the castle and hummed with curiosity.

'Like I said, I'm sure I was just hearing things, but do me a favour and be careful.'

'Will do, and thank you for your concern,' she said as she made her way up the steps.

'I know I don't have to worry about you, Ebony—you're a shrewd young woman. Traeh be with you all the same.'

Abraham played with the grey-black bristles on his chin as he sat in the waiting room of Wilheard Surgery. A slight pang sensation was whirling inside his belly, resulting from nervousness rather than ill health. He was waiting to see Sylvia, whose shift was approaching lunch break. Although Abraham was a patient man, he hoped Sylvia would come out soon. When she did, the agitation would subside.

In addition to his nerves, two other things made the wait all the more intolerable. The wooden chairs provided for patients were uncomfortable and of poor quality, which vexed the carpenter in Abraham, yet the elderly woman sitting opposite bothered him more.

With a wart on the side of her nose and a protruding bottom tooth that made her look like a ghastly witch, the woman gazed at Abraham with a cold stare, seemingly unconcerned about how uneasy it made him feel.

Abraham grinned forcefully at the older woman. Ghastly Witch maintained her stare for a few seconds, coughed into her closed hand and resumed her gaping.

Three agonising minutes passed by the time a gaunt-faced nurse walked into the waiting room. After calling Ghastly Witch's surname twice and getting no response, the nurse tapped her on the shoulder. Ghastly Witch snapped out of her trance-like stare, looked at the nurse with a friendly smile and stood up.

Abraham exhaled his relief as the nurse led the old woman away, leaving him alone in the waiting room. Now alone, he pondered what Ebony was doing. He had failed to be open about Sylvia and wondered what his daughter would think of this new friend. Abraham continued to stroke his chin. This apprehension was misplaced; he knew his daughter would be mature enough to show civility no matter whom he befriended. Anyway, he had just met Sylvia, so any announcements might seem premature.

A few minutes passed before the low creak of a door broke the silence again. Abraham turned his head to see Sylvia and then got to his feet.

'Fair noon, Abe,' Sylvia said, giving Abraham a quick kiss on the cheek. 'Sorry to keep you. Have you been waiting long?'

'No, just a few minutes,' Abraham lied. Having arrived at the surgery earlier than planned and much more eagerly than most when it came to such a place, he had had to wait nearly twenty minutes for Sylvia to get herself ready. Rickety chairs and Ghastly Witch aside, the wait had not worried him too much, and he was just happy to see the doctor again.

Abraham and Sylvia exited the surgery from the rear-most door and entered a concrete area encircled by half-built walls. The location was mainly designed for deliveries but also served as temporary storage. However, with unused or broken medical equipment, discarded chairs and beds, as well as other unwanted items, the area looked more like a dumping ground.

'Please mind the mess,' Sylvia said as the pair walked over to one unfinished wall and sat on the most even part they could find. 'When I catch the culprits, I give them a telling off. Unfortunately, the rascals have become ever more vigilant at doing it behind my back.'

As he sat down, Abraham looked round at the area. Despite the not-so-pleasant setting, it was at least quiet and private enough to talk comfortably. On the other hand, he had yet to think of anything worthwhile to say. 'It's another hot day,' he said awkwardly, squinting at the blue sky.

Sylvia ignored the statement and looked at Abraham with a bashful smile. 'It's nice to have a little break. Sometimes, I feel I don't get enough time for that. Ho hum…'

Abraham looked at Sylvia; her hair glistened in the sun. She was so beautiful, yet as he gazed into her blue eyes, he spied a trace of sadness that beset this beauty.

Abraham looked at his shoes. 'Your profession is too demanding for such things, I expect.'

'It can be, but I shouldn't complain. Compared to Pothaven, working in Wilheard is to some extent like having a holiday.'

Remnant Tales of Stilly:
Passion and Benevolence

The two jumped as the surgeries' rear door suddenly swung open. A pair of nurses tottered into the concrete square carrying a soiled mattress. The male nurse at the front end halted upon noticing Sylvia. Wondering why he had stopped, the female nurse holding the other end peered round to look outside. Sylvia lowered her eyebrows and cast a disapproving look. Without a word, the nurses turned and carried the mattress back inside.

Abraham snorted his amusement. 'You seem to have a way with other people.'

Sylvia smirked. 'I don't care much for the term *under one's thumb*, but I suppose I have a degree of influence.'

'Yes, a stern quality of a mother,' Abraham murmured. 'You remind me of someone I once knew.'

Sylvia sucked in her lips and grinned. She shifted closer to Abraham. 'I know this will sound forward, but I would very much like it if we could become more than just friends.'

Abraham blushed and cleared his throat in an attempt to give a response to the bold remark. Nothing came out.

Sylvia took the carpenter's rough hands in her own, softer ones and looked him in the eyes once more. 'I know we only met yesterday, but from what I have learned about you, it seems longer.'

Abraham could not deny that he felt the same way; being near this woman seemed natural. Even so, something about her also puzzled him.

'Perhaps,' Sylvia continued, 'you can introduce me to your daughter.'

Abraham groaned then and stood up, taking his hands from the doctor's. 'Ebony… She might not share your—or rather our—enthusiasm. You understand that since we only met yesterday, I have told Ebony little about you.'

Sylvia did not say anything, her boldness visibly ebbing.

'Can you imagine her shock if I were to walk in and declare…' Abraham paused. 'No, that's not the right thing to say. After all, you do not know her.'

Sylvia now had an abashed look about her. 'I'm sorry…'

Abraham rubbed the back of his head before moving back towards Sylvia. He knelt in front of her and took her hands once more. 'Don't be sorry. You haven't done anything wrong, and I honestly feel the same way as you—it's just… maybe we don't need to rush this kind of thing. Besides, I will surely introduce you to Ebony in no time. Do you understand where I'm coming from?'

Sylvia looked to one side. 'I suppose.'

Abraham studied Sylvia's face for a moment and gave a weak nod. 'Good. Now let's go for some lunch. This place has had more than its fair share of our company.'

Ebony marvelled at Castle Stilly. The construction never failed to impress her, no matter how often she saw it.

Despite owning features typical of a stone keep castle, such as high curtain walls, a moat and a drawbridge, its eccentricity was apparent. Architects over the years have questioned the sanity of the original designer, but in truth, the castle had been made to the will of the then King, who (probably in a fit of zeal) had ideas of peering down on Wilheard from atop the hill, exuding his authority over the peasantry below. Not wanting to lose their heads, the architects would have gone ahead with the project.

This was how Ebony imagined it, at least, and in due credit, the castle has remained standing centuries later.

Sitting in the shade of an oak tree, Ebony peered over the sun-bleached Wilheard and thought back to Ordaiest Psoui's mention of noises. She had failed to hear or see anything unusual, but perhaps that was a good thing. Town life could be dull, but trouble was never wanted.

With that in mind, Ebony once again opened her book. Would Emmanuel be able to resolve his own troubles?

Passion and Benevolence.
Elgin's Thoughts.

Although never particularly warm throughout the year, the castle is notably chillier as autumn comes. Yet, even with the season's arrival, I remember the temperature to be relatively mild the year Fordon returned.

In total, four gardens belong to the castle. The smallest (and most unloved) of them is situated to the northwest, known as Cliff Garden, so named because of its position on Wilheard's northern cliff. Separated from the other gardens and blanketed in perpetual shade owing to surrounding curtain walls, wildflowers were left to take possession.

As far as duties went, I was on top of things. Taking advantage of my free time, I went for a stroll. Making my way up the stairway and into Cliff Garden, I peered into the mass of greenery, hearing nary a whisper within. Believing myself alone, contentment passed through me, and although this solitude was a mistaken belief, my unnoticed company could not have been any more affable.

'Fair noon to you, Minach Emmanuel,' the voice of a man called. 'How very nice to see you on such a fine day.'

I smiled, not having to turn to know whom the voice belonged. 'A fair noon to you as well, Master Hosp,' I replied, now moving my attention to the sovereign knight. 'I didn't expect to see you, of all people, out today. Are you done with your oil work already?'

Elgin Hosp removed his thin-rimmed spectacles and closed the book he was reading, using his thumb to keep his place. An intelligent man, Elgin excelled in many subjects: he played multiple musical instruments, was well-versed in several foreign languages, dabbled in oil works, and (of all things) studied human anatomy. Alas, he was also a chronic procrastinator; so easily distracted by what happened around him, I wondered how he accomplished anything.

Sitting on a stone bench, Elgin palmed his naturally curled black hair from his face. 'I am ashamed to say that I have not, dear Minach. I'm starting to wonder if I will ever reach its completion.'

Elgin explained that he was struggling to put what was in his head onto canvas and that the Autumn breeze blowing through an open window had scattered loose papers onto the floor. After picking up the sheets, he wandered outside, hoping the fresh air would clear his mind.

Elgin exhaled. 'More's the pity, then, that my little plan has not panned out how I hoped—I am at a loss for focus. However, enough about me. How are you, my friend?'

I explained my own reasons for being up and about the castle.

'I see,' he answered. 'It's best to make the most of the free time one has. But tell me, Minach, is our elusive returnee still dominating your thoughts?'

I was taken aback by the question. 'You mean Lord Latnemirt?'

A smirk creased Elgin's cheeks. 'None other.'

Confusion must have been written over my face as the knight did not wait for a reply. 'Darwin told me you were watching Lord Latnemirt during the Summer Festival. I have no quarrel with that, so do not be concerned. In fact, as you will no doubt know, you are not alone in such endeavours.'

There was no denying it. Since Fordon's return to Wilheard, he had become the one name on many a person's lips. 'Lord Latnemirt is on my mind among other people,' I said. 'What is your take on him?'

Elgin tapped his fingers on his thigh and looked thoughtfully to one side. 'What is there to say that has not already been said? If you are wondering if I know what he gets up to in that chamber of his, then I am afraid I do not. Needless to say, we could always ask the man'—he pointed behind me—'he is standing over there, after all...'

Alarmed, I dashed to behind where the sovereign knight sat.

Elgin bellowed a laugh. 'I didn't know you could move so fast, dear Minach!'

'A cruel jest, Master Hosp, I don't mind telling you.'

'Apologies, my friend,' giggled the knight as he thumbed a tear from his eye. 'It would seem Darwin's levities have rubbed off on me.' He returned to a solemn composure. 'To be frank, however, I find it difficult to trust Lord Latnemirt like I used to. I think he is conjuring more than one can yet fathom, and whatever his plans, I fear we will find out sooner rather than later.'

Negative thoughts bounced round my mind. I could not deny that I feared the same.

Using the cuff of his shirt sleeve, Elgin wiped the lenses of his glasses and put them back on the bridge of his nose before reopening his book. 'Nevertheless, Minach Emmanuel, I can be a paranoid man at times. Take what I say with some scepticism.'

'If you insist.'

'About the other individuals on your mind… If I might be so inquisitive, is one such person Princess Evelyn?'

It was as if Elgin could read my mind. I told him as much.

Elgin grinned. 'Do not think that I have been spying on you as well, dear Minach.'

'You are a perceptive man, Master Hosp. I mean that most sincerely.'

'The princess worries greatly,' Elgin said. 'I think she comprehends much more than any of us, which, I believe, frightens her highness. Can I request that you watch over her?

'I always do my best by her.'

Elgin nodded and returned to his reading. 'I know you do, my friend. You are a good man.'

I went back into the castle then. My stroll no longer seemed so appealing.

'I'll see you tomorrow,' Doctor Sylvia Enpee said, waving goodbye to the last of her colleagues from the surgery. She leant against the now locked door and blew a sigh of relief, blowing loose strands of blonde hair from her eyes. At last, she was alone.

Sylvia was often the last to leave the surgery, left to roam the empty halls and ensure everything was locked. She did not mind this, though; being alone meant she could concentrate better on any unfinished work that might be left.

In fact, over the years, Sylvia had grown accustomed to being by herself. In many ways, she preferred it, not least because the ever-watching eyes were more prevalent when darkness came.

Sylvia sat in her office and blinked several times as she looked at a line of unlabelled bottles on her desk containing different medicines. She was tired, and her eyelids rebelled against her will to stay awake. Although her body wanted to sleep, Sylvia did not feel like dreaming. Abraham Gibenn's desire to take things slow had lowered her mood, and she had deluded herself into thinking that work would be the perfect distraction.

'How are you today, Doctor Enpee?' said Ninapaige. 'You look tired, girl.'

Startled by the unexpected voice, Sylvia knocked one of the glass bottles to the floor as she tried to label it. The doctor turned to find Ninapaige sitting behind her, who was now suppressing childish laughter.

'Now look at what you made me do!' Sylvia chided, staring at the shattered glass and spilt liquid. 'Now I have to clear it up, and the chemical is bound to leave a stain.'

'Are you sure?' Ninapaige replied as flippantly as Sylvia would have expected. 'It does not look *that* bad.'

'Tender spirits, are you serious?' Sylvia continued, pointing to where the bottle had fallen. 'Just look at the...'

She looked back down to the floor. The mess was gone, leaving no trace of broken glass or the substance in sight.

'See?' Ninapaige grinned.

Sylvia scowled. 'All you do is mock me.'

'Hardly,' sneered Ninapaige, taking a bottle of medicine from a nearby shelf to inspect. 'Such infantile complaints are unbecoming for a human of your standing, especially one who takes herself so seriously.'

Sylvia swore something foul at the comment, but Ninapaige simply cackled. When she stopped laughing, she handed the doctor the glass container, the same one that spilt a moment ago.

Sylvia grunted and placed the bottle on the desk. 'How about you use some of that sorcery on me—I need waking up.'

Remnant Tales of Stilly:
Passion and Benevolence

'I could always slap you in the face—that might wake you up… but what fun would that be? The best time to get into that pretty little head of yours is when you sleep.'

'I bet. Especially since you can manipulate whatever enters it.'

Ninapaige pulled her sad-looking mask from behind a shelf. Placing it over her own face, she feigned crying. 'Oh, Sylvia—you are always so pessimistic. Your hurtful words make me sad.' She tossed the mask out the window. 'But never mind. I know you do not mean what you say!'

Sylvia grimaced. 'Why are you here?'

'Actually, I came to speak about my day, but the thought of dreams has reminded me of something.'

Sylvia folded her arms and looked at the petite woman in silence.

Ninapaige went on. 'That man you have been chasing lately… the apple of your eye…'

'Abraham Gibenn?' Sylvia said.

'That's the one,' Ninapaige said. 'At first, I was apprehensive over you forcing your way into his life, but--'

'Oh but, mummy!' Sylvia blurted. 'I'm a big girl now and don't need your approval.'

'Spare me your quips, petulant child. What I have to say is important.'

Sylvia muttered something incoherent under her breath, which Ninapaige ignored. 'As I was saying, at *first,* I did not approve, but it would seem he and his daughter might need your help after all.'

Sylvia's eyes widened, her tiredness all but forgotten. 'What do you mean? Are they in trouble?'

'Do not fret, young one—they are fine. However, I have noticed an increase in attention from the very eyes that watch you, and they are now watching Abraham and his daughter. In fact, the attention is more on the girl.'

A film of sweat formed on Sylvia's brow. 'Her name is Ebony.'

Ninapaige moved behind Sylvia and placed her hands on the taller woman's shoulders. 'Easy, now. No harm will come to them; I can guarantee that.'

Sylvia placed her fingers on Ninapaige's hand. 'I believe you when you say that, but what must *I* do?'

'Things have been getting complicated for this little hamlet in recent weeks. Along with your return to the town, two other men from the past have made their presence known. That girl Ebony is like you—she is an inquisitive young woman. Certainly, she has shown great interest in Wilheard's happenings lately. Especially for one of those men.'

'You mean that vigilante?' Sylvia said. 'I have read about one in the Village Express.

'Yes… Sombie. And if he wanders Wilheard again, there is undoubtedly something nasty to follow.'

'Will you be getting rid of him?'

Ninapaige raised her eyebrows at the remark. 'I do not think that will be necessary. Besides, I would rather not tangle with Sombie.'

'So you are going to just leave him to lurk about? You have never had faith in him before.'

Ninapaige shook her head, causing her bobbled hat to jiggle. 'That is not strictly true. I have never cared much for him and do not consider him a means to an end when it comes to all Stilly's troubles. Still, times do change, and so can opinions. Besides, despite what you might think, I do not impose myself on everyone's affairs.'

'So what is your point in all this?'

'Well, as I said earlier, your mention of dreams reminded me of something. Promise not to get mad, but I have entered both Sombie's and Ebony's dreams.

Sylvia frowned but said nothing.

'Dreams are a good way of manipulating decisions. It is difficult to explain without sounding sinister, but it can ultimately persuade certain people to stay out of trouble.'

'You believe she will get herself into trouble?'

'It's complicated,' Ninapaige said, humming as she thought. 'Perhaps I should not have mentioned it. In any case, I need you to continue your little escapade with this Abraham.'

Sylvia smiled weakly. 'I won't bother asking why the sudden change of mind—I can handle that. By the way, who is the second man who has returned to Wilheard?

'Oh, yes… him. Let us just say he is someone I have known for a long time. In fact, this man is another reason I should leave Sombie alone to wander. At any rate, do not concern yourself with those two for now. Their actions are something I will watch closely.'

Sylvia paused to consider what Ninapaige said before nodding, showing she understood.

'Oh, and one last note,' said Ninapaige, moving to the back of the office and near a gap between the shelf of medicines, 'do not forget that this Abraham—as a certain Myrah Dolb so kindly enlightened you—is officially a widower. He still holds his lost wife in his heart, and it will be difficult for him to let go of her and fall for you.'

'You can change that.'

'That would be cruel after all his mourning and altogether problematic. Deep down, you understand this.' Ninapaige moved into the gap between the storage cases and out of view. 'Speaking of Myrah Dolb…'

A knock came from the outer side of the office window and startled Sylvia. She spun round to see Myrah Dolb waving to her.

'Sorry if I made ya jump, girly,' Myrah called through the glass.

Sylvia lifted the windowpane. 'Fair Eve, Myrah. I'll be out with you shortly.'

'Fine, but don't you take too long, you hear? We have a lot to talk about—I've heard about you and Abe. You can't keep all your secrets, cheeky girl!'

Sylvia blushed. *Tell me about it*, she thought as she closed the window again.

Ebony sat on her bedroom floor under the sunbeam pouring through the window.

Remnant Tales of Stilly:
Passion and Benevolence

It was almost 8.30pm, and Ebony was ready for bed. However, before going to sleep, she wanted to finish Passion and Benevolence. She was now on the concluding chapter, and if she read it now, she could finish the book before the natural light became too dim.

Passion and Benevolence.
Regicide.

Even before I begin to write this, my hands tremble.

Until my dying breath, I will never forget when Castle Stilly fell into utter turmoil. Fordon Latnemirt had been behind all the chaos. Hysteria filled hallway after hallway as royal servants and soldiers ran in all directions. All I could do was to remain as calm as possible and search for Evelyn. She was my utmost duty at the time; even with my aged body hampering my efforts, I had to find the princess and protect her as best I could. Amidst all the mayhem, I had little idea of how I would accomplish this.

With my shoulder against the walls, I wheezed as I staggered through the castle. Evelyn had not been in her tower, which was perhaps wise; alas, I was now at a loss for where to locate her. This being so, my next course of action was to find someone who would be willing to help. As fortune had it, this did not take too long.

Clement Suavlant was exiting the Ballroom. I called out to him.

'Minach Emmanuel?' The sovereign knight rushed to my side and placed an arm about me. 'Are you hurt in any way?'

I shook my head and relayed my plight.

'Then I bring you good tidings—Princess Evelyn is hidden away safely and in good company. Perhaps you would like to join them.'

'I would prefer to put myself to better use, Master Suavlant,' I said, relieved that Evelyn was well. 'I am confident I will not be a burden.'

Clement helped me upright. 'Truth be told, I am in the middle of a search myself for King Godfrey. At least I was—not long ago, I received word that he and Queen Verity are in Royal Garden. I was heading there now... that is if you insist you are well enough to join me.'

I straightened my back as best I could and gave a determined nod.

Clement returned a subtle frown before nodding in return. 'I will not persuade you to do otherwise. Stay close to me.'

The castle's population had thinned to almost nothing, but this only meant one thing: Fordon was nearby. In the southwest of the castle, Royal Garden was all but empty. As Clement and I made our way through, we spotted the king, queen and, as expected, Fordon. The sky was overcast, and rain was imminent. Alas, this would have been the least of anyone's concerns.

King Godfrey and Fordon stood near the centre of the garden. Queen Verity was a dozen paces behind her husband, her demeanour one of trepidation. Clement and I remained at a distance. Caution was vital, more so than ever; scattered about the garden were the bloodstained bodies of Wilheard soldiers. Fordon was undoubtedly aware of our presence, and carelessness would result in further bloodshed.

Therefore, we waited... and we listened.

Godfrey glared at the thinner, darkly dressed man before him, a greatsword tight in his grip. The king had gained a deep wound to his left leg, and standing was gruelling. Fordon, in comparison, was surefooted, his expression stern and his body unscathed. A curved-bladed weapon not much larger than a dagger was in the lord's possession. Stained with the blood of many, the sword had served its purpose.

Godfrey grimaced. 'You have gained much more over the last two years than you have let known, renegade. How you have ascertained such strength is nothing short of a miracle.' He choked at the thought. 'No. It is not a miracle. It is that damnable wizardry. You have always been so obsessed with it, and I see that this obsession never abated.'

Fordon remained silent.

Godfrey held an arm out and waved it from side to side, gesturing at his surroundings. 'Do you now see it, Latnemirt? Do you now see why I abhor that livnam power?' He turned back to Fordon. 'Is this truly what you wanted?'

Fordon peered round at the garden. He studied the dead and the broken castle walls about him, eventually returning his attention to his accuser. 'Would you believe me if I said no?' Fordon took two steps closer to the king, halting as the royal held his sword forward. Fordon pulled at his long, grey beard. 'Before my journey to Drieloca, there always appeared to be a mutual trust between us. Your ignorance towards ytyism is as stubborn as ever, but it is not too late for us to make amends. You can still be by my side—as a comrade. There is no need for us to fight.'

Godfrey spat at the offer, the blood in his spittle reddening the grass. 'After how you have betrayed this very kingdom, you dare call for peace? As far as I am concerned, everything you have ever said has been a lie…'

Fordon bristled at the claim. 'Wrong! Everything I have said has been the truth, including after my return to Wilheard. What I professed in the throne room is how it happened. If I have lied, it is merely by omission, but I can explain it now if you just listen.'

'Enough!' Godfrey snapped. 'Spare me your excuses. You have betrayed this kingdom, and In the name of Traeh, you will pay for this treachery with your life.'

Fordon smirked derisively. 'You know nothing of betrayal. I experienced more duplicity than you have in a lifetime. But no matter—I intend to punish all those who have wronged me.'

'I sheltered you, I fed you, I offered you succour… How have I caused you wrong?'

Fordon closed his eyes and shook his head. 'It is not you that I wish to punish.'

'And yet you destroy my castle and take the lives of my soldiers.'

'Matters of consequence. If people get in my way, then I will push them aside. As for the castle—I am surprised you have not realised by now that I am looking for something. You have hidden it better than I thought capable. Where is Omnipotent?'

A baffled look spread across the king's face. He glanced at Verity, who showed an equal amount of uncertainty.

Fordon's nostrils flared. 'Do not feign idiocy—the orb, man! The unbreakable glass orb. Tell me where it is!'

Deep creases formed on Godfrey's brow. 'You attack my castle for that?'

'Do not waste my time! Where is it?'

'I do not know. It disappeared years ago, shortly after your departure to Drieloca. I considered its vanishing a blessing from the almighty Traeh—a good riddance.'

Fordon reddened with anger, his knuckles whitening as he clenched his fists. 'Did she know this all along,' he said. 'How could she? *Why* would she? Yet more betrayal.'

'Who?' said Godfrey. 'Who is this *she*?'

Composing himself, Fordon faced Godfrey again. 'On second thoughts, I am not surprised... Where is your daughter?'

A gasp came from Queen Verity. What did he want from Evelyn?

'Don't you dare,' Godfrey growled, 'you stay away from my daughter. I will not have you harming her.'

'Do grow up, Godfrey,' Fordon rebuked, causing the king's eyes to widen. 'If I wished to harm your daughter, don't you think I would have by now?'

'Perhaps... perhaps not. I wager that my sovereign knights have always made you think twice.'

Fordon roared a mirthless laugh. 'Quite. I had considered them. But where are they now?' Fordon once again looked about the garden. 'I see only one.'

Clement murmured something illegible and tightened the hold on his own sword. He must have felt further trouble looming. I concurred, yet we remained still.

'If I go down, they will protect her from you. However'—Godfrey held up his sword—'you will have to bypass me first. With Traeh at my side, I will defeat you.'

'Do you honestly still think your god exists?' Fordon gave a cruel smile. 'Everything you see, even the very stone that forms your castle, is thanks to the ytied—they are the true creators.'

'You worship false gods now, is that it? You have truly fallen, Latnemirt.'

'I never said they are gods, neither did I say I worshipped them. Ytied are a stupendous race, to be sure—a race that is far older and greater than mankind, but they are not immortal. In fact, one of them is in this world, banished by her kind. She promised that she would make me one like her—a sibling. However, I knew this to be a lie, and her intention was merely to use me while she hid away. Still, there is a chance I can become one like them, so to speak. I have studied their ways endlessly. Ytyism, they call it—the sorcery you hate so much.'

Fordon turned the sword in his hand. 'I do not need Omnipotent, even if, in the unlikely circumstance, I could wield it. I have created my own power source—held within the sapphire embedded in the hilt. This is Ascendancy, and with it, I will destroy Rosaleen for her cruelty. Once I am done, I will use it to make this place where we live a greater world. I will be *like* a brother to the ytied.'

Godfrey had heard enough. 'We shall see if the almighty Traeh does not exist. Have at you!'

Ignoring whatever pain he felt, the king lunged at the thinner man with his remaining energy. Godfrey brought his sword down vertically with all his might, swinging it horizontally after the first strike failed to meet its target. Alas, the greatsword had become too much for him to bear, and the results of his attacks were clumsy. Fordon avoided the assault with little effort, the worst possible outcome following.

Godfrey regurgitated a mouthful of blood, choking back any scream he might have had. Fordon, with the same speed to avoid harm, had answered Godfrey's strikes by plunging the point of his bowed sword through the king's abdomen, doing so with such force that the whole of the blade entered, curving upwards and piercing the king's heart.

'You never did ask me what I wanted with your daughter,' Fordon said. 'In death, this ignorance will eternally haunt you.'

As the sword ripped into the king, sudden motion filled the garden. Verity fainted as she watched her husband's lifeless body fall onto the blood-reddened grass. I moved as quickly as possible to her side while Clement rushed to Godfrey.

Fordon stepped away from the king, indifferent and unspeaking.

Remnant Tales of Stilly:
Passion and Benevolence

As I tried to leverage the queen from the ground, I felt the soft droplets of rain on my head. Despite her collapse, Verity did not have any concerning injuries. I needed to get her under some cover to shield her from the impending downpour and protect her from the clash that was about to arise.

Clement brushed Godfrey's eyes closed and got back to his feet. 'Regicide,' he said hoarsely. 'A murder most foul.'

The sound of Clement's Longsword unsheathing from its scabbard made the hairs on my neck stand on end, the draw of the weapon akin to a dog baring its teeth.

I managed to get the queen underneath one of the arched halls lining the garden. Sitting at the side with Verity's head in my lap, I clutched at the cramp in my chest. With my energy spent, there was little else I could do now but watch.

Before that moment, I had never seen the sovereign knights in combat. Fordon peered at his new opponent with heightened vigilance but was altogether prepared for what would follow.

Without utterance, Clement leapt at Fordon and thrust the point of his sword towards the older man's chest. Fordon met the strike with a twist to the side, immediately attempting a strike of his own by aiming for Clement's torso. Unlike Godfrey, the younger swordsman effortlessly matched Fordon's pace, and their swords clashed with a resonating clang. Clement followed up the block by barging his shoulder into Fordon, almost toppling his opponent. The lord faltering, Clement seized the chance for a lethal assault, using a fallen stone ornament to vault into the air and bring his Longsword down with a savage overhead cut. The power behind the slash was devastating, and it would have been enough to slay a man ten times larger than the intended target. Having maintained his balance, Fordon evaded Clement's fury by mere inches, the sword instead embedding deep into the now rain-softened ground. This gave Fordon precious seconds to retaliate while the sovereign knight freed his weapon.

Ascendancy shone a calm but ominous light as Fordon took firm hold of his sword. As soon as Clement released his blade from the earth, a shadow rose from the ground between the two men. Forming from a purple-pink pool, the shadow moulded into human form, twitching grotesquely as it materialised. Clement remained where he stood, braced with his Longsword chest high and pointing towards the humanoid.

'Allow me to introduce you to something I have been working on,' Fordon said. He remained behind the manifestation while looking it up and down. 'This is what I call a Redifass Skirmisher. I admit it is hardly a masterpiece, but I can assure you that it is competent in its purpose and, most important of all, loyal only to me.'

Clement studied the redifass. Armour as black as coal covered its whole body, so dark that daylight and the intensifying rain seemed to disappear as it made contact with the being. Its head, reminiscent of clay, lacked facial features, yet it seemed to sense its surroundings without trouble.

The redifass swirled a weapon in its hand, an object I can only presume was a sword. As with the rest of the creature, the piece was black.

Clement grunted. 'Your tricks not disquiet me, Latnemirt.'

'That is good to hear—I would have been disappointed if it did,' Fordon retorted. 'Truth be told, this will make a good assessment as to how a redifass responds in battle.' Fordon placed a hand on the redifass's shoulder. 'Now... let us begin.'

The creature darted from its master and swung its sword at Clement. The knight parried the assault and took a step back. The redifass's manoeuvre was fluent and its strike precise, but its speed was wanting. In contrast, the figure could not compare to Clement, who, after easily evading a follow-through thrust, struck with a merciless counterattack. With a single, horizontal swing of his Longsword, Clement severed his enemy, separating its body at the hip and spraying a murky liquid. The torso of the redifass crashed with an audible thud, its remains leaving this world as it had entered.

Clement whirled back to face Fordon, who put his hands together with a single clap. 'That went as expected,' he said, a broad smile on his lips. 'I guess I need more time to perfect the redifass design.' Fordon sighed. 'Alas, all this conjuring is exhausting and requires substantial energy. I will need some time to recuperate, and there is a certain royal girl I would love to find.'

'You will stay where you are, Latnemirt!' Clement bellowed.

Fordon's grin lessened all but entirely. 'I had a feeling you would say that.' He turned to face the sovereign knight and put his hands behind his back. Three more redifass stepped out from behind Fordon as if from nowhere, striding forward to obstruct access to their master. 'Do not presume to tell me what to do, Clement. You are a man with terrifying abilities, but I have not endured all this time just for the likes of you to stop me now, and you would do well to remember that. I will become much more than you could ever hope to be.'

Fordon paced from Royal Garden, leaving Clement with his new opponents.

As with before, the knight stiffened himself into defence. The rainfall had become torrential, and Clement, without any armour other than the leather jerkin covering his chest, had become sodden. Now heavier and more uncomfortable, one wrong move could prove fatal.

It was fortunate, then, that he did not have to deal with the redifass alone.

A bowstring thrummed over the thundering rain, a steel arrow piercing the air at an unseen speed, passing entirely through the head of one redifass and embedding in the neck of a second. This left Clement with enough time to finish off the remaining humanoid, which had been distracted by the slaying of its twins.

To my right, the remaining sovereign knights entered Royal Garden, emerging from the opposite end to which Fordon had exited. As I had expected, the arrow had come from Darwin's Longbow, which remained tight in his grasp as he approached Clement and the stricken King. Elgin and Maynard jogged over to Queen Verity and me, noticing us sprawled in a darkened corner under the arches.

Elgin placed a hand on my shoulder as he knelt. 'Minach Emmanuel, are you hurt? He asked before looking down at Verity. 'Is the queen harmed in any way?'

'For... don...' I said, still exhausted from hauling Verity. 'The
King... is dead.'

Elgin shut his eyes and let out a sigh. 'I know,' he replied softly. 'It
seems our nightmare has been realised. Calm your breathing and tell me
what happened.'

'Queen Verity survives,' I continued eventually. 'She is unconscious
but physically unharmed. The shock of what happened proved too great
for her. All I could manage was to pull her here and away from danger.'

'You have done admirably, dear Minach.' Elgin said, taking Verity
from my lap and effortlessly lifting the royal in his arms. 'Leave the rest
to us.'

Maynard helped me to my feet and followed me to Clement and
Darwin.

Darwin was kneeling over Godfrey, his lank red hair spilling over the
king's body. 'This is the worst possible outcome, but you must not
condemn yourself, Clement,' he said, looking up at his forlorn comrade.
'I am certain you did all you could.'

Clement hummed a response. From his pained expression alone, I
could see that he thought otherwise. He sheathed his sword and said
nothing.

'In any case,' Maynard said, taking the king in his arms. 'We must
find Latnemirt and make him answer for this.'

As we took the royal pair into the castle and out from the rain, I
explained to the hitherto absent sovereign knights the conversation before
Fordon slew Godfrey.

'I see,' said Elgin. He briefly laid Verity on the grand table centring
the dining room. Maynard laid Godfrey next to the queen, pulling a
Stillian flag from the wall and covering him. 'We had always suspected
Fordon was deep in the darker side of sorcery. Ytyism, did you call it?'

I nodded.

There was a moment of silence before Elgin continued. 'I know not
what Latnemirt hopes to achieve, but we had best find him as soon as
possible.' The other three knights signalled their agreement. 'Then let us

make haste. I will remain with Verity until she regains consciousness, and when she does, I will take her to where Princess Evelyn is.'

At that moment, I remembered something. 'Fordon is searching for Princess Evelyn.'

Darwin placed a hand on my shoulder. Despite everything, he smiled his usual smile. 'We have taken this into account, and she will be safe for the time being.'

We had assumed Fordon would retreat to his chambers in the castle's frontal tower. To get there, we needed to head towards the throne room. No trouble arose as we journeyed through the many halls, but upon arriving at the throne room entrance, I noticed a single Wilheard Soldier lying face down in a puddle of his own blood. Instinctively, I moved to help the stricken man, only for Darwin to drag me back. The soldier, who was already dead by the time we reached him, had been placed there as a trap, and Darwin took the punishment for my actions. Plucking a dart from his midriff, Darwin examined the object between his thumb and forefinger as it disintegrated. The sovereign knight reacted almost blithely to what happened, unwilling to accept my apologies. Unfortunately, although my actions were virtuous, I could not shake the feeling that I had doomed the knight to a slow death.

I followed behind the sovereign knights as they entered the throne room. The hall was quiet, save for the downpour from outside, and at first glance, empty of anything living. Past the decorated table and to the rear of the chamber sat Fordon, seated in the largest of the three thrones.

Fordon was looking to one side, his chin resting on the back of his hand as he observed the rain through the tall windows along the east wall. Cautiously stepping more into the hall, I kept my attention on the lord, whose rain-soaked clothes still showed the blood of his victims.

'Believe it or not, I have never seen the attraction of sitting upon such opulent chairs,' Fordon said nonchalantly, not taking his gaze away from the windows. 'Being a monarch is not something many choose, I realise, but some in the world dream such a life.'

Clement tightened his grip on the hilt of his sheathed sword. 'Your ambitions surpass that of kingship. You believe you can become a god.'

Remnant Tales of Stilly:
Passion and Benevolence

Fordon blew a frustrated sigh, tapping his fingers along the curved blade resting on his lap. Ascendancy pulsated with a dull glow. At last, he turned his attention towards his adversaries. 'I know you are not as ignorant as Godfrey was, so do not pretend you are. Ytied are not gods, at least not in a way one might consider. It is true that they created us and much of what we see, but given enough time, even humans can create life. Still, that does not make us gods.'

A crack of thunder boomed overhead, shaking the very foundation of the castle.

Fordon simpered and stood from the throne. 'Ah, but I can see in your eyes that you want to know what the ytied really are, and if that is true, then listen well. There is no better time for such revelations.

'As you will know by now, I travelled into the thickets of Drieloca's dense forestry with my accompanying Wilheard soldiers. The deeper we went, the darker it became. Wildlife, which had been abundant for most of our journey, thinned dramatically before disappearing altogether, something we would eventually understand why.

'With no warning, we came under attack. At first, I thought the trees had come alive—consuming all animate beings that dare wander foolishly into their territory. Yet, when I could see through the gloom, I realised that the trees were not devouring us but rather shadows hiding within them. My company seemed unable to perceive the horrors all around, and yet *I* saw them: I saw how they butchered my men—watched as they wrenched the life from their victims' bodies, leaving nothing but a bloodbath. Although I escaped the brunt of the massacre, I did not come out unscathed. Stretching the length of my back was a deep slash. I did not feel the attack, but a searing pain soon spread. Perhaps it was because of the shock, but I lost consciousness not long into the slaughter, the shrieks of the terrified soldiers being the last thing I remember.

'When I awoke, I found myself in a place like nothing I had ever seen. In contrast to the dark of the Neffaloom forest, this place was soaked in a light so intense that it hurt my eyes. Gone were the screams of my men and the whistling of swinging swords. A silence now surrounded me: no wind, no rustling of tree leaves—not even the sound of cheeping birds. At first, my surroundings seemed devoid of anything, but this was not so. Eventually, my pupils adjusted to the harsh light. I rolled my eyes, and the first thing I saw was what appeared to be the feet of a woman. I was confident I had died, killed by those silent assassins, but the pale skin did not belong to that of a Traehen anjyl, as I had initially believed. No—this *woman* was far from anything divine, and I was far from dead.

'Before me, on a marble, throne-like seat, sat Rosaleen. For want of a better look at this figure, I attempted to stand. The gash on my back, which for a time had caused no discomfort, sent a sudden and fiery pain through my entire body. Collapsing was all I could do to lessen the pain. It was then I heard that wicked laugh for the first time—a laugh that showed this being had control over me, a power she enjoyed. I need not suffer such agony, she told me. This deep voice promised me that she could make all the pain dissipate. Rosaleen had the answers to all the questions that passed through my head. *"Your mind is blind, Fordon Latnemirt, and your questions childish. I can remedy this, as I know what you want. First, however, you must comply."* Although understanding my confusion, she insisted that it was in my best interest to obey her wishes, which she demonstrated by placing her foot on my cheek. *"Under me, you will remain if you do not, though sincerely, I want this as little as you"*.

'Rosaleen shifted her attention to the small of my back, the burning sensation ebbing away on her touch, replaced by a soothing coolness. She continued to speak, reading my mind. Indeed, she knew not only my name but also my innermost desires.

Rosaleen laughed again. *"Even now, you doubt your senses and my existence. Nevertheless, I do exist, and how all this—all that you are experiencing—is possible will become clear if you accept my offer. What say you, Lord Latnemirt?"*

'The answer came easily, so much so that I wasn't sure I had even moved my lips. Perhaps I had not. Rosaleen extended a hand for me to take; her skin was cold. As I stood, I prepared for the agonising pain to rise in my back like before, but there was nothing. For the first time, I managed to get a clearer view of my surroundings. I could see the faint outline of trees, a stream of water and clouds in the sky, but the brilliant light left everything bleached. Yet, all that seemed insignificant compared to the pallid woman now standing before me. Rosaleen, as she eventually introduced herself, is a ytied. Dressed in a silk gown, the delicate material fluttered as she moved, as did her dark hair, which stood out in the otherwise white world. Her eyes, pupil-less but full of malice, bore into my sanity.'

Fordon had made his way down from the throne dais. The sovereign knights and I said nary a word as we listened.

'Intrinsically, Rosaleen wanted me to serve under the *"you scratch my back, and I will scratch yours"* premise.' Fordon laughed then, but there was no joy in it. 'More aptly, it was *"I'll heal you if you heal me."* It was almost as if she knew me better than I knew myself. Rosaleen recognised my interest in ytiedinity and my research of their ways. She wanted me by her side, saying my strong ambitions fascinated her. Nevertheless, although she did not state otherwise, this was not all she wanted.'

A flash of lightning lit the throne room, the subsequent thunder causing me to jolt. I rested on the edge of the round table while keeping my attention fixed on Latnemirt. There seemed to be a genuine look of regret in his eyes.

Darwin cocked his head to one side. 'So what did this Rosaleen do to you?'

Fordon contorted his face with distaste. 'Rosaleen betrayed and cursed me. When she imbued in me the knowledge and power of ytyism, she exploited my weaknesses. She intensified my desires beyond self-control, filling me with hate.'

'Then let us help you, Fordon,' Darwin continued. 'Let us find a way to free you from this torment.'

'Help me? Is it not a little late for that? I have all but destroyed this castle and killed our king. Do you think the good Minach Emmanuel can remedy my ills, like how he treated yours?'

'That doesn't mean we should do nothing,' insisted Darwin. 'How can you know the result before we have tried?'

Fordon ruminated over the offer. 'Yes… liberation from this misery is a grand thought, and accomplishing such an act would be miraculous. Yet, why should I trust you or anyone else? Perhaps you should open your mind to how I feel and how I could help you understand the truth. I know what I want back from this world, and it does not involve people standing in my way.'

'That is the hatred speaking,' Darwin once more said. 'Do not let the curse--'

'Enough of this!' Fordon interrupted, his temper rising. 'I have made my intentions clear.'

The sovereign knights readied themselves for trouble, but I had one last question. 'What does this have to do with Evelyn?'

Fordon calmed at the mention of the princess's name. 'Oh yes. I almost forgot about our young princess. It would be remiss of me not to mention Phyeroc.

'Phyeroc—or Prophecy—is the one thing Rosaleen did not try to hide from me. Because of this prophecy, Rosaleen wanted, or rather needed, me. Understand that the ytied has a wound—a wound that has proved untreatable and one that has weakened her to the point where she is susceptible to Phyeroc. Ideally, she needs Omnipotent back: a spherical object in which concentrated power is entrenched, leaving it capable of endless possibilities. In simpler terms, Omnipotent is comparable to Ascendancy, although I concede that my own creation pales in comparison. I would be a fool to think my abilities can compare to that of Rosaleen's… at least, for the time being. Yet anything and everything can change, and this is where Evelyn comes in. Rosaleen told me that, in Phyeroc, the princess is a danger. I realised that Rosaleen wanted to use me to get rid of Evelyn and, in doing so, remove the threat. She had given me just enough power to get the job done. I am just a pawn to her.'

'But how?' I asked further. 'How is Evelyn a danger?'

Fordon chuckled. 'As absurd as it might seem, the life of our innocent princess is not as mundane as we all thought. Under everyone's noses, that girl has studied ytyism, and who knows what she has learned over the years. Her father would have been distraught, to say the least. Be what may, with Evelyn dead, I would be able to claim her energy.'

'So you are the collector,' Clement said. 'Yet, given your obvious distaste for this Rosaleen, you will not simply hand over the energy.'

It was at this moment Fordon's intentions dawned on me. 'You mean to use Evelyn's energy against Rosaleen.'

As if on cue, another flash of lightning illuminated the chamber, followed closely by a deafening crash. 'And now you know. It is a shame it has come to this, but Rosaleen only has herself to blame. She took the care and loyalty I felt for others, replacing it with rancour.'

Clement snorted. 'You know that the princess will not go along with your retribution, so you will take her energy by force.'

'Despicable, is it not? Generally, I do not abide such duplicity'— Fordon brandished his curved sword for the last time—'But when I am made a fool...'

'Has it occurred to you that this is all Rosaleen's intention?' Maynard said, for the first time speaking. 'She has you under her thumb even more than you thought.'

Before Fordon could retort, the duel doors leading into the throne room threw open. Elgin Hosp entered the hall, Queen Verity behind him. 'Princess Evelyn has left the hideaway.'

'So the final sovereign knight has arrived,' cackled Fordon. 'And what is that? Evelyn has absconded from the safety of her hideaway? I knew the four of you would have placed her under such conditions. You said you wished to help me, but how can you hope to do so when you cannot even keep Evelyn safe? Shall we make a game of who will find her first?'

'I never said Princess Evelyn absconded from her hideaway,' Elgin said, a look of satisfaction showing.

'And as for your game,' Evelyn said, stepping into view. 'Let me save you the trouble!'

Stricken by a ball of concentrated force, Fordon whirled from the dais and hurtled to the marble floor with a thud.

'What did I tell you?' croaked Fordon, his voice hoarse from the attack. 'The girl knows the ways of ytyism. This will make things interesting.'

Getting back to his feet, Fordon spun his sword above his head. Ascendancy shone, immersing its owner with a purple hue. Moments later, he disappeared into a haze, in his place emerging a throng of redifass. Maynard immediately ran to Princess Evelyn's side while Elgin came to Queen Verity and me. The knights led us towards the throne room balcony and out of harm's way, eliminating any redifass that got close to us. Clement and Darwin brawled with the brunt of the enemy attack, cutting their way through the monsters and spilling murky blood in all directions.

Fordon was nowhere to be seen, leaving me to wonder if he had fled. However, this was not so, and Elgin was the first of the sovereign knights to suffer his wrath.

Despite the chaos in the throne room, Elgin could sense an unseen presence nearby. He remained as still as possible for a moment, then, without warning, held up his sword as if to shield himself from an attack. Elgin recoiled as the concealed Fordon came down on him; the knight swung his sword in retaliation, striking nothing but air. No attacks seemed to follow, but (as I would later discover) Fordon had achieved his purpose. I looked at the back of Elgin's hand and noticed it bleeding. The skin about the wound sallowed almost immediately into a bruise and then turned purple.

With the redifass being no match against the combined might of the sovereign knights, it did not take long for their numbers to drop. Yet, despite their success, not all was well. Faltering, Darwin fell to one knee and clutched his waist. The poison dart that had pricked him not long before was now taking its toll. Clement slew the final redifass and wheeled to his comrade, leaping to his aid. Alas, this noble action would cost him dearly.

Losing his magical veil, Fordon appeared afore Clement, his sword clasped in both hands and raised high. Before Clement could lift his weapon in defence, Fordon plunged the curved blade into the knight's shoulder.

Maynard's eyes widened in horror as his brother succumbed to the assault.

Fordon sneered as he looked into Clement's eyes, releasing the hilt of his sword as the other man tumbled. 'As I told you, I will become so much more than you could ever hope to be. You cannot compare to me'—he kicked Darwin in the back of the head, sending him crashing down next to Clement—'none of you can.'

With Fordon visible once more, Evelyn hurled a second bubble of energy, striking the man directly in the stomach and sending him hurtling through the air. The attack was more powerful than the last, and Fordon slid several metres after hitting the floor.

Maynard ran to his brother.

The princess called to Fordon from across the room. 'You have done unfathomable harm to everything you have crossed this day, but it ends here.'

With Fordon lying motionless on the floor, Evelyn looked at her mother, Elgin and me. Elgin, like Darwin before him, was suffering the effects of the poison and was now unable to stand.

'Do you remember what I said in my tower?' Evelyn said to me. 'Our combined efforts can repel anything Latnemirt can offer.'

All eyes shifted to the other end of the throne room as a shuffling disturbed the calm. Forcing himself from the floor, Fordon coughed a gobbet of blood into his beard. 'That is the second time you have struck me down, Princess,' he said, wobbling as he stood. 'Let us see how you like it.'

Fordon swirled his hands in a circular motion. While Fordon created his magic, Evelyn attempted a counterattack, but it was to no avail. More experienced than the princess in the arts of ytyism, Fordon summoned a ball of energy in a fraction of the time and launched it at her.

I felt hopeless. Elgin was indisposed, Verity tending to him, and I was too old to react quickly enough to protect Evelyn. She would surely perish.

The energy in Evelyn's hands evaporated as she moved them to cover her mouth; Maynard had jumped in the way of the attack.

His face contorted, the sovereign knight writhed on the floor as the energy passed through his body. After a few moments of what I could only imagine being agonising pain, the shaking came to an abrupt end.

'Such benevolence,' Fordon scoffed. He reclaimed his sword from Clement's body, pulling the weapon back and forth to release it. 'After I reunite this man with his brother in death, nothing more should be left to stand in my way.'

Evelyn bombarded Fordon with minor attacks as he approached her, but this time, he was prepared for the onslaught. Fordon laughed as he quelled every projectile, none having any effect against his movement. Evelyn moved away, edging closer and closer to the balcony, slipping backwards as she trod in a puddle of rainwater that had trickled in from under the balcony doors. Bumping her head and spraining her wrist, Evelyn lay dazed.

Fordon stopped just behind Maynard; the sovereign knight rolled over to his belly, pushing himself onto his hands and knees. The princess groaned as she sat back up, her fingers pressed on the back of her head.

'Is this really whom Rosaleen fears? A girl green in the ways of ytyism?' Fordon jeered. 'Such a pity. All the same… a prophecy is a prophecy.'

Fordon thrust the point of his sword through Maynard, narrowly missing his spine. Blood gushing from his front, the knight crashed down once again. After freeing his sword, Fordon stepped over Maynard's body and continued towards Evelyn.

Evelyn struggled back onto her feet, using the throne dais as support. 'Help me, Minach…' the princess implored. 'Please!'

Fordon laughed again. 'And what do you expect the old minach will be able to do? I imagine his abilities are inferior even to yours. You are alone, Princess.'

'If you mean to kill me, Lord Latnemirt, then do so quickly. Just remember that even when I am gone, nothing will change. You will never be strong enough to destroy a ytied, and your torment will continue until your last breath.'

'I admire your spirit, but you can drop the pretence—there is nothing you or anyone can do to stop me now. Please believe me when I say I would have preferred another outcome, but such decisions have been beyond me for quite some time.' Fordon took Evelyn firmly by her bodice and pulled her closer, placing the edge of his sword on her neck. 'Do not worry. I intend to make your death as quick and as painless as possible... I hope you find peace in death, wherever that might--.'

Fordon jolted backwards as a Longsword ran him through, penetrating his torso and slicing a tuft of Evelyn's hair. With a grip that defied his debilitated state, Maynard pulled Fordon away from the princess, smashed his way onto the throne room's balcony and tossed Latnemiert over the parapets to what would be the mote water a hundred feet below.

I had moved to Maynard's side while Fordon spoke, spurred into action by Princess Evelyn's plight. Having just been attacked, I believed Maynard had a better chance over his comrades to help Evelyn before the poison took effect. Recalling the ytyism I had learned over the years, I filled the knight with just enough energy to reawaken and save her in a way I could not.

The sovereign knights, like so many others, passed away that fateful day. The aftermath was a lengthy procedure, but at least we were able to afford everyone proper burials.

No one came forward with information on Fordon. His body was not within the moat waters, but if he had somehow managed to survive the fall, especially without sustaining broken bones, it was reasonable to assume that he would have perished soon after. We are in a time where we can rest, but whatever Fordon's fate, trouble will not have left Stilly entirely.

The day of our departure fast approaches. What the future holds is in the hands of the creators, and although a corrupted man, Fordon Latnemirt came with a warning that we must not ignore. Indeed, our old friend has opened our eyes to what we failed to see, and we are now at a time when we can begin to understand the world.

Is this part of that Phyeroc of which Fordon spoke? Only time will tell.

Watch over us, our only hope. May the creators light your way for evermore.

Chapter Four

Oliath Burley had a few places to visit that morning.

Another attack occurred during the early hours, this time on the blacksmith. Oliath did not know the details of this latest incident; a few night guards handled the problem, but he had yet to catch up with them. Before dealing with that problem, however, he wanted to visit the twin owners of Blow Your Mind! and clear up a few things. That, he hoped, would not take long.

Marching towards the gunpowder shop, Oliath squinted as he glimpsed at the numerous guards patrolling the area, their armour shining harshly in the sun. Upon noticing the captain, some of the troops stopped what they were doing and saluted. Oliath returned no more than a passing nod as he walked by, ignoring a majority altogether. Nolan and Cordelia were with their boss, their presence for little more reason other than to keep him company. Then again, they held open the occasional door, which he supposed was nice. As the trio got within eyesight of their destination, Cordelia quickened her pace, opened the door to the shop front and held it until Oliath and Nolan were inside, reclosing it with a firmer-than-necessary shove afterwards.

Slouching over the counter, his chin buried in one palm, dual shop owner Whitaker Firs shifted his eyes from the newspaper he was reading and glanced at the three visitors before looking down again. Whitaker's twin sister Lilac Firs entered the customer room not long after, walking behind the counter as if she were floating. Like her brother, she regarded the visitors indifferently before peering over Whitaker's shoulder to see what he was reading.

Cordelia and Nolan exchanged looks, irked by the twin's behaviour. Oliath was less surprised at the reception, remembering previous visits.

In unison, the twins lifted their heads as Oliath cleared his throat. This caused him to frown; it was almost as if a mirror were between them. Anaemic in appearance, nearly every part of the two was pale: their skin, lips, hair… Indeed, the only thing that seemed to stand out was the red tint in their eyes. It was tricky to know what they were thinking most of the time, but perhaps that was a good thing.

117

'You are back again, I see,' droned Whitaker. He licked his finger and turned a page of his newspaper with a languid flick of his wrist. 'Did you forget something?'

'We have just come to have a second inspection... just to make sure we have not overlooked anything.'

'As you have it, Captain Burley,' Lilac said in an equally dull tone. 'Don't let us stand in your way.'

Oliath harrumphed. 'Well, don't go too far... I might have some questions for the two of you.'

Whitaker licked his finger again and turned another page. 'I'm not sure we can be of much help,' he mumbled.

Cordelia scoffed at the lack of concern. 'You seem remarkably untroubled by the whole affair. I get more upset when I spill my drink than you do getting burgled.'

'There is no use crying over spilt milk,' Lilac replied.

'Quite,' Whitaker agreed, nodding. 'Every now and then, disagreeable things happen.'

'Everyone reacts differently to certain situations,' Lilac went on, nodding as well. 'Besides, we were not burgled. All our stock seems in order.'

'Could you have overlooked something missing?' Nolan asked.

'As we said,' Whitaker began.

'All our stock *seems* in order,' Lilac finished.

Oliath grimaced. *Creepy little weirdoes.* 'Actually, I have a question about your back door.'

'It's still blown off,' Lilac said sardonically.

Oliath ignored the comment. 'On our visit yesterday, I noticed a lack of gunpowder residue on or around the door. I am not the biggest expert in explosives, but considerable force seems to have been used nonetheless.'

'It could have been kicked in,' suggested Whitaker.

'It looks like something more than a kick, I know that much. Besides, the merchant in detention does not seem the type to kick down a door. Nonetheless'—Oliath leant on the counter and moved his head closer to the twins, as if about to whisper—'I presume that you two have some knowledge on explosives and the like, seeing as you run a business that deals with the stuff. Or am I wrong, and spewing satirical remarks is your speciality.'

Oliath pushed himself back up from the counter and folded his arms.

Judging from their momentary silence, the Firs were stunned by the rebuke, even if they did not show it.

'If it was an explosive of some description, it is certainly not one from our stock,' Whitaker yawned.

'We were also puzzled by the absence of gunpowder residue,' Lilac added. 'Because of this, we are certain that if a chemical was used, it was not purchased from us.'

'I see,' Oliath said. He rubbed his chin with his forefinger and thumb. 'Were you in the building at the time of the attack?'

'We were both asleep,' answered Whitaker.

'And you heard nothing?'

'We sleep heavily,' Lilac added.'

Oliath groaned at the remark. 'Still, you would think an explosion would wake even the most comatose.'

'Who knows,' Whitaker went on. 'If an explosive at all, perhaps the substance used does not make much noise when detonated.'

Oliath rolled his eyes, fearing the two were returning to their sarcastic ways. He ran his fingers through his hair. 'Very well… is there anything you would like to add before we leave?'

'Not really,' said Lilac. 'We have been preparing fireworks for the upcoming festival. Benjamin Oswin came here requesting them.'

Oliath was about to dismiss what Lilac said but gave it more thought. Oswin was an irritating busybody who often stuck his nose where it was not welcome, but he seemed unusually more interested in Oliath's work of late. As noted in the previous meeting, perhaps Oswin was simply concerned about weapon misuse; the prospect of crazed people getting their hands on dangerous items was unnerving, but it was not as if the captain of the guard could not handle such matters.

'Thank you for your co-operation. I will make sure that someone comes to properly fix your back door.' Oliath said.

'No need,' Whitaker sighed.

'We have already arranged to have it repaired,' Lilac explained.

The Firs twins resumed what they had been doing before Oliath arrived, acting as if he had already left. Oliath again rolled his eyes and moved to the shop's main entrance, but Lilac called out to him before he exited.

'Just a minute, Captain Burley,' she said. 'There *is* something else.'

Oliath gave a sideways glance.

'Whitaker and I overheard that a man was near our shop the other day while the break-in happened.'

'A man?' Oliath repeated, turning to face the twins properly.

'Oh, yes. That's right,' Whitaker said, realising what his sister was talking about. 'Rumours of a bright light, followed by a man wielding a large sword, is the word on the street. The swordsman is good with his weapon, by all accounts.'

Oliath digested the information, pinching his chin as he thought. 'Bright light and a large sword. That light might have something to do with what damaged your back door. Do you think this man is an accomplice?'

'Maybe, but it seems unlikely,' said Lilac.

'People who claim to have witnessed the man say that they scared him off,' said Whitaker.

Oliath showed a look of disbelief. 'Civilians spooking a supposed gifted swordsman? Who are these witnesses, anyway?'

The twins shrugged at the same time, apparently unconcerned with such details.

'Thanks anyway,' Oliath muttered. He walked from the shop.

Was this the actual reason for Oswin's interest? The mention of a large sword would suggest so, but why would this swordsman run from simple townspeople? Maybe this man did not wish to be recognised.

If what the Firs said was true, then Oliath *had* to find out more.

Ebony stood up straight and wiped the sweat from her brow.

Remnant Tales of Stilly:
Passion and Benevolence

The sun's heat was almost unbearable, and shifting farmyard hay with a pitchfork that her clammy palms could barely grip was losing appeal. Yet, she would struggle on, as she had a good reason. In fact, she had three reasons for being at Dolb's farm that day. The primary purpose was empathy; Hazel Dolb often single-handedly did most of the work on the farm without complaint, but her face could not hide the strain it caused as each day passed. A little helping hand was the least Ebony could do. The second reason (even though her intentions were genuinely selfless) was that she knew to help at the farm was a way to earn a few stinneps. The final motive, albeit less flattering, was so Ebony did not end up banging her head against a wall in boredom. Now that she had finished her library book the night before, she knew that sitting about and doing almost nothing between domestic chores would ensue.

Dragging her feet towards the stables, Ebony dropped the pitchfork to the grass and fetched herself a tin mug. Using the well outside the barn, she poured water from the hanging bucket. Although clean, the water was slightly warm. This did not particularly worry Ebony, however; she was too thirsty to care.

Standing in the shade of a nearby tree, Ebony rested her back against its trunk and drank a mouthful of water. She turned her head to look at Hazel and blew an exhausted breath. Her friend moved at a constant pace from one task to another, ranging from making sure the animals were all right to keeping farming tools and other items in working order. At least she did not have to deal with customers: her mother Myrah handled that.

Hazel was used to multitasking, but her ability to do so would never fail to amaze Ebony, especially during summer. At least Colossus could relate; laying a few metres away from Ebony with his body spread limp on the grass and his tongue hanging out, the Great Dane did not appear to have the will for anything other than basking.

Ebony looked back at Hazel and called out to her. 'Would you like a drink?'

Hazel stood up from what she was doing and placed her hands on her hips, reaching her fingers to her lower back and letting out a soft groan.

'Yeah, that would be a blessing, m'dear, but you stay there—I'll get it myself.'

'This heat's too much for us,' Ebony admitted when Hazel got close. She was looking at Colossus as she spoke. 'I don't know how much longer I can go on.'

Hazel gave a pursed smile. She often did this, Ebony noticed. The expression suggested she was smug about something, but she, more often than not, did it out of habit. 'Don't worry about that, Ebs. I appreciate the help however it comes.'

Ebony murmured a response as she drank another mouthful of water, peering into the distance.

Hazel looked at Ebony and cocked an eyebrow. She could see her friend was deep in thought. 'So,' Hazel blurted, interrupting the tranquillity of the moment. 'Are you gonna tell me what's on your mind, or must I beat it from you?

Ebony shifted her eyes towards Hazel.

'Don't look at me like that, Ebs—you're thinking about something, and judging by those big brown eyes of yours, it is something exciting. You know I can't stand it when you withhold these things from me.'

'I have no idea what you are talking about.' Ebony sipped her water. 'I still have that story stuck in my head. It was a pretty good read.'

'Uh-huh,' Hazel responded. 'So you've said half a hundred times already. *"Passionately Benevolent is really absorbing",*' the farmer said, impersonating Ebony's voice poorly. ' *"Passionately Benevolent is set in Wilheard"—"Passionately Benevolent is better than your life!"*'

Ebony smirked. *I mentioned it so many times, yet you still get the title wrong*, she thought. 'It's called Passion and Benevolence, and I do not recall saying that last one.'

Hazel simpered and fluttered her eyelids.

'I was also only thinking about the same thing I have been the whole summer.'

'What? You mean that *change* thing you've been blabbering on about?'

'If by blabbering you mean mentioning once a few days ago, then yes.'

'Oh,' Hazel said. 'Well, I guess that's fine… I just thought you might have something exciting on your mind. Tender spirits! What a pity… I could really do with something more fun to think about. If only someone could satisfy this need…'

Hazel let out an exaggerated sigh then.

Ebony rolled her eyes. 'All right, I confess—I am thinking about something else, but since I was initially not going to tell anyone, you have to promise to keep quiet about it, especially to my father.'

Hazel held a finger up to her mouth and pulled a mischievous grin. 'I promise.'

'Seriously, though, you must not tell anyone unless absolutely necessary.' Ebony took a deep breath. 'I'm thinking about going into the eastern woodlands.'

'The eastern woodlands?' Hazel repeated, taken aback. 'Why?'

'I have a few reasons. The short of it is I want to go exploring, and this will be the perfect way of shaking up the monotony of my day-to-day routine.'

Faint lines of concern creased Hazel's brow. 'Are you sure that's wise, Ebs? I know that with my work always piling up, I have not been able to find out much about the blacksmith thingy, but even I can see that it would be--'

'Blacksmith thingy?' Ebony echoed, interrupting her friend. 'Has something happened to the owner?'

Hazel raised her eyebrows. 'You mean to tell me you haven't heard? Good grief, you are slow today, m'dear.'

Because of her busy lifestyle, Hazel did not often discover something of interest before Ebony, but there was a good reason why that day was different. As with Blow Your Mind!, Wilheard's blacksmith was in a part of Wilheard Ebony had little need to visit. She preferred to keep swords and other weapons inside her storybooks. She could only want candles or lantern oil from such places, which her father tended to buy anyway.

'Anyway,' Hazel continued, 'it turns out there was another attempted break-in on a business early this morning. As you now know, the blacksmith's hangout was targeted.'

'Poor Mister Blacksmith,' Ebony said. She did not know the smithy very well, including his real name, but she knew he was a nice enough person to deserve her sympathy. 'I hope he did not suffer too much trouble.'

'Funny you should say that because the old codger and his shop remain unscathed. That is why I said *attempted* break-in. But ignore that—the best part is yet to come.'

Ebony's ears pricked in anticipation, her fatigue practically forgotten. 'Go on...'

'Well,' Hazel said in a hushed tone, leaning closer to Ebony as if to make sure not even Colossus could hear, 'even though Captain Burley—that gorgeous man—arrived at the scene with his troops as quickly as possible, it ended up with him not even needing to do anything. That is, apart from taking the would-be-crook away.'

How curious,' Ebony whispered back. 'Then who intervened with the *attempted* break-in?'

Hazel smiled. 'I don't know. But at least I've got you interested.'

Ebony pouted. 'You're such a tease.'

'I know, but fear not, m'dear, as this is where you come in. You never know—your adventurous nature might be satisfied in town, and you will not need to go into the woodland.'

'We'll see,' Ebony mumbled.

The blacksmith got little work done that day.

Ordinarily, Drah Leets was not much of an attention-seeker, but he found himself enjoying the interest of the crowds surrounding his smithy that morning. The short, red-bearded man felt famous with Wilheard's soldiers acting as sentinels by keeping reporters and prying onlookers at a distance. The real reason troops were keeping the public away, however, was less flattering and not for Leets's benefit.

Oliath Burley's patience had already run dry that day. As he stood outside the blacksmith's, it had only taken five minutes for his temper to rise, and he found he was in no mood to deal with the flocks of curious town's people, and certainly not those from the newspapers.

Oliath's investigation into Wilheard's recent problems was generally non-progressive, with more questions than answers. Why were merchants and others out of town targeting shops, especially weapon dealers and other specialised places? Why do all the suspects seem lost and confused upon arrest? What is causing the intense flashes of light that witnesses claim to see near all the crime scenes? These questions were confounding, but at least he was discovering more about that swordsman the Firs twins mentioned at Blow Your Mind!. Unfortunately, what Oliath had learnt had gone from interesting to something more disconcerting. He had a gut feeling that this swordsman, despite Oliath's best efforts to prove otherwise, would make him appear inept, and that was something in which reporters seemed to take unwarranted glee.

The captain pinched the bridge of his nose; a headache was brewing. The sooner he got the information from the blacksmith, the sooner he could escape the intensifying heat.

Oliath sneered as Leets waved at the gathering of people, an idiotic grin fixed on his chubby face. 'If I can pull you away from your celebrity, Mister Leets, I would be grateful for a moment of your time. I have a few questions I hope you can answer.'

'Fire away, Captain Burley. You can call me Drah if y'like,' Leets said, too preoccupied to notice Oliath's sarcasm.

'What were you doing at three-thirty-five this morning when the—shall we say—*feat* took place?'

'Funny you should say that because I were sleepin' when a noise comin' from me roof woke me up.'

Oliath frowned at the answer. After concluding there was nothing funny about the question in any sense of the word, Oliath shook his head and pencilled *"Sleeping"* in his notebook.

'It is essential you tell me what you know, Mister Leets, so please listen carefully. What actions did you take after hearing the noises on your roof?'

'I got out me bed and thought to me-self—I wonder what that is!'

Remnant Tales of Stilly:
Passion and Benevolence

Oliath sighed and looked down at his notebook once again. *"Rudimentary attempts to investigate the disturbance"*.

'I know you had no hand in the commotion, Mister Leets, but I will assume you made some attempt to find out what was happening. Did you, for example, look out the window or step outside and see a suspicious person?'

'You know as much as me, Captain Burley. I don't think I can 'elp you...'

'Humour me, Leets. I want at least something minutely constructive to come from your mouth.'

By now, Leets had finally grasped that Oliath was losing patience. Swallowing hard, he meekly replied. 'It happened all so fast, Captain Burley. By the time I got outside, the criminal was tied up on that pole'—Leets pointed to the pole in question—'but as for the one who did it...' he gave an exaggerated shrug.

'Very well. Thank you for your cooperation, Mister Leets.' Oliath turned round and ran his fingers through his sweat-matted hair.

Nolen Shakeston and Cordelia Lawford, standing several paces behind the captain the whole time, sneered as much as their boss at Leets's manner.

'Tender spirits... it's like trying to get blood from a stone,' Oliath grumbled. 'How is the suspect?'

'We asked a few of the morning guards that had been on patrol, sir,' Cordelia answered. 'According to them, the suspect is under the same care as the other detainees.'

'Good,' Oliath said. He was pleased with the pair's efforts as always, but even this could not raise a smile from him. 'If only the mayor would give me permission to question the suspects. I'm sure the results would be better than we currently have.' He shot a disapproving glance at Leets before looking back to his lieutenants. 'The suspect is a woman this time, I hear.'

Nolen and Cordelia looked at their boss silently.

'It just doesn't make sense. Who are these people, and what are their motives?' Oliath said rhetorically.

'The female apprehended displays the same confused temperament as the recent others, sir,' said Nolen.

Oliath nodded in acknowledgement, but it was something he had already guessed. 'That is what confuses me, Shakeston.'

Oliath tilted his head backwards and thought for a moment. 'Mister Leets! I have one last question if you would oblige me. Have you got any notion—I don't care how trivial you might deem it—as to why your shop might have been targeted?'

While Oliath listed what Leets said in his notebook, Cordelia and Nolen talked between themselves.

'Have you read The Wilheard Chronicle today?' Nolen asked his female counterpart.

Cordelia gave a slow, single nod. 'I swear the Vultures get a thrill out of writing the nonsense they call news.'

'Precisely why I do not read any of the papers,' Nolen snorted. 'I don't know how you put up with that rubbish.'

'It keeps my mind occupied. Besides, the Vultures sometimes come up with information that we overlook.' Cordelia stared off into the middle distance. 'Speaking of which, with this new character on everyone's lips, the reporters certainly have something interesting to write about.'

'That's a good point. The more the Vultures write, the more we will find out.'

'Perhaps, but it would be folly to rely on them too much—they have a habit of embellishment.'

Nolen shook his head at the notion.

'Mind you,' Cordelia went on. 'I am always searching for ways to better myself. This vigilante's work intrigues me. Perhaps, if we find him, we can test his technique with our own. And as you know, terrible accidents can happen when undertaking such *tests*.'

Nolen grinned. 'That is very true. Not only does the boss not need the extra trouble, but if we eliminate this nuisance ourselves, the Vultures would have something worthwhile to write about. I would love to see the look on their stupid faces when they no longer have reason to criticise our efforts.'

The lieutenants chuckled at the thought but stopped after they realised someone had overheard them.

A man heavily dressed in beige-coloured clothing and wearing a wide-brimmed hat approached the two. He was tutting as he walked. 'Come now… surely even you two would not stoop to such underhandedness.'

Nolen and Cordelia growled inwardly. There was no need to guess whose voice it was; only one man had the nerve to provoke them so openly.

'It's a little hot for such clothing, Theryle,' Nolen sneered while folding his arms. 'Dressing like that in this heat would definitely fry someone's senses. Then again, I see it has had no effect on yours.'

Dexter Theryle stopped under a metre in front of the lieutenants, not once losing the impertinent look on his face. 'Perhaps you should be less worried about my wellbeing and more concerned with your inability to quell your frustration with the Vultures. Or am I wrong in thinking that those repugnant bulges on your faces—which look remarkably stress-related—are, in fact, normal?'

'What do you want, you little narcissist?' Cordelia asked before Dexter could say anything else.

'The others and I have carried out our duties. I am here to report our findings to Captain Burley.'

'He is busy,' snapped Nolen, holding out his arm to stop Dexter from walking past. 'You may tell us of your findings.'

'May I?' Dexter retorted. 'That's very kind of you, my rottweiler friend, but I am not obligated to share my knowledge with you dogs. I will wait until Captain Burley is available.'

'Learn your place, cretin!' Cordelia seethed, the words hissing through her teeth. 'You do not deserve the praise the boss gives you. Everyone knows your loyalties stretch only as far as your purse.'

'Calm yourself, pooch. Go and find a fountain to lap from—it will cool your head.'

Nolen and Cordelia clenched their fists. It was taking all of their self-control not to thrash Dexter. Yet, before any violence could materialise, there was a much-needed interruption.

'Theryle!' Oliath called, pleased to see him. 'I thought I could hear you. Come closer, man.'

Dexter tipped his hat mockingly at the lieutenants before pushing between them.

Oliath smiled and patted Dexter firmly on his upper back. 'Tender spirits, Theryle! Are you not hot in all that winter attire?'

'You'll be surprised to hear, sir,' said Dexter as he dusted the sleeves of his coat, 'that it reflects the sun's rays rather nicely.'

'If you say so, but never mind that for now. By the look on your face, I trust you have some good news for me.'

'Yes, sir,' Dexter answered, taking a moment to look at the crowds. 'But perhaps we should take this somewhere else. The Vultures don't need to hear our conversation.'

'Agreed,' said Oliath, beckoning to Nolen and Cordelia. 'I could do with getting some shade anyway. My head is killing me.'

Benjamin Oswin was a little chilly: an oddity in summer.

He was sitting inside a room with thick stone walls. He did not have much choice on the matter; because of his type of work, he moved from room to room, which seemed to range from stuffy and well-lit to cold and shady. It could not be helped, though. Perhaps when he stopped for lunch, he could have a walk to the eye surgery to get Mayor Basil's glasses fixed. That ought to give him a chance to obtain a bit of sun and fresh air. For now, though, he had one last interview.

Led in by a nurse, a man with a round head and belly entered the room. The man, a merchant from Thane, spotted Benjamin sitting next to the table in the centre of the room and took a few nervous steps closer.

'Please take a seat, sir,' Benjamin said, getting to his feet as the other man entered the room. He gestured an open hand at the chair on the opposite side of the table and smiled warmly, causing his moustache to smile, too. 'I understand that you have been through quite a bit, and I promise I won't keep you long. I just hope we can clear up a few things.'

129

Remnant Tales of Stilly:
Passion and Benevolence

As the merchant sat down, Benjamin nodded a *thank-you* to the nurse, who then left, closing the door behind her.

The merchant looked down at the papers laid neatly in front of Benjamin, avoiding eye contact. Although not generally shy, the merchant was uncomfortable being there, and his timidity resulted from embarrassment.

'So… Mister Relles, is it?' asked Ben, looking at the heading of the topmost sheet of paper and then at the man before him.

The merchant nodded.

'Good. My name is Benjamin Oswin'—he shook Relles's hand from across the table—'I am Basil Wolleb's assistant. Mister Wolleb is the mayor of Wilheard and has tasked me with asking a few questions. You are under no pressure to answer any of them, but any help is appreciated.'

Benjamin smiled again. Relles managed a half smile in return.

'So tell me, Mister Relles, I have written in front of me that you are from Thane. What brings you to Wilheard?'

'I's just on a delivery, sir. I make the trip every season.'

'I see,' Benjamin replied. 'And what is it you deliver?'

'Mainly sauces and other preservatives. My main supplier is Mrs Whickett's Recipes.'

Benjamin murmured in acknowledgement. 'Very well. Can you tell me what you were doing the morning you were apprehended?'

The merchant stuttered, outwardly abashed and unsure what to say.

Ben continued questioning. 'What I mean to say is that there is a lot of confusion lately involving people from out of town. As you will have been informed, you were involved in some disturbances. Can you elaborate on what happened?'

'All I can remember is that I's just reaching eyeshot of this here town when I started feeling dizzy-like. Before I knew it, I's getting a thumpin' headache and terrible chest pains…'

'Chest pains?'

'Yes, sir, an' I's sweatin' all over.' Relles waved his hand over his face and torso.

Benjamin wrote a few notes. What Relles told him was similar to other suspects. 'Some locals say they noticed bright flashes of light and a loud crash, which they likened to lightning and thunder. This was close to the place where you were found. Can you tell me more about that?

'I cannot remember anythin' like that…'

'What about the damage you caused. It is very peculiar—as if you have some otherworldly powers, as silly as that may sound. What did you do exactly, and is it relatable to the former question?'

'I cannot remember!' Relles covered his face and sobbed in frustration. 'I dunno what 'appened or why I'm even 'ere.'

Hearing Relles shout, the nurse re-entered the room with a Wilheard Guard. Benjamin held his hand out for them to wait at the door. 'I'm sorry if I have caused you any distress, Mister Relles. That will be all for now, and thank you for your help.'

After the nurse led the merchant away, Benjamin sighed as he sat back in his chair. He rubbed his arms from the chill and looked through the piles of paper. All the suspects suffered from the same symptoms, but what had got into them in the first place? These were otherwise ordinary individuals, and it made no sense.

Benjamin imagined this was how Oliath Burley felt.

By the time Ebony returned to Dolb's Farm, it was approaching mid-afternoon.

As she made her way to the stables, the main thing on her mind was how Hazel would react to her findings. Additionally, she wondered how her friend would respond when she told her that doing the extra research only made her want to explore the forest even more.

Climbing over the wooden fence nearest the barn, Ebony walked round the back to see if Hazel was about. Sure enough, she found her friend shifting farming equipment. Hazel had pulled a few tools outside the barn doorway and was now tossing other smaller objects to one side. Colossus, still lounging in the sun, watched his owner as she busily searched for something.

'Are you not busy enough already to be clearing out?' Ebony said, carefully stepping into view of Hazel and ensuring one of the farmyard projectiles did not hit her.

Hazel stood up straight and turned to look at Ebony. 'Not quite, m'dear. I have got some unwanted guests.'

'I see,' Ebony said, not actually paying much attention to the farmer and more concerned with what was on her mind. 'Anyway, I have returned with my discoveries. Of course, you'll have to forgive that this is all based on hearsay.'

'I expected no less,' Hazel responded, tossing a tin bucket out of her way.

Ebony went on. 'Even though the attempted attack happened to be on the Smithy, Mister Blacksmith was pretty much the only one not to know who prevented it. By the time he came outside, Captain Oliath was only just arriving.'

'The blacksmith's name is Drah Leets, and I know about that already.'

'Fine, but let me continue. The would-be-crook turned out to be a woman, but according to reporters, she seemed to be in a state of confusion like the last few suspects that targeted the other shops.'

'I know that too.'

'Will you be quiet, Hazel! I'm just getting to the good parts.'

Hazel smirked. 'Sorry, Ebs.'

Ebony cleared her throat and continued. 'Here's something interesting I overheard. According to some of the town's night watch and a few citizens, the shadow of a man wearing a coat with longish hair was seen sprinting towards the eastern woodland. They are convinced he is the one who scuppers the attempted break-ins.'

'A coat, you say? That is interesting, but are you sure these witnesses are not mistaking this shadow-man with that unusual guy… oh, what's his name…? Dexter Theryle?'

'Well, as I said, the man in question also has long hair. I do not know Mister Theryle all that well, but he has short hair as far as I can remember. Besides, I don't think the coat is as big as Dexter's.'

'Fair enough,' Hazel huffed. 'Also, Dexter always wears that big hat— he's a bit weird…'

Ebony chuckled. 'He probably thinks the same about you.'

'Probably. Anyway, what else did you find out?'

'Well… um… Not much,' Ebony said.

Hazel raised an eyebrow. 'Are you sure? I'm not convinced.'

'Well…' Ebony lightly bit her bottom lip. 'I'm sure I heard one of the witnesses say that the shadow-man had a… sword.'

'A *sword*?' Hazel exclaimed. 'Oh, Ebs, please tell me you are not still planning on going into the woodland after hearing that.'

Ebony winced, shrinking her head into her shoulders.

'Tender spirits, Ebony! For a bright girl, you sure can be a dunce.'

'Come on, Hazel, give me some credit. I have put some thought into the idea. If the vigilante were dangerous or bad, surely the good deed this morning would not have occurred. In any case, I can handle myself, and I do not intend to rush into the woodland just yet. I will continue to gather more information so that I have the best chance of planning ahead.'

Hazel shook her head and sighed. 'I know how wise you are, m'dear, but it still sounds stupid. Not only that, what would your pop think if he were to find out?'

Ebony did not respond. She looked down at her feet.

'You are as stubborn as you are smart. I know I cannot stop you when your mind is set on something. To be honest, I wish I could go with you, but I'm too busy.'

Hazel kicked a small hay bale, causing a brown rat to scurry out from hiding. 'Get it, Colossus, get it!' Hazel cried, pointing at the rodent.

Colossus pricked up his ears upon hearing his name. Catching sight of the rat, he watched it bolt into the farmyard, towards a bush, and then out of sight. The hound looked back at Hazel, yawned and laid his head down again.

Hazel grumbled. 'What's wrong with you, you dippy mutt? I swear—that dog's as much use as transparent clothing.'

'Mean, but witty.'

'You liked that, huh?' Hazel said, folding her arms. 'I've got more where that came from if you're interested.'

'Perhaps another time. There are things I must do and places I must go.'

133

'I know,' the farmer said, her face stern. 'Just you mind yourself, m'dear.'

The soft glow of oil lanterns, which hung above doors of numerous buildings, lit the stone streets of Wilheard. With darkness looming, the air was cooler and calmer.

Walking alone down a cobbled path, Dexter Theryle pulled his coat closed. Although not cold, his heavy eyelids made him long for his bed. His home was in sight, but that only gave Dexter partial gladness; as soon as he walked through the door, he knew that Wiley would be there and would want an update on today's meeting with Captain Oliath Burley.

Opening the door to his home, Dexter stepped wearily indoors and sighed. Two of his housemates were watching him as he entered.

Wiley Penrose, a thin man with round glasses, sat at a large table with his head resting in one hand. A deck of playing cards lay scattered in front of him. To his left was Meddia Penrose, a timid sixteen-year-old girl with a cute face. She sat atop a wooden stool, her back straight and legs crossed.

Despite sharing his name, Meddia was not related to Wiley. He was, however, a mentor and father figure in her eyes, and she followed him nearly everywhere. Childish for her age, Meddia's behaviour towards Wiley was clingy, but this did not bother him. She had been that way since he found her lost, walking along a road outside Wilheard several years ago: cold, hungry and with a look of confusion in her eyes. Wiley knew little of Meddia's upbringing (or how long she had been alone), which, thanks to a lack of communication skills, he concluded had been poor. Whatever the circumstances, be it that her parents had died or abandoned her, Wiley had tasked himself with helping the girl in any way he could.

As he always did after arriving home, Dexter hung his coat and hat on the hook next to the front door, not saying so much as a fair eve as he went through the routine. Wiley disapproved of this behaviour and occasionally tried to break the habit, yet Dexter was not a man to break easily; he liked his space after arriving home and refused to adequately acknowledge anyone until he had sat down.

More docile than her mentor, Meddia was content to leave Dexter alone, not speaking until someone else broke the silence.

Trudging towards the table, Dexter slumped into the chair opposite his friends and rolled his neck, causing the joints to crack audibly. He looked round the room. 'Where's Priory?'

'Out flat on his bed, staring at the ceiling in a drunken, trance-like stupor, no doubt,' Wiley said, unsmiling. 'Why?'

'Because what I have to say concerns all of us.'

'I can go and get Rida if you want,' Meddia said, looking at Wiley, who, in turn, looked at Dexter for an answer.

Dexter picked up one of the playing cards and toyed with it. He tossed it back on the table. 'No… that won't be necessary, but make sure he is informed by tomorrow afternoon.'

Meddia bobbed her head in acknowledgement. She got along with Rida Priory better than anyone else did.

'Ok… as you know, I met up with the boss during the afternoon to discuss our movements in his investigation and then asked what we should do next. First of all, Wiley, I will say that the boss was pleased with your conclusion about why these particular businesses were targeted. He had not considered it would have anything to do with glass stones and other materials, so well done on that.'

Wiley gave a single nod, inwardly delighted for the commendation and contented with the knowledge that Oliath Burley appreciated his efforts.

'Oliath would appreciate it if you, as you have likely guessed, can also find out the appeal of such objects,' Dexter added before looking towards Meddia. 'As for your work, Meddia, the boss is happy that you and Rida have unearthed some potential witnesses in the investigation. He said that he will interview them sometime.'

Meddia pulled a toothy grin. 'Ah, it weren't much.'

'No, Meddia, you should have said it *wasn't* much—or even better—*was not*,' Wiley corrected. 'Anyway, you should not be so modest. You did well, and I am sure you did all the hard work while Rida just watched as he picked his nose.'

Meddia tittered. That had not necessarily been true, but it sounded funny nonetheless.

Wiley turned back to Dexter. 'In any case, besides continuing our scouring of the town, what does Captain Burley have in mind for us now?'

Dexter sat up in his wooden seat, giving a shrug as he rested his arms on the table. 'That's it, to be honest. I'm sure you heard about the blacksmith incident this morning—it would seem a foreign vigilante is sneaking about town. The boss seems to think that we will see more of this stranger, and I am inclined to agree.'

'So can I infer that we are to find out more about this vigilante?'

Dexter glanced at the thinner man. 'You two and Rida can do so, yes.'

'Why won't you be doing so, too?' Meddia asked.

'I will, in my own way,' Dexter replied. 'I've got my eye on one particular woman.'

Wiley looked unimpressed. 'Can I ask who that might be? I hope this woman has something to do with the investigation.'

'Of course—and to answer your question, I am referring to the carpenter's daughter. You know—the one up that hill to the south of the town?'

'Ebony Gibenn?' Meddia pouted with confusion. 'What's so great about her?'

The two men looked at the teenager.

'Do you know this person?' Wiley asked.

Meddia looked down at her bare feet and played with her toes. 'Not really. I know who she is because I see her at Bookish Charm sometimes. I did what you ordered, Wiley—I looked at some books.'

'I did not *order* you to look at books, Meddia; I simply suggested it to improve your reading. But never mind that. Tell us about this Ebony Gibenn.'

Meddia looked downwards once more. 'I don't know her really—she seems nice, I s'pose. She likes reading those big books with little words.'

Meddia raised her hands as she spoke, exaggerating how thick she remembered the books to be.

'Yes, and I have noticed that she is a curious woman,' Dexter added.

Wiley smirked. 'You have your eyes on everyone these days, don't you?'

'I like to think I am a perceptive man. Besides, I feel I can relate with this Ebony Gibenn. Like her, I consider myself the curious type. I would love to know what she gets up to in her spare time.'

Sitting on a lone tree stump to the border of the eastern woodland, an equally lone figure stared impassively at the colours now filling the horizon, lighting the star-speckled darkness with a warmer yellow.

The man, his eyes filled with uncertainty, thumbed his hair behind his ear and scanned the rooftops of Wilheard. The time, according to the town's clock, was early, and he knew that very few people would have yet arisen from their slumber. All the same, caution was no less critical; lingering in the air, a particular menace pricked his senses. Although faint, this threat was rank enough to put him on edge.

What was this foulness? The man did not know. As of late, there were many questions to which he could not find the answer, but he knew at least that it was a threat that could not escape him… or something he could escape in turn.

Various people had fallen afoul of the threat; once targeted, the victim would lose control of body and mind. Thus far, the lone man had confronted every victim as delicately as possible, and although he disliked interfering in the duties of others, his help averted starker consequences. Vexingly, such actions had earned him the title of vigilante.

Despite this, Wilheard's current circumstances were not what brought the man to the town that morning. A puckish, imp-like woman had been invading his dreams and thoughts of late, and although she had proved elusive, the vigilante knew that she was within this part of Stilly. As far as Wilheard's troubles went, he was dubious over whether she might be involved. Even though she was capable of delving into one's subconscious, brainwashing and control did not seem to be her intention. Whatever the imp's reasoning, she insisted on drawing the man's attention to Wilheard. Was she merely playing with him? Using him as a pawn for bigger things? If true, then so be it; he would play her games for now. In time, he was confident all would become clear.

As the vigilante peered over the town below, two individuals, roughly three hundred yards from each other, caught his attention. The more noticeable of the two, a young man walking with straddled footsteps, shambled down a lane unoccupied by Wilheard's night watch. This man shared the same irregular characteristics as the previous victims. The second individual, an older yet swifter man, was shifting between shadows, carefully ducking notice from patrolling guards. The latter man appeared to be a crook, but his actions were crude: he was making hard work of avoiding detection.

The thief could wait; the other man posed more danger.

The vigilante stood and patted his torso, checking the pouches round his waist. There were no weapons on him: his current desire. He had left his sword hidden in the woodland for the time being. Force beyond his bare hands would not be necessary, and he had no reason or intention to brutalise his targets. Besides, his weaponry only added needless weight and rattling when moving, which had become apparent in previous nocturnal undertakings.

Clinging to the shadows, the vigilante dashed behind buildings and through passages. The night guards were exceptionally watchful over Wilheard's border that evening and seemed to be keeping a close eye on certain parts of the vicinity woodland. As a response to the actions of recent strangers, he could appreciate the precautions, but it would make his endeavours more taxing.

Shifting his attention upwards, the man examined the length of nearby rooftops. When it came to stealth, jumping from roof to roof, especially on tiles, would usually be the last option to choose, but since the buildings were mostly adjoining, jumping was not a worry. Furthermore, the patterned projections on a nearby wall would provide a silent way up.

138

Remnant Tales of Stilly:
Passion and Benevolence

With scarcely a sound, the vigilante followed the stretch of the buildings, his loose-fitting coat fluttering as he moved. It did not take long before he closed in on his target. While minding the night guards, he silently returned to ground level and walked round to confront the young man.

As the vigilante turned a corner, he paused a moment after spying a whimpering dog. The small, yellow-brown hound had been following the young man that evening, a sad and confused disposition about it due to being unable to approach its master. It could not figure out why the man was suddenly acting so hostile and had not long ago shirked an unprovoked attack. When the vigilante showed up, the dog swopped his whimpering for a growl, sensing that this unknown individual had come to harm its master. Despite a desire to protect the young man, the dog dared not approach the stranger and scurried backwards into the crevice of a nearby building, keeping the vigilante in sight. Subsequently, the growling got the attention of the target, who, after hearing his pet, wheeled round.

Salivating through clenched teeth, the young man's face contorted with anger upon noticing the vigilante, darkness filling his eyes. He wore gloves with iron nails poking through the fingertips, making for a makeshift weapon. This was a new addition from past victims, indicating the target had expected a clash.

With outstretched arms, the young man lunged at the vigilante, staggering as the latter dodged the clumsy attack. Veering round, the young man attempted to claw at his opponent, slashing first with his left hand and then his right. The vigilante sidestepped the first slice, snatching the young man's wrist as he attempted the second. This gave him a chance to strike back.

Thrusting upwards, the vigilante drove his palm squarely into the young man's chin, forcing the victim off his feet and knocking him cold. Immediately taking the target by the waist, he carefully laid him down.

Stepping from its crevice, the dog barked.

'Over here!' The distant call of a Wilheard soldier sounded from nearby. 'The noises are coming from over here, I'm sure of it!'

The vigilante was out of time. Removing the gloves from the floored target, he tossed them to one side. With his affair complete, he returned to the rooftops and left as silently as he had come, staying only long enough to see the dog lick the face of its sleeping master, finally able to approach once again.

Now for that crook...

Remnant Tales of Stilly:
Passion and Benevolence

Chapter Five

If one were to take the time to get to know Ebony, one would find that she goes from curious to captivated rather quickly when it comes to certain subjects.

The mysterious vigilante from the eastern woodland had visited Wilheard numerous times in the past five days. On his latest visit, as with previous instances, he appeared when it was dark, and although his actions proved altruistic, his motives remained unexplained. Fortunately, with more townsfolk learning about the vigilante, overhearing new information should be simpler.

Ebony did not have the moral pressure of work today; Hazel had other helpers on the farm, and her father was again out meeting his newest friend. Ebony had almost forgotten about her conversation with Abraham a few days ago, what with all the excitement about Wilheard lately. Frankly, Ebony was not as concerned as before; so long as her father was happy, so was she, and if that meant she could get on with her own thing without worrying, then she could not see a problem.

In the same part of New Market Square, perched on the usual barrel, Harold Dolb minded his fruit and vegetable stall while pulling on the styled hairs that formed his moustache. Gazing into the surrounding crowds, Harold did not notice Ebony approaching, the full force of her inquisitiveness in tow as she strode along the cobblestoned street.

'Fair morn, Mister Dolb,' said Ebony.

Harold jerked from his daydreaming. 'Oh... fair morn, dear. I didn't see you there.'

Ebony forced a smile. She often caught him off guard, as did light-fingered children.

'So what can I do for you, young lady? Have you come for the usual?'

Ebony looked at the various vegetation neatly arrayed on the stall table. Even though she was out for leisure, getting a few things for tonight's meal would not hurt.

'I heard that vigilante has been busy lately,' Ebony said while selecting some goods. 'Exciting, wouldn't you agree?'

'If you say so, dear,' Harold replied, his tone full of apathy. 'Hard to ignore it all, if I'm honest.'

Despite the drab response, Ebony continued with her questioning. 'What do you know about the incidents?'

'Not much, I'm afraid. I know as much as I read in the papers.'

'Are you sure? Even though you are surrounded by gossipers, you have not heard anything?'

Harold smirked as he continued to prepare Ebony's order. 'If I didn't know any better, I'd say this was an interrogation.'

'Sorry, Harold. It's just that I'm really interested in what's going on.'

'I noticed—and I understand, dear. You're still young. I tell you what, if I find out anything, you'll be the first person I tell.'

'Thank you.'

'Then again,' Harold continued, 'I did overhear a couple of my customers nattering to one another about all kinds of nonsense. Old girls that talk a lot, they are. One said that ol' Vincent is in the know. She said—very excitedly, I might add—something about the vigilante being athletic, fast, strong and all that.'

'Great!' Ebony said, dropping two copper stinneps on the stall and turning to leave. 'I need to go to the butchers as it happens.'

'I thought as much. Don't you want these, though?'

Ebony wheeled round and looked at the brown-paper bag in Harold's hand. 'Oh yes,' she said, her cheeks reddening. 'Thank you.'

Harold watched Ebony dart off and chuckled to himself. 'Young'uns these days.'

Like Ebony, Oliath Burley had developed an ever-increasing desire to learn more about this outsider. His reasons were very different from hers, however, which was something his temper reflected. Yet, there had been a bit of luck for the captain of the guard.

Remnant Tales of Stilly:
Passion and Benevolence

One of the assailants apprehended by the vigilante early that morning was a known offender nicknamed The Snake, a title owing to his distinctive snigger, which (because he habitually laughed through his teeth) resembled a hiss.

It would later transpire that, when attempting a burglary on the sibling-run shop Blow Your Mind!, Snake had assumed attention on the place would have dwindled. Even though he had managed to avoid the night guards, he did not evade the notice of the vigilante. Because Snake was a common crook, Oliath should not have any restrictions when interrogating the prisoner, unlike the other recent detainees. If he could squeeze a droplet of information about the vigilante from Snake, that would be progress. Still, as with the other people in custody, and to avoid any accusations of going against orders, Oliath decided it would be best to consult Mayor Basil Wolleb before any questioning.

Sitting in the usual leather chair opposite the mayor, Oliath fidgeted as he waited (as always) for the older man to acknowledge him. With his stomach churning, he hoped that would come soon; even though Oliath was shielding his nose with his forefinger, it did not block the stench of the office entirely. Oliath had never got used to the smell and accepted that he perhaps never would. How Wolleb and Oswin managed baffled him no end.

Seemingly unaware of Oliath's discomfort, Basil leisurely read the notes Oswin had presented him. Basil was balancing his reading glasses on the bridge of his nose, which sat askew thanks to only having one arm.

Oswin scoffed at the risible display. 'Have you still not got those things fixed? It has been four days since they broke.'

'Four days is not all that long, Benjamin. Besides, I am just too busy.'

'Don't talk piffle!' the assistant exclaimed. 'You have had many an opportunity. I have even offered to do it for you numerous times... Tender spirits, I'll do it now!'

'No...! Thank you, Benjamin. I promise I'll do it later today...'

Oswin did not believe that but declined to argue further.

'So what do you think, Mayor?' Oliath said, feeling he had been patient long enough.

Basil gently tossed the spectacles onto his desk and clasped his fingers behind his neck. He gazed at Oliath for a long moment. 'It seems you are slowly progressing, my good man.'

Oliath grumbled. The mayor referred to the information the *Other Four* had discovered over the past few days. He supposed it *was* progress. 'Slowly… That is a word I seem to be hearing a lot lately.'

'Indeed,' Oswin said, lifting a folded newspaper to read the captions below various sketches. 'The news reporters feel you have exhausted your efforts.'

Oliath sniffed at the comment, coughing after inhaling the room's odour. 'I'm aware of their opinions. The Vultures like to think they have everything figured out.'

Oswin Nodded. If there was one thing the pair could agree on, it was their opinion of the newspapers. As far as Ben was concerned, reporters were arrogant, verbal brutes that twisted almost everything; the way they misrepresented Oliath was disgraceful. Whilst this was the case, the papers provided some healthy information, especially regarding the mysterious man from the forest. Oswin highlighted this.

'Oh, yes. The vigilante was another thing I wanted to bring up,' Wolleb said, peering over Oliath's written report again. 'Do you really see this chap as a concern?'

Oliath stared at Basil incredulously. Was he serious? 'With all due respect, Mayor Wolleb, I did not think of you as someone who endorsed vigilantism.'

Basil curled his top lip. He knew Oliath disagreed with him when the captain called him Mayor Wolleb. Regardless, he shrugged off the remark. 'With all due respect, Captain Burley, I hardly see this stranger as a civilian taking the law into his own hands. At least, I say that judging from the results. There is a degree of professionalism—if I can put it that way—and perhaps you will eventually see the stranger as an ally rather than a hindrance.'

Oliath sneered but covered the disdain with his hand, which he was still using to shield his nose. 'Be that as it may, Mayor, I worry when a stranger, apparently wielding a large blade, creeps about town. I—or rather we—must

144

put the public's safety first. Besides, a vigilante *is* a vigilante, no matter how one sweetens it. You don't pay me for nothing.'

Basil slouched in his chair and removed his hands from his nape. 'And that money I pay you comes from public tax, m'lad. The community do not seem perturbed by this stranger's presence, but'—Basil held up his hand before Oliath could argue—'that is only presumption, and I have not asked anyone their *actual* opinion. In addition, I can understand how you might feel frustrated. So… what do you propose?'

Oliath faintly raised the left corner of his mouth in triumph. 'Give me the right to question suspects.'

Basil groaned. 'Please, Oliath. We have already--'

'Hear me out, sir,' Oliath interrupted. 'I don't wish to question the detainees—Oswin can have them. As I mentioned in my report, one of the men taken into custody this morning is The Snake, a repeat offender. I hope you will--'

'But you wish to question the crook under the same circumstance and not over his actual crimes,' Basil said, taking his turn to interrupt. 'He is unlikely to know much about the other suspects. Besides, you only want this vigilante character because of your insecurities.'

Oliath scowled at the remark, causing Basil to apologise. 'That was harsh of me… I take it back.'

'Please, Mayor Wolleb,' Oliath said. 'If only I can get hold of this vigilante and question his motives, then perhaps—if all parties are willing—we can formally integrate him into the law.'

'If all parties are *willing*?' Basil repeated scornfully. 'Everyone in this room knows you are not *willing* to go through with such a proposal, Oliath, and therefore, the answer remains a firm no. I know how you feel—really, I do—but Wilheard is suffering eccentric problems as of late and, to be frank, it needs an eccentric helping hand. Leave the outsider be.'

Basil looked down at his desk and sorted through the piles of paperwork, signalling that he was finished with the conversation.

Unable to maintain his calm further, Oliath stood up and slammed his fist on the desk, bringing it down with such force that the room seemed to shake. 'FOOLISHNESS!' he roared, his face contorting with rage.

Basil rose to his feet to meet the captain eye-to-eye once more. 'Calm yourself, man!' He yelled back. 'How dare you act so indignantly—and to such a degree?'

The two men exchanged glares for a moment longer, Oliath striking the desk once more with his open palm before marching from the office.

Lost for words, Benjamin remained silent as he waited for his heart rate to slow to its average pace.

Basil leant forward with his hands on his desk so that his arms supported his weight. He looked down to the opposite side of his desk.

Benjamin closed the office door, not once taking his eyes off the mayor. 'Are you all right?' he asked, his voice quiet.

'You know,' Basil said, tittering. 'I'm glad the desk was his only victim...'

Benjamin moved closer to the desk and looked at the visitor side; Oliath had left a noticeable crack in his wake. He ran his middle finger over the damage, reaching from the top of the desk's surface and round to the underside. Although pleased to see Basil unperturbed, Ben could not bring himself to feel the same way.

Basil looked up at his assistant. 'I'll be fine if you are, my good man, don't you worry.'

'What does this mean for Oliath?'

'Not much... I will not dismiss Burley from his duties if that is what you mean. Honestly, I expected him to react this way—I have known him too long not to guess what he wanted from the beginning.' Basil sat heavily back in his chair and pinched the bridge of his nose. 'With that in mind, and I loath to say it, we had better keep an eye on the lad. You know as well as I do how rash he gets when his temper is high.'

Remnant Tales of Stilly:
Passion and Benevolence

Sitting outside her favourite tearoom on Efflorescence Way, Sylvia Enpee looked morosely into the crowds as she swirled the remainder of her coffee. The drink had gone cold, and she did not intend to finish it. Sylvia was waiting for Abraham to finish his drink, not realising that he had done so minutes ago.

Abraham Gibenn stared at Sylvia for a long moment. She did not seem content; that was clear, but he could not figure out why. Reaching into his trouser pocket, he pulled out a bronze coin. 'A stinnep for your thoughts,' he said, gingerly tossing the coin onto the glass-based table.

Sylvia glanced round at the stinnep before looking back at the passing people. 'That phrase reminds me of someone.'

'My daughter says it every so often.'

Sylvia sighed. She placed her arm on the back of her chair and rested her chin in her palm, continuing to swirl the cold coffee with the other hand.

'Well?' Abraham said. 'Are you going to tell me what's on your mind?'

'I was thinking how well we seem to get along,' Sylvia replied somewhat sullenly. 'We met here... in this exact place.'

Abraham wondered for a moment why Sylvia told him this; he knew she was not really thinking that. 'I suppose we do,' he said, lost for words. 'I have enjoyed every moment.'

Sylvia did not respond, but Abraham had expected as much. Deep down, he knew what she was *really* thinking, even though it raised questions: *why was she so desperate to meet Ebony? What does it all mean to her?* Abraham had noticed soon after befriending Sylvia that she was someone who rushed into things, but this seemed curiously pushy.

Abraham breathed in preparation to say something more but held it as Sylvia spoke. 'I know you felt as uncomfortable as me in the shop.' She was referring to the butcher shop they had visited the previous day. 'Regardless of our discomfort, what Vince said was not far off how I feel—we are not young anymore, Abe, and there is little reason for us to take our time on such matters.'

'Oh... that.' Displeasure creased Abraham's face. Despite Sylvia's bluntness, he could not argue with what she said.

He thought back to when he and Sylvia were in the butcher shop. Vincent had commented on how nice it was to see another woman in Abraham's life and said that the two were a good match. Vincent also mentioned how nice it was to see a void filled so quickly. That had not been the butcher's exact words but rather the gist of it.

In truth, Abraham agreed with Sylvia and Vincent. He was not getting any younger and longed to fill the emptiness in that part of his life. Sylvia was a good woman, Abraham was wise enough to see that, and Ebony would surely see things the same way. Now was a good enough time to move on; his dear Luanna would not deny him as much, and his daughter would only want him to be happy.

Abraham gazed in the same direction as Sylvia. 'At the end of the week…'

Sylvia frowned, turning to face Abraham. 'End of the week?'

'At the end of the week, I will take you to my cottage and introduce you to Ebony. If she is about, of course, but I see no reason--'

Cut short from his sentence, Abraham desperately tried to maintain the balance of his chair as Sylvia leapt to embrace him. 'Oh, thank you, Abe, thank you!'

Although this reaction increased Abraham's suspicion, her joy was enough to keep him quiet, as was the embarrassment of onlookers staring in their direction.

Sylvia stood back and straightened her clothes. She thanked Abraham again before sitting down, a satisfied quality about her. 'I'm very grateful. You don't know how much this means to me.'

That is an understatement, Abraham thought. He smiled and kept quiet. *What **does** meeting my daughter mean to you?*

Jangling the familiar chime of the bell, Ebony entered the butcher shop, an empty room greeting her.

Remnant Tales of Stilly:
Passion and Benevolence

Entering the shop floor, Vincent peered across the room to see who was disturbing his lunch break. Noticing who the customer was, he smiled and moved closer to her. ''Ello, young Ebony. Didn't expect to see you back 'ere so soon.'

'Well, I can never get enough of a good bit of meat, Vincent,' Ebony said. 'I hope I wasn't disturbing you.'

'Nah,' Vincent lied, licking bits of his food from his teeth, his closed lips bulging.

'Are you sure? If you're in the middle of lunch, I can come back in an hour or so.'

'Don't be silly, lass. I'm always 'appy to 'elp you out,' Vincent insisted. 'By the way, I 'ope that chicken you got last time went down a treat.'

'It certainly did. It was most delectable, and I loved that sauce.'

'Marvellous. So what will it be today? I'm afraid I'm a bit short on some things, so you've got to bear with me.'

Ebony scanned the meat on offer for a moment. Although she had not initially entered the shop as a customer, she thought it would be rude to blurt out any questions without buying something first, especially when she had indeed interrupted the man's break. 'May I have some of those sausages, please?'

'Ya certainly can, lass.'

After wiping his hands, Vincent wrapped his giant fingers round a row of pork and moved them to the preparation table. Watching the butcher do his job from behind, Ebony cleared her throat and proceeded with her first question. 'So… what is this I hear about an elusive swordsman of late?'

Vincent grunted as if amused by the question. 'I thought so,' he said, not turning to look at Ebony. 'See it in your eyes that you got more on ya mind than sausages.'

Ebony pulled an uneven smile. 'Well, I heard that you know something about the vigilante. If you don't mind sharing, I would appreciate any information.'

'What makes ya think I know anythin' interestin' about all that stuff?'

'Harold said two women had spoken to you about the vigilante.'

Vincent paused a moment to think about what Ebony said. 'Were these women wearin' silly 'ats by chance?'

Ebony shrugged. 'I don't know. Harold did say that they were talkative, though.'

Vincent grunted, once again, with apparent amusement. 'Aye, I know exactly who-ya talkin' about—couple of old chinwaggers is what they are. Poor Harold and I are always getting it in the ear. Traeh bless their little gossipin' hearts!'

Ebony covered her mouth to hide a chuckle.

'Anyway, lass,' Vincent sighed, continuing with his work, 'those old birds have an 'abit of exaggeratin' even the smallest things. What did ya 'ear?'

'One of the women apparently said something about the vigilante being athletic and having above-average speed and strength.'

'Like I told ya—exaggeratin'.' Vincent turned to Ebony and placed the sausages, wrapped and ready to sell, on the serving counter. 'Well, I can tell ya this—I saw a fella jumpin' about on the rooftops the other night. Although I weren't able to get a proper look, I did notice 'im heading towards the eastern forest. A peculiar fella, and very quick he was too, but as for the great strength... a load of nonsense. Then again, he probably *does* have a lot of strength to move the way he did.'

Vincent sighed again.

'Thank you. I knew I could count on you for interesting information.'

'As always, you're very welcome, love.' Vincent said, sighing for a third time as he pushed the produce towards Ebony. 'As for the pork—I believe ya know the price by now.'

Taking a few stinneps from a small purse, Ebony placed the coins into the butcher's hand and took her order from the counter. 'Is something the matter, Vincent?'

Vincent looked up from the money. 'Pardon, lass?'

'You sound as if something is troubling you. Is there anything I can help with?'

Remnant Tales of Stilly:
Passion and Benevolence

Vincent cleared his throat and shook his head. 'Kind of ya to ask, lass, but I were just thinkin' to me self. In fact, what we were just talkin' about has had quite an effect on me business. One of the people that the vigilante took out 'appened to be my main supplier of sauces and stuff.'

'Similar to the sauce I bought the other day?'

'Mrs Whickett's Recipes,' Vincent said. 'Aye, that's the one.'

'I'm sorry to hear of your troubles.'

'That's all right, love—everyone faces setbacks now and again. But just in case you were wonderin', I don't know the details of what 'appened, just that he was found tied up outside that gunpowder place and that two confused mares were wanderin' the streets with a riderless cart.'

Ebony gave an apologetic nod. 'I hope it all works out for you.'

'Cheers, lass. Anyway, on to a more cheerful topic,' Vincent said, folding his tree trunk arms, a grin creasing his cheek. ''ow's your father and 'is lady friend? She and 'im make a grand couple, don't-cha think?'

'I knew it!' Ebony blurted, almost choking on the words. 'He has been seeing a woman!

Cringing, Vincent looked down at the ground and scratched the back of his head. 'Sorry, lass. I thought you knew.'

'That's all right, Vincent, don't worry. I had my suspicions anyway,' Ebony said. She thought to herself then. *Why did he keep it such a secret?*

Ebony forced a stupid-looking grin. 'I guess I'll talk to Father about the matter later. A fair day to you.'

With that, she left the shop, leaving its owner abashed.

Who could this woman be? Perhaps Ebony should have asked Vincent. *I guess it doesn't matter*, she thought as she moved out of view of the butcher shop. Even if he were to answer, Ebony believed that she had bothered the man enough for one day, and he should be allowed to enjoy the rest of his lunch in peace.

Petulance grew inside Ebony as she walked away. *At least I no longer have any reservations about my plans. If Father is entitled to his secrets… then so am I.*

Elated: that was probably the most appropriate word to describe Sylvia's mood at that moment; she was practically skipping as she made her way along New Market Square.

The time was early evening. Various merchants and stall owners were packing up for the day, and their exhausted looks showed they were glad it was over. Like the shopkeepers, Sylvia had had a long day, but she was far from restful with the recent turn of events.

If Ninapaige did not already know, Sylvia imagined that the little woman would show at least some happiness about the news, and being dusk, the likelihood of Ninapaige showing her face typically increased.

As Sylvia reached out of earshot from fellow towns' people, she heard a *psst*-ing coming from a small area to the back of a nearby shop.

'Psst...! Doctor Enpee—over here!'

Sylvia turned her attention to the voice. In a darkened corner, amid various wooden crates and other discarded items, she spied Ninapaige wearing a cheery-faced mask and gesturing for the doctor to come closer.

'You look happy,' said Ninapaige, her violet eyes glowing from the hollows of the clay mask. She removed it. 'What have you been up to today?'

Sylvia did not answer. She was too busy looking about for other people. 'I hadn't expected to see you until dark. Are you sure you want to be out here when there is still so much light?'

Ninapaige gave Sylvia a grin. 'I am not so careless that such things pose a risk. I can keep myself out of trouble... unlike someone I know.'

Nervous, Sylvia had not noticed the gibe. 'What if someone hears us whispering?'

'Then I'll be out of here in the blink of an eye. In the worst-case scenario, people will think you are talking to a wooden box and losing your mind.'

'Thanks a lot,' Sylvia sneered, 'that puts my mind at ease.'

'Keep your voice down, girl!' hushed Ninapaige. 'If you are *that* worried about others hearing us, then we should talk telepathically.'

Remnant Tales of Stilly:
Passion and Benevolence

'You know I have never got the hang of that. You complain that what I say—or rather *think*—sounds muddled and incoherent. You also berate my efforts as childlike.'

Ninapaige inhaled through her mouth, displaying mock offence. 'That was unwarranted. Do you honestly see me as the petty type…? I never *complain.*'

Sylvia tutted at the remark, which caused Ninapaige to chuckle.

'Do not worry so much, young one,' Ninapaige went on, smirking and taking hold of Sylvia's hand. Drifting through the air, she led the doctor between the buildings more. 'Trust me… we will be all right in here.'

On closer inspection, Sylvia could see why. The lack of sunlight in the passage, coupled with wet patches dotted about the floor and walls, left little to be desired. Sadly, it did not take much imagination to guess what these patches were.

Sylvia placed a hand over her nose and mouth.

'So,' said Ninapaige, continuing the conversation. 'Tell me what has put that bounce in your step.'

Sylvia looked at Ninapaige. Perched on a stack of brittle wooden boxes, the imp had an out-of-place grin that suggested she could not smell the foulness in the air. 'I'm guessing you already know the answer to that,' she replied, her voice nasally. 'I thought you were always watching me.'

'I cannot always be watching you, at least not these days.' Ninapaige simpered. 'But why should that matter? I do very much enjoy hearing about what you get up to.'

'Abraham has finally invited me back to the cottage. He says he will let me see Ebony at the end of the week.' Sylvia breathed a sigh of happiness, clumsily inhaling through her nose. She pinched it closed again.

'I must admit, it is nice seeing some colour in your cheeks.'

'Well… it has been a while since I've had reason to smile.'

'It is a shame that the greeting will happen at the end of the week. That girl has really taken an interest in Sombie's actions.'

'The *girl* is called Ebony… and as for Sombie, a lot of people have taken an interest--'

Ninapaige interrupted. 'I mean to say, Sylvia, that the girl plans to go into the eastern woodland. I realise Sombie's presence has caused a stir in the village, but Ebony has taken an exceptional interest. She intends to go looking for him.'

Sylvia furrowed her brow. 'How do you know that?'

'As I said, I am not always watching *you*. Sadly, there is little you can do for the girl.'

Sylvia bit down on her bottom lip, worry once again clouding her mind.

Ninapaige closed her eyes and tilted her head to one side, raising her palms into a shrug. 'Yet, you know how melodramatic I can sound, and it is not as if Ebony is in any danger. I may not be omniscient, but not much escapes my notice. As it happens, Sombie is wandering about for more reasons than he comprehends. When the two meet--'

'Keep Sombie away from her!' Sylvia sputtered. 'Please! I have never been too trusting of him. He can be a brute, and he lacks emotions.'

'I would argue that you simply repeat what I have said, but that is only because a novice made him that way. It is hardly surprising, though—you humans have never quite got the hang of ytyism. Anyway, he is not completely devoid of feelings, outwards or otherwise...'

'You are digressing, Ninapaige,' Sylvia said, a hint of impatience in her eyes. 'Besides, for all the years I have known you, you have told me to trust no one but yourself. Have you changed your mind?'

Ninapaige snapped out of her daydreaming. 'Apologies. If you are unsure of Sombie being near Ebony, then I will do what I can to keep him at bay. I will warn you, though, that she does not share your apprehension.'

'She is only young,' Sylvia argued.

'Unless you have a long grey beard or a face like cracked earth, you humans all look like children to me, and she does not seem much younger than you, in my opinion. Do you remember when we met in the forest?'

Not again with this, Sylvia thought. She closed her eyes and sighed. When she reopened them, Ninapaige was gone, leaving behind the cheery-faced mask on a wooden crate.

Remnant Tales of Stilly:
Passion and Benevolence

Chapter Six

Sitting on the edge of her neatly made bed, Ebony Gibenn stared out the window at the yellow sky and listened to the clock down the hall from her bedroom.

Tick... tock... tick... tock...

Her belly churned. The usually calming sound was doing nothing to relax her, yet she could not put her finger on the actual cause of the twinge. Most likely, it was a sign of nervousness; then again... was it guilt? Whatever the reason, she could not sit on the bed much longer, and changing her mind was out of the question. This was not necessarily because she had been planning this moment for days, nor because she was ready to leave the house with her basket of essentials: she owed this to herself. The tedious routine in her life needed to change, and this was a big step into achieving that.

It was perhaps fortunate, then, that Ebony had something on her mind to help distract her. Once again, she had not slept particularly well last night, but when she had managed to drift off, she had had a strange dream that she would not quickly forget.

In the dream, Ebony stood in a long, stone hall. She vividly recalled that warmth flowed through her despite the cool-looking atmosphere. Eventually, she walked down the corridor, glancing at the dusty objects about her, looking for something to display her reflection. The windows stretching the entire hall length did not reflect anything despite their relative cleanliness. Ebony glanced through the glass and at a garden below, which kept flowers, small trees and various stone sculptures. Above it all, a blue sky.

Footsteps echoed from the farthest end of the hall. Walking to the end of the corridor, Ebony turned a corner to see a man. He held a guitar in his right hand, the strings of which thrummed as he dropped the instrument to the floor. Could this be the same man from her previous dream? He bared a striking similarity, including an obscured face.

The approaching man walked towards Ebony with determined strides, the narrowing lasting for an eternity. He approached her slightly to her right and placed one arm round her upper back. Tilting her backwards and positioning his other arm about her waist, he moved closer as if to kiss her, yet stopped before making contact.

Interrupted by a child-like laugh, the man raised Ebony upright once more. Looking in all directions, she tried to find the location of the laughter. Yet, despite sounding close by, she saw no one.

The man turned his back to Ebony, his grip tightening round the hilt of a large sword. Undoubtedly, he had heard the laugh as well. Did he recognise it?

Without turning to look at Ebony, the man spoke in a tone barely louder than a whisper. *'Stay safe, Princess...'*

Upon waking, Ebony had sat up and looked towards the open window. Something had been sitting on her sill at the time, but it leapt away before her sleep-hazy eyes could focus.

Must have been a cat, Ebony thought. It would not have been the first time one had climbed into her bedroom. Perhaps she would close her window at night from now on, especially with all that was happening in Wilheard lately.

Thinking back to the dream, Ebony considered who the man might have been. Perhaps unsurprisingly, considering how much she had overheard recently, he fit the description of the vigilante. Still, Ebony had not seen the elusive man, and she did not know what his face looked like—just like in the dream.

Waking from her reverie, Ebony opened the lid of her wicker basket to ensure she had what she wanted: a corked bottle of water, two shiny red apples, her pocket watch and a three-inch, folding pocketknife, just in case. Perhaps most importantly, Ebony had the treasured crystal heart that her mother had given her. For luck,

Barefoot and tiptoeing, Ebony walked down the upstairs landing and passed her father's bedroom, pausing to look at the snoring man in his bed. He had reverted to his usual quiet self last night as the two ate dinner. Ebony had also been silent during the meal, but she had made sure not to show what was on her mind. This had not mattered anyway: Abraham had been too wrapped up in his thoughts to notice.

Remnant Tales of Stilly:
Passion and Benevolence

Making her way to the base of the staircase and slipping into her shoes, Ebony stepped outside the cottage and gently pulled the front door behind her until it clicked. Turning towards the eastern woodland, Ebony shut her eyes and took a deep breath. The clean morning air filled her lungs and reached the pit of her belly. The churning sensation had changed from nervousness to one more akin to excitement. It was finally happening: the first proper step in breaking from the monotony.

She could hardly wait to see what lay ahead.

Sitting in his favourite room of The Repose, Captain Oliath Burley adopted his usual position of leaning on the back legs of a wooden chair with his feet on the table.

As expected, Cordelia Lawford and Nolan Shakeston were the only others in the room. This was probably just as well; considering the captain's current temperament, staying out of his way was for the good of everyone else's health. This was what Oliath wanted anyway. His lieutenants were the only ones he could tolerate at the time.

Laying open on the other end of the table to Oliath was the day's The Wilheard Chronicles. He had not bothered even to glance at its pages: they invariably contained the usual disparaging words, and the tutting coming from Cordelia served only to confirm that fact.

Damnable Vultures! Oliath cursed inwardly. *They are enough to drive a man to drink.* The captain of the guard rubbed his chin. Now that he thought about it, he would kill for a cold pint of bitter ale. It would go down well and complement his equally bitter mood. A troubling thought to admit, especially so early in the day.

'That fool Basil is undeserving of your contempt,' Nolan said, reading Oliath's mood. 'Try not to let it bother you, sir.'

Oliath did not answer. It was too late for him not to get upset. He tilted his head to one side, looked through the nearest window and watched the townspeople flit about outside.

'What is our plan of action now, sir?' Cordelia asked. 'There is still a list of people we could question.'

'That can wait,' Oliath said, not taking his gaze away from the window. 'Theryle and the rest of his crew are still scouring for information amongst the people, and I have instructed Wilheard's guards to listen out for anything suspicious. Besides, I have something else on my mind.' He turned his attention towards his lieutenants once again, furrowing his brow. 'I feel we have no choice but to act without authorisation from now on.'

'You say that as if we will think lesser of you, sir,' said Nolan.

Cordelia hummed her agreement. 'When you know something is for the best... well, you need only give us the order.'

When you know something is for the best... Oliath, forcing a grin, looked back out the window. 'I have always tried to be a good man, but if I always adhere to certain principles, how can I claim to be doing what is right?'

'What will you have us do, sir?' asked Cordelia.

'Well,' Oliath said, removing his feet from the table and leaning forward. 'Taking into account your personal abilities, I have separate tasks for you both. Lawford, with your stealth skills, I want you to break into the mayor's office and get the prison block's rear door key. If you tread carefully—which I know you will—you will not attract attention. That twerp Oswin confiscated my keys, so they should be hanging near his desk.'

Cordelia acknowledged her orders with a nod.

'After that, Shakeston, I will need your speed and acrobatics. The back door to the prison can only be unlocked from the inside. When Cordelia hands you the key, you will enter the prison blocks from the roof. There are a few ceiling entrances, one that leads into a storage room, so you should not be seen. Seeing as no one tries to break *into* prisons, maintenance to the outside is limited. Years of weather damage will have weakened the latches, and they should break with a bit of force. To prevent suspicion, avoid any patrolling guards until we are together. They will not question anything as long as you are with me.'

Nolan nodded.

'As for me,' the captain added, 'I will watch out for patrolling guards outside and be sure to distract any.'

The plan made sense in theory: guards had no reason to question Oliath once inside. Unfortunately, this did not apply to those standing at the prison's main entrance. Oswin would have informed them of any temporary restrictions, even those placed on their captain.

'This all sounds very exciting,' Nolan said. 'It is enough to make one's heart race.'

Oliath smiled, this time more genuinely. 'Hold your enthusiasm for now. After all, we will need the cover of darkness. I suggest you spend daylight preparing for when the time comes.'

Ebony often walked along the eastern edge of Wilheard. With a library book under her arm, she would search for a tree to sit beneath where she would not be disturbed. Nevertheless, strolling on the border of the woodland was not the same as walking within.

Even during her explorative younger years, Ebony had not wandered far into the forest; at the time, it was the one place that spooked her. Although this childhood fear had since faded, owing to what happened to her mother, the notion of going into such a place alone was not something she had ever entertained. With that in mind, she found it ironic that she would do so now, especially with a sword-wielding vigilante on the loose. Such a man should have been reason enough to stay away, yet it had had the opposite effect.

Why was this? Ebony could not put her finger on it, but she had been seeing life from a different perspective as of late. Indeed, she was excited, not afraid. Unfortunately, this excitement would not last.

After an hour and a half, Ebony sat down on a grassy knoll to rest. Pulling an apple from her basket, she took a bite and stared along the foot-trodden path she had been walking. Grass, leaves and airborne insects glistened as light poured through the treetops; it was all very pretty. Such a sight should have been relaxing, but she was instead troubled. The pang she had felt earlier that morning continued to somersault about inside her belly, and this time, it was definitely guilt-related.

Remnant Tales of Stilly:
Passion and Benevolence

I have betrayed my father's trust, she thought as she took another bite from the apple. *And what would he think? Especially after what happened to Mother.*

Had eagerness for change clouded Ebony's sense of reason? She had avoided letting her father know of her intentions, as he would have tied her up while she slept. Of course, this was only because he loved her.

But...

Ebony put the apple to her mouth as she tried to think of an excuse to justify her actions. Was it all worth the heartache she might cause? Without taking a bite, Ebony tossed the fruit and watched it hit the ground with a thud, bouncing and throwing up dust before rolling to a stop. She leant her elbows on her knees, placed her face in her hands and blew a loud sigh. Cursing to herself, she watched through her fingers as insects gathered round the discarded apple.

What a disappointment this has been.

Ebony would need to think about heading home soon, which would be challenging since she had not been paying much attention to the route. She fumbled about in the basket once more and pulled out the crystal heart her mother had given her. Luanna was probably in the spirit world somewhere, Ebony imagined, watching and mentally punishing her daughter for this indiscretion.

Ebony placed her hands on the grass, ready to push herself up. However, before she could do so, she halted upon hearing a distant cough. It had come from behind her.

Could it be the vigilante?

Gingerly getting to her feet and brushing the dust from her dress, Ebony listened carefully for further sounds. Sure enough, she heard someone mumbling.

Ebony shifted in the direction of the voice, using the foliage about her as cover. She was nervous, evident in her now trembling breaths. Was sneaking up to this yet unidentified person a good idea? What would happen if this individual mistook her for that of a stalking predator? Conversely, if she instead strutted towards this person, who turned out to be hostile, would she not just be putting herself in danger? It was as if what Hazel said before only now made sense. Seeking an unknown man with a huge sword *is* stupid.

No, Ebony told herself. *I'm letting my imagination get the better of me, that's all. I'm not a child—I can handle myself.*

Between a patch of large trees and a dried, water-woven groove, Ebony came across an embankment. The mumbling was now clearer, a man's voice coming from the other side of the levee. Placing her hands on the slope, Ebony adopted a crawling position and climbed. Keeping her head low as she shifted her fingers through the grass, she peered over and spotted a thin man standing by a heavily damaged statue. With a scroll in one hand and a pencil in the other, the man appeared to be taking notes.

His scruffy appearance notwithstanding, the man did not fit the description of the vigilante one bit. Long hair? No. This man had brown, curly-tipped hair that barely reached the top of his ears. Then there was the clothing: instead of a simple coat, this man wore a lurid red shirt and an equally loud purple jacket with no sleeves. In contrast, the grey trousers were a pleasant sight but were tucked into checked socks that matched his shirt.

This man was either unconcerned with how ridiculous he looked or was colour-blind.

Ebony gazed at the man, who seemed to be a scholar, for a while longer. Judging by his stance and how he strolled about with his hands cupped behind his back, he had the mannerisms of someone older, and the smoking pipe hanging from the corner of his mouth only reinforced this impression. He was, apparently, a traveller: among his possessions, blankets, rope, pegs and a simple cooking pot.

Despite his eccentricity, Ebony reasoned that the man would not be a threat, which was fortunate considering she needed to ask for directions.

Standing upright and making her way down the other side of the embankment, Ebony cautiously walked towards the man, keeping her basket where she could quickly reach into it if the need arose.

'Yes,' the man mumbled aloud as he brushed the blemishes from the sorry-looking sculpture. 'Very intriguing.'

Ebony stopped several paces away from the scholar and continued to study him. She hoped he would eventually notice her, but after what seemed like a minute, she realised that he, with his back turned, was far too engrossed in his research to see who (or even what) was around him.

'Um… excuse me, sir.' Ebony waited for a reply from the man. After getting no response, she tried again. 'Fair morn… I'm sorry to bother you, but--'

Interrupting Ebony, the scholar continued to witter aloud. Was he really *that* immersed in his work? It was as if she was not even there. 'I see… truly fascinating,' he said, scribbling something on his scroll before consulting another on his waist.

Clearing her throat, Ebony tried again to get the scholar's attention, this time a little louder. 'Pardon me! Can you hear me?'

Slowly looking up from his scroll, the man turned his head so Ebony was just about in view. Taking a moment to study the woman, he eventually looked into her eyes, displaying no alarm or surprise.

'Fair morn to you,' The man said with a well-spoken accent. 'Can I help you?'

Ebony parted her lips and smiled, taking a step closer. 'Actually, I was hoping you could. I'm a little lost, and I wondered if you knew the best way back to Wilheard.'

The scholar did not answer, staring at Ebony as if she had something stuck in her teeth. She closed her mouth.

'Assuming you know where Wilheard is,' she added, pondering if the man was as crazy as dress sense.

'I do most definitely know where Wilheard is, Ms.,' the man said, placing the scroll back in its pouch. He removed the smoking pipe from his mouth, tapped its chamber with his finger to release any embers and then put it in a pocket.

Ebony blew a sigh of relief. 'That's good. I am sorry to bother you, but can you point me in the correct direction?'

'I can do one better than that, dear girl,' the scholar continued, his tone much friendlier than a moment ago. 'It just so happens that I am heading to that very hamlet. I have been on the road for a while and expected to arrive today. If you like, I can accompany you there.'

'That would be lovely. Thank you.'

The scholar scratched the back of his head. He was flattered that this pretty woman would put such trust in him. 'That is quite all right, dear girl. Incidentally, my name is Alim Larring, and it is an honour to meet you.'

Alim held out his hand for Ebony to shake. She gawked at him in return.

'Is something the matter? I am terribly sorry if I have upset you some--'

'No... sorry. I am Ebony Gibenn,' she said, now shaking Alim's hand. 'It's a pleasure to meet you.'

'Very well, Ms Gibenn. I will have you in Wilheard in no time. Can I request a favour, though? he asked, looking at the statue behind him. 'If it is not too much trouble, I would very much like to continue studying this magnificent artefact. I promise I will not be much longer.'

'By all means,' Ebony said. 'I'm in no hurry.'

Ebony sat on a fallen tree branch and watched Alim as he resumed his research. She could see that the statue, although smoothed by years of rain and the forest's climate, resembled a man. Yet, not all the damage looked natural, and the whole area of the eyes had been defaced. The left eye and upper nose had a deep slash, whereas the right eye was wrecked, a cracked hollow in its place.

This made her curious. What is the statue? How old is it? Why is it in the middle of the forest?

Ebony wiped the sweat from her forehead and exhaled, drumming her fingers on her lap as she waited. Although she did not wish to disturb Alim, asking a few questions would not hurt. Besides, he looked like the type who would happily share his knowledge.

Standing up from her seat, Ebony walked closer to Alim. As before, he was fixated on his work and failed to acknowledge the woman alongside him.

'So... what is this anyway?' Ebony asked in a clear voice, making sure Alim heard her the first time.

Alim did not answer straight away; he continued to jot down notes. 'This, my inquisitive friend, is a significant part of my research,' he replied enthusiastically. 'Is it not just magnificent?'

Ebony gazed once more at the slanted stone, staring at the broken eyes. 'But who is it supposed to be?'

Remnant Tales of Stilly:
Passion and Benevolence

Tilting his head forward, Alim gazed at Ebony over the top of his spectacles. 'You… are a resident of Wilheard, correct?' he replied, his tone implying that she should already know.

'Yes,' she said, unfazed.

Still gazing at Ebony over his glasses, Alim raised the corner of his mouth into a smile. 'My dear girl, this is the last king of Stilly—King Godfrey.'

Ebony nodded.

'Have you never seen the King's face before, Ms Gibenn?' Alim asked, taking his smoking pipe from his pocket and sprinkling tobacco into its chamber. 'Forgive me if I come across as arrogant, but seeing as you are from Stilly's capital, I must admit some surprise if not.'

Ebony explained the extent of her knowledge. She remembered being taught a little about the royal family in school and had even heard stories from Vincent Sawney. Then there was the story Passion and Benevolence, but Ebony did not mention that.

Alim placed the pipe to his lips. 'I see. In that case, feel free to ask some more questions. Perhaps I can help enhance your knowledge.'

'Very well,' Ebony continued. 'How old is it?'

'I'm afraid it's difficult to say exactly.' Alim drew four short breaths on his pipe. 'Hazarding a guess, I would say about three centuries old.'

Ebony slid her fingers along the length of what was left of the statue's mouth. 'Time has been remorseless.'

'Quite, but it would be unfair to blame natural causes for all the damage,' Alim said. 'A rhetorical question for you, Ms Gibenn: What is the statue doing out here, in the middle of a forest, of all places?

Ebony looked at Alim without saying anything.

'Well… I cannot give a proper answer to that. Sorry—that was a daft question. Then again, I can give a theoretical answer.'

Alim placed his pipe on the plinth and hopped up to the back of the king's head. He was more agile than he looked.

'Up here'—Alim called to Ebony—'is certainly not something caused by weather damage.'

Ebony squinted at Alim from below. 'What is it?'

'Come up and take a look for yourself, dear girl.'

Starting from the statue's base, Ebony traced Alim's route with her eyes. Her knees wobbled. 'I'd rather you describe it to me.'

'But of course, it was silly to suggest such a thing,' Alim said, misinterpreting Ebony's fear of heights for etiquette.

Alim explained to Ebony that there was damage to the back of the king's head: a hole deep enough for him to insert half his arm.

'That's peculiar,' Ebony said. 'What could have caused it?'

Alim shifted his glasses and looked at the hollow for a second longer. 'Well, I can't say for sure, but it does have a distinctive fist shape to it… as if someone punched the stone.'

Ebony raised her eyebrows. 'Punched it?'

'I know, I know, the very thought is ludicrous. But consider this…' Alim hopped down from the bust and made his way round to its left side, beckoning Ebony to follow him. 'Take a gander at these scuffs.'

Alim brushed his fingers across numerous markings on the Stone King's cheek.

'They look like drag marks,' Ebony said after a moment's thought.

'Agreed. Yet, if you look at the depressions on the ground, you'll notice they do not match.'

'Well, if what you say is accurate, and the bust is over a few hundred years old, then surely the marks will have faded to some extent.'

'That is true enough,' Alim admitted with a shrug,' and I did consider this myself. Yet none of this is as logical as one might think.'

Ebony chuckled. 'But someone punching a hole in pure stone *does* sound logical?'

Alim returned a light-hearted *humph*. 'You have me there, but I did say it was only speculation. Speaking of which…'

Alim paused midsentence and looked towards the statue one last time.

'What is it?' Ebony asked.

'Never mind… I was just thinking about my grandfather. I follow in his footsteps, you see. He was—bless his soul—an unusual sort of chap. Mind you, I'm told I share these traits.' Ebony watched as Alim bundled all his possessions into a sack before slinging it over his shoulder. 'Righto, Ms

Gibenn. I thank you for your patience, and now it is time for me to uphold my end of the bargain. Onwards to Wilheard.'

Ebony walked by Alim's side as he led her down a trail. The track was broader than the one Ebony had taken earlier, and judging from the various hoofmarks and cartwheel imprints along the way, it was a popular route.

Five minutes passed when Ebony decided to break the silence.

'You say you follow in your grandfather's footsteps.'

'That's right. Quite the adventurer he was. I was always fascinated by his work as a lad, and I suppose that nowadays, I am much like him when it comes to the weird and wonderful ways of life. One could say it is my dream to rediscover his work.'

To live life by following a dream. That was something Ebony envied. She looked at the bag on Alim's back. 'I presume this dream of yours involves a lot of travelling. It must be nice to see the wider world.'

'You could say that. I have become a bit of a drifter in recent times, but I manage to earn a bit of coin by doing various jobs here and there.'

'I see. Where do you call home?'

'Central Thane.'

'How long have you been travelling?'

'Since the beginning of spring. I spent some time in villages between Thane and Wilheard, but mostly, I am on the road.

'I have never visited Thane. I hear it is a busy and bustling place, full of excitement.'

'It has a nice gransanture,' Alim replied, his tone lacklustre. 'Thane is nice if you like what is on offer. The surrounding villages have some character. I needed to escape the place for a while—too much noise.'

Ebony pursed her lips. *You will like Wilheard, then,* she thought. 'So what brings you all the way here?'

Alim regained his enthusiasm. 'Well, there is King Godfrey's bust, of course, but I fancy there will be more titbits of information in Wilheard itself. I love discovering new things, especially when they are out of the ordinary.'

'I like learning about the unfamiliar, too,' Ebony replied. 'I imagine that I could learn a lot from you. Your grandfather seems the interesting type as well.'

Remnant Tales of Stilly:
Passion and Benevolence

'Thank you, Ms Gibenn. It is nice to find someone who shares my interests. In fact, if you really are interested, then I have something that might fascinate you. Take a look at this.'

Alim reached into a pouch on his waist and pulled out a scroll. Holding the item out for Ebony to take, he pulled away again before she could touch it. 'However, I have a word of warning,' he said, sounding serious. 'What is on this scroll *is* unusual, to say the least, but you must promise to take it seriously. I cannot abide being laughed at.'

Ebony gazed stony-faced at Alim. 'I promise.'

Carefully unravelling the paper, Ebony looked inside and found two hand-written lines of what looked like foreign lettering. She scanned the symbols several times and looked up at Alim, who smiled at her over his shoulder. 'Are these glyphs of some sort?'

Alim nodded. 'You may have overlooked them, but similar symbols are carved on the king's plinth. Curiously, and considering the state the rest of the stone is in, these symbols are very clean and clear—as if only newly engraved.'

Ebony looked back at the paper. 'They are not something I recognise.'

'I am not surprised,' Alim said, shifting his glasses and retaking the scroll from Ebony. 'The symbols are esoteric, but that is because they are from—as far as I know—a lost language.

A lost language, Ebony mused. 'How interesting.'

'It certainly is, dear girl,' Alim said as he placed the scroll back in its pouch. 'But I'm sure they are more than just random scribblings.'

'What do you mean?'

'Well…' Alim hesitated. 'It doesn't matter. Forget I said anything.'

'Are you worried I will find it ridiculous? I promised I wouldn't laugh.'

He chuckled. 'It's not that, dear girl, trust me.' Taking his smoking pipe from a belt pouch, Alim placed it in his mouth. Taking some tobacco from the same pocket, he sprinkled it into the pipe's chamber and lit a match on a nearby tree. 'Anyway… I think you have heard quite enough about my research and me. How about telling me what brings you into the forest. I am curious as to what makes a woman wander into a place she is unfamiliar.

Ebony grimaced, her cheeks reddening. After meeting Alim, the reason for her being in the forest had slipped her mind. She looked to where she was treading. 'I was looking for someone.'

'I see,' Alim said, peering at Ebony over the top of his glasses. 'Judging from your relaxed demeanour, I presume this person is not technically missing. Did you find who you were looking for?'

'No,' Ebony said. 'And you are right about the person not being missing. Then again, I don't think he even wants to be found.'

Alim looked forward once more. 'How troubling.'

'Maybe. I admit, though, that I don't know the person.'

Alim tilted his head to one side, puzzled by what Ebony was saying. 'I hope you do not mind my saying so, Ms Gibenn, but this all sounds quite bizarre. Why would you seek out a complete stranger?'

'I understand your confusion, but this person—a man, more specifically—is a bit of a hero in Wilheard. From what I have overheard, he has been seen coming in and out of the eastern woodland. I was hoping to maybe talk with him.'

'I see.' Alim puffed on his pipe. 'Still, it is rather brave, to say the least, seeking out someone you do not know.'

Ebony gave an exaggerated shrug. 'In any case, the man is said to play a musical instrument.

Alim stopped walking, his mind digesting what Ebony was telling him. 'Music, you say?' He adjusted his glasses and looked into the middle distance. 'Is the tune from a guitar by any chance?'

'Yes. Well, at least I think so. That is what I have been told.'

'In addition, does the said man wear tatty clothing, wield a large sword and ride a shire horse?

'That is very accurate,' Ebony answered with surprise and excitement. 'Minus the shire horse, that is.'

Alim drew from his pipe again and resumed plodding.

Ebony jogged to Alim's side and waited for him to say something. 'So you know this person?'

'Not exactly,' Alim murmured. 'Indeed, I am in the same position as you, dear girl. I have not met this man, but I overheard similar anecdotes in the last town I visited.

After a thirty-minute walk, the pair reached the edge of Wilheard, exiting the woodlands from a different place to where Ebony had entered.

'And here we are, Ms Gibenn—back in Wilheard as promised.'

Ebony smiled at Alim. 'Thank you very much. Have you visited Wilheard before? If you are staying for a while, perhaps I can return the favour by showing you about.'

Alim scanned the rooftops of the town before him. 'As a matter of fact, this is my first visit to Wilheard, and a guide would be very nice. I hear there are several historical sites in the capital.'

'Now you mention it, there is one particular statue like the King's bust.'

'Wonderful,' Alim said. 'By the by—about that elusive person. It just so happens that I am also interested in learning more about him. If, like today, you are feeling curious, then you are welcome to join me for another stroll in the woods. I must admit, it would be nice to have company for a change. That is if I have not already bored you to tears.'

Ebony laughed. 'If I am not imposing, I would love to.'

'Not at all,' Alim chirped, placing his pipe in the usual corner of his mouth. 'I hope to see you in the near future, then. For now, though, I think I will look round for an inn. Cheerio.'

Ebony watched Alim walk away for a moment and then headed home. As she neared the cottage, she spotted Hazel leading a horse and cart up the hill from New Market Square. The farmer was on her morning delivery, and this was her last stop. Ebony had made a one-off request for her friend to deliver a couple of pints.

'This heat sure is a killer. I hope you're grateful for me bringing this to you,' Hazel called as she saw Ebony pacing towards her.

'I have more sympathy for this poor thing,' Ebony said, stroking the horse on the nose, causing it to whinny.

'I thought you might,' Hazel winked. She placed her hands on her hips and looked down at the town below. 'So, m'dear, who's the scruffy bloke I saw with you a moment ago?'

Ebony looked at Hazel with surprise. 'You saw us?'

'Of course. There is not much you can hide from me, Ebs. In truth, the extraordinary clothes of the guy caught my attention first, but then I saw you standing next to him.'

Ebony wrinkled her nose and looked back at the horse. 'Fair enough. Anyway, that *scruffy bloke* is Alim; he is my new friend, and from what I could gather, he is a scholar.'

'Is he now,' Hazel replied. 'Did you meet him in the forest?'

Ebony stopped stroking the horse and looked towards her friend again, this time with less surprise. 'Yes,' she admitted, expecting a look of disapproval in return. 'I guess I really can't hide anything from you.'

'Come now, m'dear, it doesn't take much imagination to guess what you have been up to. Your desire to go moseying off into the forest grew stronger every day. Besides, I saw you coming from that direction.'

'I guess so,' Ebony conceded.

Hazel moved to the back of the horse and reached into the cart for the milk. She placed it in the shade of the cottage. 'Anyway, did you and Mister Scruffy discover anything interesting?'

Ebony explained to Hazel what she saw.

'That sounds fun,' Hazel said. 'But you did not find *you-know-who*?'

Ebony shook her head.

'Well, that's probably for the best, m'dear. I'm glad you're making a *change* to your life, as you put it, but seeking strangers in forests is not something you should make a habit of. Saying that, I should probably check out this Alan chap… see what he is all about.'

'Firstly, his name is Alim, not Alan. Secondly, I know how cheeky you can get when it comes to men—I don't want you pestering him.'

'Any friend of yours is a good enough friend for me,' Hazel said, pursing her lips.

Ebony smirked. 'Don't pester him.'

'You can be so bossy and serious sometimes,' Hazel said. 'Speaking of serious, you'll never guess who came to the farm this morning.'

Ebony shrugged.

'He is tall, muscular and handsome enough but wears an expression similar to a tortoise.'

Ebony thought for a moment. 'Oliath Burley?'

Hazel nodded. 'He was asking questions about our elusive friend from the forest, wondering if I knew anything.'

'What did you tell him?'

'I wasn't able to tell him anything. But he also asked if you were about.'

'Me?' Ebony said, biting her bottom lip. 'What would he want with me?'

'Probably the same as he wanted from me—answers to his questions. Don't worry yourself. I didn't tell him your plans, and it is improbable he knows of them.'

Ebony's brows knitted. 'All right. I can't imagine I will be of much help.'

'To be fair, I think he wants to talk to you because you live near the eastern woodland. Everyone knows that is where that vigilante keeps coming from. Perhaps he is just making the rounds. Y'know… talking to as many people as possible and all that?'

'I suppose that makes sense.'

'Then again, maybe he has a thing for you.' Hazel winked at Ebony. 'Perhaps his questions are just an excuse to speak to you.'

'Well, I don't know about that—I can't imagine I'm his type.' Ebony said. 'Besides, that woman who always follows him gives me the creeps. I don't think she likes me.'

'Cordelia Lawford? I don't think she likes anyone, so I wouldn't take it personally.' Hazel walked back to the mare and took a firm hold of its reins, pulling the horse round to face the other direction. 'In any case, I've delivered your milk, m'dear. It won't last long in this heat, so put it in the cool as soon as possible.'

'All right,' Ebony replied, collecting the produce from where Hazel had left it. 'Thanks again. I'll see you soon.'

Sitting in the hollow of a tree, Ninapaige chuckled to herself. She had forgotten how enjoyable it was to tease humans, especially the ones who tried to catch her. Things were progressing nicely, and those under her watch were all doing what they should be doing; all it took was a little persuading.

Still, Ninapaige was concerned. That girl Ebony had perhaps been a little too easy to impel, and although she was searching for Sombie, as planned, she was also walking into danger. Unsurprisingly, Sombie was aware of Ebony's movements, and with him watching over her, matters would not be so bad. Yet, his refusal to reveal himself to the girl irked Ninapaige somewhat.

Ninapaige closed her eyes. She wondered what Sylvia would think. After all, by making Sombie and Ebony aware of one another, she effectively did the opposite of what the doctor wanted. Not that her disapproval concerned Ninapaige; even with everything she had been through, Sylvia was callow regarding such matters. Why should that girl decide what was best? All the same, it was unfortunate to impose on others' affairs.

Ninapaige snapped her eyes open; she could sense Sombie nearby. With Ebony out of the forest, he had again shifted his attention. She giggled and left the tree.

Who knew that entering dreams could bother a man so much? In truth, she no longer needed to do such a thing and letting events pan out naturally from now on would prove just as effective. Then again, why stop when the chase was this much fun?

Standing in the shadows of night-darkened trees, Oliath Burley looked across the empty pathway towards the prison blocks. He was feeling tense.

Hitherto, there had been no reason for the captain of the guard to be surreptitious; considering his line of work and general repute, most people, especially Wilheard's guards, would not question his presence anywhere in town, yet loitering near the prisons at night would be suspicious on any occasion, and he could do without the headache of being spotted. Even if

172

most guards were oblivious to the restrictions, Oliath knew he was going against the mayor's orders and felt more at ease keeping out of sight.

'Everything is going smoothly, sir,' Cordelia said, emerging from behind a separate tree. She moved to stand nearer her boss, having noticed his anxiety.

Oliath kept his eyes on the handleless back door of the prison block. It had only been five minutes since Nolan had sneaked into the complex, but it felt longer.

'Shakeston is more than capable of carrying out this task. He will not be much longer, I know it.'

'I have no doubt, Lawford,' Oliath whispered, his tone frustrated. 'I have no qualms about your or Shakeston's abilities.' He sighed and gave the starry sky a cursory look. 'Forgive me if I come across as annoyed, but you know I would rather it not have come to this. All this sneaking about is… demeaning.'

Cordelia did not answer. Her captain's voice was full of shame. This was understandable; avoiding the law he strove to uphold was something that would never have crossed his mind.

'Finding the key was not a problem, then?' Oliath asked. 'It can be difficult to avoid knocking things over while fumbling about in the dark.'

Cordelia murmured at the pitiful remark. Oliath did not usually participate in idle conversation, let alone start it. 'As I said, sir, all is going smoothly. According to The Wilheard Chronicles, two of Wilheard Hall's back windows were smashed the other week. It did not take long to find them during my search round the building. I was faced with an empty room.'

Earlier in the day, Oliath noted that the patrolling guards about Wilheard Hall had dwindled over the weeks. Even though he did not attempt to distract what was left of the patrolling troops, Cordelia had no problems getting past them. Ironically, Oliath was at odds as to whether this was a good thing. Cordelia was a remarkable woman when it came to her abilities, so it was somewhat forgivable, and considering the circumstances at the time, he was grateful for any incompetence from the guards.

Cordelia continued her report. 'The key was near Benjamin Oswin's desk, as you said it would be, sir. Frankly, I am glad I found it quickly—the stench of that room is not something I can stomach for long.'

Oliath grunted, amused by the comment. It was nice to know he was not the only one.

The prison's back door slowly opened, barely making a sound as Nolan pushed it. Looking round one last time, Oliath and Cordelia stepped from the shadows and dashed towards the lieutenant.

Oliath patted Nolan firmly on the back. 'Any trouble?'

'No, sir, the halls are quiet. I was as quick as possible. Did I take too long?'

Oliath shook his head. 'They say time passes quickly when one is having fun. It turns out this is not one of those times. Let's get this over with.'

Sitting on an old wooden chair with uneven legs, a solitary prison guard gently rocked back and forth, humming to himself as he stared dreamily at the ceiling. Sometimes, he wondered why he became a guard; it was so dull at times that he secretly wished there was more trouble in Wilheard Prison. If only one of the lags broke out from his cell or something. That would be fun—chasing a criminal through the halls. It would be better than sitting on the outside door leading to the cells of petty criminals. Those bums were unlikely to cause any trouble.

Disturbed by footsteps echoing along the empty corridors, the prison guard sat straight. Oliath marched into view with a dogged expression, triggering the guard to jump to his feet and salute his superior. Maintaining his stance, the guard watched Oliath stride towards him, unable to take his eyes off the captain's thick arms-of-muscle as they motioned back and forth with every stride.

'Um… fair eve, Captain Burley,' the prison guard said. 'Come to interrogate a few delinquents? I've got to admit, I wasn't expecting anyone to--'

'I am here to see The Snake,' Oliath interrupted, showing he was in no frame of mind for talking.

The prison guard tightened his lips together and stepped towards the cellblock door. The lock released with an audible clunk as he turned the key, followed by a creak as he pushed the door open. Oliath entered as soon as the way was wide enough.

Not taking long to find the cell he wanted, Oliath peered through the rusty bars. The light pouring inside was low; the oil lanterns in the passageway provided barely more than the moonlight shining through the opening on the far wall. Of course, even with the jail covered in shadow, there was nowhere for the man within to hide.

Oliath palmed the metal bars. 'Wake up! I want to talk with you, Snake.'

Shifting from a stained mattress, a bony, middle-aged man stepped up from his cell bed and out from the shadow covering it. Snake stared at Oliath from the other side of the bars. Having been asleep, the thief's face was drawn and showed he was not happy to have been awakened. Wrapping his hands round the top of two bars, Snake stretched his back and let out a wide-mouthed yawn, showing his yellowed teeth as he unleashed his foul-smelling breath. 'I was wondering when you might show up, Burley. Couldn't whatever this is about have waited till morning?'

Twisting his face, Oliath stepped back a pace after inhaling the crook's rank breath. 'I must attend to far more pressing matters during the day than the likes of you.'

'O' course you do,' Snake said, characteristically hissing through his teeth as he tittered. 'I noticed you've got your work cut out for you these days, what with this stranger hanging about town. Perhaps your uselessness is finally being challenged.'

'It's hard to feel offended by someone with the brain of a newt. You're the idiot that gets captured repeatedly,' Oliath countered. 'Furthermore, you were stupid enough to try and burgle a building under guard watch. Didn't you realise that the gunpowder shop had been targeted recently?'

Snake grunted and moved away from the bars, turning his back on Oliath. 'Yes, well… I ain't the one who's got to live up to the town folks' approval—and I know you've been struggling to get information on that geezer from the forest.' He turned back to face Oliath, baring his discoloured teeth into a crooked smile again. 'But I came face to face with him.'

'Do you think I am here for any other reason?' Oliath said, pressing on with the interrogation. 'I won't beat round the bush with you, Snake—I want answers tonight, and if you hope to get out of here any time soon, you will cooperate.'

Snake once again hissed through his teeth, showing his amusement. 'You know, I was actually thinking about getting a tattoo of a snake on my wrist. I'm getting quite fond of that name.'

The metal bars of the cell made a low ringing sound as Nolan thumped them. 'The captain of the guard asked you a question! You would do well to answer it.'

'Oh-ho!' laughed Snake, 'quite a temper on this one. You must be rubbing off on him, Burley.' The crook turned back to face his interrogator and hissed once more. 'I was hoping you'd beg a little, but you can't even manage a *please*. Lucky for you lot, I want to tell what I know.'

Oliath and his lieutenants listened carefully for Snake's answer. The prison guard, who was still standing nearby, leant closer too.

The Snake went on. 'If you hope to take this geezer head on, you may have your work cut out. As you know, he ain't exactly outgoing, and I don't think he'll take kindly to your roughness.'

'Get to the point,' Oliath said. 'I know how elusive he is.'

'Yes, but have you heard about his skills? He is fast... and unusually strong for his size. He didn't appear to be anywhere near as large as you and all that, but... well, he didn't have any trouble tossing me about, that's for sure, and I wouldn't be surprised if he beats you up too.'

'We will always have the captain's back if he requires it,' Cordelia put in. 'No man has been able to best the three of us together.'

Snake curled his lips. 'If you say so, but this ain't no ordinary man we are chatting 'bout. There was definitely something unnatural 'bout him. I saw it in his eyes.'

Oliath rubbed his chin as he processed the information. 'There has been talk about Wilheard of the vigilante's extraordinary abilities. I admit, though, that I dismissed the rumours as childish hyperbole. What about weapons? I've heard he wields a large sword.'

'He didn't have a sword when I saw him, but I don't know about other weapons. He could have anything under that coat of his.'

'If he did not have his sword when dealing with you, then perhaps he is not as violent as I might have feared.' Oliath said. He accepted that the vigilante had yet to do anything beyond leaving his victims unconscious and bound. Regardless, he was still not at ease.

'Tender spirits!' The Snake continued. 'Good thing he didn't have a sword on him. I'd hate to see what he can do with one o' those. Trust me, Burley, that geezer has certain powers... powers that ain't human.'

Oliath frowned at the remark but did not pass comment. He gazed pensively at the prison guard for a moment. Before he noticed Oliath was looking at him, the guard had been staring at The Snake with a daft expression glued to his face, more confused than intrigued at the conversation. He snapped to attention upon realising the captain was looking at him.

'What did the vigilante look like?' Oliath asked, turning his attention back to the thief.

The Snake closed his eyes and thought for a moment. 'He is nothing special, really—longish brown hair, a bit of stubble on his face... he wore dirty clothes that looked as old as me. Like I said, he is quite muscular and about as tall as you are. Handsome enough for a geezer—he had a nice set of teeth on him...'

'That's enough,' Oliath snorted, combing his hair back with his fingers. 'Perhaps someone can mock up a wanted poster. I appreciate your cooperation.'

At last, Oliath had acquired some much-needed information. Now, it was a matter of what to do with it.

Remnant Tales of Stilly:
Passion and Benevolence

Chapter Seven

Adulthood does not allow most people to experience boredom. One might become fed up, but this is arguably not the same as boredom.

Being bored and fed up tended to go hand in hand with Ebony. When she was on top of all her chores and errands, if she did not find something to do quickly, boredom was the one thing that soon set in, followed by peevish behaviour and eventually misery. Being at home was a problem when she got like this, as she tended to get fidgety and sick of her surroundings. Often, if Abraham did not throw his daughter out of the cottage first, he would do his best to distract her. Yet, her father was not there.

Naturally, books had been on Ebony's mind as she puzzled over what to do with her free time. It had seemed like ages since she finished Passion and Benevolence, and it was about time she borrowed another book.

As Ebony thought about Passion and Benevolence, something occurred to her.

'Of course!' Ebony blurted, disturbing her own thoughts. 'Alim Larring... I knew I recognised that name. I wonder if Alim knows a Ted Larring.'

It only took Ebony a few minutes to reach Old Market Square. Upon entering Bookish Charm, her only hope was that no one had borrowed Passion and Benevolence since she returned it. Showing Alim the novel when she next saw him would surely arouse further interest.

On her approach to the library, Ebony noticed the figures of two people through the building's cloudy windowpane. She recognised one of the silhouettes (the short, slightly hunched-backed man with a walking cane was Albert Comyns), but who did the other belong to?

Albert was examining the taller man standing before him, a mixture of confusion and vexation on his face. It tickled Ebony when she discovered why.

Alim was standing next to the bookcase that made up the left wall of the library. Despite Albert standing directly in eyeshot, the scholar did not seem put off. Ebony recalled that he was good at ignoring people about him as he studied, which she guessed was a blessing considering he came from the busy Thane. No doubt, that was where he learned it.

Cradling a large book in one arm, Alim hummed as he read, switching back and forth from certain pages. 'I see,' he muttered. 'Very interesting indeed'.

Neither man had noticed Ebony enter the building. 'Well, fancy meeting you here, Mister Larring,' she said, interrupting the silence.

Alim peered at Ebony over his glasses, whereas Albert wobbled ninety degrees and squinted at her.

'Fair noon, young Ebony,' Albert said with his usual gravelly voice before shuffling towards her. 'Come for another book, have you?'

'That had been the plan, but now I'm drawn to what Alim is doing.' Ebony looked back towards the scholar and gave him a thin smile.

Alim returned a grin. He looked to have made himself at home; several tomes were on tables and chairs, bookmarked by other books.

Using his cane to steady himself, Albert shifted once more on the spot and turned back to Alim. 'You know this bizarre young man?'

'Albert!' Ebony tutted. 'That is very uncouth of you.'

Alim's smile grew, showing no offence. 'No harm done, Ms. Gibenn. Furthermore, if I might be so bold as to reply for you, the answer is yes— Ebony and I met yesterday in the woodland.

Ebony cringed.

'The woodland?' Albert echoed, the wrinkles on his forehead deepening. 'What were you up to in the woodland, girl?'

By now, almost everyone knew about the mysterious vigilante from the eastern woodland; typically, opinions varied.

'Oh, just for a walk. I wanted to look at all the beautiful nature.'

The librarian's expression remained unchanged. He was not impressed or convinced by the answer. Alim's shoulders bounced as he chuckled inwardly. Although he knew the truth, it did not take a genius to surmise why Ebony hid it. She placed a covert finger on her lips, gesturing for Alim to keep hushed.

'Young lady, I might be an old fart, but I am not a *silly* old fart. Anyway, it is none of my business what you youngsters get up to.' The ninety-four-year-old turned and walked back to Alim. 'As for you, young man, be sure that you are careful with my books,' he said, tapping a hardback on the table with the end of his walking stick. 'Especially the one in your hands—thirty years I have been studying that book. I hope your mitts are clean.'

'My "mitts" are indeed clean, old boy,' Alim replied calmly. He dabbed his index finger on the tip of his tongue and turned a page.

'Don't be licking your fingers before turning a page, either. I don't want spittle on my books.'

'Very well, old boy.'

'And stop calling me old boy!'

Ebony approached the men and placed a hand on the librarian's hunch. 'I'll be sure to watch him, Albert.'

The elderly man's lips twitched as he looked between the pair. He made a dismissive wave. 'Thirty years,' he repeated, 'and you only needed thirty minutes.'

With that, Albert hobbled from the room.

Alim smirked as he watched Albert leave. 'Spirited fellow. I think he likes me.'

Ebony sighed in relief, placed a hand on Alim's shoulder, and peered at the book in his arm. 'He can be for his age. What are you reading, anyway? It certainly has Albert worked up whatever it is.'

Alim placed his thumb on the page he was reading and closed the book. '*Perception of Nonentity*,' he said, showing Ebony the front cover. 'That old chap keeps harping on about how he has researched this tome for many years, only to now interpret some of its meaning. He believes I have come to understand it all in only a short time, but that is not so. I have been studying subjects like this practically all my life.'

'What's it about?'

Alim looked out the window, his green eyes darting as he tried to find an answer. 'There is no easy way of explaining it.'

Ebony made small nods. That was understandable if Albert had been reading the book for three decades, as he claimed. 'Very well,' she said, thinking of a way to rephrase the question. 'What do you intend to learn?'

Alim gave a languid shrug. 'As much as possible.'

Ebony raised her eyebrows. Getting an answer from Alim was like felling a tree with a dinner knife.

'I suppose,' Alim continued, 'if I were to highlight anything in particular, I would say that I am trying to find out more about those symbols on King Godfrey's plinth.'

Ebony nodded again.

Alim raised the corner of his lips ever so slightly then. 'Speaking of which'—he turned a page—'do you remember what I said about those symbols?'

'You mentioned that they are from a language of some sort.'

'That's right,' Alim replied. 'The world is full of mysterious things.'

He selected a book from the middle of the stack on the chair and handed it to Ebony. She scanned the title:

Interpreting the Obscure

'It looks ponderous if you'll forgive my saying so.' Ebony said.

'Do you believe in magic, dear girl?'

Ebony was taken aback by the unexpected question. 'I've not really thought about it.'

After running a finger along the bookshelves, Alim selected yet another book from its place. 'Well, do you believe in spiritual beings or acts of divinity?'

'I don't practise religion if that's what you mean, and I cannot say I have witnessed anything otherworldly.'

Alim returned the same book to the shelf. 'That will be a no, then…'

Ebony wrinkled her nose. 'I admit I believed in fairies and pixies as a child. As an adult…' she paused, 'as you said—the world is full of mysterious things.'

'That is logical, dear girl, but you seem to be evading the question.'

'Very well,' Ebony conceded. 'Why not—I am open to the suggestion that mankind is capable of extraordinary things, including magic.'

Alim finally looked at Ebony, gazing at her over the top of his glasses like before. His expression remained impassive. 'Do you mean that?'

Ebony gave a hesitant nod.

'How frightfully absurd!' Alim guffawed. 'You have a unique imagination...'

A thumping sound from above followed Alim's laughing as Albert struck the floor, presumably with his cane. 'Quiet down there!' the elderly man's muffled voice called. 'You are in a library, not a circus!'

The pair winced at each other.

'Anyway, dear girl, I merely jest,' Alim said, his voice now hushed. 'In truth—and if you mean what you say—I am relieved. That book is not as dull as you might think.'

Ebony smiled. 'I guess I made the age-old mistake of judging a book by its cover. It will be nice to learn something new. That is if I can understand it.'

'Learn something new, eh?' Alim repeated. 'That reminds me.' He looked down at the piled books and scanned the spines for a certain hardback. He pulled one out. 'Here you go, dear girl—this should jog your memory on some of Stilly's historical personages.'

Ebony took the book from Alim. She read the title and opened it to one of his bookmarks, finding a list of Stilly's royal timeline.

Archives of Stilly: Volume one

Sanine Lineage.

- *King Theodore Sanine. 1278SN-1360SN, aged eighty-two years.*
  - ○ *Queen Mikki (maiden name unknown) Sanine (spouse to Theodor). 1285SN-1375SN, aged ninety years.*
- *Queen Teri [Olvewhort] Sanine (retained maiden name (daughter and successor to Theodore and Mikki)). 1323SN-1379SN, aged fifty-six years.*
  - ○ *King Ithel Olvewhort (spouse to Teri). 1328SN-1379SN, aged fifty-one years.*
  - ○ *Prince Paul Sanine (sibling to Teri (rejected throne inheritance)). 1325SN-1390SN, aged sixty-five years.*

- o *Prince Olann Olvewhort Sanine (son to Teri and Ithel (died without inheriting the throne)). 1350SN-1375SN, aged twenty-five.*
- *King Doran Sanine (son to Paul, successor to Teri (aunt)). 1355SN-1444SN, aged eighty-nine years.*
  - o *Queen Charmion [maiden name unknown] Sanine (spouse to Doran). 1362SN-1448SN, aged eighty-six years.*
- *King Godfrey Sanine (son and successor to Doran and Charmion). 1400SN-1466SN, aged sixty-six years.*
  - o *Queen Verity [Pothelm] Sanine (spouse to Godfrey). 1406SN-1467SN, aged sixty-one.*
  - o *Princess Clover Sanine (sibling to Godfrey) 1404SN-Unknown.*
- *Queen Evelyn Sanine (daughter and successor to Godfrey and Verity). 1440SN-Unknown: abandoned throne in 1468SN.*
  - o *Possible spouses or children are unknown.*

Half a dozen paragraphs were printed on the adjacent page to the list that briefly explained Castle Stilly. The book then detailed the separate generations of the Sanine Lineage, all of whom inhabited the castle. Ebony read through the royals' varied stories, starting with the brilliant and ambitious King Theodor, followed by the life of tragic-laden Queen Teri.*

'How are you finding it?' Alim asked, interrupting Ebony's reading. 'Interesting, no?'

'Rather sad,' Ebony replied with a faint sigh. 'The castle has had a troubled history.'

'Ah, you must be referring to the Second Generation rule of Queen Teri. I agree it is very tragic. There are more in-depth volumes on the different royal generations if it appeals to you.'

'No, thank you,' said Ebony,' 'this is sufficient, I think. I may borrow it. If you were not after it first, that is.'

'By all means, dear girl. Of course, you'll have to get the attention of that cranky old boy.'

'I heard that!'

Remnant Tales of Stilly:
Passion and Benevolence

Alim and Ebony wheeled round in surprise as Albert called from the doorway to the back of the customer floor. The pair was astonished that the librarian had managed to sneak up on them. He sounded displeased at Alim's comment, but it was difficult to tell under the masses of bushy white hair that covered his face.

Ebony spoke before Albert could lash out at the poor scholar. 'I've chosen a book to borrow.'

'Very well, young lady. Bring it to the front desk.' Ebony did as asked and waited for Albert to go through the usual routine of stamping loaned books. Albert looked to Alim after pushing the hardcover to Ebony. 'How about you, young man? Are you finished browsing, or will you make me wait longer?'

Alim pulled a nervous face. He walked to the front desk and plopped down a pile of hardbacks. 'I feel my welcome has expired. I'll take these if it is all right with you.'

Albert grunted. 'Before I go through the routine, I will tell you I have several membership offerings. I already know that you are not from Wilheard. Depending on how long you intend to stay—and if you plan to borrow further books—then I suggest you choose one. It will be expensive otherwise.'

'While you decide, Alim, I'll wait for you outside,' Ebony said with a smile. Alim nodded in response.

Sitting on the shallow wall of the water fountain with the pretty but sad-faced sculpture of Old Market Square, Ebony ran her fingers through the cool water. After ten minutes of waiting, she saw Alim walking towards her. He was holding the library books under both arms. 'Are you all right?' she asked him.

Alim placed the books on the fountain's stone edge and blew a soft whistle. 'I think I'm growing on the old boy.'

Ebony grinned and looked at the book stack. 'Tender spirits!' she uttered. 'I forgot all about that book I wanted to show you.'

Alim looked at Ebony. 'Which book would that be?'

'A story called Passion and Benevolence. It is written by--'

Remnant Tales of Stilly:
Passion and Benevolence

'Ted Larring?' Alim interrupted, finishing Ebony's sentence. 'Ted Larring is the interesting grandfather I told you about.'

'So, he's your grandfather... I wondered if there was a relationship. The world may be mysterious, but it sure is small.'

'It truly is. As for Passion and Benevolence, I borrowed it yesterday. I heard the book was in Wilheard—truth be told, that is one of the reasons I am visiting this charming hamlet.'

'You heard the book was in Wilheard?' Ebony mused. 'You make it sound as if there is only one copy.'

'Well...' Alim scratched the back of his head. 'As far as I know, there *is* only one—my grandfather only paid for a limited publishing. There used to be three in Thane, but one got gravely damaged, and the other two lost or stolen.'

'I see. How fortunate at least one still survives. So, how are you finding the book?'

'As interesting as I imagined. I read it before snuffing my candle last night.'

'You read the whole book in a night?'

'Yes,' Alim said, replying as if this was typical of most people.

'I thought I read fast. In that case, what *did* you think of it? I suppose you found it amusing in the light of your research.'

'It was an insightful read. My dear grandfather has given me much to think about after reading the note at the book's lattermost page.' The thought of his grandfather made Alim chuckle. 'Indeed, the old coot still has a knack for intriguing me, even beyond this mortal coil. I knew that I would not be disappointed.'

Ebony had not heard the second part of what Alim said. 'A back note?' She repeated.

'That's right—the one on the thinner paper.' Judging from the nonplussed look on her face, Alim presumed that Ebony had overlooked the note. 'I see. The fact that you may have missed the note is hardly surprising. Whether intended or not, it is pretty well hidden. Here's a thought,' he continued, glancing at the books under his arms. 'I'm going to The Wooden Duck now to drop these off. Since explaining the note to you will not be as fun as showing it, how would you like to tag along? Do not worry, Ms Gibenn, I mean nothing ungentlemanly by inviting you to a tavern.'

Ebony gave a coy look. 'I have no doubts. If that is your wish, then lead the way.'

'Good show. I think I might need help with carrying the books, anyway.'

See Appendix for more details.

'How is the planning for the Summer Festival coming along?' Basil Wolleb asked his assistant.

Benjamin Oswin stared blankly at the Stillian flag to the other side of his desk. He had heard Basil speak but did not catch what he had said. *Now the slamming for the bummer festival is becoming too long! That can't be right.*

Confused, Benjamin turned to Basil with a frown. 'Now the *what*, Mayor?'

'I was wondering how the preparation for the Summer Festival is going.'

'Oh... It is going well.'

Basil turned his attention to Ben. 'You seem unfocused, my good man. That is not like you?'

Benjamin sat back in his chair and placed his hands behind his head. He gazed up to the ceiling. 'I was just thinking about the people I have been interviewing lately—The Possessed.' Benjamin and Basil had coined this term for the group of outsiders. 'The latest two being the woman related to the blacksmith Mister Leets and a man the night guards found down a back street. A dog had been with him.'

'Oh, yes—I remember now. How is that going?'

'Slow,' Benjamin replied. 'Which makes me all the more relieved that I am interviewing these people, not Oliath.'

Basil hummed. Because of how the captain had acted the other day, he was inclined to agree. He looked at the crack on the far side of his desk.

'In any case,' Benjamin resumed, 'I have found out that The Possessed all suffered from the same symptoms prior to their actions, most notably head and chest pains, rise in body temperature and loss of consciousness.'

'Tender spirits,' swore Basil under his breath. 'And they still have no recollection of what they did or their encounter with our elusive friend from the woods?'

Benjamin shook his head.

Basil hummed again. 'No wonder Oliath is becoming aggravated with this investigation. I can relate, you know—I don't like things happening in my town that I cannot figure out, even if this vigilante means well. I mean, he must be here for a reason, and he showed up not long after these possessed folk started causing trouble. What do you make of him?'

'I think the vigilante is here for more than what we have seen. He is watching for something... or someone.'

'What are you getting at, man?'

Benjamin shrugged and wiggled his moustache. 'I'm not sure.'

'You have one of those faces,' commented Basil. 'You've got a bad feeling again.'

'You know me, Mayor,' said Ben, pulling a weak smile. 'I worry too much.'

'Well, I think we are all a little apprehensive,' Basil said. 'You have been keeping an eye on Oliath, right?'

'As you instructed, but I only see him a few times during the day.'

'During the day...' Basil echoed. 'I wonder if Oliath sleeps much.'

'Sorry, Mayor?'

'Nothing, I was just thinking aloud. Don't worry about what Oliath gets up to from now on. He may be an angry so-and-so at times, but I trust he is sensible enough not to get into too much trouble. Mind you, it would be interesting if he brought this vigilante in.' Basil turned on his chair and looked out the window. 'Anyway, you keep to your usual business from now on, Ben. For starters, tell me in more detail how the Summer Festival is coming along. I need a bit of cheering up.'

Typically, the walk to The Wooden Duck from Bookish Charm was a fifteen-minute journey. Thanks to Alim's curious nature towards anything old or slightly out of the norm, however, the trip ended up taking an extra ten minutes.

Being the tolerant type, Ebony did not mind the delay in reaching their destination, yet the anticipation of discovering what was hidden in Passion and Benevolence prompted her to move Alim onwards.

By the time the pair reached The Wooden Duck, Ebony's pocket watch had read 11.54am. Since it was close to noon, some of Wilheard's residents were out for their lunch, and during that time of day, Efflorescence Way was teeming with the hungry. Being part of the same street, the old tavern was no exception.

I'm glad Father is not here, Ebony thought as she shifted past the increase of people. *He would not like seeing me following a stranger into a place like this.*

Ebony expected not to see her father in The Wooden Duck as she and Alim arrived. Abraham opposed crowded places, and even if he and his new lady friend often went to the pub (which she suspected they did), it would not have been then.

Reaching the lodgings of The Wooden Duck (a T-shaped hall at the top of a stairway), Ebony and Alim exhaled in relief, glad that they had got away from the crowd downstairs. Since there was no one about, the landing was quiet, save for the muffled voices below and the giggles coming from a closed door belonging to one of the rooms; the playful growls of a man, followed immediately by the squeaks of his company, caused Ebony to blush.

Abashed, Alim quickly led Ebony further down the corridor and to his own accommodation, promptly closing the room door after he and Ebony had entered. 'Phew,' he exclaimed. 'Let's shut all that noise out, dear girl.'

Although modest, the room had ample moving space due to the minimum amount of furniture: a simple bed fit for only one; a bedside cabinet, atop which sat a candelabrum and a leather-bound book titled Traehen Scripture; and lastly, a small desk, which was filled with books and scrolls. Above the desk was a cross-hatched window.

Alim opened the window on a slant. 'Have a seat, dear girl,' he said, pulling the chair from under the desk. Ebony thanked him and sat next to the window.

Alim sifted through the cluttered desk. 'You'll have to forgive the mess. I have never been one for orderliness,' he said as he searched for Passion and Benevolence. 'Ah-ha—there you are, you rascal!'

Alim turned Passion and Benevolence over onto its front and opened the book to the back page. At first glance, the inside looked no different to any other book: a plain inlay covering the board cover. Moving his fingers to the book's spine, he tugged at the paper. With the page loosened, he gestured for Ebony to open it.

Balancing on Ebony's fingertips, the paper felt roughly half that of the other pages. Hidden on the inside were six hand-written paragraphs.

Note

In all my years of study and exploration, I have never encountered anyone as fascinating as the bygone Minach Emmanuel Grellic. If, like me, dear reader, you cannot resist the escapades of life's lesser-known secrets, then it is of great fortune you are reading this.

Firstly, I apologise for the way I present this passage, but I have my reasons. Although I do not wish it to detract from Emmanuel's work in any way, I cannot—and will not—avoid its inclusion entirely. These are my beliefs, and I hope whoever might read this is open-minded enough to consider their plausibility. With that in mind, as I said before, if one is like me, one will question Emmanuel's anecdote.

I will not reiterate too much of the book but reflect on parts I deem relevant to my discoveries.

Remnant Tales of Stilly:
Passion and Benevolence

If one is familiar with Stilly's history, one will know that many of the characters in this book were more than fictitious: King Godfrey, Queen Verity and Princess/Queen Evelyn being the most obvious. However, one would be hard-pressed to find anything on other characters such as Fordon Latnemirt or the sovereign knights. Although there is evidence of their existence, reasons for why the information is so tricky to come by are apparent once found. Regarding the latter example, their tragic yet complicated fate determines why. How much of Emmanuel's narrative is factual is anyone's guess, but I digress.

The very mention of magic in historical documents is next to none. Is this due to Godfrey's revulsion towards anything beyond Traehen or the Naitsir faith? It is known that the last King of Stilly would strike anything he did not like from history; however, the same cannot be said about Evelyn, who assumed power after her father's death. Nothing was stopping her from exposing everything about the subject. After all, Evelyn supported "magic", and this book (or its original) would probably not have come to fusion. In theory, perhaps she decided to obscure any knowledge. There are many reasons why she would do such a thing, Fordon Latnemirt's use of magic being one such.

One might conclude the story of Fordon's betrayal as just that: a story. But what of the evidence in Wilheard's eastern woodland that suggests otherwise? A king's bust, gravestones, and the unusual engraved symbols accompanying them. I will be astonished if this book is nothing but fantasy.

Ted Larring

Ebony looked up from the book and stared blurry-eyed out the window. Alim had been studying her face as she read the passage, a slight smile on his lips as he waited for a reaction.

Remnant Tales of Stilly:
Passion and Benevolence

'So this…' Ebony said after a long pause, 'this story is *not* a story?'

Alim moved to the open window and leant on the sill. He pulled out his smoking pipe and sprinkled some tobacco into the chamber. He was still smiling. 'If that is what you want to believe, then I will not argue… but there is only one way to find out. Did you notice the symbols at the bottom?'

Ebony looked back to the foot of the page and scanned the glyphs written there. 'These look similar to the ones on your scroll,' Ebony mused, looking where Alim was still standing.

The scholar drew on his pipe and exhaled the smoke out the window. He nodded at Ebony. 'I believe I neglected to mention yesterday that these are Pentominto letters. I have a basic alphabet of the glyphs written on parchment somewhere. It was one of the many things my grandfather bequeathed me.'

'I'd love to see it sometime,' Ebony said.

'And I'd love to show you'—Alim peered round the room—'now even, if I can think where I put it.'

'So you can speak this language?' Ebony asked as she watched Alim rummage about.

'Only the tiniest bit, I'm afraid,' he replied, almost apologetically. 'In fact, I am mostly translating the symbols from that parchment… Where is that blasted thing?'

'That's all right. Perhaps you can show me another time.' Ebony stood up from the wooden chair and walked to the window; the breeze from outside felt nice against her face. 'I presume you have translated those letters.'

'For the most part. To the point where it might mean something, at least. But it only suggests what I was going to do anyway.' Alim took another lug on his pipe. 'I will be going back into the woodland—tomorrow, that is.'

'That's great. I'll go with you,' Ebony blurted. 'That is if you can put up with me, of course.'

Alim scratched the back of his head; he seemed apprehensive. 'I will be more than happy for you to come along, dear girl. As I said before, the company would be nice. However… I fear people who know you better will be against it.'

'Oh, don't you worry about old Albert. I am more than capable of looking after myself.'

Alim puffed on his pipe as he considered Ebony's response. 'Very well, Ms Gibenn. I was planning it to be early morning. Say… six-thirty? There will be plenty of light for such an expedition by then.'

'All right. I can meet you by the forest entrance, where we entered Wilheard?'

'A capital idea—that will be something to look forward to. For now, allow me to escort you from this place.'

Sitting next to the large table in the living room, Wiley toyed with a single playing card.

Wiley and Meddia Penrose and (regrettably) Rida Priory had arrived home a few hours ago, and with their day behind them, it was now time for the three to rest. At least, that was supposed to be the idea. Rida was snoring upstairs, probably askew on his bed and dribbling as he slept, but Wiley and Meddia were wide awake.

Dexter had not arrived home thus far; he rarely did so at the same time as the other three. Despite its regularity, the wait never became tolerable for Wiley, who preferred not to rest until he and Dexter had swapped the daily information and perhaps a bit of repartee.

Wiley picked up another playing card from the top of the deck and bent it back and forth between his fingers and thumb. Sitting about with little to occupy his attention was wearisome, and finally kicking back to rest became more tempting with every passing second. Resisting this urge, he shifted his attention across the room to see how Meddia was passing the time.

Meddia, sitting cross-legged on the sofa at the far end of the living room, hummed quietly to herself as she stared out the nearby window. She was picking at her toenails, an absent-minded habit of her's that made Wiley frown.

'You should not do that, Meddia,' Wiley said softly so as not to sound as if he were scolding the girl. 'It is not a particularly clean habit. Besides, you will only make your toes sore.'

Meddia ceased picking and unfolded her legs. She continued humming, swapping the picking for fidgeting.

Wiley turned his attention back to his cards and sighed. He thought back to what he had done during the past twelve hours. As with the previous day, Wiley, Meddia and Rida decided to look more into the recent break-ins. Drah Leets's Smithy had been as decent a place as any to continue investigating, providing he could keep Meddia and Rida under control. Meddia, who generally stayed close to her mentor, had been the easiest to manage; her child-like curiosity, which led to her fiddling with several objects, needed only the smallest dissuasion. Rida always required that little bit more work. The lard bucket always seemed to have his mind on something that had nothing to do with the current task. In fact, Wiley suspected Rida used the investigations as an opportunity for other devious activities, and Priory was nothing if not good at hiding things.

The suspects targeted places selling hazardous materials, yet Wiley, as he had already determined, did not believe they were interested in these but rather in the other artefacts the shops had in common.

What was it about glass, particularly jewellery, that attracted these individuals? Wiley believed himself a lateral thinker, but this one had him mystified. Although the people detained were unfamiliar to him, they did not seem to be petty thieves.

To his credit, Rida had been the one to put the relevance of the jewels forward, even if that had been unintended. Thinking aloud and remembering the jewellery from previous visits, he had asked what the individual businesses used them for. Whether or not Rida cared for the answer to his musing was anyone's guess, but it had at least Wiley curious. Then again, the answers merely confirmed what Wiley would have already guessed: the glass, most of which was relatively low in value, was for decorative purposes. Drah Leets, for example, used them for custom-ordered weapons, while the Firs twins at Blow Your Mind! decorated oil lamps and candelabrums for the more ostentatious of customers. But what of the oil refinery and even the chemical and powder shop from a few weeks back? As far as Wiley knew, those two businesses did not have much jewellery lying about, yet they were targeted all the same. Wiley felt close to getting an answer to this riddle, although not as close as he hoped he would be by now. Perhaps a little bit of spying would help. Wiley was not nearly as good at skulking as Dexter (be that a good thing or not), but he was not altogether bad at it either. The problem was knowing whom to track and when to track them.

The topic of glass and jewellery also reminded Wiley of one of his visits to Bookish Charm with Meddia. While she busied herself with finding a fun book to read with him, Wiley browsed the pages of a book the elderly owner had left on the serving desk. He could not recall the book's name, but he remembered it to be a bizarre read, delving into the subjects of myth, paranormal connections, magic and hidden human abilities of all things. As he glanced through the pages, he came across a section specifically on crystals. The chapter went on incessantly about how jewels and the like are an excellent source for restricting things, or even good at, in the book's own words: *"holding an abundance of substance for later use, allowing for more profound effects."* Although interesting, it was altogether too fanciful for Wiley's tastes.

The front door's lock clicked open, waking Wiley from his thoughts. Dexter entered through it.

Looking wide-eyed at Dexter, Meddia silently waited for him to say something. Wiley made a low coughing sound to get the other man's attention. As expected, Dexter held up his hand in a way that asked for patience while he removed his hat and coat. Although demanding space until he sat down, judging from his peculiar smile, Dexter appeared eager to tell everyone about his day.

Dexter sauntered to the table and sat opposite Wiley. At first, he did not say anything; he picked up Wiley's deck of cards and gave them what appeared to be a random shuffle.

'I have been keeping an eye on a pair of diamonds today,' Dexter said, tossing the top card from the pile, leaving it face-down in the table's centre.

He gestured for Meddia, who had since padded her way over, to turn the card.

Meddia dragged the card closer and turned it, smiling her usual toothy grin upon noticing it was the Two of Diamonds. She was very impressed.

Wiley smirked, watching the other man continue to shuffle the cards. 'I have been looking at glass-made things myself today… Of course, you have diamonds of a different kind on your mind.' Wiley sat forward in his chair. 'Is Ebony Gibenn one such diamond?'

'Correct,' Dexter said, flicking another card on the table. 'With an unusual man in her company.'

Meddia eagerly turned the card over. It was the Joker.

'Perhaps that is a bit harsh,' Dexter explained. 'The man is odd, but certainly no buffoon.'

'I see.' Wiley said. 'I hope you got something out of observing these diamonds of yours.'

'I did.' Dexter flicked yet another card. Meddia snatched it up, revealing the Two of Spades. 'They are going back into the eastern woodland, it seems, to dig up its secrets.'

Meddia giggled, now understanding the relevance of the card.

Wiley murmured, mildly amused. 'Very well. I see you enjoyed finding this out.'

'Yes,' Dexter said, tossing one last card, this time for Wiley to turn over. 'Despite Miss Gibenn's friend being an unusual character, he comes across as the learned sort.'

Wiley turned the card. The Ace of Hearts.

Meddia frowned at the choice. 'Why that card?'

'A man after my own heart,' Wiley smirked. He pitched the card back towards Dexter and leant into his chair again. 'Do not think too deeply into it, Meddia. Dexter simply means that this man and I share similar interests. 'But enough parlour tricks for tonight. Does this have anything to do with the break-ins or the vigilante?

'Gibenn and her friend are interested in the vigilante, among other things, but I will need to find out more.'

'As you have it,' Wiley said. 'Do we have orders?'

'Nothing new,' Dexter groaned, reclining in his chair and placing his hands behind his head. 'I haven't spoken to the boss today, but I'm sure he would appreciate any news, no matter how small, so just keep an eye out.'

Wiley grunted in a way that indicated both bemusement and disappointment. 'Is that it? That is why you have come home with a curious smile? I expected more from you tonight.'

Dexter chuckled. 'You don't need to know *everything* I get up to, my friend. Meddia, be sure to let Rida know you should all keep your ears to the ground.'

'He means to continue listening for anything that might interest Captain Burley,' Wiley added to save any potential confusion, not that he needed to: she had heard the saying before.

'Ok,' Meddia said, rushing off to Rida before Dexter could tell her there was no urgency.

Dexter grinned as he watched Meddia bound up the stairs, waiting for her to go out of sight before he turned back to Wiley. 'To be honest, I am glad she has gone—there is something else I wanted to tell you, but I think it is best not to fill the girl's head with strange thoughts.'

Wiley sat forward, his interest rekindled.

'I followed Miss Gibenn and her strange friend into the Wooden Duck Inn. Although reluctant at first, I pursued them upstairs to one of the rented rooms.'

Wiley scowled.

'Do not think me a creep,' Dexter continued. 'Despite some liveliness sounding from one end of the corridor, it wasn't like that with these two. I tailed them because of something they said before reaching the Inn, so I knew what to expect. Anyway, I stood on the landing and managed to eavesdrop on their conversation--'

A bump, followed by one of Meddia's gleeful cackles, sounded from upstairs. From the sound of it, the girl had managed to sneak up on Rida as he slept.

Wiley rolled his eyes.

Dexter continued. 'As I said before, Miss Gibenn and the scholar—that is what her friend is, by the way—are going back into the woodland to uncover

196

some secrets.' Dexter grimaced for a moment and gazed at the ceiling. 'Admittedly, I'm not convinced the pair's conversation has much to do with the ongoing investigation, and I am purely observing them out of personal interest.'

Wiley made a soft humming sound. 'You really do enjoy spying on people.'

'Spying is such a mischievous word… I prefer *necessary scrutiny*.'

'Call it what you want, so long as you can achieve something useful out of it.'

'Oh, but of course.' Dexter smiled. 'I'm sure that whatever I get from the pair will interest the boss.'

Wiley nodded and reclined in his chair once more. 'Then, by all means, don't let me stand in your way… What holds the pair's interest, anyway?'

'Something about ancient history in Stilly.' Dexter stood from his seat. 'However, there is also something paranormal about their exploring. The scholar used the word magic at one point.'

Wiley pursed his lips. *That's a coincidence,* he thought, thinking back to that book in Bookish Charm.

Dexter interrupted Wiley's reverie. 'I appreciate that it sounds ridiculous, but I hadn't planned to divulge that information. Anyway, if you are interested, I will tell you how it goes tomorrow evening.'

A moment ago.

Doing as Dexter had asked, Meddia bolted up the stairway, taking two steps at a time as she headed for Rida's whereabouts.

The girl skidded on the dusty wooden landing, making a position-perfect stop outside Rida's room. Looking through the open door, Meddia covered her mouth with her fingers and giggled as she spied the portly man. Lying on his back, one leg raised against a wall with his head hanging off the bed, Rida snored as a trickle of saliva formed at the corner of his mouth.

Remnant Tales of Stilly:
Passion and Benevolence

Meddia stepped into the room and crept towards the bed, barely making a sound as she moved. Although she had successfully sneaked up on Rida almost a dozen times in the past, his reaction when jolted awake never failed to amuse her. Indeed, having done this many times already, she had become quite the master; she knew the position of all the creaky floorboards and was skilful when bypassing the various bits of rubbish Rida left scattered.

Rida bounced upright as a sudden weight landed on the other end of his bed, waking him instantly from snoring. Meddia shrieked with joy as Rida startled awake, her mouth open wide as she chortled. 'I got you again!' she exclaimed.

Puckering his lips and wrinkling his nose, Rida gazed at Meddia with sleepy eyes. He yawned and scratched the top of his head with one hand while scratching his belly with the other. He continued to look at the girl in a way that suggested he was trying to guess who she was, but after a long moment, he seemed to figure it out and smiled. 'Ya sure gave me a jump.'

Meddia gave a broad smile, baring her teeth. 'I'm getting better at sneaking, don-cha think? Maybe one day I'll be as good as you and Dexter.'

Rida continued smiling and nodded. His eyes widened seconds later; Meddia had reminded him of something.

Rida shoved one hand under his bed pillow and made a groping motion. Turning his head to give the girl a sideways glance, he paused, keeping his hand under the pillow. 'Promise ya won't tell nobody 'bout what I'm gonna show ya…'

'You should have said *anybody*, not *nobody*,' Meddia corrected. 'Wiley told me… I think. Something like that.'

Rida did not hear what Meddia said. He looked to the open doorway, back to the pillow, and then to the adolescent. 'I knows I can trust *you*, Meddia.'

Slowly bringing his hand out from underneath the pillow, Rida removed the item he had been hiding and placed it between him and the girl on the bed. Meddia gasped the moment she saw the object. It was a sword.

Rida made a shushing sound.

Reflecting the glow of a nearby candle, the well-polished blade glinted orange. Despite not holding much knowledge or interest in such things,

Meddia considered the sword pretty. She had never seen one with a curved blade before, and the sapphire embedded in its hilt made it look even more special.

'Where did you get this?' Meddia asked, not taking her eyes off the sword.

'Found it lyin' 'bout today.'

Meddia looked at Rida. She knew what he had *actually* done, and it was not the first time. 'You stole it from Mister Leets?'

Rida shushed the girl again.

'Why?' Meddia whispered.

Rida shrugged. 'It were jus' lyin' 'bout. I liked the look of it.'

Meddia pulled a worried expression and looked at the sapphire, which shone in the candlelight. The weapon really did look lovely. Expensive, too.

Uneasy and not knowing what to think about Rida's thievery, Meddia stepped off the bed and turned her attention back to what she had come to say in the first place. 'Dexter says we should continue keeping our ears to the ground.'

Rida gave the girl a stupid look that suggested he did not understand.

'It means we should carry on listening out for anything the boss might like.'

Rida nodded and placed the curved weapon back under his pillow, laying his head on it.

Meddia wheeled 180 degrees and tottered towards the door, once again sidestepping the various bits of rubbish. As she reached the exit, she turned back to Rida, who had been watching the girl as she walked away. 'You shouldn't take things that don't belong to you. You might get in trouble—you might get me and the others in trouble, too.'

With that, Meddia left, leaving Rida to think about what she had said.

Chapter Eight

Ebony held her pocket watch in her palm and rocked it from side to side, watching as the morning sunlight glistened along its silver edge.

The time was 6.26am.

Despite feeling tired the night before, Ebony had not slept well, but this was down to excitement (or nerves) rather than bad dreams. Returning to the woodland excited her for several reasons, most notably because few others knew about it. Her father would be furious if he were to find out, but she pushed the thought to one side. Everyone had little secrets, including him.

Just short of jumping from her bed, Ebony was out the front door within five minutes, putting on her brown dress and collecting the things she thought she might need before putting them in her wicker basket. She arrived at the meeting point about ten minutes early but did not mind waiting as long as Alim kept to the agreed time.

Ebony dropped her watch into the wicker basket and reached into a pocket on her dress' front, removing the heart-shaped crystal her mother had given her. Although not worried for the morning ahead, Ebony had instinctively brought the jewel with her. As always, perhaps it would bring good luck.

Ebony scanned the various streets and buildings across Wilheard before turning her attention towards The Wooden Duck, where she expected Alim to appear. She had seen nearly a dozen people wandering about, primarily Wilheard soldiers, all of whom she gave a passing glance while making sure not to seem suspicious. Other people up and about were those preparing for the annual Summer Festival. Their presence worked in Ebony's favour to some extent, as they would divert possible attention away from her. Fortunately, she did not have to worry for too long as Alim was the punctual type and far better than Ebony when arriving on time.

Clumsily fiddling with his smoking pipe, Alim looked unsteady on his feet as he made his way up the sloped route towards Ebony. He was slightly hung-over yet had a smile despite a sore head.

Remnant Tales of Stilly:
Passion and Benevolence

'Fair morn, Mister Larring,' Ebony said. 'Pardon me for saying, but you look a little worse for wear this morning,'

Alim continued grinning, placing the stem of his pipe on his bottom lip and ruffling his already unkempt hair. 'Fair Morn, Ms Gibenn... This town sure has a lively group of people, let me tell you.'

'Are you all right?'

'Fine, dear girl—as you pointed out, worse for wear—but fine all the same.'

Ebony smirked. 'You look as if you had fun last night.'

Alim tittered, still rubbing his head as he looked towards the ground. 'Indeed. Despite initially keeping to myself with a flagon of ale, I managed to get tangled up in the merriment of a nearby group led on by a lively blonde-headed woman. I'm still not sure how, mind you.

A lively blonde-headed woman, Ebony thought. She knew a farmer who fit that description.

Alim continued. 'There was singing and dancing and drinking... I refrained from the former two, but not so much the latter.'

'Well, you'll get little sympathy from me, I'm afraid,' Ebony chuckled. 'But it is good you are enjoying Wilheard's nightlife.'

Alim took a puff on his pipe, ditched the remaining tobacco from the chamber and placed it in a waist pouch. 'Just so. Shall we be off?'

It was nearly two hours into the journey when the pair stopped for a rest. This was on Ebony's request, who seemed to suffer more from the humid atmosphere than Alim. She swallowed a mouthful of water from one of the flasks in her basket and offered Alim some. He declined, too busy studying a flower he had picked. Ebony shrugged and took another sip. Despite the amount of time the two of them had been inside the forest, she had a feeling that they had not delved as far as they could; everything interested Alim, all of which seemed to demand a closer look.

'What fantastic petals,' Alim uttered, twirling his picked purple and yellow bloom by its stem. 'I've not seen one quite like this before.'

'They say you shouldn't touch exotic-looking things found while travelling,' Ebony said. 'That is very true, dear girl. Alas, you don't see much in the way of colour in Thane.'

Remnant Tales of Stilly:
Passion and Benevolence

Ebony swallowed one last mouthful of water and returned the flask to her basket. 'What is Thane really like? I know it is busy, but what of the city itself?'

'It certainly is busy… full of stone buildings and the like. I admit it has a lot of history to discover, but there is only so much a man can see before he needs to go farther afield.'

'I suspect your grandfather thought the same way. What about your parents?'

Alim's smile faded. He sighed. 'My grandfather always wanted to learn more… not so much my parents.'

Ebony frowned. She recalled Alim had not been so keen to talk about his home the last time she mentioned it. Perhaps his parents were the reason. 'I'm sorry. I seem to have touched upon a raw subject.'

Alim flicked the flower away. 'No need to apologise, dear girl. I admit that my last visit with my parents was less than gracious—at least with my father. He does not have and never has had any interest in his father's—that is my grandfather's—past time, and he has likewise never been pleased that I showed interest.'

Ebony had nothing to say, so she simply nodded.

Alim continued. 'My mother seemed more apathetic to my interests. I got no trouble from her but little support, either.'

'I'm sorry,' Ebony repeated.

'Like I said, dear girl, there is no need for apologies. I won't let such minor complications deter me.'

'That's good,' Ebony said. 'At least you now have someone interested in your journeys. If you need any support, I can always lend an ear.'

'Appreciated,' Alim said, his smile restored. 'What about your parents, dear girl? Do they share your zeal for exploration?'

Ebony wrinkled her nose. 'My father doesn't have an exploratory bone in his body, and I am not sure he ever has. He is quite happy to keep to what he knows. As for my mother… well, she *did* like to see new places, I suppose, but…'

Ebony sighed.

'I'm sorry, Ms Gibenn. Is your mother…?'

'She disappeared about ten years ago during a storm while travelling to Thane. There was a large search, but no one found her body.'

There was a moment's silence.

'That puts my family troubles into perspective,' Alim said. 'I'm terribly sorry.

'That's all right,' Ebony said. Like you, I'm not going to let others' opinions stop me from living my life. Besides, my mother would not want to hold me back.'

'That is what life is all about,' Alim said. 'It is good that you--'

Alim ended his sentence prematurely and turned his attention in the opposite direction to Ebony.

Getting to her feet, Ebony looked in the same direction as Alim. 'Are you all right?'

Appearing as if listening for something, Alim did not answer straight away. 'Did you hear that?' he said eventually.

Ebony listened for anything out of the ordinary. Moments later, she heard what sounded like the strum of a guitar. Without warning, Alim bolted in the direction of the sound. Not wanting to fall behind, Ebony snatched her basket from the ground and chased after him.

Alim was quicker than Ebony, yet she was nimble enough to keep him in sight. As she weaved between trees and leapt over mounds, she could not determine from which direction the sounds were coming, yet the more she sprinted, the clearer they became.

Darting behind a large tree, Alim temporarily left Ebony's line of sight. As soon as she made her way round the same tree, Ebony saw that Alim had come to a halt, but so had the strumming.

Out of breath, Alim leant one arm against a nearby tree and closed his eyes. Ebony joined him and sat down with her back against the trunk. She clutched one of Alim's trouser legs. 'You're a fast one,' she panted. 'I won't let you... run any farther until I... have caught my breath.'

In between panting, Alim chuckled. 'I haven't run... like that in a long while. Sorry... if I surprised you. I promise that... I won't leave you behind, dear girl.' He eventually steadied his breathing. 'Well done for keeping up with me, all the same.'

Remnant Tales of Stilly:
Passion and Benevolence

Once she had regained her breath, Ebony stood back up. 'Do you know where we are?' She asked as she gazed round.

'Somewhat. I cannot be entirely certain, but I believe the bust of King Godfrey is five hundred or so metres over there'—Alim gestured vaguely to his left—'and if I am correct, then we are south of the statue. Do you know what that means?'

'We are behind the statue?' Ebony replied. She felt a little silly for saying that, but from Alim's nodding, it must have been the correct answer.

'That's right. We are *behind the king*,' he said emphatically. 'I forgot to mention. That parchment I told you about yesterday—the one with a basic form of the Pentominto Alphabet on it. Well, I found it not long after you left and got to work translating that script in my grandfather's note. I believe it reads, "Into the woods; follow directly behind the king. The lonely grave; find nothing within.".'

'Sounds like a rhyme,' Ebony said. 'It has a sadness to it.'

'The words do have a particular darkness to them. Talk of graves and loneliness can arouse such feelings, I guess.'

'I suppose so. There is a point to the words, I assume.'

Alim hummed in contemplation. 'I'd be surprised if there isn't—my grandfather was not a man to write senselessly. Unfortunately, the only part that makes sense so far is the first. How far behind the king one must follow is anyone's guess. We will need to ponder more on the matter, wouldn't you agree, dear girl?' Alim looked at Ebony and waited for an answer, yet her mind was elsewhere. 'I said, wouldn't you agree…?'

Ebony placed an index finger on Alim's lips. 'Hold that thought,' she said, looking round. 'I think I heard something.'

'Is it more strumming?' Alim whispered.

Ebony shook her head. 'I heard rustling.'

The pair crept towards where the sound was coming from. Ebony stayed just behind Alim, her hand in her wicker basket and clutching her pocketknife. As they got closer, Alim gestured for Ebony to keep back. She stopped where she was and watched as he sneaked nearer, carefully looking into the nearby foliage. What happened next gave both of them a start.

From the bush, a badger jumped just to Alim's left. He stumbled back and landed on his rump. As soon as it touched the ground, the badger bolted in the opposite direction from where Ebony was standing. It paused a moment to look at the two humans, snorted, and then ran away.

The pair giggled.

'I think you woke him from his sleep,' Ebony said, putting the knife in her dress pocket before helping Alim back to his feet.

'I must have.' Alim brushed himself down. 'It seemed a bit ill-tempered.'

Regaining their composure, the two again listened for anything over the sounds of cheeping birds and rustling leaves. A short while later, they looked at one another.

'Is that running water?' Alim said, taking the words from Ebony's mouth.

Several yards behind the bushes from where the badger had pounced stood an ivy-concealed wall of sarsen stone. Taking a few steps back, Ebony and Alim noticed that the wall stretched about a hundred metres in either direction. Following an easterly route, the structure eventually led to a pile of boulders amid felled trees. The boulders had come from a nearby cliffside, and judging from the damage, Alim reasoned that the rocks fell in a landslide, most likely caused by a storm.

Alim pulled his smoking pipe from its pouch, tapped a stone that made part of the rubble with the chamber butt and then sprinkled tobacco into it. He took a few steps back and puffed on his pipe as he lit it. 'Seems this debris once formed an entrance.'

Ebony had come to the same conclusion. She closed her eyes and again listened to the distant trickling of water. 'I do not remember seeing an obvious way past the wall. Then again, I did see--'

She re-opened her eyes and saw Alim scaling the wall, using the knots of ivy to hoist his way up. 'What are you doing?'

Yanking himself to the top, Alim whistled in amazement as he peered at what was now before him.

'What do you see?' Ebony called again from below.

Alim sat so that his legs were on either side of the wall. 'It's breathtaking, dear girl. Come take a look.'

Ebony's eyebrows raised in the middle.

Alim scratched the back of his head upon noticing the worry on Ebony's face. 'You don't have to worry about propriety with me, dear girl.'

'It's not that, honestly. It's just… I don't feel comfortable climbing up there.'

Alim thought for a moment. 'Oh, I see. Not one for heights, eh? Don't worry, I understand.'

'That's good. Anyway, I was going to say that I saw what looked like an opening not too far along'—Ebony pointed to a tree just round the curvature of the wall—'I'll go and have another look.'

'Very well,' Alim said, standing up atop the stones and making Ebony's stomach turn. 'I'll follow you round. I promised I would not leave you behind, after all.'

It did not take long for Ebony to relocate the hole. Regrettably, even after using her hands to brush away vines and other bits of greenery, the gap was too small for her to fit. She knelt down and peered through.

'How does it look, dear girl?' Alim called.

Ebony puckered her lips while continuing to study the gap. She shook her head.

Alim eased his way down the wall and looked at Ebony from the other side. He glanced at the edges of the opening and then stood again. Still peering through, Ebony watched as he walked off, only to return a moment later with a tree branch.

'Ok, Ms Gibenn, stand back.'

Alim poked at the inside of the hollow, causing parts of it to crumble, and after a couple minutes of prodding and scraping, he gave the wall a kick. The stone directly above the hole dislodged, causing the insides to loosen further.

Clearing the hole from the remaining fragments, Alim looked through to Ebony once more and grinned. 'There you go, dear girl—a bit of initiative gets the job done.'

Ebony raised the corner of her mouth into a smirk. 'You vandal.'

She inspected the hole again. The entry was certainly wider: enough for her to squeeze through, at least. Her concern now, however, was whether it would be safe to do so.

With her belly inches from the ground, Ebony pushed her basket through the hole and then slid her hands to the other side. Alim remained near the opening the whole time, ready to help.

As she wriggled along the floor, Ebony's dress snagged on a root. Fortunately, with the breadth of the wall only two feet, she was already most of the way through. She held out her hands for Alim to take.

Alim pulled Ebony free from the hole and helped her to her feet. 'Are you all right?'

Ebony looked down at herself. She was a mess; grass stains and dirt covered her front, while the right side of her dress had torn near the thigh. 'It has been a while since I got this filthy—I am glad I chose my brown dress. This will take a bit of explaining to Father.'

Standing side-by-side, Ebony and Alim gazed about the enclosure in wonderment. Trees, mounds and rocks surrounded a spring of clear water. Everything looked largely untouched by human hands.

'Who would have thought such a place existed in Wilheard's woodland,' Ebony uttered. 'It is beautiful.'

'Without a doubt,' Alim agreed. 'This place is calling to be explored. Do you mind if I... have a look round?'

'By all means—I think I'll do the same,' Ebony said. 'Keep your climbing to a minimum, though. I might want to see what you are doing after a while.'

Alim gave a pleased nod, speaking as he walked away. 'Don't worry. I suspect I won't need to do much in the way of climbing. Give me a call if you need me.'

Ebony watched Alim plod towards the spring and then make his way round the water's edges. Getting his attention may prove difficult if the king's bust was anything to go by.

Never mind, Ebony thought as she removed her shoes, leaving them alongside her wicker basket. She approached the spring and looked down into its waters; she had never seen her reflection look so clear beyond that of a mirror. She dipped a finger into the centre of her face, causing the image to ripple. The water was more tepid than it appeared.

Remnant Tales of Stilly:
Passion and Benevolence

Ebony waded to the middle of the spring and peered up at the towering trees, their leaf-covered branches stretching towards the centre of the spring and casting vast shadows. The overhanging branches did not block the light entirely, though; the blue sky shone amid them.

A sense of serenity washed over Ebony then. Any troubles she might have had were left on the other side of the wall. Ebony closed her eyes and took a deep breath. It seemed ironic that she would appreciate such an ambience. Notwithstanding recent occurrences, tranquillity was not something Wilheard lacked.

Ebony's eyelids snapped open upon the call of her name.

'Ms Gibenn,' Alim cried from the west of the spring. 'Come take a look at this, dear girl. You won't believe what I have just uncovered.'

Droplets of water splashed up Ebony's legs as she paced towards Alim. She followed him across a path of smooth rocks and under willow branches until they reached what appeared to be a dead end.

Alim moved towards the cliffside and squatted. After scraping away at some moss, he looked back to Ebony and gestured for her to come closer. She crouched next to him and examined the cleared patch.

'There are signs of carvings under all this,' Alim commented as he continued to scour the stone. 'I find that generation of moss build-up tends to protect this kind of thing from a lot of wear and tear. The different seasonal temperatures deteriorate stone over prolonged periods, and...'

Alim continued to chatter away as he worked, eventually clearing the cliffside to the point where Ebony could see an elongated stone.

'I should probably feel guilty,' Alim wittered on, 'removing the mould will only expose what lies beneath to sudden atmospheric change. At least I will be able to chronicle our findings.'

'Vandal,' Ebony said playfully before shifting her attention to the ground. 'Is it just me, or does the soil look like it has been disturbed?'

Alim hopped back a pace and looked at the earth. He brushed his fingers along the top. 'Quite right—it looks like someone has been here already. It is as if an excavation has taken place... *The lonely grave; find nothing within.*'

'Do you believe this is the grave in your grandfather's hidden note? Do you think he exhumed the remains?'

Remnant Tales of Stilly:
Passion and Benevolence

Alim furrowed his brow as he pondered the question. 'I cannot see what he would gain from such a grisly act. Besides, from what I remember of the old boy, that wasn't his style when exploring. He would certainly do many things while investigating a site, but his notes were the only parts he would generally take away.'

Ebony nodded and looked back to Alim. His frown remained.

'A stinnep for your thoughts,' Ebony said.

'These pointed marks on the stone'—Alim indicated several scratch lines along the middle of the carved cliffside—'They do not coincide with someone trying to get into the grave. Rather, it is as if someone was trying to claw out.'

Ebony gave the markings a closer look. Indeed, it was as if someone had tried to prevent their own burial. She moved her hand over the scratches; each one was thinner than her own fingers, yet too spaced apart for someone smaller to have made them. Whatever the case, the prospect made her shudder.

The distant noise of falling stones sounded then, startling the pair.

'Just a few loose boulders, no doubt,' Alim reassured.

Ebony shuddered again. 'This place is starting to give me the creeps.'

'You're not alone there,' Alim admitted. 'In any case, I am unable to read what is on the stone. It is a mixture of Pentominto and archaic Stillian. I'll quickly jot it all down, and we'll be on our way. That is, if you don't mind, of course.'

Alim and Ebony retraced their footsteps, again ducking the willow branches before making their way round the spring.

Brushing the soles of her feet and putting her shoes back on, Ebony nodded towards the wall and to where she had entered. 'You are stronger than you think. That explains the crumbling sound from a moment ago.'

The hole Ebony had crawled through earlier had caved in, the sarsen stone now spilling outwards and away from the spring. Alim was surprised his actions could have caused such a collapse. 'Well, at least we can pass a lot easier.'

Ebony picked up her basket. 'I'll grant you that… you vandal. At least no one was hurt.'

Remnant Tales of Stilly:
Passion and Benevolence

Ebony and Alim left the spring, stepping over the fallen stones and returning towards Wilheard.

'It has been quite an eventful morning so far, wouldn't you agree, dear girl? Alim chirped. 'We made some superb discoveries, albeit we did not find the source of that strumming.'

Ebony did not answer; her mind was elsewhere. She pulled out her pocket watch. The time was nearing 9am.

Alim patted Ebony on her upper arm. 'Are you all right?' he asked her, failing to get much of a response. 'I hope you are not disappointed about today's trip.'

Ebony stirred from her inattention. 'Oh, not at all. I was just seeing how long we have been exploring.'

'Is that it? Something seems to be troubling you.'

'Well. It might just be paranoia, but…' She paused. 'Don't worry, I'm just being silly.'

Alim gazed at Ebony for a moment but did not question her further.

Indeed, something was bothering Ebony, and this was visible from the look on her face. She could not shake the feeling that something was nearby, and her anxiety only worsened when she heard what sounded to be a low growl.

Ebony froze on the spot. 'D-did you hear that?' she stuttered.

Alim slowed to a stop and nodded. 'Stay behind me, dear girl, and keep close.'

With Alim leading the way, the pair edged onwards while closely examining their surroundings. Nearly a minute later, the two walked round a thicket of bushy trees and came face-to-face with something unexpected.

'Tender spirits!' Alim exclaimed. 'A brown bear!'

Motionless, the two gazed at the animal with dread. The bear, evident by the staining about its snout, had been gorging on raspberries. Now sensing the presence of the two humans, it looked away from its meal, took a moment to sniff the air and then rose onto its hind legs.

Alim slowly took hold of Ebony's arm, ensuring not to make any sudden movements. 'Astonishing to find a bear in this region of Stilly,' he whispered. 'I'm no expert, but I know the last thing we should do is panic. Whatever you do, don't run.'

The bear roared in displeasure, its eyes wide and arms clawing at the air in a display of dominance.

Another deep growl sounded, but this time, it had not come from the bear.

In the space of a second, the bear slammed to the ground, an attack from its right rendering it instantly unconscious. An even bulkier creature had lunged at it as if from nowhere, pouncing like a predator on smaller prey.

Ebony and Alim remained stationary. Nothing could have prepared them for what they now faced.

Standing on four legs, the creature was eight feet of revolting malice. Half the size larger than the bear, the monster was unparalleled to any one animal Ebony had ever seen: its flattened face, loosely akin to that of a bulldog, had two oversized canine teeth that extended from its lower jaw and out from the mouth, reaching to either side of a stumpy, up-turned nose. Its torso was similar to a bull's, albeit devoid of any fur, as were its disproportionate legs: the hinds shorter than the fore.

The monster brought its head down close to the bear's, exposing its teeth at the unconscious victim and giving an intimidating growl. At first, it seemed unaware that anything else stood nearby... until it raised its eyes level with the terrified humans'.

Alim sprang into action, causing Ebony to gasp as he forced her along. Without letting go of her, he leapt between two close-standing trees. The monster, which immediately gave chase, bound the bear and thundered towards its new targets. As Alim pulled Ebony through the trees, the beast lunged, only to become wedged between the trunks, its lower teeth biting mere inches from the intended prey. Ebony and Alim stumbled forward from the force but remained unharmed.

The trees quivered on impact, the ground they were rooted in quaking from the beast's sheer power. Lurching back to their feet, Ebony, followed by Alim, lingered only long enough to see the creature wrench itself free, pushing and snapping the trees apart as if nothing more than rotted timber.

Taking advantage of the surroundings, Ebony and Alim continued running. Although managing to keep ahead of this unknown predator, they could not escape it entirely. Unable to pursue through the thickets, the creature moved to more open ground so that it was galloping on the other side of a dried ravine from its targets.

Salivating with rage, the monster kept its eyes on its prey to avoid losing them. This worked in Ebony and Alim's favour as the beast, through a lack of attention, staggered over rocks and fallen trees on several occasions. Unfortunately, this slowed it only temporarily.

Realising they could not outrun the beast forever, Alim did the unthinkable and stopped sprinting.

'What are you doing?' Ebony yelled incredulously.

'It's no use,' Alim panted. 'We can't outrun this thing forever. Keep moving in the same direction. We needn't both perish—I'll serve as a distraction.'

'No! I cannot do that... I will *not* do that! We must get out of this--'

Before Ebony could finish arguing, the monster was once again upon them. Being its closest target, the creature launched at Alim, only to land on something far more pointed.

In a moment of impulse, Alim had kicked up a tree branch and planted it into the ground. The branch passed the creature's fangs and penetrated the roof of its mouth. The makeshift stake snapped under the immense weight, succeeding in forcing the beast to one side but knocking Alim down in the process.

Hoisting itself upright, the beast shook its head to loosen the broken spike from its mouth, ultimately using its front paw to get the job done. A gush of tar-black blood followed the splintered wood. Watching Alim stand, the monster growled gutturally, a new and intense hatred awash in its eyes.

'Get out of here, Ebony!' Alim yelled, tossing a nearby rock at the creature and then running in the opposite direction as her.

Ignoring Ebony, the monster resumed its chase of Alim, spewing a trail of darkened saliva as it ran. If Alim had been able to look, he would have seen how terrifying his situation was; every tree or bush that might have served as an obstacle to the creature was decimated.

Remnant Tales of Stilly:
Passion and Benevolence

Upon reaching him, the monster barged Alim with the flat of its face, managing enough force to immobilise the man. The chase over, it halted and turned to find its victim, snorting in triumph.

Alim groaned. Dazed and exhausted, he was unable to comprehend exactly what had happened. He looked upwards at the light shining through the gaps in the trees, his spinning head blurring his vision.

The monster plodded over to Alim, positioning itself so that the man was between its front legs. The creature stared at him, its teeth bared and fixed into a silent growl. A string of drool hung from its fang, spilling onto the cracked glass of Alim's spectacles that, despite everything, had remained in place.

Blurred... focused... blurred... focused...

Alim watched an indistinct paw hover in front of him, gradually increasing in height. It looked huge. Tender spirits! Were those claws emerging from its fingers?

Alim closed his eyes. He did not feel the paw hit. The attack must have been too swift. He was dead... or at least that was what he had convinced himself. He could still feel the same dull pain in his lower back where the monster had barged him, and his head hurt with the same stubborn ache. Surely, this should no longer be so.

Alim reopened his eyes. His vision was still unfocused, yet he was able to see someone. Had an anjyl saved him? Alim could see the shape of a being to the creature's rear. Did anjyls exist after all?

'... Alim... Alim...'

The anjyl was shouting his name; she was trying to tell him something.

'Alim... get up! Quickly!'

Alim recognised the voice then.

The beast roared as a sharp pain shot through its back leg. Rushing up behind the monster, Ebony thrust her pocketknife into its thigh. She had dropped her basket while running through the forest but remembered that she had placed the knife in her dress pocket (next to her lucky charm heart) after the badger encounter.

The attack forced the monster to lose balance, its paw landing away from Alim's head.

'Alim!' Ebony called again. 'Hurry! We need to--'

The monster kicked its injured leg backwards, striking Ebony and knocking her off her feet.

The blade had snapped in the creature's leg, yet it ignored the pain. It turned its attention away from Alim and lumbered towards the woman. Stricken with fear, Ebony's limbs seemed to freeze. Her eyes widened, and her lips trembled as the monster lowered its head to its front paws. It was preparing to pounce.

'Ebony!' Alim yelled in dismay. If only she had got out of there when she had the chance. There was nothing more he could do for her now except hope she felt no pain for what would follow.

The monster sprang towards Ebony, bounding at least six feet into the air. Without a doubt, it would crush her.

As if appearing from the very heavens, the figure of a man leapt down from the tops of the trees, tackling the monster mid-air and smashing it to the ground with an earth-shuddering thud.

Blurred… focused… blurred… focused…

Alim's eyesight remained poor, and his broken glasses hindered his vision further. Was it a man he could see? The figure was tall, had brown hair and was holding what appeared to be a sword almost as big as the wielder himself.

Ebony feebly pushed herself up from the ground using her elbows. The man who had intervened stood almost motionless, staring impassively at the creature, unafraid and waiting for it to make the next move.

The monster righted itself and shook its head, dizzy from the knock it had endured. As expected, it turned to face its new adversary, belligerence exuding from its very being. However, unlike earlier, the creature paused; as if nervous, it shifted from side to side, snorting with irritation before letting off one last roar and attacking.

While the battle between the swordsman and the beast commenced, Alim finally managed to regain some balance and staggered towards Ebony, scooping her up in his arms and moving her from harm's way. 'Are you all right?' he asked her as she lay on his lap.

Ebony responded with a murmur and continued to look towards what was happening. Her eyes were barely open, and she was on the brink of falling unconscious.

'Everything is going to be all right. Just relax,' Alim whispered, looking towards the swordsman as well.

As the monster lunged with its mouth open wide, the swordsman grabbed it by the throat and slammed it onto its back.

Ebony's eyelids flickered in a futile attempt to stay open. As they closed, she heard the monster choke one last growl, followed by the sounds of a quick, yet unpleasant, death.

She slipped into unconsciousness then.

'It's this way, Wiley,' Meddia said, trying to hurry her mentor along.

Wiley smiled faintly. 'I have not forgotten where we live, Meddia.'

Meddia did not hear the remark. Dexter had given her the task of finding Wiley as quickly as possible, and find him quickly she had done.

Wiley maintained his smirk and bimbled behind the girl, hands in pockets. Meddia had failed to tell him what all the fuss was about, and she often got excited about matters that did not warrant the drama, yet this felt different.

"Dexter has summoned you". These had been Meddia's exact words. Wiley did not expect the word *summoned* to pass her lips ordinarily and that at least stirred some curiosity. Maybe there was a genuine reason for her haste. Incidentally, this was the first time Dexter had arrived home first in goodness knows how long. Wiley would avoid the urge to show his palm while he hung his coat and hat up before allowing the other man to speak. The idea was droll, even if a bit mean, especially since he was wearing neither of those things and would have to mock the actions.

Meddia jogged ahead when her home came into view and burst through the front door, forcing it to slam against the coat hanger on the other side.

Wiley tutted at the behaviour and prepared to give the teenager a lecture, yet the sight of Dexter gave him pause.

Dexter was pacing the width of the living room, wringing his hands together and mumbling to himself. Wiley had not expected to see such a man: gone the characteristic smile and air of self-confidence, replaced by an ashen wreck wearing his guise. Theryle did not seem to realise that anyone had entered the building, even with Meddia's uncourtly arrival.

Wiley called out to Dexter.

Dexter stopped marching and turned his head, glancing at the other man in a way that suggested he did not even recognise him. 'You will not believe the day I have had,' he said eventually before continuing the pacing.

'He's gone cuckoo,' Meddia whispered to Wiley. She was at a loss for anything appropriate to say or do, but she was sure her mentor would know how to handle the situation.

Wiley placed a comforting hand on her upper back, not taking his eyes away from Dexter. 'Do me a favour, Meddia, and go to your room for a little while. If you want, you can talk to Rida… just give me a minute to chat with Dexter.'

The girl did as instructed, speaking not a word as she darted up the stairs. Wiley now knew why she had been in such a hurry—the poor girl would have had quite a shock upon seeing Dexter, and it must have been a relief when she managed to find her mentor.

'Dexter.' Wiley stepped in the other man's path. 'Dexter. What has got into you?'

'I can't believe it,' said Dexter, the marching and hand wringing unceasing. 'I've had hours to digest it all, but…'

Wiley seized Dexter by the shoulders and shook him. 'Snap out of it, man! You are delirious. Tell me what has got you so worked up.'

Dexter's head swung back and forth as Wiley shook him, the latter moments away from adding a slap, but Theryle managed to utter something that made Wiley stop altogether.

Released from Wiley's grip, Dexter dropped to the sofa behind him. In an instant, he ended his panicking and sunk into the cushions with a sigh as if

216

too tired to worry any further. With darkened skin sagging under reddened eyes, his face certainly displayed as much.

'You have seen better days,' Wiley said. 'Can I get you something? Water, perhaps.'

Dexter blinked and gave a barely noticeable shake of the head.

Wiley sighed through his nose and sat next to Dexter, his gaze not once straying from the other man.

'It was supposed to be easy, Wiley—like any other day.'

Wiley took a moment to remember what Dexter had planned for the day past. If he recalled correctly, Theryle had wanted to track and follow Ebony Gibenn and a male associate.

'Yes, his name is Alim Larring,' Dexter said after Wiley asked. 'I followed the pair into the woodland as planned. Naturally, I kept out of sight as best I could, hiding behind bushes and climbing trees as I tried to keep up with the two. Yet, perhaps I have lost my touch—I am not as good as I once thought.'

Dexter revealed everything then. He told of the guitar sounds Ebony and Alim chased, the enclosed spring the pair inadvertently found, and even the supposed gravestone.

'The wall's collapse was my fault,' Dexter reflected as he continued his tale. 'That Alim had weakened the stones, but I was the one that caused them to give way. I was lucky they did not notice me.' Dexter swore as he remembered the incident. Wiley urged him to continue with his anecdote. 'Well, I say that *they* didn't notice me, but I got the attention of something altogether different... a bear of all animals.'

'A bear?' Wiley repeated dubiously. 'In Wilheard?'

'Yes, a bear—in Wilheard,' Dexter said, Wiley's reaction vexing him. 'Yet that is not the strangest thing of all. The bear caught sight of me when I disturbed its sleeping—it was resting between a cluster of boulders, and I had not seen it until I heard it practically breathing down my neck. In any case, I didn't hang about—I quickly got away from the animal, and it eventually lost interest. However, be it because of the bear, Ebony and Alim, or even me, the attention of something else was stirred... something which should not exist anywhere, let alone in Wilheard.'

Dexter continued explaining, talking about the beast with tusk-like teeth, how it hounded after Ebony and Alim, and how the vigilante came at the right moment to save the two.

'It happened all so fast. I wanted to help Ebony and Alim, but I felt powerless. What could I have done?' Dexter said, breathing another long sigh as he closed his eyes, seeing it all unfold again in his mind. He looked back to Wiley. 'You don't believe me, do you? That's all right... the boss was the same.'

Wiley remained solemn as the other man spoke. If not for Dexter's shaken state, such words would be difficult to trust.

'When did you tell Captain Burley of all this?'

'As soon as I got out of the forest.' Dexter shrugged. 'About noon, I guess.'

Wiley looked at the time. It was approaching 5 o'clock. 'And it has taken you this long to tell me about it? What have you been doing during that time?' He shook his head. 'Never mind, you do not need to answer that. I am sorry—you have clearly had a frightening experience. What did Captain Burley have to say?'

'He had many questions, but they were mostly to do with Ebony Gibenn, her scholar friend and the vigilante... especially the vigilante.'

'I see,' Wiley said. 'It is good that you have explained all this to Captain Burley. He can deal with what happens next. As for you, Dexter, the best thing you can do is get some rest—you look in need of a bed.'

Chapter Nine

Ebony woke to the sound of dripping water. Someone placed a damp flannel on her brow, its coolness soothing the aching in her head.

Her eyelids were heavy, but she could hear familiar sounds: the ticking of a clock... the soft creaking of floorboards... the ruffling of a quilt.

She was home and in her bed.

Opening her eyelids was more arduous than she could ever have imagined, and what she got for the effort made her regret even doing so; the light pouring in from her bedroom window stung her eyes, restoring the headache. Everything was indistinct, including the person sitting at her bedside, who could have been no more than a foot away.

'Perhaps you should keep your eyes closed a while longer, m'dear,' suggested a female voice. It belonged to Hazel. 'I can tell by the redness that they hurt.'

Ebony swallowed; her throat was hoarse. 'How long have I been sleeping?'

Hazel placed a hand on Ebony's nape and brought her head forward, pressing a cup of water to the stricken woman's lips. 'The best part of twenty-four hours,' she said, laying Ebony back down.

'Twenty-four hours,' Ebony repeated. 'Then my eyes have been closed for long enough.'

Ebony tried to sit up, only for Hazel to press her back down. 'I draw the line there, m'dear. You still need rest, whether you like it or not, and you can't just be rushing off.'

Hazel removed the flannel from Ebony's forehead and leant closer to examine her eyes. She gently widened them.

'Ouch!' Ebony complained. She tightened her eyes after Hazel dripped a liquid into them. 'That stings!'

'Sorry, Ebs. At least that should ease the soreness in the long term.'

Ebony sighed and let the eye drops get to work. The stinging dulled within a minute, easing entirely soon after. She rolled her head to one side and looked at her friend. 'I suppose I am not very popular right now.'

'Not with your pop, as you would expect. Sylvia managed to calm him down, though.'

'Sylvia?'

'Your dad's lady friend—Doctor Enpee?'

Ebony looked away from Hazel and towards the sloped ceiling. 'Father's lady friend, huh? It is nice to finally know her name.'

Hazel pursed her lips. 'Sorry, m'dear. I didn't realise the two of you hadn't met.'

'That's all right, Hazel. I'm sure I will get the chance soon. Then I can put a face to the name.'

'Well, that might not be for a while—They have gone out for a walk. Your pop still needs to cool off a bit. That might not be easy in this weather, mind.'

Hazel chuckled at the small joke, but Ebony remained sombre. 'He'll want to throttle me, I imagine. That is after I recover from my current state.'

'To be fair, m'dear, he would have every right to do so. You'll find, though, that his relief outweighs any anger. Which reminds me… he told me to clip your ear if you woke while he was out, but we can just pretend I did so.'

That made Ebony smile despite her situation.

Hazel exhaled audibly from her nose. 'I said going into the woodland was a bad idea, Ebs.'

Ebony did not respond, but the shame was evident on her face.

'Never mind that, though,' Hazel said. 'At least you are safe. Y'know, it was Sylvia who nursed and mended you—being a doctor and all.'

That made Ebony think of her mother Luanna, but she pushed the thought aside when she remembered someone else. 'Tender spirits! How could I forget about Alim?' She tried to sit up again, groaning as she did so. 'I hope he was not too badly hurt. Did he even return with me?'

Hazel once again restrained Ebony. 'Yes, and you will be pleased to hear that ol' Scruffy is fine. He said he was all right, but Sylvia insisted on checking him over a little, and she will likely do so again later. In fact, that might be sooner than expected—I believe she and your father planned to go to the surgery after their walk.

'That's good,' Ebony sighed in relief, relaxing again.

'You'll have to thank him later,' Hazel said. 'Although he says otherwise, Alim must have carried you most of the way back home. I spotted him while out on my milk round. I admit that seeing you strewn in his arms gave me quite a shock.'

Ebony grunted. 'I always imagined that being carried by a man would be more romantic... Oh well.' She looked back at her friend. 'What did Alim tell you?'

'He seemed unwilling to say much at first, but considering the situation,' Hazel shook her head. 'Mind you, I'm not surprised. He was probably worried about loosening his tongue. A man can't talk about monsters and superhuman swordsmen without sounding like he is having you on. See where I'm coming from?'

Ebony wrinkled her nose.

Hazel shrugged. 'I dunno, Ebs. I suppose I would believe it more if it came from your mouth.'

'I trust everything he said is true.'

'Even about the bear?'

'Yes, even about the bear.' Ebony shifted her legs out from under the quilt. Hazel moved to stop her friend, but this time, Ebony was insistent. She sat on the edge of her bed; the sudden change to an upright position made her head spin. 'You know we could not possibly be making this up, don't you? Why would we?

Hazel did not answer.

'Besides,' Ebony continued, 'why else would I be in such a state?'

Hazel shrugged again, not wanting to contradict her friend. It would have seemed unfair to put Alim in any negative light, especially since he brought Ebony home. 'I believe you, m'dear. Your pop is—or at least was—less convinced, but Sylvia will have persuaded him. In fact, your dad was ready to bite Alim's head off, but Sylvia was quick to side with him. She seemed to believe him straight away.'

'This Sylvia is starting to sound more interesting by the minute,' Ebony said. 'Did she say why she believes him?'

'No,' Hazel answered, shaking her head. 'Perhaps it was just the way Alim said it all. He could've just said that he found you unconscious in the woodland. Of course, I would have known he was lying. Anyway, Sylvia said that you mumbled his name while sleeping, which kinda indicates you know him.'

'She watched over me while I slept?'

'Don't sound so surprised, Ebs. As much as I would like to have been with you the whole time, I needed some sleep, too. Besides, with Sylvia being a doctor, who better to keep an eye on you when you are like this?'

'I appreciate that. It's just...' Ebony grumbled. She had still yet to wake up properly, leaving her unable to think straight. 'I am sorry for being churlish. I would have just... I mean... I would have preferred to meet Sylvia in better circumstances.'

'She was of a similar mind,' answered Hazel.

Ebony attempted to stand up then.

'Ebs, what are you doing?'

Ebony's knees shook as she got to her feet. Her legs were stiff, as expected, and the strength would take a moment to return. Thankfully, Hazel was quick to lend a shoulder. 'I don't know what you want me to say, Hazel. I have no doubt that what Alim told you is the truth, but I would like to speak with him myself. I want to know what happened when I fell unconscious.'

'Fair enough, but you can't just go rushing out the door, m'dear. Besides, Alim needs to rest too, and like I said before, Sylvia will want to check on him again.'

'I know,' Ebony said, 'but I'm not going to lie about in my bed all day, and certainly not after what I went through in the woodland. Thinking one of those monsters coming to the town makes me uneasy.'

'That is if there are any more,' Hazel said. 'Let's be serious, Ebs—I have never seen such monsters before, and I don't know anyone else to have even hinted that such things might be real.'

'I can't argue with that,' Ebony said, resisting the urge to scowl at Hazel's comment. 'All the same, I cannot just ignore such thoughts.'

By now, Ebony had regained enough balance to stand unaided. She looked down at herself; she was wearing a nightdress but could feel bandages underneath. Ebony took a few steps towards her wardrobe, cringing on the last step as a dull pain passed from her waist to her ribs. Doing her best to ignore further discomfort, she changed into one of her blue dresses.

'Oh, I almost forgot,' Hazel said as she helped lift Ebony's left arm into the dress's sleeve. 'The hunky Oliath Burley came round no fewer than three separate times while you slept. I'm not sure how he found out, but he seems to know about your little—shall we say—adventure into the woodland.'

Ebony blanched. 'R-really? If he knows, then who else could know?'

'I didn't mean to make you worry, m'dear. Oliath has been the only one to drop by… at least if you don't include those two that make up his shadow.'

Ebony thought on this a moment but eventually shrugged it off. 'Well, that might not be such a bad thing. If anyone should know about what happened to Alim and me, it should be Captain Burley. Do you know if he has spoken to Alim?'

Hazel shook her head. 'Not that I know of, Ebs.'

'In that case, perhaps I shouldn't go too far. I guess I needn't ask, but please stay with me, Hazel. I might need your support in more than just my step, and the last thing I want is to be alone.'

Sylvia looked out the window of her office and at the clouding sky.She was desperate to calm her thoughts until Alim Larring arrived for his medical, but nothing outside seemed to work as a distraction.

The end of the week was supposed to be a pleasant experience: Abraham introducing her to Ebony, the two women becoming firm friends swiftly. Instead, Abraham had taken the doctor to his cottage under circumstances she would never have wanted.

With Alim arriving shortly, Abraham had decided to wander round to the back of the surgery. He was not allowed in Sylvia's office when a patient was present, but he was likely not to stray far. Indeed, now that he had calmed down, he probably wanted to have a word with Alim, although Sylvia still preferred not to give him a chance.

Sylvia shifted her thoughts back to Ebony. *Everyone is all right. Ebony and Alim are alive, and that is what matters the most.* In principle, this was all she needed to tell herself, but the nagging questions at the back of her mind were proving difficult to ignore.

How could this have happened? That was a good question, but the next seemed more significant. *Where had Ninapaige been?* **She** *was supposed to look out for Ebony.* **She** *had promised that no harm would come to her.*

Sylvia was in two minds as to whether she wanted to see Ninapaige after all that had happened. She was livid, and it might take a lot of the imp's otherworldly power to hold her back. Then again, Sylvia knew there would be an excuse. She wanted to hear that, at least, before subjecting Ninapaige to her fury, and it would have to be a perfect excuse.

This would take place sooner than she anticipated.

Sylvia continued to look out the window. *Rain is the last thing I want to see,* she thought.

'It is needed, though,' came the near child-like voice of another woman, sounding from behind Sylvia. 'The trees and grass are rather parched. They will enjoy the respite from the dry air. Likewise, I tire from all the heat and look forward to some rain.'

Sylvia did not jump from Ninapaige's sudden appearance for the first time in a long while. Indeed, she did not react at all, at first pretending as if the little woman was not even there. 'If you are reading my thoughts, then you know what else I am thinking.'

Many of the words passing through Sylvia's head at that moment were vulgar, to say the least. She had come knowing that the reception would be frosty, and she understood why. All the same, Ninapaige smiled. 'These clouds have been a long time coming, but I suppose the past was going to rear its head eventually.'

'Don't pretend it never happened!' Sylvia snapped, the words seething through her teeth. 'You said you would take care of things.'

There was a moment pause then. Ninapaige cleared her throat. 'Without a doubt, things are about to get much more hectic—sooner rather than later. Yet, something else travels with those dark clouds, and--'

Remnant Tales of Stilly:
Passion and Benevolence

Then, in a sudden loss of control, Sylvia brought her arm round to where Ninapaige was sitting; her hand curled into a fist, she swung with a horizontal swipe, aiming for where the imp's head should have been. Somehow, she missed her target by a metre.

'I said *don't!*' Sylvia's eyes reddened as tears formed. 'You don't even have the dignity to show remorse for your failings. They could have been killed!'

In an instant, the room's atmosphere darkened. A chill filled the room, and the surrounding furniture shook. Sylvia knew then that she had done something like never before: she had upset Ninapaige.

'You dare?' fumed Ninapaige, her composure disappearing. 'You push your luck, child—you *provoke* me, child. I have done more for you than any human deserves—I did my utmost to protect, guide, and nurture... and now you say *this*? You selfish little wretch. How dare you!'

Sylvia cowered, a tear falling from her eye.

No harm came to the doctor; as quick as the air had intensified, so too did it calm.

Ninapaige, her anger diminished, looked at Sylvia levelly. 'You must understand, young human, that you are not the only one with whom I must contend. Despite your accusation, I *did* watch over the girl, and the boy with her. Despite what you wanted, I admit that I led Sombie to them. He is much better at protecting others than I am.'

'I-I am so sorry,' Sylvia stuttered. 'It's just...'

Ninapaige placed her hands on Sylvia's cheeks and lifted the doctor's head until their eyes met. 'I understand your feelings. Nevertheless, and as I said, something more blows with those dark clouds. It affects everyone, not just you, and even though I might have inadvertently made you believe otherwise, my powers are not absolute.' A smile returned to Ninapaige's lips then. It was all she could do to lighten the mood. 'I hope you do not attack all your patients like that.'

Sylvia managed a chuckle, thumbing the tears from her cheeks. 'Now that you mention it, Alim Larring should be here shortly.'

'Is that for an examination, or so you can question him?'

'Perhaps both. Alim aside, maybe it is time to reveal a few secrets.'

Ninapaige nodded. 'You might be right, and I am through arguing over the subject. I will not interfere, lecture or even give excuses, but heed my advice—trouble will accompany whatever you say or do. I have always done what I deem right, and I will leave you to do the same from now on.'

'I understand. You must be tired of all this,' Sylvia said. 'You must be tired of me … I know I am.'

Sylvia looked out the window again. Alim was heading towards the surgery. She turned to find Ninapaige, ready to suggest the smaller woman leave. As expected, however, she already had.

'Thank you for your co-operation, Ms Gibenn. I won't take up much of your time.'

Captain Oliath Burley sat down where indicated. Folding one leg over the other, he removed his notebook from a trouser pocket and looked through the untidy handwriting that filled the pages.

Sitting on the sofa opposite Oliath, Ebony looked to the floor as an uncomfortable silence filled the living room. Butterflies fluttered in her belly; she was uncertain whether she should be saying something.

Cordelia and Nolan were also present, standing like statues to either side of Oliath with their hands clasped behind their backs. To Ebony's side sat Hazel, who, unlike her friend, appeared relaxed. The blonde smirked at the giant lieutenants, amused by their stiffness.

Ebony took a moment to look out the window behind her. The weather was turning. 'Those rain clouds look ominous,' she said eventually, her voice barely louder than a whisper. 'Can I offer anyone a drink of tea?'

Oliath gave a broad smile that made him look as though he was in pain, an obligatory response on his part rather than genuine gratitude and one that showed he was unaccustomed to pleasantries. 'A kind gesture, Ms Gibenn, but as I said, this should not take long. I would like to get home before those—as you put it—*ominous clouds* begin pouring.'

Remnant Tales of Stilly:
Passion and Benevolence

Oliath took a deep breath and looked up from his notes, gazing directly into Ebony's eyes. 'At six-thirty yesterday morning, I have eyewitness report that you and one male accomplice by the name of'—he rechecked his notes—'Mister Alim Larring entered the eastern woodland. May I ask your intentions?'

Ebony dithered, looking towards Nolan and Cordelia, whose eyes seemed to narrow as she thought of a suitable answer. 'I... I mean, *we* were exploring something of historical value. It has something to do with Stilly's past, specifically Wilheard's. Alim is a scholar.'

'So I have heard,' Oliath said, scribbling new notes. 'And you were simply interested in his work?'

'Yes.'

Cordelia scoffed at Ebony's answer. This, in turn, made Hazel sneer.

Oliath continued. 'I see. Forgive me for saying this, but there have been rumours that you have shown an interest in the vigilante who—I guess one could say—lives amongst the trees. To tell the truth, Ms Gibenn, my investigation into this individual has been rather slow. I have also heard that you might have had a close encounter with said man. Can you confirm this?'

Ebony's mouth opened, but no words came out. She was amazed how Oliath had come about such information.

Hazel was also curious. 'The hills have eyes and the trees ears, it seems.'

Oliath smirked. 'I have my ways of obtaining information. These assets are a necessity at times, and I hope you do not think that I abuse my authority.'

'Of course not, m'dear, but perhaps you could put your *assets* to better use. Maybe they can search for the vigilante directly.'

'They have their limits, Ms...?'

Hazel grinned. '*Miss* Dolb—and it was just a suggestion, m'dear.'

Oliath's upper lip twitched. 'Ah, yes... I remember you now. You're the one who works on the farm.' He turned his attention back to Ebony. 'One of my employees claims that he was in the woodland near the same time as you, Ms Gibenn. For whatever reason, I do not know—perhaps it was just another attempt to find this vigilante. In any case, my man states he spotted you and Mister Larring intermittently and that you ran into a bit of trouble.' Oliath unfolded his leg and sat forward. 'It so happens that this employee of mine is in a state of shock. He mentioned something—not to put too fine a point on it—far-fetched. I might be able to accept his tale more willingly if someone else can provide similar accounts. That is, someone as noble as you, Ms Gibenn.'

Cordelia scoffed again. Hazel snorted back.

'Well, it sounds as if your man knows as much as—or even more than— me.' Ebony moved one hand to her side, placing it on her midriff and where the bandages lay. 'Alim and I were attacked by a creature I had never seen before. I am uncertain what happened precisely, but I believe the vigilante saved us. He means no harm.'

This time, Nolan made a noise, coupling it with a sneer.

Oliath nodded. 'If you say so, Ms Gibenn, but I must insist that all concerns are handled by the proper authorities.'

'Can I ask another question, m'dear?' Hazel blurted. 'Is it necessary for your guard dogs—no offence intended—to be here? Forgive me if they have a cold or something, but there does seem to be a lot of unsavoury noises coming from your side of the room.'

Oliath regarded Hazel with a frown. He gestured for Nolan and Cordelia to go and stand outside, which they did promptly, glowering at the two women as they walked away.

Oliath looked out the window behind Ebony. The rain had already started: sporadic droplets beat against the windowpane before meandering down and onto the sill. He closed his notebook and stood up from the chair. 'Thank you for your assistance, Ms Gibenn. It seems your description matches my man's story.'

Ebony looked down to the floor without saying anything.

'If you have any more information about what we discussed, be it new or something you forgot to mention, please don't hesitate to come directly to me. If it concerns the vigilante, it would be best not to speak with Benjamin Oswin. The Vultures have a tendency to find out things when he does.'

'Vultures?' Ebony repeated.

'Reporters, Ms Gibenn,' Oliath explained. 'I can say from experience that things become hectic when that lot catches onto something. Believe me when

I say they are persistent and rather irritating, and you do not want them pestering you every moment of the day. Let's keep knowledge of your escapade to a minimum if possible.'

Closing the front door behind Oliath, Ebony turned to Hazel. 'I feel this was not the most official of visits.'

Hazel yawned with apathy. She had not considered such a thing. 'How so?'

'Well, he specifically mentioned Mister Oswin. Oliath said it is because of reporters, but I think there is another reason he wants me to stay away from Benjamin and go straight to him about the vigilante.'

'Yeah, now that you mention it, Ebs, I don't think that Ben and Mister Hunky get along too well.'

'What makes you say that?'

'Wilheard Hall is just down the street to the farm. I oft see Oliath and Ben getting each other's backs up. At least, that is how it seems.'

'Maybe.' Ebony folded her arms and closed her eyes. 'Anyway, judging from Captain Burley's word use, I'd say he dislikes the vigilante—or at least does not trust him.'

'True,' Hazel nodded lazily. 'You'd think Oliath would be a little thankful for the help.'

'I don't know. When the vigilante first showed, I overheard news reporters talking down to Oliath. They tried to cover it with flattery, but their questions ultimately criticised his efforts.'

'Don't think too much about it, Ebs—I have a feeling everything will make sense soon. For now, I think I'll take you up on that cup of tea you offered earlier. Just listening to the rain is making me cold.'

Sitting on the sofa in the living room, Wiley listened to the rain hammering on the roof of his home. It was loud, and he could barely hear himself think for the racket. He supposed that he had little to think about anyway.

Excluding Dexter, Captain Burley had not spoken to him or any of his housemates in the past day, leaving him lethargic from doing nothing.

Upstairs and in his room, Dexter lay in solitude. Wiley had not seen his housemate for several hours, but that did not concern him; he assumed that Dexter was sleeping, yet that was not a certainty. Theryle was not about to forget what he had seen in a hurry, whatever that truly was, and Wiley imagined the man wanted to be left alone to make sense of it all. If Dexter, on the other hand, was asleep, then Wiley commended him.

Blasted rain!

Rida was probably asleep despite the noise, but that would not have surprised Wiley. When it came to the unreasonable and Rida, not much did surprise him. Incidentally, Wiley noticed that Priory had been unusually quiet lately. It was as if the little man were hiding something. That, if true, would not surprise Wiley either. All the same, it did not particularly interest him; the less he thought about Rida, the less annoyed he would feel.

After a futile attempt to think of something constructive to do, Wiley gave up and turned his attention to Meddia, who was standing in front of a window. Initially, she had been content simply to watch the downpour saturate everything outside, but she soon moved onto entertaining herself with the condensation on the windowpane, drawing obscure pictures with her finger before her breath re-misted the glass. Wiley admired the girl's ability to amuse herself so easily. In fact, it made him almost envious.

Contrary to Wiley's belief, Meddia's interest in her doodling was waning. With the thick clouds forming a depressing gloom over the town, the girl tired from looking outside before long and turned from the window. Bounding across the room, she leapt onto the cushion next to her mentor, causing the both of them to bounce. For once, Wiley did not react to her behaviour. He continued to look where she had been standing.

Meddia stared wide-eyed at Wiley, looked to where he was gazing, and then back towards him. 'What-cha thinking about?' she asked eventually.

His thoughts interrupted by the sudden question, Wiley stirred from his daydreaming and looked at Meddia blankly. Whatever he had been thinking about, it had since faded. Wiley repositioned his glasses on the bridge of his nose and shifted his attention back outside. 'It is hard to think of anything for all the noise.' He looked back to Meddia and smiled. 'Are you looking forward to the Summer Festival? It should be up and ready in a few days.'

Meddia beamed and nodded. 'Yes. I hope it don't rain, though.'

'You hope it *doesn't* rain. Come now, Meddia, I have taught you better than that,' Wiley corrected.'

'Sorry,' Meddia pouted. 'I hope there will be fun games at the festival— especially that Disc Toss game. I like that one.'

'Yes,' chuckled Wiley, thinking back to last year's festival. 'You were really good at that one.'

Indeed, Wiley seemed to remember that the girl had been much better than everyone else who played. The aim of Disc Toss was as simple as the name suggested: fling the five discs provided at one of several slits cut into a wooden board. The board stood just over two metres away, and directing the discs into the targets, which were only three times the discs' thickness, was tricky enough, yet the marks behind the board were the real goals. The challenger needed to hit the target through the gap with enough force so the prize perched atop it tumbled down. No matter how carefully Wiley trained his throw, he could not get the discs through his chosen target. The heavy-handed Meddia, however, was far luckier. Tossing the discs almost haphazardly, she won a prize on her second attempt. That was just as well, as the first disc had made a resonating *thwack* as it struck the board, ricocheting and missing an onlooker by mere inches.

Wiley again woke from his daydreaming. He murmured softly. 'It would be a shame for the rain to spoil such an occasion.' He stood from his seat and walked to the same window from which Meddia had been looking. 'Let us hope this is a one-off summer storm. Still, this is quite the downpour. I cannot remember the last time I saw one quite like--'

Before Wiley could finish his sentence, he was cut off by the sound of someone rushing down the stairs. He turned to find Dexter, who had sweat streaming down his face.

'Dexter?' Wiley said, giving the other man a look of concern. 'Whatever is the--'

'Can't you hear it?' Dexter interrupted. 'Another one of those *things* is outside… It is in the town—I can sense it.'

A distant rumble of thunder sounded then as if to complement Dexter's panic.

Meddia raised her eyebrows into a worried frown. She looked towards Wiley. 'What *thing*? What is Dexter talking about? Are we in trouble?'

Wiley did not answer the girl; instead, he chose to walk towards her and put a consoling arm round her shoulders. 'Calm yourself, Dexter. You look half-asleep... are you sure you heard what you think?'

'Do *not* treat me like a fool, Wiley!' Dexter snapped. 'I can sense it... I recognise the sound of their movements—even that stench they carry. You did not see what I witnessed within the forest. How can you possibly tell me to keep calm?'

This time, a louder clap of thunder followed Dexter's words, making Meddia flinch. She wrapped her arms about Wiley's midriff and squeezed.

Wiley moved his hand over Meddia's ear and enveloped her head into his chest. 'I do not mean to patronise you, Dexter, but tender spirits, man, you are upsetting Meddia!'

Dexter sniggered mirthlessly, a toothy smile spreading across his face. 'Really? A pity to be sure, but the girl is not exempt from this creature's malice, and she will suffer these horrors just like everyone else in this damned town.'

Wiley's mood dropped then. 'Stop this nonsense now! Even if what you say has a single shred of credibility, do you honestly believe your current behaviour is at all appropriate?'

Dexter's grin melted away. He gave Wiley a searching look. 'You still don't believe me?'

Wiley did not answer; he concentrated on Meddia's well-being.

'That's all right. I understand.' Dexter moved away from the stairs and towards the front door. 'I appreciate your misgivings—I would be the same in your position, truth be told.'

Dexter dragged his long coat from the stand, swinging it over his shoulders and shrugging it on.

Wiley let go of Meddia and darted towards Dexter. 'Where do you think you're going? You plan on going out there in this weather?'

Dexter ignored the questions and proceeded to put on his wide-brimmed hat.

'Are you out of your mind, man?' Wiley said, placing a firm hand on Dexter's shoulder.

Dexter batted Wiley's arm away and shoved the taller man into the table that centred the room, causing one of the chairs about it to topple down with him. Wiley grimaced and placed a hand on his lower back.

Another crash of thunder sounded, shaking the foundations of the building.

Dexter straightened his coat, keeping an eye on Wiley. 'How can I prove this to you if I don't go outside? You should come as well, but it doesn't matter if you don't—you'll see it soon enough. I need to face my fears, anyway, so whether you come or not is up to you. Just don't get in my--'

Dexter did not finish what he had intended to say. Meddia, who had sneaked up behind the man as he spoke, jumped at him, knocking his hat off in the process. She clung to his back, wrapping her arms and legs about him and eventually causing him to fall. Wiley took advantage of the moment and pinned Dexter down with Meddia's help.

Dexter squirmed to escape the detention, but his attempts proved futile. The combined strength of his friends was too much for him, especially in his weakened state. After only a short while, he gave up, panting from exhaustion.

Letting Dexter go, Wiley and Meddia stood up from the floored man and stepped away. Dexter slowly sat up and wrapped his arms round his knees. 'Look out the window and tell me what you see,' he said.

Wiley did as asked and peered through the rain-streaked glass. 'I see people coming out from their houses.' He frowned.

'Yes… I can hear them shouting.' Dexter remained where he was. '*They* can hear it too.'

'What's goin' on down 'ere,' Rida said, taking everyone in the living room by surprise. He was standing at the foot of the staircase. 'I woz tryin' to sleep, but I can't do that wiv you lot makin' all this noise.'

Wiley sneered. 'Sorry to have disturbed you, my lord. If it is no trouble, do us all a favour and go back to that hole you call a living space and--'

Remnant Tales of Stilly:
Passion and Benevolence

Before Wiley could finish his rejoinder, a creaking from the house's roof cut him off. The spine-chilling sound made its way from one end of the building to the other, stopping above where Wiley was standing. A resonant growl followed, piercing through the roaring rain.

Meddia returned to her mentor's side. 'What was that?' she trembled.

'*That* is the sound of one of those creatures,' Dexter answered, standing up from the floor, 'and when you see it, you will wish I had lied.'

It seemed night had come early.

Standing under the entrance porch of her home, Ebony peered down at the rest of the village. Visibility was low: the rain was so torrential that everything appeared smudged, and the dull light of candles and lanterns was barely noticeable. Most of the glow, Ebony guessed, was from inside households, but some of the dotted light seemed to be floating along the streets and roads, darkness concealing the carriers. Although most of the lanterns likely belonged to Wilheard Guards, Ebony wondered if civilians had ventured outside for the same reason as she.

There was a flash of lightning, followed shortly by a grumble of thunder.

Hazel peered outside the front door of the cottage to find Ebony. 'Come inside, Ebs,' she said, beckoning her friend. 'You'll catch a fever at this rate, and ya still need a little more time to mend. Trust me, that growling you heard was just thunder.'

Ebony did not respond; she shuddered and continued to gaze into the downpour. The growling she had heard a moment ago had definitely not been thunder. 'I wonder where Father is,' she said, not looking for a response. 'He and that Sylvia have still not come home.'

Hazel shifted outside to stand closer to Ebony. 'They are taking shelter elsewhere, I imagine, as you should be.'

Ebony again chose not to respond. She lifted her attention towards Sanct Everard. Out of all the buildings, the soft light illuminating the stained-glass window fronting the sancture was the most noticeable, albeit also muted by the rain. Peering farther north, Ebony noticed another light source different from all the others.

To the top of Castle Way, coming from the easternmost tower of the castle itself, shone what appeared to be mauve fire. Although not much brighter than the other specks of light below, it stood out all the same.

Why was there a fire in the castle at all? The edifice was sealed to the public and had been for many years.

'Can you see that?' Ebony said, pointing. 'There… in the castle.'

Hazel peered to where Ebony was pointing. Hidden in darkness, she could not see the castle itself until lightning struck, yet it did not take long for her to spy the flame.

The distant shriek of another woman pierced through the storm then. 'Up there on the hill… near that cottage! What is that thi—?'

A boom of thunder drowned the woman's voice before she could finish what she had to say. However, Ebony and Hazel soon realised the reason for the woman's panic.

Stepping from the shadows, a beast emerged at the south of the cottage: tusk-like teeth, thick limbs, and the body of an oversized bull.

Ebony instantly recognised the creature. Ignoring the pain of her bruised body, she snatched a stunned Hazel by the wrist and pulled her into the cottage.

The monster darted from behind the building and leapt towards where the two women had been standing. Slipping on the sodden grass, it crashed into the cottage, obliterating the porch and cracking the surrounding walls as it wedged into the doorframe. Unperturbed, the creature attempted to claw into the house, using its fangs to strip whatever got in the way.

Escaping from the backdoor via the kitchen, Ebony led Hazel down the hill and towards New Market Square. The two women ran for what seemed like an eternity, not looking back to see if the monster had realised they were no longer in the cottage. Ebony's hair and clothes, quickly saturated by the downpour, clung to her skin. She could barely see what was before her but heard crashing all around. The monster that had attacked her home was not alone, and Wilheard was in tumult.

Remnant Tales of Stilly:
Passion and Benevolence

The wailing of terrified people, the ringing of steel and the snapping of wood filled the streets. The breaking of timber came from shop stalls and temporary fixtures used for the Summer Festival; the steel was that of swords, spears and other weaponry belonging to Wilheard's infantry. How long could the soldiers last against such unfamiliar foes? Undoubtedly, as frightened as the civilians, the guards would have been unprepared for such an attack.

Ebony's grip slipped from Hazel's hand. She halted and wheeled round to find her friend, who was now jogging in a separate direction.

Hazel signalled for Ebony to follow, waving her arms in large semi-circles. 'Over here! We can take shelter in the barn. I left the dog there.'

Hazel threw shut the barn doors and latched them with a wooden bar.

Ebony lit an oil lantern and hooked it onto one of the low-hanging beams. The animals sheltering inside the barn were agitated, upset by the storm rather than the monsters, which had yet to reach the farm. The horses were particularly uneasy, snorting and flicking their heads while clumping the stone floor with their hooves. Hazel tended to them first.

Ebony kept close to her friend and did her best to help calm the other animals while keeping an eye out for Colossus, who, potentially distressed by the storm as well, could be hiding in one of the stables. Even though her parents were in the windmill, Hazel had left the Great Dane in the barn to sleep while she was away. If she had known a storm was coming, she wouldn't have done so.

From the barn, all Ebony could hear from the outside was the thundering rain, the shrieking of the townspeople now too distant. Could that mean monsters were nearby?

Without warning, one of the cows let out a horrified low, spooking the other livestock again. Ebony rushed to the offending animal and caressed its muzzle to calm it. A sudden gust of wind rattled the barn doors, fighting against the latch holding them closed. From a broken corner of the left door, something scurried in from the rain and into the shadows.

Ebony jolted with surprise. At first, she wondered if it had been a rat, yet the snake-like hiss that followed moments later suggested otherwise. She alerted Hazel and edged towards her friend, not taking her eyes away from the shadow. The two women moved to the middle of the barn and farther from the doors. The livestock and horses continued to show their anxiety, capable of seeing in the darkness what the humans could not.

Another hiss emanated from the same corner, followed by the creature stalking into the light: its skin was as black as tar and looked just as slick. With the legs bowed and outward facing, the creature reminded Ebony of a lizard, although its neck was far longer and capable of bending in multiple places.

Ebony and Hazel moved even farther into the barn as the creature crept closer. Ebony shifted her eyes from side to side, hoping to find something to use as a weapon. A pitchfork or another farming tool was bound to be nearby, but she did not want to make any sudden movements.

It was then that the worst possible thing happened.

Hazel tripped, stumbling onto her rump and inadvertently pulling Ebony down with her. As feared, the sudden movements prompted the lizard to dash over to the women, slinking towards them with frightening speed. Upon reaching the two, the creature reared and splayed its fingers. Although it did not have much in the way of claws, the three layers of razor-sharp teeth in its mouth would have little trouble tearing into flesh.

Bounding over the floored women, Colossus barged the serpentine creature with the flat of his head. Caught unawares, the creature had no time to react and hit the barn floor with a slap. Despite the painful sound, the lizard was untroubled by the assault and regained its footing within seconds.

Lightning flashed as the Great Dane let out a throaty growl, his teeth bared fully and to inimical effect. The creature hissed in response, its attention now fixed entirely on the dog. The two glared at one another for a moment as if waiting for the other to make the first move. In the end, timed with the delayed boom of thunder, Colossus made the first strike.

Colossus dived towards his opponent with an audible snap of the jaws, following up with a downwards swipe of his paw. The lizard evaded the first attack with a graceful twist but failed to dodge the successive cuff. Although recoiling from the hit, the creature recuperated instantly, jumping the dog with an assault of its own.

Colossus yelped as the lizard sunk its layers of teeth into his nape. A moment of struggle ensued as the two battled to drag each other down. Even though the Great Dane was by far the stronger of the two, the lizard won the scuffle, pulling the canine off balance. Ironically, this had been a fatal error. Its jaw locked, the lizard failed to let go at the crucial moment, the sheer mass of the hound essentially crushing it.

Colossus seized the advantage in a heartbeat. The dog closed its teeth about the lizard's long neck and bit hard, the helpless creature opening its mouth into a silent scream. Colossus proceeded to finish his victim, pitilessly shaking the lizard until he was satisfied that it would not get back up.

Colossus dropped the now-decapitated creature and lumbered towards the two women, panting with exhaustion. He placed his chin on Hazel's lap and looked dolefully at her. She smiled and gently brushed her fingers over his injury.

'Do you still think he's as useful as transparent clothing?' Ebony tittered.

Hazel wrapped her arms round the Great Dame's neck. 'Rats are for cats—Colossus prefers a challenge.'

Ebony moved her attention back to the lizard. 'Is it... decomposing?'

Hazel stood up and gathered the hanging oil lantern. She moved closer to the corpse, the yellow light revealing all. Ebony joined her friend, shadowed by Colossus. The hound sniffed at the disappearing creature, its remains forming a black puddle before all traces of it vanished entirely. With it gone, the barn animals calmed significantly.

Ebony stepped away from where the lizard had been and peered out the shutter to her left. With the rain persistent in its intensity, visibility remained low, but she could just about see the silhouette of someone (or something) approaching the barn.

As the unknown approached, the silhouetted figure cleared, revealing a shire horse and a man as its rider. The rain-soaked man reined the horse to stop and studied the barn momentarily, stopping his gaze at the shutter where Ebony was standing. Moments later, the rider dismounted the animal and, to Ebony's alarm, drew a large sword.

Ebony leapt from the shutters, telling Hazel what she had seen. The two women backed away from the barn entrance, expecting the worst. This caused Colossus, who noticed the tension in the air, to prepare for further trouble. The Great Dane growled as the barn doors rattled several times before coming to a still again. Heartbeats later, the sword's blade pierced the centre of the doors and sliced the wooden latch in one stroke, instigating panic among the livestock all over again. The hinges screeched as the barn doors parted. Colossus lowered himself to the ground, waiting for an excuse to lunge at the intruder.

Expressionless, the man strode into the stables and came to a complete stop. With his sword tight in hand, he studied Ebony and then Hazel. Colossus grizzled at the stranger and backed himself towards the women. The swordsman glanced at the hound and then switched his attention back to Ebony.

As the man gazed at Ebony, she stared back. Drenched in rainwater, he almost shone in the yellow light of the lantern; his brown hair hugged his face while his clothes, including a threadbare coat, drooped over his body, accentuating the muscles beneath. His longsword glinted in the dim glow, showing damage from extended use. The lack of blood on the steel gave the impression the wielder had not used it recently, but Ebony wondered otherwise.

The swordsman placed his weapon back into the scabbard hanging from his hip. 'I have been watching you—as have *they*.' He took a single step forward, which caused Colossus to grumble further. 'I mean neither of you harm. Control the canine.'

Hazel knelt to calm Colossus, who ceased growling but continued to watch the stranger.

The swordsman looked up from Hazel and towards Ebony again. 'My words are directed at you, my lady. You... you share her comeliness.'

Ebony frowned at the remark but made no reply.

The man continued. 'Your life is in peril. These creatures that plague this hamlet are here for you and your friend.'

Ebony shuddered at the man's words and looked at Hazel. 'You say, my friend--'

'Not her,' he said curtly. 'I refer to the scholar with whom you entered the woodland.'

'Alim…? What have we done to deserve this?'

'I insist we make haste from here. You must come with me for your safety and for the good of Wilheard's people. Answers will come in time.'

Ebony once again looked towards Hazel. The farmer gave a thin smile. 'You best do what he says, m'dear. I'm sure I'll be all right—I have a good guardian.' She stroked the top of Colossus's head.

Ebony glanced at the swordsman, stepping towards him cautiously. She had been uncertain what to say, but what the man said next took all words from her breath.

'My lady. My name is Maynard Suavlant, and I ask for your trust.'

Oliath muttered a curse as his stomach churned. He could not deny it, not least to himself: he was nervous and dumbfounded. A lot was going through his head, particularly Dexter Theryle, who had been telling the truth all along.

Oliath dwelled on this for a long moment. He had little reason to question what most people said to him, and Dexter, albeit eccentric at times, was no exception. Yet, when he came hurtling towards Oliath, almost tripping over his own feet with talk of odd creatures and even a bear… well, what was the captain to think?

Ebony Gibenn was also on Oliath's mind. Before their meeting, he had pictured her as a wild child, but this had not been the case; Ms Gibenn was pleasant enough to talk to, and although he did not know much about her, he wanted to. Olitath could not say the same about her friends: the spirited Hazel Dolb and that scholar. He had yet to meet with the latter, and even the name had slipped his mind, but he imagined the man would be an oddball.

Admittedly, and putting aside her congeniality, Ebony's account of what Dexter told him earlier had done little to change Oliath's thoughts on the anecdote.

The bang of a pistol woke Oliath from his musing. He harrumphed at the sound. Guns, specifically flintlocks like the Lunsser pistol, were still relatively new in Stilly, even more so in Wilheard. Oliath had been dismissive of their introduction, refusing to acknowledge them as a replacement for a blade. The Lunsser, in particular, seemed far too cumbersome to be advantageous; the wielder needed to reload the thing after a single shot.

No. Oliath knew what he liked, and what he liked worked well.

Tightening a leather vest about his midriff, Oliath moved to gather his breastplate, gauntlets and an old steel helm. He had always been fond of the helmet despite a design that merely covered the wearer's cranium and eye area, leaving the neck and face exposed. Undoubtedly, the blacksmith Drah Leets had intended it to be worn with further armour. Regardless, on its own, the helm had served Oliath well in the past, and as he fastened its clasps under his chin, he knew it would serve him again that night.

A line of dirks lay to his right, perfectly fitted into a customised belt. Although not initially crafted for throwing, Oliath had trained to use them as such, favoured the weight and size of the blades compared to a standard throwing knife, which he considered insubstantial to any significant effect. Like the belt, the daggers were tailor-made, their hilts thinned and straight. Use was arguably more awkward than the Lunsser, but at least far more convenient for a follow-up attack. Still, the dirks served only as a secondary attack and were no substitute for his primary weapon.

Oliath lifted a sword from its mount and held it at eye level: a sabre with a short blade that projected seamlessly from a silver hilt and pommel. Although thin, the sword was strong, and the intended use was just as effective as any other. Indeed, a tactless man had once misguidedly belittled Oliath for owning the weapon, likening it to a child's. After a demonstration, the said man left the captain's presence in a worse state than he had arrived.

Oliath smirked at the memory as he studied the sword. Candlelight traced the length of the steel, imbuing it with an orange sheen that emphasised its short, inventive and deadly quality.

Oliath was ready to face whatever awaited him outside. Whether they were prepared for him was another matter.

Ebony had never ridden a shire horse before.

Named Lithe, this shire was for anything but pulling carts. As its name suggested, the stallion was supple, faster than any horse she had seen. Bolting over the rain-covered ground and sending water under hoof splashing high, the horse came to the side of each enemy before they could react, allowing Maynard to end them with a single swing of his sword. The weapon, despite its over-used condition, had no problem cutting through its victims, creating cascades of dark blood with every swipe.

Keeping her arms wrapped about Maynard's waist, Ebony tried not to pay much mind to his massacring. She watched townsfolk run about in all directions, trying to avoid the splintered remains of wrecked festival structuring. Many of the people were making their way to the safety of Sanct Everard, either by their own volition or with the encouragement of Wilheard's troops. By now, the soldiers had gained the upper hand over their enemies, but this had come at a cost. Scattered, broken and discarded were spears, swords and bits of armour, some of the weaponry immersed in red-tinted water. This was a disconcerting sight, but with a lack of any human bodies, Ebony remained hopeful that it was not as bad as it appeared.

Among the soldiers, Ebony caught sight of a taller, more muscle-bound figure.

Oliath Burley, standing in a grassy open, tossed his curved sword from hand to hand. With his back hunched, he moved with sideways steps, his legs poised and ready for the beast standing before him. By now, the monster infestation had reduced to almost nothing.

Maynard wheeled Lithe round to face Oliath. 'These creatures are called suoidi,' he said to Ebony.

Ebony and Maynard watched Oliath from a distance, who now seemed to be talking to the adversary. The suoido cocked its head at the man as if trying to fathom the spoken words. Oliath, with the help of Nolan and Cordelia, had already taken down two suoidi, but now the captain was alone, face-to-face with another and nary a Wilheard soldier for an ally.

'Are you going to help him?' Ebony asked Maynard, looking over his shoulder.

There was a moment's pause before Maynard answered. 'The man wishes to demonstrate his standing. My interference will merely bruise his already fragile ego.'

Ebony furrowed her brow at the comment but did not question further. She continued to observe Oliath.

Oliath and the suoido simultaneously made a move for each other, the man gaining first blood by slashing at his enemy's side yet failing to affect its movements. Subsequently, the suoido followed with an attack of its own, swinging the top half of its body sideways and towards the captain in an attempt to gore him with its tusks. With speed unusual for a man his build, Oliath dodged the assault with a twist before kicking at the suoido's head to distance himself from the creature again. He rolled as he landed, coating himself in mud.

As the battle continued, it became apparent that the downpour hindered Oliath. The clothes underneath his armour were saturated, and his boots sank into the sodden grass beneath. In contrast, the suoido, seemingly built for such conditions, continued its assault with little impediment.

Oliath, arms outstretched, leapt to one side to evade another charge by the suoido, landing in a puddle of water and dropping his sword. He raised himself to one knee, palmed his mud-soaked hair from his face and reached for his belt. The suoido turned to find the man once again, letting out a roar as a knife sunk into its front-left leg. Protruding from the limb was one of Oliath's dirks, thrown so hard that the blade pierced the suoido's skin entirely. The beast jumped back into action, defying any pain. Oliath flung two more dirks, the first dagger striking the monster's chest, the second planting into the throat, sending the beast crashing down. Oliath, as quick as he could muster, regained his footing and reclaimed his sword. Standing over the suoido, he plunged the weapon deep into its belly and twisted. The suoido growled, thrashing its legs before coming to a complete still.

Oliath released the sword, leaving it embedded in his fallen enemy. He allowed himself to fall back, his landing cushioned by a waterlogged embankment. He lay still, inhaling and exhaling with heavy breaths.

Ebony, continuing to watch from behind Maynard, sighed in relief. Her belly had been fraught with worry throughout the battle, but now it was over. 'He did it,' Ebony uttered to Maynard. 'I hope he will be all right.'

Without a shred of concern, Maynard dismounted Lithe, swinging his leg over the shire's head and landing with a splash. He detached a simple bow from the horse's side, nocked an arrow to its string and then raised the weapon, aiming it in Oliath's direction.

'What are you doing?' exclaimed Ebony.

Hearing the shrill of a woman's voice, Oliath looked to his left, noticing Ebony and the vigilante for the first time. However, he did not get the chance to react to their presence.

Reanimating, the suoido pulled itself upright and rammed its tusks to either side of Oliath. The captain, still flat on his back, seized the fangs in both hands and pushed, every muscle in his arms bulging as the beast used its body weight to push down on him. Oliath pulled at the suoido's tusks, twisting its head from side to side to escape immediate harm and force the creature off balance, but it was no use; the suoido was brawnier, and its teeth were getting closer to his face.

Maynard loosed the arrow, the bowstring twanging as the projectile launched at a ferocious speed. The arrow swerved away from Oliath, who at first looked to be the target, and into the side of the suoido's neck, the tip piercing right the way through and becoming lodged. In an instant, the monster slacked, all energy pouring from its lifeless body. Oliath hurled it to one side and resumed gasping.

Only now did the suoido disperse, as its ilk always did in death. Soon after the felling of the monster, the rainfall quickly calmed, stopping entirely a minute later.

Ebony put her arms about Maynard as he saddled Lithe again and set the horse into motion. The shire sauntered over to Oliath and stopped, snorting and shaking its head. Maynard, looking at Castle Stilly as he rode over, now turned his attention to Oliath. He studied the stricken man for any grievous injuries.

Ebony peeked over Maynard's shoulder and towards the castle. The mauve light she had spied from home had since vanished.

'You...' Oliath sputtered, spitting a globule of red from his mouth. 'I want a... a word with you. Do not... do not go anywhere...'

Maynard did not answer Oliath, nor did he follow the order.

Ebony looked around as she heard the call of Oliath's title. 'Captain Burley!' called Nolan and Cordelia, the pair looking for their boss. 'Where are you, sir?'

'He will be all right,' Maynard told Ebony, spurring Lithe towards Sanct Everard.

Abraham could hardly believe what he had just seen. Like almost everyone in Wilheard, the suoidi had shocked him, appearing from the shadows in all their inexplicable and disgusting form.

How could monsters like that possibly exist? A reasonable question, Abraham thought, yet there was another at the fore of his mind: was Sylvia a sorceress?

Abraham was grateful for her actions, of course, but in all the time he had come to know Sylvia and understand what she was all about, she did something that threw this notion into the wind.

Feeling their way through the empty, darkened halls of Wilheard Surgery, Abraham followed the sound of Sylvia's whispering as she led him by the hand. A short while later, the pair reached a room.

Sylvia fumbled about the space, finding what she wanted moments later. The hiss of a matchstick interrupted the silence, illuminating the room in an instant; she ignited a lantern and placed it on a hook hanging from the ceiling. 'There are flammables scattered about the room, so don't be tempted to move the lamp.'

Abraham took a moment to study his now visible surroundings. Judging from the arrays of beakers and jars containing coloured liquids, they were back in Sylvia's office.

Remnant Tales of Stilly:
Passion and Benevolence

Sylvia looked out the window at New Market Square, her hands pressed against the glass. 'At least the rain has passed,' Sylvia commented. 'I wonder what *she* is up to.'

Sitting in the patient's chair, Abraham remained silent, looking at Sylvia via her reflection. He did not need to say anything for her to know what was on his mind.

'I am familiar with all this... the monsters, I mean.' Sylvia pushed herself from the window and sat on her desk chair. Leaning forward, she ruffled her wavy blonde hair, moving her hands along her scalp with frustration. She nodded to the window and at the blackness outside. 'Those things are called Suoidi. Ninapaige has only ever told me their name—I do not know where they come from, but I don't really care to know... not anymore. All I need to understand, as everyone in Wilheard should, is that they are vicious creatures created to strike terror in the unsuspecting and kill any threat to their master.'

Abraham looked puzzled. 'Who is—?'

'—Ninapaige?' Sylvia interrupted, guessing the question. 'I have never figured that out, but I know she means well. She does not say much about herself or her past, and she knows a lot more than she conveys, even when it comes to my supposed importance. I am a product of hers, so to speak, right down to my abilities.'

Abraham thought back to a little while ago. Having left the surgery earlier, he and Sylvia used one of Wilheard's tearooms to shelter from the rain. The sky had quickly darkened, and the initial drizzle turned into a downpour. As time passed, and the rain did not abate, mutters of exasperation filled the shop, but these complaints soon wavered when the growls of something other than thunder rumbled from outside. The mere form of the beasts, or suoidi as Sylvia had termed them, was enough to send the other people in the tearoom darting to the rear of the building and down into the basement.

'*Livnam!*' a man had squealed, upending a table as he stood. '*Traeh has brought the apocalypse down on us for our blasphemy and sins! Quick, to the basement!*'

Remnant Tales of Stilly:
Passion and Benevolence

Although now curious about what the man got up to in his day-to-day life, Abraham put the thought aside. He was inclined to follow the others but paused when he noticed Sylvia had not moved.

Sylvia had not attempted to escape, but it had not been fear keeping her rooted. After studying the suoido, she walked out from the tearoom and into the rain. Incredulous, Abraham almost tripped over himself to pull her back in, but she was already outdoors before he had the chance.

Sylvia stretched her forward and moved them in a circular motion. The suoido, its body stiffening as it became encapsulated in a bubble, rose into the air. Sylvia clapped her hands, and the bubble popped, a mass of black liquid pouring from where the beast had been moments before and muddying the rain-soaked ground. Sylvia lost her balance then, but Abraham had been there to catch her.

Abraham awoke from his daydreaming, disturbed by Sylvia sighing. He looked up to notice a bead of sweat roll down her rose-red cheek, glinting in the candlelight.

'At the tearoom… was that magic?' he asked, feeling foolish for even speaking such a word.

Sylvia smiled thinly and nodded slowly. 'You could say that. More specifically, it is ytyism. I know very little of it, and even what I do know is clumsy.'

Abraham grunted. 'From what I saw, you are amazing.'

Sylvia tilted her head backwards, using her fingers to brush her hair behind her ears. 'Ytyism is complex, and even the smallest spells can look impressive when mastered.' She sighed once again. 'What a mess this has become. I guess what people say is true—there is no escaping destiny. Where could *she* be?'

That last part roused a response from Abraham. He swore aloud and stood from his chair abruptly enough to make Sylvia jolt. 'Ebony! I can't believe my daughter even slipped my mind for a moment. Some father I am. Quick, we need to…!'

Sylvia jumped to her feet and pulled back on the man's arm. 'It's all right, Abe. Ebony is a capable young woman.'

Sylvia's tone sounded a little too calm for Abraham's liking. He snatched his arm away. 'How can *you* say such a thing?' he said, more curtly than he had intended. 'You have only met her once, and even then, she was unconscious.'

This was all it took to make Sylvia cry.

Guilt replacing worry, Abraham groaned and closed his eyes. 'I'm sorry…'

Sylvia wiped away her tears. 'Ebony is a survivor—that is what I truly meant.' The doctor sat back down and shook her head. 'Besides, Sombie… I mean… *Maynard* is probably with her.'

Maynard; the name did not sound familiar to Abraham. 'That isn't that scholar's name, is it?'

'No, he is Alim Larring. Maynard is,' Sylvia paused, 'Maynard is the one people are calling a vigilante.'

'That man from the forest?' Abraham was almost lost for words. '*He* is with my daughter?'

Sylvia gestured for Abraham to calm down. 'I don't know, but he will not harm Ebony if he is. I know what he is like. We have even crossed paths.'

Abraham sat back down and said nothing.

'Ninapaige said I would know the right time to reveal my secrets.' Sylvia cupped Abraham's hands in hers. 'Do you remember when we met down Efflorescence Way? That was by no means our first meeting. What I am about to tell you will be difficult to believe, but it is important that you listen carefully and that you do not interrupt me. I have no doubt that my words will shock you.'

'I advise against tarrying too long, my lady. There are other matters to which we must attend.'

Ebony acknowledged Maynard with a nod, even if she had yet to find out what those matters were.

Remnant Tales of Stilly:
Passion and Benevolence

She looked about Sanct Everard. In all her years, the sancture had never seen such activity. The building was packed: all the pews had filled quickly, and many townspeople lined the walls, pillars and the dais north of the sancture where the pipe organ sat.

Standing with Ebony, Maynard watched the congregation from the south of the sancture; numerous people shuffled aimlessly about the building, too anxious to keep still. A few individuals paused to study the vigilante, but if any of them recognised him, they did not explicitly show it. Perhaps they did not care who he was. Ebony considered that a good thing: having seen him in action, she knew Maynard had fierce capabilities, and if someone were to provoke him… she did not want to entertain the thought. Yet Ebony did not believe he would harm anyone unjustly—she *knew* he would not. Not if this man was the same Maynard Suavlant she had read about.

Could this really be the same Man? That is unlikely, indeed an impossibility. Ebony reflected back to when Maynard introduced himself in the barn. Was Passion and Benevolence more than a story? What would Alim make of this?

Alim Larring, like many others, had also taken refuge in the sancture. Ebony sat beside him and rested her back against one of the hall's pillars. She gave her account of what happened.

'I see,' Alim muttered, glancing towards Maynard as he listened to Ebony's tale. 'You have proven to be very formidable, dear girl. How do you feel physically?'

'Bruised and a bit tender. How about you?'

'Similar as far as bruises are concerned, but when it comes to during the storm, I got off rather lightly in comparison. Following my visit to the surgery, I returned to The Wooden Duck. After everything that happened, sleeping had not been easy, and at the time, I just wanted to be in the company of others, so I stayed downstairs of the inn. At any rate, I watched as the weather worsened and… well, that is when the monsters showed. Suoidi, did you call them?'

Ebony nodded. 'And you went outside?'

'Like most everyone else, it seemed,' Alim said, patting himself down in search of his smoking pipe. 'I heard growling before seeing the suoidi. I got caught up in the crowds when the main hubbub started and eventually ended up here.'

Ebony yawned; she was unsurprisingly weary. Left to her thoughts for a moment, she tried to gather her mind. Ebony thought of her father, her friends, and even the cottage. She also thought about what would happen next. Was it worth trying to plan what actions to take? What could she do? She had never experienced such difficulties before.

'Fair eve, Ms Gibenn,' asked a familiar voice. The voice was that of Ordaiest Caleb Psoui, which, despite being dulcet, caused Ebony to jolt. 'Sorry if I frightened you.'

Ebony tittered and placed a hand over her eyes. 'No, I'm fine. You didn't really frighten me,' she said, smiling.

Caleb knelt beside Ebony. 'Forgive me if I am imposing, but I saw you from across the sancture. How are you doing?'

'Reasonably, all things considered,' Ebony said. 'I would ask you the same, but I can already tell that you are busy.'

The ordaiest smirked and looked to one side. 'I would never in a hundred years have thought I would witness something such as this. Still, I am sure that with Traeh's love and support, we will all get through these trying times.'

Maynard cast his eyes in Caleb's direction then, as if disapproving of what he said. He rolled his shoulders before moving his attention forward once again.

Caleb did not notice the apparent displeasure and continued speaking. 'I see you have made new friends since we last met.'

'Of course—forgive my rudeness. The gentleman to my left is Alim Larring. He is a scholar.'

Alim and Caleb shook hands and exchanged a friendly nod. Caleb stood and turned to Maynard next. 'And this well-built figure would be…?'

'Maynard Suavlant,' Ebony answered.

'Caleb held out his hand for Maynard to take. 'It is an honour to meet you, Mister Suavlant. Please do not presume me rude, but would you happen to be the same man I have heard rumours about lately?'

Maynard looked deeply into Caleb's eyes, his expression po-faced. 'That would depend on the rumour.'

Caleb lowered his hand and placed it behind his back with the other. 'I refer to a rumour about a certain vigilante helping this little province. Again, I hope you do not take offence, but if you are the same man, then I would add that your movements are very surreptitious.' An awkward silence followed, interrupted by Caleb again. 'I apologise if I have overstepped. I see you are the taciturn sort, so by all means, disregard my questioning, Mister Suavlant.'

Unspeaking, Maynard continued to study the ordaiest.

Caleb changed the subject. 'That is a sizeable sword you have there. I do hope it only unsheathes when justified.'

Maynard moved to face Caleb properly; he stood a head taller than the ordaiest. 'I keep unto myself, which is a preference and not the fault of any man. I understand that my words are terse, and my emotional quality wanting.' Maynard held out his hand; his skin was cold to the touch. 'I bear you no ill; my sword will remain sheathed in your sancture.'

Finished, Maynard turned away once again.

Ebony pushed herself up from the floor and stood next to Caleb. 'Have you seen my father by chance?' she asked. 'Maybe you have seen a woman called Sylvia Enpee. She is a doctor—blonde hair, I believe. She is a friend of my father's.'

Caleb shook his head gently. 'I'm afraid not, and I do not believe I have met this Sylvia you speak of.' Upon seeing Ebony's disappointment, he placed a sympathetic hand on her upper arm. 'I am sure they are safe and sound. I suppose there is little to smile about at present, but perhaps this will lift your spirits. That story you were reading not long ago… Passion and Benevolence, was it? Well, it may surprise you as much as it did me, but after much rummaging, I believe I have found some information on the book's author in the sancture archives. The papers I uncovered are old— dated near the same period as the original book. I must say, however, the writing style is enigmatic at best, including several passages of symbols.'

This piqued Ebony's curiosity. 'That sounds about right—the esoteric nature, I mean. Alim might be able to make something of it.'

Remnant Tales of Stilly:
Passion and Benevolence

Alim had jumped to his feet after the mention of Passion and Benevolence, his curiosity also captured. 'A most thrilling discovery, Ordaiest Psoui.' Alim shifted his glasses. 'The original author's name is Emmanuel Grellic. My grandfather translated and rewrote the--'

Before Alim could finish his sentence, Maynard, who had been listening the whole time, interrupted. 'Emmanuel Grellic?' the swordsman repeated.

'You are familiar with this name?' Caleb asked.

Alim interrupted the brief silence that followed. 'I knew it! You *are* the same man, however preposterous that might sound.'

Ebony grinned, pleased that Alim had come to the same conclusion. Maynard Suavlant... the sovereign knight. Still, how could this be possible?

'With respect, I am not the man you think me to be,' Maynard said flatly. 'The individual of whom you speak died many years past.'

Alim opened his mouth as if to dispute this but decided against it. There was a morose quality to the vigilante's words.

Maynard continued. 'Even so, I would be obliged to see these documents. I have my own questions.'

Without warning, the doors of Sanct Everard flung open, their wood-and-iron framework vibrating as they crashed against the walls. Ebony peered round a pillar and saw Nolan Shakeston and Cordelia Lawford stride into the building, shadowed by their limping captain. Oliath Burley looked scarcely better than when Ebony had last seen him: he was still caked in mud, his attire drenched.

The hall went eerily silent. Dozens of people looked up, their eyes drawn, gazing at the imposing figures. A few people towards the further end of the sancture, unable to see through the congregation, jumped for cover, fearing monsters had come back to finish them off. Closer to Oliath, one man chose to run from the building altogether, perhaps dreading trouble of a different breed.

Oliath ran his fingers through his matted hair, then wrung his hands together. 'I am looking for a man,' he announced, his voice echoing about the chamber. 'This is a man I'm sure many of you have heard about lately— roving about our town as though his actions are above reproach. The man of whom I speak is heralded as a hero on occasion. Undisputable even by me, he has done many a good deed. However'—Oliath wagged his finger—'this man is *not* above Wilheard's jurisdiction.'

'I have had a brief encounter with this vigilante. He is tall—about my height—has longish brown hair and most notably carries a Longsword. I do not wish to antagonise or make an enemy of the man but rather talk reason with him.' Oliath stepped forward, wringing his hands tighter as he looked at sections of the crowd. 'I have cause to believe this individual is among you, as the horse he rides is standing outside.'

All eyes shifted from Oliath and towards the pillar next to which Ebony stood. The captain turned his attention in the same direction, quickly spying Maynard. The very sight of the vigilante caused him to clench his hands into fists.

Oliath, followed by Cordelia and Nolan, limped towards Maynard. He stopped a foot in front of the swordsman and looked him directly in the eyes. Maynard remained motionless, an unconcerned look about him. Caleb moved to intervene before anything could materialise, yet Nolan, who took hold of the ordaiest's shoulder, held him back.

'I do not want trouble here, Captain Burley,' Caleb said, not bothering to struggle against Nolan's grasp. 'This is a house of Traeh—a place for peace. I ask that you respect the Naitsir faith and stay all acts of menace.'

Oliath continued to glower at Maynard, the anger emitting from him unwavering. If he had heard Caleb's plea, he gave no indication to show it.

'You're a hard man to pin down,' Oliath said softly, a smirk breaking onto his face. 'Outside, I believe I told you to stay where you were.' He shifted his attention to Ebony, looking at her over Maynard's shoulder. 'Ms Gibenn. I seem to remember you promising me something. It was along the lines of: "If you know anything about the vigilante, come straight to me". Well… from where I'm standing, you cannot get much closer to him than at the moment, and if you do not know something about him by now, then you never will.'

Ebony did not respond; instead, she looked down at her feet. This earned her a grunt of contempt from the lieutenants.

Alim stepped more into view then, moving to Ebony's side. 'Now steady on, old boy. Dear Ebony here has not long been in this man's company—I can vouch for that, as she has been mostly with me as of late.'

Oliath turned his attention to Alim, looking the scruffy man up and down. He folded his arms. 'I see... and you must be that scholar I have heard about. Alan...?'

'Larring. *Alim* Larring,' the scholar corrected.

The captain snorted. 'That's the one... I wanted to have a word with you, as well.'

Oliath stepped away from Maynard and turned his back for a moment. He peered at the various stained glass windows lining the upper walls and considered the holy figures filling them. 'I like to think that I am a reasonable man. Truly, I want no tension between us, Swordsman, but there will be if I do not have your respect and compliance.' He turned back, thrusting a finger towards the group and raising his voice. 'I want all of you to come with me— the vigilante, the scholar... and you, Ms Gibenn. The three of you can explain yourselves in confinement.'

No one moved. Maynard, standing rigidly on the spot, remained unperturbed.

'So,' Oliath went on, gesturing towards the sancture doors. 'Are you going to come quietly?'

'No,' Maynard replied bluntly. 'The other two are not going with you either.'

Oliath, taken aback by the retort, blinked. He sniggered through clenched teeth. 'The temerity of this one!'

Oliath motioned to Cordelia, who handed him a pair of shackles. He moved closer to Maynard. 'Today has been a trying day, Swordsman, and I am not prepared to let you make it any worse. Now, put your hands behind your back!'

Oliath shoved at Maynard's arm in a show of dominance, which proved a mistake.

Spurred into action, Maynard placed one hand on Oliath's chest and pushed with enough force to throw the captain off balance. Losing his footing, Oliath crashed into Nolan and Cordelia. The lieutenants caught their boss, steadied him back up and then unsheathed knives.

'You impudent mongrel!' Oliath seethed, unclipping a dirk of his own.

Maynard instinctively reached for his own blade, ready to defend himself. However, before he could draw his weapon, Ebony moved to his side. 'Please,' she said. 'Don't do this. You said that you would keep your sword sheathed.'

Caleb had also taken a hesitant step forward by this time. 'No violence, Captain Burley, I beseech you!'

'ENOUGH!' Oliath roared. 'I am sick of people questioning my authority—telling me what I should do and how to do it. I know my duties! I have served this town for years, long before this pest encroached on our lives. The least you fools could do is acknowledge that fact. Now, lest you make me *really* angry, I suggest no one get in my way. Let me do my job.'

'Your job?' a voice boomed from behind Oliath. 'If you intend to remain in your position by the morning, man, you will stop your foolishness this instant.'

Oliath about-turned to face this new confrontation, knowing whom the voice belonged.

Mayor Basil Wolleb stood by the entrance of Sanct Everard, flanked by a dozen soldiers. Basil was livid, his white beard unable to hide his disappointment. Beside Basil was Benjamin Oswin, his own moustache slanted into a look of disapproval.

It turned out that the man who had run from the sancture earlier had been the one to find the mayor.

Basil stared at Oliath for a long moment. 'I thought we had a deal, Captain,' he said eventually.

Oliath clenched his jaw in frustration, annoyed by the mayor's sudden and unwanted appearance. 'Mayor Wolleb,' he managed without swearing. 'All I want is this man... that is *all*. Please allow me to arrest and question him. That is all I ask of--'

'We have already been over this subject, Oliath,' Basil snapped. 'Since when has spitting in the face of amity been noble? That does not set a good example, and you cannot just start arresting the innocent.'

Oliath screwed his face in anger. 'This man is a VIGILANTE!'

'And how many, besides you, care? Are you so filled with inadequacy and envy that it clouds all reason? Tender spirits, man! Have you already forgotten about what has just happened? This character helped *save* us from those creatures.' Basil held up his hand and shook his head before Oliath could argue further. 'I'll hear no more on the matter. I suggest you leave before we both do something we will later regret. If you can, get yourself seen to by a doctor while you're at it—you look in terrible shape.'

Oliath sneered. 'Have it your way, then!' he growled, throwing the shackles to the floor and causing them to clank.

Basil watched as Oliath went out of sight before looking to one side. He gazed at Maynard, then at Ebony, and lastly at Alim. He shook his head sullenly. 'I really hope I have made the right decision... I really do.' Basil walked to leave Sanct Everard, calling back as he did. 'In fact, Stranger, I hope you can prove me right by making things as they were... Everything as it was.'

Maynard did not say a word to Basil, keeping silent until the mayor left. Whatever he had initially planned, he now seemed to have reservations about rushing into them. He turned to Ebony and Alim. 'Perhaps the two of you should rest here a while. We can decide what actions to take tomorrow.'

The time had just gone midnight, and all but one room at The Repose was empty.

Oliath slammed his bitter ale down on the table and croaked a profanity. To say things were not going his way would be an understatement; matters had never been this difficult before, and the recent discrediting of his authority was more than he could bear, even when it came from his supposed superior.

Several hours had passed since the sancture incident. Oliath had not bothered seeing a doctor; he bandaged his own wounds before recuperating alone. By the time he had arrived at The Repose, he had regained most of his strength. Sadly, the same could not be said about his forbearance.

'Unbelievable,' Oliath muttered, characteristically running his fingers through his hair. 'I did not think even *he* would go that far to protect the vigilante… after all I have done for this town.'

Cordelia and Nolan, listening to their boss's bemoaning, gathered the *he* in question was Basil Wolleb. Oliath had been thinking aloud for a while now. The *Other Four* were also in the room, choosing to sit away from the captain and leave him to his complaining. Keeping silent, Dexter and Wiley listened as Oliath spoke to his lieutenants.

'That bloated mayor doesn't deserve to hold such a position,' Nolan put in. 'His aptitude staled years ago.'

'I agree with Shakeston,' Cordelia continued. 'That man should not be giving orders to you, sir. You are far more suited for such responsibilities.'

Oliath placed his feet on the table and rocked on his chair, entertaining the idea. He swallowed the remainder of his beer with one large gulp and sucked on his teeth. 'No. You two know me better than that—I do not care for such responsibility. Can you imagine me sitting in the Mayoral Chair? I don't mind staying in front of that desk, but I expect the man behind it not to treat me with such open disdain.'

'If you say so, sir,' Nolan said. 'You have done a lot for Wilheard, and I believe rewards should reflect efforts.'

Cordelia nodded in accord, pushing a refilled beer mug to her captain.

Oliath grumbled his thanks to the both of them. He rocked his chair farther back and stared out the window where he could see Castle Stilly. 'Did any of you see it?'

A silence befell the room, no one understanding the question.

Oliath continued, keeping his eyes on the edifice. 'There is someone in the castle. I saw a man in the chamber above the gatehouse… I think that is the throne room. I noticed a figure when that vigilante peered towards Castle Way.'

Everyone looked out the same window as Oliath and towards the castle.

'We are going up there,' Oliath declared, throwing back his drink. 'Right now… All of us.'

Remnant Tales of Stilly:
Passion and Benevolence

Reaching the castle did not take long, despite Rida's unfit stature, which slowed the rest of them down. Initially, Oliath had been happy to let him catch up, but Rida had a nasty habit of wandering when no one was looking. He wanted to keep everything low-key, and sneaking up to the castle at night could look shady. Conversely, many people would likely not care what the group was up to; after all the upheaval, why should they. Regardless, Oliath did not want the attention, and no one was permitted to enter the castle without good reason. Even so, getting inside should not prove difficult with Nolan's skills.

In truth, Oliath was not too worried about guards and soldiers seeing him. He still had power over them, despite the reprimand from the mayor, and he could make any excuse he wanted. Then again, the vigilante was also on his mind; the swordsman could be watching, and they would not even know about it.

'How are you doing, Shakeston?' Oliath whispered harshly as he waited for the other man to unlock the thick wooden doors of the gatehouse, which was beneath the raised portcullis.

'Almost there, sir,' Nolan replied, picking at the final lock. 'These locks might be large and many in number, but they have become rusty and brittle over the years.'

Oliath agreed that an abundance of locks lined the entrance, but that was understandable if the townspeople were expected to stay out. It seemed altogether strange, however, if someone was within the keep. How could anyone get inside without interfering with the outside locks? If the original occupants truly wanted to keep out intruders, it seemed unlikely that the castle would have other entrances. Oliath supposed there was always the possibility of secret entries.

Cordelia and the *Other Four* were at the farther end of the drawbridge, looking for anything that could be a hindrance.

Meddia, clearly nervous, stayed close to Wiley, taking hold of his hand like a little girl. He did his best to reassure the teenager but could not help but feel the same, a slight pang of anxiety rolling in his gut. He would rather be somewhere else, but Captain Burley was insistent they all entered the castle to investigate, and he was the boss. All Wiley could do was hope this would all be over presently.

Albeit quieter than usual, Dexter had calmed significantly from earlier and seemed eager to go into the castle and find out what was inside. Surprising even to him, Dexter had quickly got used to the fact monsters existed in Stilly, and he had a feeling some would be within the keep. All Theryle wanted to do was prove his abilities, particularly in fighting. He had decided that no good came from sitting about cowering and now was the perfect opportunity to demonstrate to Oliath that he was just as good as Nolan and Cordelia.

Rida seemed blissfully unaware as to why the group was even at the castle. Sitting at the end of the drawbridge, he busied himself by jamming his finger in his ear, only to wipe whatever he found inside onto his trousers. Although unaware of what was happening (if he even bothered to think about it), Rida was quietly excited about entering the castle; a lot of things to find in there, he reckoned, and providing his greed did not get the better of him, he could add more to his secret stash. Then again, he doubted if anything could beat his latest find: the short, curved sword with the beautiful sapphire. He kept that one on his person for safekeeping.

A soft snap sounded as Nolan broke the final lock to the castle's entrance. At last, the group could move on.

Oliath stepped through the partly opened doors, closing them once again after Rida waddled his way in. Pushing the farthest doors of the gatehouse open with his foot, the captain, his lieutenants and Dexter drew swords and then made their way inside.

The group found themselves in the foremost courtyard. Barren in its heyday, plant life had now taken over: Ivy was widespread, wrapping round pillars, statues and other structures; weeding climbed like beanstalks, as tall as the curtain walls; and even fully-grown trees had broken through the stone ground.

Oliath lowered his weapon and scanned his surroundings. It was like peering into a jungle. Navigating in the dark would prove difficult if everywhere else was in a similar state of disarray. However, this did not put him off his mission, and he ordered his team to find a way into the central part of the castle.

Not long after giving the command, Rida surprised Oliath by pointing out that he had already found something not far to the left of where the group had entered. Rida had not waited for permission before looking about the courtyard and had already come across a vine-covered entrance. Hacking at the foliage with Nolan, Oliath cleared the way, kicked open the rotted wooden door and found a passageway.

All was dark, the other end of the corridor out of view. Before entering the castle grounds, the group had relied on moonlight, which had been altogether insufficient. Yet, with the mass of greenery blocking what windowpanes remained, even that was now gone. It was fortunate, then, that Wiley had anticipated such a hindrance; he pulled a candle from his pocket, followed by a tinderbox, both of which he had taken from The Repose. Moving his hand along the wall to his left, Wiley found a rusted sconce. Removing the torch from its bracket, he forced the candle into the hold and lit it.

Oliath praised Wiley and took the torch from him, using it to find a spiral staircase a short time later. The way was tight, and the steps steep. Oliath listened long enough for anything that might be at the top, but all was silent. He led the way, treading softly. Although he could not hear any movement, he knew someone was in the castle: the captain could sense it and would find the individual before the night's end.

Once again, the group came face-to-face with darkness, a spacious hall lined with archaic armour and ornate objects. Oliath held the flame above his head, inspecting his surroundings for movement. Everything remained in place, not even a rodent disturbing the silence. Oliath relaxed his shoulders and sneered with dissatisfaction, handing the sconce back to Wiley. He watched Rida for a moment, who, although exhausted from climbing up the stairway, managed to claw back enough energy to examine anything inanimate. Meddia, who had also become more relaxed as the group made their way through the castle, joined Priory, prodding anything that took her fancy. The pair stopped with their fiddling soon enough when a crash of metal-on-metal rang out, resonating along the length of the hall. Oliath had struck the closest suit of armour with the pommel of his sword. Weary of tiptoeing, he hoped to rouse a response from within the castle. He *knew* that someone else was there.

Sure enough, something sounded: a whirring coming south from where the group stood.

Oliath turned his attention in the direction of the noise. 'That must be where the throne room is. Let's go!'

Thrusting his foot into the centre of the double doors, Oliath leapt into the Throne room with his sword drawn.

Murmurs of astonishment interrupted the silence, the whole group amazed at what they saw. Unlike the rest of the castle, the opulent throne room was immaculate. As with the hallway leading up to the chamber, the hall was outlined with knight armour, but unlike the ones seen before, these suits were unaffected by the ravages of time: intense, elegant and polished so that they glinted in the fiery light that also lined the walls.

'You were right, sir,' Dexter said as he gaped. 'Someone *is* in the castle.'

Oliath moved farther into the throne room and looked down at his reflection on the gleaming marble floor. In the centre of the area was a decorative round table of Traehen design with several chairs round it. As with the floor and armour, the furniture looked as if it had never been in use, devoid of even the minutest scratches on its surface. To the farthest end of the room and upon a dais were the thrones, three in total, with the middle one more grandiose than the other two. To either side of the thrones stood identical, elongated doors covered with shutters. Presumably, they led to the balcony.

Rida's eyes lit up when he entered the throne room. Never had he seen objects so shiny in his life. Swords, daggers and spears; clubs, maces and hammers. Such tools of war had no right to be so beautiful. Each was lovely, yet one particular item took Rida's fancy.

A shield with a mirrored surface, embraced in the arms of one set of armour, distorted Rida's reflection as he approached, making his head appear even rounder than usual. Rida smirked at his image, taking a moment to amuse himself by pulling a few faces. The shield really was fabulous, much better than the day-to-day chaff he usually saw. Sadly, the boss was unlikely to let him keep it, and there was no way Rida could sneak it out unnoticed. This was a shame, but he would, at the very least, examine it more closely.

Rida placed his hands on either side of the shield and gave it a tug, only for it to remain stubbornly in place. Disregarding the likelihood of drawing attention, he persisted, the suit of armour shaking as he pulled. Priory put his foot on the knight's leg for extra leverage and even tried to open its fingers with his teeth, but to no avail.

Puffing, Rida took a step back, collared the sweat from his forehead and glanced over his shoulder to look at the others in the chamber. As expected, he had gained some attention, but only from the Penroses: Wiley shook his head with small, denigrating motions while Meddia simply grinned.

Ignoring what the pair thought of him, Rida looked back at the armour and peered towards the helm. 'Stupid thing!' he declared, giving the suit a pathetic kick on the shin.

Rida turned his back on the row of knights and walked towards the others. However, as soon as he did so, he heard a creak come from behind him. Snapping his attention back to the armour, his nerves rattled, Rida gazed again at the suit of armour. Had he managed to dislodge the shield after all? It appeared to be in the same position, but something seemed different. He glanced to see if his team had heard anything, but no one was paying him any mind. Backing away with small steps, Rida continued to scan the figure.

'The hand,' Rida gasped, noticing that the knight's right hand had moved behind the shield, 'that thing's movin'!'

Irritated by Rida's sudden outburst, Oliath turned to the shorter man, ready to dish out some choice words. However, he was stunned into silence before opening his mouth.

Animating before Rida's very eyes, the suit of armour brandished a short-handled war hammer from behind the shield and raised it above its head. Rida spun and made for an escape, his clumsy form causing him to stagger. Ironically, this blunder saved his life.

Rida's ears rang as the iron hammer crashed inches from his head, chipping the marble floor. The knight lifted the hammer once again and positioned itself directly over the floored man, Rida covering his face with both arms to hide from the horror. Once again, luck was on his side. As the hammer reached full height, Meddia screamed in alarm, distracting the knight.

Nolan rushed behind the knight and grabbed its weapon with his right hand, locking his left arm about the armour's shoulder. Before the figure could react to Nolan's interference, Oliath was upon it; having acquired a hammer of his own, the captain smashed it into the side of the helm, hitting with so much force that the armour split and flew clean off, sending the knight crashing down.

Oliath leapt towards the knight and thrust one knee onto the breastplate, using his other foot to pin the knight's fighting arm. He raised his hammer again, ready to deliver a gruesome end, but a glance at the fallen enemy's face made him hesitate.

Oliath's eyes widened. 'What is this? He said, unable to take his attention away from what he was looking at. 'A livnom?'

A grey, bulb-shaped head devoid of facial features slumped from the top of the armour. Eyes, nose, mouth, ears, hair… there was nothing. Oliath stared at the figure for a long moment, but before he could finish the creature, Dexter pushed a sword into its cranium.

Dexter removed his weapon with a grunt and stepped away. Oliath did the same, the body inside the suit evaporating as he stood. No one spoke, but there was no time for words; more knights lining the throne room came to life.

Rida dived towards the table and scrambled towards the single leg supporting its round top. Wiley and Meddia, also not trained for such confrontations, followed Priory on Dexter's recommendation, who reassured all three that he would keep the knights away.

Five suits stirred: three from the left of the room's entrance and two from the right, where the initial one had come. Oliath, Nolan and Cordelia moved towards the three suits of armour to the left, leaving Dexter to deal with the remaining two.

Cordelia made first contact, ducking a horizontal sword swing from the knight closest to her before twisting and slashing at an exposed part of its leg. The knight dropped to one knee, a dark liquid spurting from the wound. Cordelia moved in quickly to finish her enemy before it could recuperate, a messy demise ensuing as she slid her blade under its chin. Oliath and Nolan performed similar attacks, locating their enemies' weak points and downing them quickly. More suits awakened immediately, replacing their fallen counterparts in superior numbers.

Dexter was having more difficulty battling his opponents. Forced into sidestepping their consecutive (and incredibly precise) slashes, he was left with only clumsy attempts at retaliating, which failed to cause meaningful effect. This continued until one of the knights noticed three pairs of legs under the table centring the room. The being turned its attention away from Dexter and paced towards the table, kneeling to peer underneath. It stared at the frightened trio for a long moment as if trying to figure out who, or what, they were. After a while, it swung its sword at them without warning, aiming solely for their throats. Fortunately, the knight's reach was half a metre short.

Wiley deduced that the being had a simple understanding of human body parts; it seemed to recognise that the head and neck were the most vulnerable areas but was oblivious that attacking the legs could also be effective.

'Keep your heads back!' Wiley barked at the two on either side of him.

The knight made a second and third swipe for the group, causing Meddia to squeal in distress.

'Hold on!' Dexter called, finally gaining the upper hand with his now single opponent.

Dexter knew it was down to him to help his friends. Oliath, Cordelia and Nolan, who were taking down the knights at a high pace, found themselves getting closer and closer to being overwhelmed. With every enemy dropped, another replaced it, and with the lines of knight armour diminishing, the faceless humanoids simply appeared in their true form, emerging from thin air.

Thrusting his weapon under his enemy's gardbrace (a piece of armour that covers the top of the wearer's shoulder), Dexter twisted the blade to force the knight to drop its sword. With his opponent injured, Dexter mounted its back and plunged a knife into the nape with as much strength as he could muster, flooring the knight and toppling with it. Scrambling to his feet as the being underneath the armour dispersed, Dexter snatched a piece of the suit off the floor and threw it at the one next to the table.

Despite the awkward frame of the armour, the being had persisted in its attempts at getting closer to the three underneath the table, the tip of its sword inching closer with every swing. The fragment of armour that Dexter flung struck the knight on the cuisse (thigh armour), causing it to turn its attention back. Moments after doing so, the knight received a fatal blow to the head, a well-placed knife landing in the slit of the helm.

Dexter had not been the one to deliver the fatal blow.

Having taken advantage of the interruption, Rida brandished the curved blade he had been hiding under his belt and stabbed at the knight. Black blood gushed from the visor, and the humanoid crashed to the floor.

A deep hum filled the throne room, causing everything to rumble, followed by an intense light that filled the area.

Oliath instinctively shielded his eyes with his arm, squinting as he watched the remaining enemies inexplicably erupt into colourful puffs of smoke. The light died seconds later, taking all traces of the humanoids with it and leaving nothing but scattered piles of armour.

A sickly cough from near the thrones caused all seven group members to wheel round simultaneously. As if simply stepping from a hiding place, an aged man clad in a dark grey robe revealed himself. So emaciated was the man he looked dead on his feet: the gown covering him practically hung from his shoulders, his forearms and steepled fingers extending from the sleeves like branches from a small tree. The man's beard, perhaps the healthiest feature on his otherwise bald head, was long and straight, but even this seemed almost too much for his face to bear, which sagged in every possible way.

Oliath studied the stranger for a long moment, saying nothing.

'You are even more impressive than I first thought,' the fragile man croaked, directing his words towards Oliath. 'Your combat abilities are extraordinary. This, it would seem, is a blessing for the both of us.'

Oliath glowered at the stranger. This had to be the man he saw from outside. 'Who are you?'

'Fordon Latnemirt,' the ailing man answered, smirking at Oliath's arrogant tone. He sat on the centre throne with a sigh. 'And *you* are Oliath Burley—Captain of the Guard.'

Oliath, although perturbed by the stranger's knowledge, showed no outward concern and maintained his scowl.

'I know who the rest of you are, too. Nolan Shakeston and Cordelia Lawford—Burley's lieutenants. Then there is Dexter Theryle, Wiley and Meddia Penrose...' Fordon gestured languidly at each group member as he spoke his or her respective name, pausing as he got to the remaining group member, 'and finally, we have you, Rida Priory.'

'Fordon Latnemirt... I recognise that name!' Wiley blurted out then. 'But how is this possible? How are you even real?'

Fordon wheezed a feeble laugh at the incredulity. 'All your questions will be answered in time. For now though'—he looked back to Rida—'you have something that belongs to me.'

Everyone looked at Priory. Dumbstruck, Rida stood with a gormless expression, the short, curved sword he had used to slay the knight still in his hand.

'I have searched high and low for that sapphire,' Fordon continued. 'Indeed, the longer my search, the more my strength has deteriorated. Using the ytyism arts in my condition has taken its toll. It is risible to think that I did not consider the likes of you to have it all this time, Rida—the master thief. With Ascendancy, my energy will be replenished. Hand it to me!'

Rida looked down at the sword and pouted. He was hesitant to approach the creepy old man.

Oliath stepped forward, holding his hand out to stop Rida. 'So everything that has occurred in Wilheard recently, from the mindless people breaking into buildings to those foul monsters... it is all because of you?'

Fordon scowled at Oliath with frustration.

'And that vigilante,' Oliath went on. 'He has something to do with you, hasn't he?'

'I have nothing to do with the sovereign knight, his decisions, yearnings or otherwise,' Fordon said vehemently. 'Irrespective, and although he does not realise it yet, Maynard and I ultimately have the same goal. He wanders lost, his mind stuck firmly in the past. I do not believe for one second that he will see things my way, no matter how I articulate them, so he is nothing but a hindrance. I have but one ultimate desire, which I have planned for

centuries. If I cannot get him to understand what must be done, then...'
Fordon paused momentarily and smiled. 'I know you do not want this
vigilante in your town. He has made you feel inadequate—turned the people
against you. I know these things, and if it pleases you, I can help you
eliminate him. Of course, your wishes must not interfere with--'

'That's enough!' Oliath interrupted. 'Do you take me for an idiot? Do you
think you can manipulate me so easily? I neither want nor require your help,
old man. You are coming with me!'

'Do not be a fool!' Fordon roared, standing from the throne and drawing
what little power he had left. 'Give me Ascendancy NOW!'

Before anyone in the hall could react, a mysterious force snatched the
curved blade from Rida's hand. The sword darted through the air, Fordon
catching the hilt with a grunt. As soon as he did, an unseen force caused the
throne room to tremble again.

Oliath raised his weapon, triggering Cordelia, Nolan and Dexter to do the
same.

'Yes!' Fordon hissed, a blue wave of light enveloping him. 'This is it...
this is what I have longed for—the first stepping-stone to removing the
corruption in this world.'

The blue light intensified to blinding incandescence, forcing Oliath to
avert his eyes. 'What *are* you?' he called to Fordon.

'What am I?' Fordon repeated, the light dimming once more. 'I am but a
man, like you, of flesh and blood.'

Oliath gazed back to Fordon, his eyebrows joined in disbelief. Although
still gaunt, Latnemirt no longer appeared sickly. All his lethargy gone, the
older man stood straight and without effort, his skin a healthy pink and very
different from the ashen it had been moments ago.

'You are no man!' Oliath insisted. 'You may resemble one, but you are
something beyond this world.'

Fordon laughed. 'I will view that as a compliment.'

Oliath snorted and raised his sword once again in defiance. This made
Fordon shake his head.

'Oh, Captain Burley, do not play the buffoon. You have remarkable skill,
and it would be a shame to waste it all here.'

Remnant Tales of Stilly:
Passion and Benevolence

In what seemed like nothing more than a second, Fordon jumped from the dais and dashed towards Oliath. Before the captain had a chance to react, Fordon thrust a fist into his stomach, forcing Oliath to double over and drop his weapon. As expected, Nolan and Cordelia responded to the attack on their boss by moving to his side, yet even they found themselves unable to match the old man's newfound speed, and he simply barged them to the floor.

Oliath grimaced. How was this possible? How could an elderly man floor such seasoned warriors alone and with little effort?

Dexter, standing with the other three in the group, remained where he was. Fordon gave the *Other Four* a glance before looking back to Oliath. 'Do not make an enemy of me, Captain. It would be a shame to kill a man of your calibre.'

Oliath spat to one side. 'What do you want?'

'Compliance and order. Trust me when I say that I want no harm to befall you, this town, or even Stilly. Nevertheless, I insist I have yours, and everyone else's, cooperation.' Fordon stepped closer to Oliath and knelt next to him. 'As you have proved, not everyone will submit to my commands. You may not have the control you desperately want over Wilheard's people, but perhaps you can lead everyone down the right path. Before I forget, there is one individual I seek, one you no doubt know, especially now that she is with the sovereign knight.'

Oliath thought about this for a moment. 'Ebony Gibenn...?'

Fordon cackled. 'The very girl. She is a pretty one, is she not?'

'You want me to bring Ebony to you?' Oliath said, shifting to his feet.

Fordon moved away from Oliath and towards the throne room balcony. He opened the shutters and peered over the night-darkened town below. 'No. Even though I do not believe you will carry out such a task, it will not be necessary. I am confident that the girl will come to me, as will Maynard Suavlant.'

'So what *do* you want from me?'

Fordon wheeled round, sending his grey gown into a swirl. 'In time, you will know. I do not expect you to trust me, Captain of the Guard, nor do I particularly care. Equally, I feel inclined to tell you what this is all about.'

The old man's smile twisted into something unnerving. 'After all, you owe it to those who follow you, at least, to find out what you have got them into.'

Chapter 10

In the early morning light, the damage the suoido had caused to the cottage was plain to see, but Ebony overlooked this. She and her father were reunited, and that was far more important.

Ebony had stayed in Sanct Everard the whole night; evident by the creases under her eyes, she had slept little. Almost everyone around her, including Alim and Hazel, was in a similar state of fatigue, except for Maynard, who was just as alert as the night before despite not resting. Maynard had left not long after escorting Ebony to the cottage without bothering to say where he was going. He had done the same throughout the night but always returned a short time later.

Abraham yawned periodically, each accompanied by a guttural sound as he breathed back out. Like the others, he was exhausted, yet Ebony could see that there was more to the redness of his eyes. When she asked what was on his mind, her father reacted as though he had been doused in water, his whole body shuddering. 'There is a lot on my mind... I don't know if I can accept the truth of it all.'

Before Ebony could question further, Abraham placed a hand on her back and directed her into the remains of the cottage. He motioned for Hazel and Alim to wait outside, the two acknowledging with a nod.

'Stay here for a moment, sweetheart,' Abraham said, taking Ebony through what was left of the front hall and into the kitchen where she would be safe from falling debris. 'I just need to speak to Sylvia.'

Ebony did as her father bid and stood at the kitchen entrance, watching as he walked into the living room and closed the door. For a moment, there was a steady silence, the loudest thing being her breathing.

Abraham, Hazel and Alim were already acquainted with Sylvia, having met the doctor, among other times, while Ebony was unconscious. If there had been disquiet between any of them before, there was no sign of this now, certainly not between Alim and Hazel, who were chatting outside in an idle fashion. Ebony could only hope her introduction to Sylvia would go just as smoothly, but she was puzzled about why she had to wait in the kitchen.

Ebony leant against the broken doorframe of the kitchen and listened for any talking. Sure enough, she heard indistinct voices coming from the living room.

She crept closer.

'It's a relief that Ebony is all right,' the muffled voice of a woman said, it no doubt belonging to Sylvia. 'Will you be showing her in?'

'I suppose so,' Abraham replied. 'I just don't know if she will understand.'

'There is no better time than now,' the woman continued after a heavy sigh.'

There was a moment's pause before Abraham spoke again. 'Still… how do you think she will take it all?'

'The same as you, I expect, but neither of us can be sure about that. Anyway, are you certain you don't mind me being alone with Ebony?'

'Of course—there is no reason for me to mind. To be honest, I don't think I can stomach listening to it all again so soon. My sobbing will only make it sound worse than it actually is…'

The living room door creaked open, the conversation ending immediately. Ebony moved her head through the opening and peered inside. The room, which had survived the attack, was in the same condition as always: in the middle was a small, rectangular table with two aged sofas on opposite sides. Standing close to the door, Abraham placed his hands on his hips and looked down upon seeing his daughter. Across the table from her father and sitting on the settee was a blonde-haired woman with rosy cheeks. The woman sat with her back straight and her hands clasped in her lap. At first, she seemed embarrassed even to glance at Ebony, but eventually looked up and into the younger woman's eyes.

Ebony stepped into the room and stopped a couple of metres away from her father, standing at the edge of the room and by an open window. She studied the other woman. 'You must be Sylvia. It is a pleasure to meet you at last.

The woman nodded and offered Ebony a timid smile, folding her arms about herself as if she were cold.

Ebony glanced at Abraham again, who was still looking at the floor in silence. She looked back to Sylvia. 'I must admit that I know little about you, but I hear you are a doctor.'

This comment caused Abraham to let out a soft cry, which made Ebony worry. 'Father, are you all right?'

Abraham wiped his eyes with a sleeve and looked up at his daughter, forcing a smile. 'Just feeling a little poorly. I'll leave the pair of you to discuss things.' He stepped out of the living room then, letting out another heart-breaking sob as he did.

With her father gone, Ebony looked back to Sylvia. The doctor was straight-faced. 'My father has not spoken much about you. I suppose he hasn't had the chance, considering I have seen little of him lately. That said, when I have seen him, he has been in high spirits, which has not been the case for a long time.'

Sylvia squeezed her eyes shut in a way that suggested the comment made her uncomfortable. This aroused Ebony's curiosity.

'And yet,' Ebony continued, 'on our first true encounter, I see him crying. That is also something I have not seen him do for a while, and I am willing to bet it is not because of what has recently happened.'

Sylvia did not say anything, responding only by patting the empty cushion next to her. Ebony pursed her lips at the gesture, choosing instead to sit opposite.

Sylvia spoke then. 'I do not suppose Maynard has told you much.'
Ebony frowned.

'I'm not surprised,' Sylvia continued, noting Ebony's confusion. 'Ninapaige said he was almost as clueless as me regarding the future and why we find ourselves where we are. I will explain who Ninapaige is in a moment, as well as how I know Maynard.'

Her frown fading, Ebony sat back and took a heavy breath. A desire to hear more filled her brown eyes.'

Sylvia tittered, a broad smile spreading on her face. 'I recognise that look… at least some things don't change. That is a comfort considering what *has* changed. When Ninapaige did this to me all those years ago, I did not see

272

it for the kindness she intended—the past ten years have seemed like more of a torment than a blessing.'

'Ten years?' Ebony repeated, the relevance of the number playing on her mind.

Seriousness washed over the doctor then. 'Sylvia is not my original name.'

'What's that supposed to mean?' Ebony asked.

Sylvia gave a crooked smile. 'I'll never forget your face when I handed you my lucky charm. The expression you held suggested I was crazy, and this makes me smile even now.'

Ebony blanched. Goose pimples pricked her skin.

'Do you remember, Ebony,' Sylvia said softly, 'the heart-shaped crystal I gave you?'

Ebony's face twisted as a sharp pain suddenly exploded in her belly. Doubling over in her seat while clutching her middle, she almost retched.

This reaction made Sylvia twitch. She was unsure if comforting the younger woman by touch was wise.

Ebony looked up once again, tears welling in her eyes. 'How can you be so cruel? My mother is dead. You cannot be her... you just can't!'

Seeing Ebony in such distress also caused tears to form in Sylvia's eyes. 'I am not Luanna—that has not been my name for a decade—but I *am* your mother, and that will never change. You must believe me when I say that none of this is my fault. I had no choice.'

'No choice?' Ebony snivelled. 'You have been gone for ten long years—assumed dead without any sign that you still lived!'

Sylvia shook her head. 'It was not as simple as coming home—and seeing me as I am now, surely you can afford some appreciation as to why.'

'No,' Ebony said hoarsely. 'You are lying! My mother is *dead*. How dare you play with other people's emotions in such a way?'

'Do not be so stupid, Ebony!' Sylvia snapped, fighting back her own tears and hurt feelings. 'To accuse me of such sadistic behaviour is unfair, and I have no cause to hurt you, especially in such a way.'

Sylvia rubbed her temples. Such a revelation was never going to be easy.

Remnant Tales of Stilly:
Passion and Benevolence

Ebony was hugging her knees. She was a mixture of emotions: anger, sadness and confusion, to name the strongest. At first, all she had wanted was to strike the woman sitting opposite her, but now she just wanted to hear the truth. 'This Ninapaige you mentioned. Did this person do this to you?'

'When it comes to the birth of Sylvia, yes. However, this is all because of the mess I found myself in, which all started a few days before even parting Wilheard.'

Ten years ago…

It was an early autumn morning: the air was crisp, and the sun glistened on the dew. Holding her hands above her head and connecting her fingers, Luanna stretched as she looked over the tranquil Wilheard below. The rain clouds from the night gone were heading north and making way for a bright but chilly day.

Thane, the largest of Stilly's provinces and the closest region to Wilheard, was nearly sixty miles away. Two of Luanna's work colleagues, with whom she usually travelled, had made the trip to the city a month earlier to carry out dull and pernickety tasks that were neither applicable nor appealing to her. Indeed, spending as little time away from home as possible was far more enticing to Luanna. Besides, she was quietly excited about making such a long trip alone.

The time for Luanna to prepare for the journey was upon her, and she had several jobs to do. One errand in particular was on her mind, and being the more enjoyable of the tasks, she was going to deal with it first. Luanna had often flirted with the idea of taking an alternative route to Thane, which involved going through the eastern woodland, something her travelling companions had always insisted against in the past.

The task was simple enough: stroll through part of the eastern woodland and make sure all was passable. Despite not taking such a route before, Luanna knew that others had travelled through the forest in the past, and all she needed to do was find a popular trail. Travelling by horse and cart would result in a few days' journey if all went smoothly, but considering the time of year, that might not be easy, and fallen trees or swampy areas were a couple of potential hindrances. Fortunately, the trek through the woodland was a minor part of the journey, after which the rest would be familiar and straightforward.

Luanna yawned and turned her attention to the cottage, glancing towards Ebony's bedroom window. Thinking back to the day before, she recalled talking to her daughter about the morning walk and had accepted Ebony's offer for a bit of company. Yet, Ebony was still wrapped up under her bed covers and sleeping away. Although it was out of character for Ebony to be asleep at such an hour, Luanna did not have it in herself to wake her daughter.

Clasping her hands behind her back, Luanna smiled before sauntering towards the trees.

As she made her way deeper into the woodland, Luanna shuddered and wrapped her arms about her chest and shoulders. Despite the nippiness in the air, the autumn leaves and water droplets falling from the saturated tree tops looked beautiful in the pale morning light, which made the walk pleasant enough.

That was until she stepped in a puddle.

'Tender spirits!' Luanna lifted her foot from the puddle's murky water and shook it. The muddy trails she had found so far were discouraging, but she was not about to give up.

Backtracking, Luanna left the path she had been following and took a thinner route beyond some uneven rocks. Although narrower, the track seemed suitable enough for a horse and cart, and finding a way over the stones should not be too much of a problem. She continued a while longer, ensuring the path remained passable. Walking parallel to a channel of brown water, she eventually came to a section where the stream shallowed, allowing her and, more importantly, the horse to cross and continue on the path she had originally planned to take.

Perfect, Luanna said inwardly. *This idea is as good as I knew it would be.*

Remnant Tales of Stilly:
Passion and Benevolence

Taking a deep breath, Luanna smiled broadly, something in the distance catching her eye as she did. Walking round trees and bushes to get a better look, Luanna came face-to-face with a large and heavily damaged bust sitting upon a plinth. The plinth was covered in engravings, which were unusually clear when contrasted with the otherwise heavy damage to the statue.

This was the first time Luanna felt the livnam eyes watching her from within the shadows. She would later realise that the bust represented Godfrey Sanine, and the etchings were Pentominto. Lamentably, she would also come to understand a curse had been placed on the statue, one that would destroy her life.

Outside the woodland once again, Luanna felt more relaxed, and the rest of her day passed with relative normality, despite having to face a lecture on keeping promises from a disgruntled Ebony, who happened to be going through one of her impulsive moods at the time. Indeed, when Luanna saw her daughter that day, the younger woman was wearing a yellow dress so bright that it threatened to blind anyone caught looking at it for too long.

Luanna would spend the next few days with Ebony to make up for the broken promise, which kept her busy until departing from Wilheard.

Walking home from the surgery on the penultimate evening of departure, Luanna buttoned her coat and gazed at the orange clouds in the otherwise dark sky. Despite warm colours, there was no heat in the air. She shivered and shifted her glance towards the silhouette that was her home. Dull candlelight glimmered from the cottage's ground-floor windows. She gazed at the light and folded her arms tightly about her chest.

An icy gust hit Luanna then, making her shudder more. The double layer of clothing was doing little to keep the cold at bay, and she could not wait to get into the warmth of the cottage. Yet, by the time she reached the foot of the hill leading home, she stopped; she had heard a growl, and it had come from what sounded like the eastern woodland.

Luanna looked at the edge of the forest. The snarl had been deep, undoubtedly belonging to something huge. She turned her attention back to the town; few people were outside, and they were all distant. She scanned the trees for movement, softening her breathing to listen for further growls.

A short time later, Luanna spied a pair of Wilheard guards from west of New Market Square. The two men were making a circuit of the town, and judging by their march-like gait, they took their line of work very seriously.

Luanna waited for the guards to walk closer before getting their attention.

'Excuse me, gentlemen,' Luanna called. 'I don't mean to be a bother, but I was wondering if you could put my mind at rest.'

Both guards halted, stiffening to attention.

'We can but do our best, ma'am,' the guard standing to the left of Luanna said. 'What seems to be the problem?'

'Well, you see... I was wondering if you, by chance, heard a growling just a moment ago.'

'Growling, ma'am? No, ma'am,' said the man on the doctor's right.

Luanna pursed her lips. She was convinced she had not imagined it. 'Are you sure? It came from the woodland over there.'

Luanna pointed to the east. The guards looked in the direction she indicated and then back to her.

'Most likely a fox, ma'am—at the most a stray hound,' the left guard continued. 'Critters tend to attract dog senses, you see. Fret not, though, as we shall go and take a closer look.'

Luanna smiled faintly. She was sceptical of the growl being canine. 'A dog, eh? Must be as big as a bear.'

The men exchanged glances.

'A bear, ma'am?' the right-side guard said. 'In Wilheard?'

'I wasn't suggesting there is a bear, just that the dog must be large. The growl was deep, I mean. Don't worry, gentlemen—I was only joking. In any case, I will sleep easier tonight knowing that the two of you had a quick look for me.'

The left guard nodded. 'As you have it, ma'am. For now, you best head home and escape this cold.'

'All right. Thank you.'

'Fair eve to you, ma'am,' the other guard said, finishing the conversation.

Luanna continued slowly up the way leading to the cottage, keeping an eye on the guards as they prodded at bushes and peered round trees. She felt a twinge in her stomach, fearing something was about to jump out from the darkness at any moment, yet nothing did.

Perhaps she had imagined the growl, and her mind had got the better of her.

Stepping inside her home, Luanna gave the woodland one last look before shutting the door.

Ebony sat in silence as Sylvia, a woman claiming to be her mother, relayed her story. Ebony's eyes were raw from crying, but they had since dried.

Everything fit into place, and Ebony remembered it all well. There was little reason to doubt anymore that Sylvia was, in fact, Luanna, although the doctor made it clear that she did not feel comfortable being referred to by the latter name.

'It seems inappropriate to call myself Luanna anymore. Although I still feel the same, the woman I used to be is now just a part of me—an old soul inside.'

Ebony looked to the floor. She was unsure of what to say, and so said nothing.

Sylvia grunted. 'I never thought I would say that, but it is no less the truth.'

'But how?' Ebony said, barely louder than a whisper. 'And why?'

Sylvia sighed. 'I guess the *why* is not as complicated as it would seem. Everything I have said leads up to that, and this is where Ninapaige comes in. I have many regrets, and it is still painful to think about how it came to this. My decision to go through the woodland was reckless, but I will not dwell on that now. When it comes down to it, this all started with finding that bust of Godfrey Sanine. The statue has a curse placed on it, which is why you and Alim are also hunted.'

Remnant Tales of Stilly:
Passion and Benevolence

Ten years ago…

Luanna pressed the heart-shaped crystal into Ebony's palm and closed her daughter's fingers. 'Look after this, Ebony. It is very precious—handed down to me from my mother, who got it from her mother, and so on.'

Ebony opened her hand and admired the jewel. 'It is beautiful. It's hard to think it is so old.'

'It has been well looked after, and I expect you to continue caring for it. After all, it is more than just a pretty crystal.'

'Oh?'

Luanna nodded and smiled. 'It is a good luck charm.'

'I see,' Ebony giggled.

'It's true!'

'Then perhaps you should take it with you on your journey.'

'No,' Luanna insisted. 'I want you to have it. After all, not only will it bring you luck, it will remind you of me.'

Ebony wrinkled her nose; it was evident by the look on her face that she would have preferred Luanna to stay home altogether. She would miss her mother, especially since Luanna planned to be away for the next few months.

'Thank you,' Ebony said.

'You're welcome.'

Luanna turned to Abraham, her husband.

'See you in a few months,' Abraham told his wife, giving her one last kiss before she left. 'I love you with all my heart.'

'You soppy old thing!' Luanna chuckled. 'Then again, I cannot deny that I feel the same way.'

With all her goodbyes done, Luanna moved to the horse that would accompany her on the trip and stroked its muzzle. Myra Dolb, a long-time friend of Luanna's who worked on Wilheard's farm, had loaned the mare.

Luanna tugged on the horse's reins to set it off, pulling the cart behind. 'Look after your father for me, Ebony.'

Ebony and Abraham waved as Luanna walked away, watching her until she disappeared from view.

Remnant Tales of Stilly:
Passion and Benevolence

Half an hour into the journey, Luanna's belly settled down. From the day's beginning, she had been full of nerves, which she had expected considering the lonely conditions, but now that the journey was underway, she felt calmer, mainly thinking how nice it was to be away from the surgery for a change. Furthermore, Luanna was pleased that her planned route was even more accessible than she had imagined; the horse and cart had manoeuvred over the rocks and along the trail comfortably. Everything was going well, and for a time, Luanna had even forgotten about the growling two nights earlier. Unfortunately, this was not to last, and as the weather turned, so too did her frame of mind.

Luanna pulled the hood of her coat over her head and trudged on. The rain intensified, seemingly with every step, saturating the rotting leaves covering the ground and emitting a pungent smell. She looked skywards at the branches' remaining foliage: a large raindrop landed on the centre of her forehead.

Sighing, Luanna turned to the mare. 'Don't worry, girl,' she crooned, removing wet leaves from its back. 'We will be out of here soon, I promise.'

The soothing words did little to calm the horse's nerves, which had become agitated soon after the rain had started. The weather, however, was not the cause of the mere's distress, and as the rain thundered on, it grew more skittish. Its ears twitched, and nostrils flared; it could sense something that Luanna could not.

The horse whickered and pulled back on its rein, forcing Luanna to stop abruptly.

'What on earth has got into you?' she complained, tugging on the mare's harness.

The horse's neck craned forward as Luanna pulled on its head, but its hooves remained firmly on the spot.

With a huff, Luanna gave up struggling with the horse and dropped its harness. 'The longer we stand here, the more we get wet. You do realise that, don't you?'

The mare shook its head and looked back to where they had come. Shielding her eyes from the downpour, Luanna looked in the same direction. With the black clouds overhead, the forest was dark, and Luanna could not see far into the distance. After a few seconds, she looked back to the horse, its attention still fixed backwards.

'I'm surprised you can hear or see anything for all the rain,' Luanna muttered. 'Whatever is holding your interest, I can only imagine that it is small and nothing to fret over... you daft creature!'

The horse glanced at Luanna as she spoke, but after another shake of the head, followed by a snort, it returned its gaze.

'Fine,' Luanna groaned. 'If it will make you feel any better, I will chase whatever is bothering you away. How does that sound?'

With a smile, Luanna brushed her hand over the mare's ridged nose. Pacing in the direction she had come, she reached about five metres from the horse and cart before slowing to a stop. In the distance, amid a cluster of trees, the shape of something unexpected came into view. Bulky and with piercing eyes that seemed to glow in the darkness, the silhouette of a beast glared back. Moments later, and if only to reveal itself, the beast stepped out from the trees and stopped in the trail's centre.

Luanna gaped at what was before her in a state of paralysis, the first thing she noticed being the tusks protruding from its jaw. This monster, with which she would later become familiar, was a suoido: a brutal creature primarily designed from the curse placed upon the King's bust.

Unable to control her body fully, Luanna shifted her feet backwards, dragging them along the waterlogged ground. Noticing the slight movements, the suoido grumbled, saliva foaming from the lower part of its mouth. The beast remained where it was for a while, only moving into action when the doctor made a sudden dash.

Luanna sprinted back towards the horse, aiming for the cart in the hope she would find a makeshift weapon. Haplessly, and with the ground so sodden from the rainfall, a puddle thick with mud enveloped her boot and forced her to stumble. Without looking to find the suoido, Luanna instinctively rolled under the cart, leaving the beast to crash headlong into the wagon.

Luanna crossed her arms over her face as the Suido collided with the cart, somehow avoiding serious injury as it exploded into hundreds of pieces. Stumbling back to her feet, she ran from the trail and towards a mass of trees.

The suoido, recovering from its clumsiness, shook its head and pushed itself upright before looking around to relocate its target. However, before it could continue the chase, it suffered another blow.

After destroying the wooden cart, the suoido subsequently freed the horse from its constraints. Galvanised into a high level of panic, the mare reared onto its hind legs with a deafening scream, coming back down and performing a powerful rear kick that struck the suoido in the side. Hit with a force that not even a monster its size could withstand, the Suoido toppled onto its back, letting out a roar as it splashed to the ground.

The suoido was far behind now. At least, that was what Luanna hoped.

Leaves rustled and twigs snapped next to Luanna's ears as she haphazardly pushed onwards, gasping for breath. How far had she run? She was uncertain, but all she could do—all she wanted to do—was keep going.

So she ran, not stopping even when the aching from her legs spread to her ankles and made its way up to her hips, lower back, and shoulders. So exhausted was Luanna that she struggled to keep herself upright.

Luanna fell onto her front, tripped by a protruding tree root hidden beneath a carpet of leaves. She turned her head to one side and panted. With her eyes closed, Luanna listened to the ongoing rain thrashing everything around her. Mercifully, that was all she could hear.

Luanna pushed herself up and leant on the closest tree. Her breathing slowed to its regular pace and the aching in her limbs faded. Soon, she would be able to move again without much trouble.

Luanna quivered. Her clothes, caked in wet mud, were heavy. She did not know which way to head to get home but knew she could not stay where she was. Picking the most likely direction, Luanna plodded ahead. Maintaining balance was difficult in her state, and she slipped several times.

I will have to be careful with that, Luanna thought as she spied a steep slope to her right.

She rested against a tree and looked down the incline. Indeed, falling down the slope, which looked more like a cliff, would be the moment that defined her misery.

A rustling of leaves sounded above Luanna, waking her from her brooding. Pushing herself from the tree, she squinted into the branches. She could not see for all the foliage, but with every breath she took, the rustling seemed to get closer and closer: so close that whatever was shifting within the trees must have been no more than two metres away when it finally stopped moving.

Luanna held her breath and listened intently, but besides the persisting rain, she heard nothing. Letting out a sigh of relief, she calmed once again.

'There you are,' a high-pitched female voice said then. 'I wondered where you had got to.'

Awash with alarm, Luanna stepped away from the voice, doing precisely what she had wanted to avoid. Tilting backwards, she waved her arms to stay level, but as gravity took hold, she eventually lost her footing.

Luanna threw her arms forward, digging deep into the muddy cliff edge. She grunted as her fingers took the full force of her weight, stopping the fall in an instant.

'Oh dear!' the mystery woman said, moving into view. 'This is quite a predicament.'

Luanna twisted her head to the side and looked down the slope; the drop appeared even steeper than it had a moment ago. She cringed, whimpering as she looked back up. 'W-who are you?'

Standing at no more than two feet tall with a head ever so slightly too large for her shoulders, an imp dressed in yellow and grey clown-like attire peered down at Luanna, her hands on her hips and a devilish grin fixed to her face.

'Ninapaige,' the imp answered. 'And you are Luanna. I would shake your hand, but that might not be wise right now.'

Luanna did not answer. She did not know who Ninapaige was or even how the jester knew her name, but none of that seemed to matter.

'Lu-a-nna,' Ninapaige continued, syllabling the name in a flippant tone. 'I must say, that name of yours is rather insipid on the tongue.'

'Please,' Luanna sobbed. Her muscles were burning. 'Please help me.'

'Help you?' Ninapaige laughed cruelly, causing her silver hair and jester hat to bob. 'And how do you propose I do that? Not only are you out of my reach, but I am one-third your size. Do I look like an ant to you?'

Luanna felt her body slip. 'Stop it! Just stop it!'

Although continuing to smile, Ninapaige's laugh settled to a titter before stopping altogether. She folded her arms. 'You're right… I should not laugh at others' misfortunes. You must forgive me—levity is one of the only things that keep me going these days.'

'Please…'

'All right, all right! I heard you the first time!' Unfolding her arms, Ninapaige raised her right hand. Following a flick of her wrist, something behind Luanna snapped. 'Now, whatever you do, child, remain calm and take hold of this…'

Luanna did not have a chance to question what Ninapaige was doing. Soaring past the doctor's ears with a hiss, a tree branch embedded into the muddy slope beside her. Startled by the sudden impact, Luanna lost what little grip she had left, the last thing she heard being the imp's mocking.

'I told you to remain calm!' Ninapaige called just as Luanna disappeared from sight.

Staring skywards with blurry eyes, Luanna lay motionless at the bottom of the slope. She felt nothing: no warmth, no coldness, not even pain. Her body was numb, as if already dead and simply waiting for her mind to follow suit.

Luanna knew then that she was dying, but before her sight darkened entirely, she saw the same yellow and grey figure approach.

'You poor, poor girl,' Ninapaige whispered softly, all gaiety gone from her voice. 'You have met an unfortunate end.'

Luanna's lips moved as she tried to speak, but all that came was her final breath.

Ninapaige placed her fingers over Luanna's mouth and made a hushing sound. 'I am always so very sorry when faced with death, but the end of a certain life is sometimes necessary for a new one to begin. You will be safe from now on, believe me. I am the only one who can help you now.'

With that, Ninapaige closed Luanna's eyes for the last time.

Remnant Tales of Stilly:
Passion and Benevolence

Luanna could smell burning wood. She lay still and listened to the crackling of kindling, giving off an intense heat that she could feel on her back.

All was dark. Was she blind? Luanna could not even tell if her eyes were open. Was she then dead? Unlikely, but something was amiss.

Luanna felt weak and sore but most noticeably stiff. She wiggled until she flopped onto her back; her arm had fallen asleep where she had been lying on it, but the sensation soon returned, her fingers tingling as she moved them once more.

Shifting her hands to either side, Lanna felt her surroundings: straw... feathers... leaves... all on a stone floor. Was she in a barn? If so, it was empty, and she could not hear any livestock or smell any evidence that there ever had been. If her presumption was correct, and she was in a barn, why was there a fire?

Luanna continued to scrabble about. Every time she prodded, rubbed and scratched, everything she touched felt somehow unusual.

Footsteps interrupted Luanna's musing as someone padded over, stopping to her left.

'Can you feel me?' the familiar child-like voice of Ninapaige asked, taking Luanna's limp hand in her own, smaller hands. She gave Luanna a gentle squeeze. 'Does this hurt?'

'Yes... No,' Luanna said, answering both questions with a gravelly voice that did not sound like her own.

Ninapaige responded with a titter. 'Something is awry, but you cannot put your finger on it, can you?'

'My skin feels different,' Luanna groaned.

'Tingly?'

Luanna tried to shake her head before grunting 'no' instead. 'It feels... strange. Not my own.'

There was a brief silence, followed by a simple response from Ninapaige. 'Perfect.'

Ninapaige let go of Luanna's hand and sat on the doctor's midriff. She prodded at Luanna's face, massaging her cheeks, temple and forehead before tracing her finger down her nose.

'Your eyes will ache for a while, but you should at least be able to use them,' Ninapaige said, running her thumbs over Luanna's eyelids to encourage them open.

'Have I been sleeping a long time?' Luanna asked.

There was another pause, and although Luanna could not see Ninapaige, she knew the imp was smiling. 'You could say that, girl... you have been asleep your whole life. My, my! What lovely blue eyes you have.'

'I have brown eyes,' Luanna corrected.

'Really? I must be imagining things, then. Mind you, blue eyes *are* typical of someone whose hair is as blonde as yours.'

'I'm a brunette,' Luanna again argued.

Ninapaige got up and moved away from Luanna. 'If you say so. Anyway, if you are going to attempt standing, do so slowly. Believe me, neither you nor I want to see you get hurt... at least not again.'

Carefully placing her hands to either side, Luanna pushed herself into a sitting position, groaning as she shifted upright. Her eyes stung, but her vision eventually cleared. Looking around, Luanna first noticed that it was dark outside. As she had deduced, she was in a shack, the hay and feathers she had felt a moment ago now visible. The crackling of fire came from her right, and although the cabin did not contain a hearth and burned on nothing more than a pile of tinder, this did not seem to be a problem. The flames did not spread, and the smoke escaped from a sizable hole in the ceiling. Control of the fire was a result of Ninapaige's sorcery, a power Luanna quickly realised the imp possessed.

Ninapaige, apparently busying herself with something, was sitting cross-legged atop a stool and facing away from Luanna. The sight of the little jester once again startled her.

'Where are we?' Luanna asked. Her voice still sounded unusual, but her throat was at least clearer.

'Pothaven.'

Luanna thought about the answer for a moment. 'Pothaven... that's in Thane.'

'Yes. To the border of Thane, at least.'

Remnant Tales of Stilly:
Passion and Benevolence

Luanna pushed herself to her feet, doing so slowly to avoid falling. It was as if she had never used her legs before.

'You have likely already noticed, but I have cleaned your clothes.' Ninapaige said, still not looking at Luanna.

Luanna looked down at herself. The clothes she had muddied and torn while running were as fresh and clean as when she first put them on.

'There is some food and water over there if you are interested,' Ninapaige pointed.

Luanna glanced at a rickety table in the far corner of the shack. A small selection of fruit lay scattered on its top, a mug of water to the back. Her mouth was dry, and her stomach rumbled, but the last thing she cared to do was eat or drink.

'I like to think I am pretty endowed when it comes to creating new faces,' Ninapaige said, finally turning to look at Luanna. She held up an earthen mask with a broad smile. 'And I don't mind saying you are perhaps my best work.'

Luanna bristled, oddly disgruntled by the remark despite not knowing what it meant.

Ninapaige spoke on. 'You have already experienced a terrible thing, and I say with a heavy heart that you face sad times ahead. I hope these smiles will help ease the pain.'

Luanna uttered something rude under her breath. 'Tender spirits! What are you talking about?'

'That is a filthy tongue you have,' Ninapaige laughed. She hopped down from her perch on the stall and walked towards the shack's exit, pushing the door open and stepping outside.

Luanna instinctively followed, hobbling as she placed one heavy foot before the other.

A brisk wind brushed Luanna's face as she entered the open air. The sky was clear, filled with countless stars and a pail-white moon that had since replaced the rain clouds; the moon was bright, allowing Luanna to see her surroundings clearly, and judging from the trees around her, she was still near the forest.

Remnant Tales of Stilly:
Passion and Benevolence

Luanna spied Ninapaige roughly ten metres from the barn. She was standing beside a puddle.

Ninapaige, who appeared to be admiring her own reflection, was wearing the mask she had shown inside, the varnished clay gleaming in the lunar light. Although aware of Luanna's presence, the imp said nothing and continued to look down at the muddy brown puddle. Stepping closer, Luanna kept her eyes on Ninapaige, only looking away when her own image came into view.

Luanna opened her mouth to gasp, but nothing came out.

As she leant forward and looked into the puddle, the reflection of another woman stared back, a woman she did not recognise, who seemed to mock Luanna with an identical look of disbelief. Luanna moved her hand to her face and gently stroked her hair; the woman in the puddle moved with perfect synchronisation, caressing her own blonde tresses. She did not want to believe it, yet the evidence was clear: the woman gazing back at Luanna *was* Luanna. As Ninapaige had said, it all made sense: blue eyes, blonde hair, and even her voice and skin.

Luanna jolted as Ninapaige cackled. The jester had now removed her mask and gazed at the distraught woman with violet eyes.

'I do not much like your name,' Ninapaige said glibly. 'Have I already told you that?'

Luanna did not reply. Her breathing quickened as her composure crumbled.

Ninapaige went on. 'Indeed, a new face needs a new name. How about… Sylvia? I adore that name. It brings back such fond memories.'

'What have you done to me?' Luanna said, dropping to her knees.

'I have freed you from your problems, girl. That beast that chased you— the suoido—there are more where that came from, and worse, I can tell you that now. These creatures have lost their hunt, and although you will not yet understand my reasoning, you will in due time…' Ninapaige whistled a sigh, a smile returning to her face. 'So… *Sylvia*, what to do with you. For now, I suppose that I will need to teach you, so to speak, how to live this new life I have bestowed upon you.'

Luanna straightened herself and looked away from her reflection. She stayed silent, making Ninapaige wonder if she had even been listening. Luanna's body shook with a multitude of emotions, her mind in a state of confusion. She did not know what to think or do but knew she did not want to stay there. So she ran into the night-darkened forest, not once looking back.

'Don't be too long, Sylvia!' Ninapaige called. 'You have a big day tomorrow.'

Luanna ignored Ninapaige, the imp's laughter fading into the distance as she sprinted away.

In the denseness of the forest, the moonlight abandoned Luanna, leaving her almost blind. The thickets scratched her skin, and the dampened ground restricted her movements, but she pushed on, not stopping for anything she could outpower.

Luanna grunted as she ran headlong into something tall and unflinching, knocking her backwards. Dazed, she looked up to see what stood before her, finding the vague shape of a man.

'Who… are you?' Luanna uttered.

Clad in what sounded like steel, the man knelt next to Luanna. 'Maynard Suavlant, my lady,' he replied. 'Your face is not what I expected to see.'

Scooped up by the man, Luanna lulled her head to one side. Physically and emotionally exhausted, she fell into a deep sleep moments later.

Ebony no longer felt sad or angry; relief replaced these emotions.

At any other time, what Sylvia said would have seemed little more than a tall tale, but it was all too easy to believe, given the circumstances.

Yet what did it all mean, and what was Ninapaige's purpose?

'I awoke in a small house,' Sylvia went on. 'The owners—the parents of Ordaiest Caleb Psoui, and likewise devout believers in the Naitsir faith—took me in after Malcolm Psoui found me on a path leading into Pothaven. He and his wife Rose looked after me until I felt ready to leave.

Remnant Tales of Stilly:
Passion and Benevolence

'Malcolm introduced me to Pothaven and its residents, and it fortunately didn't take long to find a job in the local under-staffed surgery. I stayed with Malcolm and Rose for a few months before getting my own place. I decided to keep the Sylvia persona, as Ninapaige wanted. It wasn't long before Ninapaige came back to me. She would go on about how well I was doing and how it was all for the best. Ninapaige often said she was keeping an eye on me, and she always seemed to know what I was up to, even when I returned to Wilheard.'

'How did you explain what happened?' Ebony asked. 'Malcolm and Rose must have had a lot of questions.'

'Certainly, amnesia would not suffice. I confirmed that I had been travelling, stating that an animal had attacked me and that I had been helped by an unknown man. Of course, I did not mention the other details. I didn't even say that I came from Wilheard, but no one wanted to pry anyway.'

'What of Maynard?'

'I did not see Maynard at all. I believe he, like Ninapaige, watched over me, but not to the same extent. I guess it was misleading to say I knew him. In truth, I know only what Ninapaige has told me.'

Ebony nodded. 'Ninapaige was referring to Maynard... when she said not to trust anyone and that only she could protect you?'

'Yes. Ninapaige made that point particularly clear, stating that any other help would be inadequate. She would speak derisively about Maynard's possible support and sometimes referenced his past as a reason not to trust him, although she seldom talked about that.'

'So Ninapaige did not—or does not—trust Maynard?'

'I assumed as much at first, but now I'm unsure. Ninapaige would often joke about evading him, although she has never told me what he wanted from her. Ninapaige sees Maynard as a brute—unrefined. She calls him *Sombie* for his sombre and emotionless personality. Ninapaige's thoughts of Maynard had an influence on my own opinions. I cannot say that I trust the man fully—I don't know him well enough to do so, and I did not want him near you despite Ninapaige's reassurance that he would bring you no harm. I guess that has all changed now, and even she seems willing to let him roam about town.'

'Ninapaige is *willing* to let him roam?' Ebony repeated. 'Why would—?'

'It does not matter why. I do not know if Maynard is the best help you can get, but that is up for *you* to decide.'

Sylvia stood from the chair and moved to the window behind Ebony. She gazed at Hazel and Alim, who were chuckling at what the other said. 'We should take advantage of what rest we have,' Sylvia uttered, her voice unable to hide her exhaustion. 'After all that talking, I need a little break. You look in need of some sleep, too--'

No sooner had Sylvia finished speaking, Ebony startled the woman by wrapping her arms about her. Ebony smiled as she squeezed.

'It has been ten long years since I last had the chance to do this.' Ebony stepped away from Sylvia, her smile lingering. 'The last twelve or so hours have been hard for me, but that somehow does not compare to the hardships you have endured. You certainly need to rest, and I reckon more than a little.'

Ebony looked out the window at her friends, also noticing Maynard returning from whatever task he had set himself.

'What do you intend to do?' Sylvia asked.

'I believe there is more to why Ninapaige put you through all this and even why Maynard seems to have a particular interest in my wellbeing. I intend to find the answers.'

Ebony turned back to her mother and embraced her one last time before leaving. 'I looked after father as promised, and he needs you now as much as you need him. Don't worry about me—I know I am in safe hands. '

Chapter 11

Not long after taking its light away from Wilheard, the summer sun brought it back for a new day.

Maynard peered around at his surroundings. Despite what had befallen the town not three days ago, all was quiet. The presence of the vigilante in Wilheard was well known by now, and few sought to trouble him. Despite this, and even with most people avoiding the outside at any hour, he kept hidden from view. He had never been particularly social, even before he found himself in this time.

Even so, it seemed Maynard could not escape everyone's attention. Sylvia, alone and morose, hummed a tune as she walked the edge of the eastern woodland. Maynard spotted her before she did him.

Sylvia smiled wanly as she spied the swordsman, who was making his way up the hillside and in her direction. 'You look like a man who wants to be alone.'

'A mutual desire on your part, my lady.'

Sylvia chuckled at the comment but did not deny it. 'Strange, isn't it? I never want to be away from my family again, but I guess I still need a little time to myself. Then again, I am glad I have found you.'

Maynard watched as Sylvia wrapped her arms about herself. 'Are you cold?'

'Hmm? Oh, no, I'm fine. I was just thinking.' Sylvia sighed. 'I confess that I had reservations about you—before you found my daughter, that is. Now I believe you are her best help... and perhaps best for Wilheard.'

'What do you believe is best for Wilheard, my lady?'

'I don't quite know. I wish I did, but Ninapaige has kept me in the dark.'

'Ninapaige?' Maynard repeated.

'Do you know her?'

Maynard shook his head. 'I have heard the name and rumours of her origin, but we are not acquainted. I do know, however, of your relationship with this Ninapaige and her impact on your life.'

'Well... I cannot deny that I have got used to this identity. Luanna is no longer of this world.'

292

Maynard did not answer.

'Anyway,' Sylvia continued, 'Ninapaige knows of you. Very well, from what I can tell. She knows of your return to Wilheard, what abilities you have gained and... and which ones you have lost.'

'I see. I could learn a lot from speaking with this Ninapaige. Mayhap she could even show me the correct path.'

Sylvia shrugged. 'If you managed a meeting with Ninapaige, you would be lucky to get anything from her. She has learnt and seen many things but is reluctant to share most of them. She claims that she has told me all I need to know, and as I said, that is why I am glad to have found you. Do you know about the statue of King Godfrey? The one in the woodland?'

The mention of the past king gained Maynard's full attention.

'I feel their eyes on me, but I am no longer in any personal danger from the monsters. Ninapaige told me not long after I became Sylvia that the threat died with Luanna. I don't know if you are aware, but that particular statue is cursed—a sorcerer placed a spell upon it, which is engraved on its base. She did not tell me much after that, saying it is no longer my concern. Like I said, Ninapaige knows many things but only reveals what she wants. Perhaps she wanted me to pass this information on to you.'

Maynard bowed his head in acknowledgement. 'Very well. In the meantime, I have requested appropriate defence arrangements be made.' He looked towards the castle. 'I will enter Castle Stilly when all is prepared.'

'There is someone inside, isn't there? I know there is. Ninapaige mentioned him while talking to herself. He is the sorcerer I mentioned... the corrupted man.'

'The corrupted man,' Maynard repeated. He closed his eyes and folded his arms, considering all the information. 'Fordon Latnemirt. He is blinded by his desires and consumed by hate. I tried years past, as I will try now, to bring him to reason. Alas, I fear such endeavours are futile.'

'We must all do our best,' Sylvia comforted. 'In the meantime, perhaps you should get your sword worked on.'

Maynard looked down to his waist. 'I plan to, my lady.'

'That's good.' Sylvia gazed at the horizon. The sun had already crept up from behind the distant hills. 'I guess we should get to it. The smithy should be open now. I should go and check on Ebony and my husband. They won't appreciate me wandering off alone.'

'Gratitude for the tidings. I wish you good fortune,' Maynard said, walking away.'

'To you too, Sombie,' Sylvia whispered with a chuckle.

'Have you seen Oliath lately, Ben?' Mayor Basil Wolleb asked his assistant, breaking a perfect silence.

Gazing blurry-eyed at the floor, Benjamin Oswin did not answer; his mind was elsewhere. He was not often without something to do, and he was eager to progress beyond twiddling his thumbs.

'Are you ignoring me, man?'

Benjamin snapped his eyes towards Basil. 'Sorry, Mayor... did you say something?'

Basil hummed and turned to look out the window behind him. 'I was just wondering if you had seen Oliath.'

Benjamin shifted his attention back to the carpet. 'Not since he stormed from Sanct Everard.'

Basil sneered at the thought and stroked the white bristles on his face. That had been two days ago. 'Blasted man! He could not have chosen a more inconvenient time to disappear. Instead of stropping, he should be here organising Wilheard's troops. He is the captain of the guard, after all.'

'I can go and have a look for him,' Benjamin offered, standing from his chair.

'No, don't trouble yourself. Besides, I would prefer you to stay here and help me.'

Benjamin grumbled and sat back down. He jutted out his chin and shuffled his already straight bow tie for the fifth time that morning. 'Could we acquire extra help from Thane?'

'Getting to Thane would take too long. We would not be able to get anything in a reasonable time.' Basil continued to fondle his beard as he watched guards patrolling the otherwise empty Old Market Square. 'Do you have any experience in managing soldiers?'

A short, unintentional burst of laughter forced its way past Benjamin's lips. *Me?* He thought. *Such an attempt would surely get a rise out of them.* 'No, Mayor, I fear I lack the authoritative physique to even try. If I had a booming voice like yours, perhaps, but otherwise… not a chance.'

There was a momentary silence.

'Do you know someone who does?' Basil asked.

Benjamin closed his eyes and thought for a moment. 'Now that you mention it, I believe the butcher is trained in such things. He has regaled me—among others—with tales of past feats. In fact, he once told me--'

'That is a fair point. I forgot about Vincent,' Basil interjected, turning back round to face his assistant. 'Perhaps you can talk to him. While you're at it, try and think of as many people as you can.'

Ben's mood lightened. Now, he had something to do. 'A grand idea, Mayor. I'm on it.'

Before Basil could say anything else, Benjamin was out the door. Basil shrugged and looked back to the window, returning his thoughts to a few hours ago.

It had been dark outside, too early for the sun to rise. Basil, alone in the office, had been wide awake. Unable, or simply unwilling, to sleep, he peered at the room's only source of light: a single candle flame piercing the blackness, its movement almost hypnotic as the gentle flow of air from the open window set it to flicker. The atmosphere had been peaceful, but that changed when the unexpected visitor appeared.

'I recommend that you prepare a defence, Mayor of Wilheard,' a clear voice said from the other side of the office window.

Basil had leapt from his chair and clutched his chest in fright. 'Tender spirits, man! Have you no civility? You can't go about sneaking up on people like that.'

The vigilante, known as Maynard Suavlant, remained inexpressive, appearing neither amused nor apologetic. 'In addition, I advise that you prepare for an opposing assault.'

Basil listened carefully as Maynard spoke of what had happened days ago, explaining his understanding of the situation and what was likely to follow.

'This is an enemy you will not have encountered in the past,' Maynard continued. 'I will be there to help protect your town and face the foe directly, but I require your support and for you to take command of your force.'

Basil straightened himself and stepped closer to the window. 'What do you expect me to do?'

'I ask that you prepare. Nothing more. How you go about these arrangements is your prerogative. All that I ask is that you are ready by the morrow's dusk.'

'You're pushing it a little fine, aren't you? That is quite a request, lad, especially against something—as you put it—unlike anything I have faced before.'

'Hard times demand strong responses.' Maynard moved from the open window. 'I wish you good fortune.'

Basil awoke from his daydreaming and stood up from his desk. *No good will come from sitting here,* he thought. *With or without Oliath, I must get to work.*

It had not taken long for Ebony and Alim to locate Maynard, who, when they found him, was leaving Drah Leets's workshop. The pair, their cheeks pink from rushing about, was slightly out of breath.

'Sylvia… said I might find you… here,' Ebony panted. Maynard gave her a fleeting look and waited for her breathing to steady. She continued speaking once she had done so. 'I take it your sword is being worked on. What are you planning on doing now?'

Maynard flexed his fingers in a way that showed he was ready for action. While his sword was in for repair, the blacksmith had provided him with a temporary replacement. Although considerably smaller and not as durable, the weapon would suffice if a skirmish arose. 'There are a few matters I need to attend.'

Alim, who had retrieved his smoking device from a pocket while Ebony was catching her breath, drew on the pipe as Maynard spoke. 'Is a visit to Sanct Everard among your intentions, old boy?'

Maynard did not reply.

Alim took another puff on his pipe and exhaled. 'Forgive my presumption if not, but I imagine that would be where you would find some answers.'

'Of course,' Ebony murmured. 'I almost forgot about what Ordaiest Psoui had said. He mentioned that he has some ancient writings by Emmanuel Grellic.'

Maynard closed his eyes for a moment. 'It is my hope that I can finally understand how Emmanuel lived. Mayhap my own situation will become clearer.'

'I dare say it is,' Alim said. 'I admit that I am interested in discovering more, too. That is if you don't my nosiness.'

'I require that you *do* accompany me, friend—as I do you, my lady. We all have our fate.' Maynard, upon noticing Ebony's frown, added, 'I cannot say with certainty what the answers are, nor can I predict what lies ahead. However, we must not falter—everything, in time, will become clear.'

Ebony smiled weakly to show understanding, but, in truth, her head was filled with more questions than she could count.

Caleb Psoui ushered Ebony, Alim and Maynard into a side room of Sanct Everard.

As it had been two days prior, every section of the sancture remained covered with townspeople, too afraid to go back home after the attack on the town and preferring to take refuge under the roof of their god. Some people within Sanct Everard were asleep, but this had more to do with the constant anxiety draining their energy rather than the hour of the day. Additional members of the congregation mumbled prayers of comfort while others paced about in what little space was available. The remaining simply slumped in various sitting positions, their glassy eyes showing nothing but solemnness and self-pity.

Although mostly Whilheard's infantry, other people wandered the streets. The soldiers were grateful for the lack of civilian activity in many ways, as it helped keep people out of harm's way. Conversely, they were also happy to assist people who had chosen to brave the outside, primarily the individuals bringing food, water and other supplies to those who remained in the sancture.

Caleb closed the room's door with a gentle push, preventing the iron handle from rattling as best he could. 'I am pleased you came when you did,' he said. 'Those notes from that Minach Emmanuel you have been studying, I believe, have some very intriguing pieces of information. Regrettably, I understand little of the content, but I hope you have more luck.'

Caleb pulled three aged rolls from a simple wooden shelf and gently parted one of the yellow-brown papers across a table. He placed small anjyl stones in each corner and then stepped away. Maynard was the first out of the group to step forward, followed by Ebony and then Alim, who stood at either side of the swordsman. The faded lettering, written in an archaic form of Stillian, made little sense to Ebony. She looked towards the other two and wrinkled her nose.

Alim slowly made his way down the page with a heavy frown that showed deep concentration. Although capable of deciphering the script, it would take him a while.

Fortunately, Maynard did not suffer such limitations. He read a legible section, rewording the text so the others could understand.

1468SN.

It has been a little over six years since the death of King Godfrey Sanine and the sovereign knights who sought to protect this land from the renegade Fordon Latnemirt. Wilheard (or rather Stilly) enjoys peace from such extreme dangers, yet anxieties within the castle have not lessened.

Remnant Tales of Stilly:
Passion and Benevolence

My dear Queen Evelyn Sanine, the only daughter of Godfrey and the beautiful Verity, who was taken by illness a year ago, is at a loss. Although she has adapted to her duties as monarch well, she is fretful that, even with Fordon's demise, life will not remain so tranquil; the roots of the evil that corrupted the once loyal Latnemirt have not parted this world.

Queen Evelyn has confided many of these fears to me, and I cannot deny that I share them. We have been aware of the hidden world truths for too long—and of Phyeroc—which caused me to question my faith. Still, now is not the time for such confessions. The Queen and I have already decided what we must do.

The sovereign knights' bed of rest are scattered throughout Stilly. Although marked with stones, their locations are a secret to all but the men who lay them. I am one such man and shall lead my Queen to their whereabouts.

Alas, this journey is not temporary. We must abandon the town where Castle Stilly dwells; our reasons for such an act are also secret, but knowledge of this will eventually spread. Select few will carry the words, yet even they will not know where we part.

Fordon Latnemirt shall return more powerful than ever before. There is no doubt between us of this belief, and although Phyeroc speaks even further of more terrifying evils, Evelyn and I will combine our might and knowledge to prepare for such inevitabilities. We have already begun doing so by way of her father's bust. As before, Fordon will face opposition, new and old.

Forgive us, those for whom this will concern: you deserve not what will follow our actions. Understand that we face calamity, and we hope you consider us worthy of your protection. Confusion will be upon you, but falter not, as all will become clear. I regret that I must limit what words I ink to these pages, but I hope they find you well when the time arrives. Rest assured that, with effort, you will come to understand.

*One man's hope is another man's bane. To protect loved ones is to deceive them. Misperception eventually begets understanding. One is **not*** *traitorous. One is **not** misbegotten... We must all fight for what we believe.*

Minach Emmanuel Grellic.

Maynard stepped away from the table and left the others to gaze at the sheet of paper.

Ebony turned to the swordsman. 'Phyeroc... I have read that word before.'

There was a momentary silence. Maynard gazed at the sun light pouring through a stained glass window. 'A prophecy,' he said simply.

Alim elaborated. 'I believe the term was mentioned in Passion and Benevolence. Phyeroc is the Pentomino word for prophecy. Do you remember what I told you about Pentominto—the foreign letters we found on the statue of Godfrey? I do not know as much as I would like when it comes to the subject, but if my grandfather's notes are anything to go by--'

'Pardon mine interrupting you, friend,' Maynard said. 'This statue of King Godfrey... I have heard it mentioned numerous times lately. I am aware of a curse and the reason monsters target certain people.'

Alim nodded and pondered a moment. 'I see. I guess that would explain what happened in the woodland.'

The thought caused Ebony to shudder despite already understanding the truth. 'Sylvia... She told me about the statue and the suoido. Still, why would the statue be cursed?'

'We should locate the bust immediately,' Maynard said, leaving the room. 'You have my gratitude, Ordaiest.'

With that, Caleb Psoui found himself alone.

Dexter groaned as he looked through a small opening with a view of the outside world. Wilheard soldiers lined the length of a short but sturdy barricade stretching the lower sections of the hill leading up to Castle Stilly.

'I didn't realise Wilheard had that many soldiers,' Dexter mumbled, removing his hat. He traced the garment's brim with his eyes. 'They even have cannons down there.'

Wiley muttered a response. 'I wonder who is organising them, seeing as Captain Burley is occupied.'

Dexter squinted at the many faces below. 'I can't quite tell.' He re-donned the hat and groaned for a second time. 'I guess it matters little. We won't have much involvement in all of this.'

Wiley grunted. 'Are you telling me you want to fight against the soldiers?'

'Of course not! I simply meant that we have been forced into this dungeon-like room as if we were children. Sat here, we are no use to anyone.'

Wiley offered a sympathetic nod. 'As irritating as it might seem, I'm sure Captain Burley is simply looking out for our wellbeing. It is obvious that he does not trust this Fordon Latnemirt, and I believe he wants to keep us away from the old man.'

Dexter tightened his lips. 'Still, we are sitting in the soldiers' main line of fire.'

'Do you honestly think an order to destroy the castle will be given? I hope they will not be so brutish regarding such a historical landmark.'

'Respectfully, Wiley, what you *hope* will not happen and what actually *might* happen are different matters.' Dexter rested his chin in his palm. 'Faced with what the town has seen recently, such a move is hardly an impossibility. Still, I hope you're right.'

'Why can't we leave this room? It's cold in here,' Meddia complained. Until now, the teenager had been keeping to herself by making friends with a mouse hiding within the cracks of the walls.

Wiley leant back and gazed at the ceiling. 'I guess we *could* leave the room if we wanted, but we have been advised against it. Walking about the castle would probably not be a good idea at the moment.' Wiley attempted to lighten the mood. 'Besides, this place is *ginormous*—it would take days to see it all! Do not worry, Meddia. After all this, I promise we can do something more fun.'

Meddia pouted. 'All right,' she said innocently. 'But if Rida has gone exploring, I don't see why we can't.'

Wiley and Dexter turned their attention to Meddia before looking to all corners of the room.

'Tender spirits!' Wiley exclaimed. 'How does he do that?'

'Rida does what Rida does best… whatever that is.' Dexter shifted himself to his feet and straightened his coat. 'Besides, I agree with Meddia. This room is on the chilly side. If we go and explore a little, we could probably warm ourselves.'

'Oh?' Wiley said hesitantly. 'What if we run into trouble?'

'If you are referring to those things we encountered in the throne room, then I don't believe we will have any problems.'

'You do not *believe* we will have any problems?' Wiley repeated emphatically.

'I know, I know… I cannot be certain, but when you think about it, those faceless anomalies only attacked us when we got closer to that old man. They must be under his complete control. Anyway, we should follow Rida's example and do what *we* do best—investigate.'

Although apprehensive, Wiley could not deny that he felt the same. 'I guess you have a point. However'—he leant closer to Dexter, softening his tone—'we must be careful. We may not be a concern for the old man now, but if we discover something that he would rather we not, which is very likely, then we will become just that—a concern. I know you will be fine, and I am not worried about me, but I want Meddia to be safe.'

Dexter gave a subtle nod, seriousness in his eyes. 'I understand. I do not want her or anyone to get hurt, but let's be more proactive, all the same.'

Wiley stepped away from Dexter. 'Very well,' he said, clapping his hands and getting a rise of excitement from Meddia. 'But we stay together.'

'There is something I have been meaning to ask you,' Ebony told Maynard.

Remnant Tales of Stilly:
Passion and Benevolence

Ebony was close to the swordsman, walking a fraction behind him. He gave her a sideways glance.

'I know you are the one I have heard playing on the guitar. That melody you play is called Ballad of the Deity. My mother taught me the tune on piano as a child, as did her mother. I was told it is an old melody passed down through my family. I should not be too surprised that others might know it, but I am curious... where did you learn it?'

There was a momentary silence before Maynard answered, with only the soothing rustling of the woodland trees disturbing the calm. At first, it seemed that he did not know how to respond.

'A long time ago, a woman dear to this kingdom taught my comrades and me the notes. Despite our theories, we were unsure of her reasoning, but she was insistent.'

'Are you referring to Queen Evelyn?' Ebony interjected.

Maynard continued to look ahead. 'Just so, albeit she was but a princess last we met. How much, pray tell, do you know about Evelyn Sanine?'

With some help from Alim, Ebony recounted critical parts of what she knew, explaining what she had read from Passion and Benevolence and what they had learned from Ted Larring's notes.

'I see. Mayhap your knowledge is greater than mine own,' Maynard said after Ebony finished explaining. He went back to what he remembered. 'The princess told us sovereign knights that, if we found ourselves lost, the melody would allow us to see the way. The theory was that we would not need to find our path as it would find us. You are the one I sought, but it seems you sought me, too.

'Princess Evelyn and Minach Emmanuel were very secretive and shared their activities solely with each other. Even King Godfrey knew not of what they hid. Alas, despite Godfrey being a kind man, these clandestine exploits owed to the king's well-known intolerance towards anything that deviated from his faith.'

Alim, who was leading the way into the forest, turned round so that he was walking backwards. 'Yet, the sovereign knights knew of these secrets... all the same, you kept that knowledge to yourself, didn't you?'

'Yes,' Maynard responded, a trace of shame in his voice.

'Not to question your loyalty,' Ebony said, 'but what made you withhold such information from the king?'

Maynard did not answer, again as if he were unsure how to do so.

Alim stopped walking then. 'It's because you believe in Phyeroc. Did Evelyn and Emmanuel ever suspect this?'

Although his face would not show it, Maynard's eyes could not hide his feelings. 'King Godfrey entrusted us to uphold his law—his beliefs. We were torn between what we considered best for Stilly and our loyalty. We did not wish to deceive our king, but we trusted the actions of the princess and minach. Whether Emmanuel and Evelyn were aware of our knowledge…'

Maynard did not finish what was on his mind.

'Could these beliefs not have coexisted?' Ebony asked. 'The sovereign knights performed their duty. Surely it was in Godfrey's interest to trust the people around him, whatever his beliefs.'

'King Godfrey would never have accepted such differing views, even from his most trustworthy subjects. When Latnemirt attacked the castle, I wondered if we had made the right decision in hiding this knowledge. Regardless, after the regicide of Godfrey, we continued to serve, and we fought to the end. At least, I thought it was the end.

'I am in an era that is not mine, and until recently, I have been adrift for almost forty years. What I do know is that Wilheard is in danger, and as a sovereign knight, I must protect her. Alas, circumstances have changed, and despite what abilities I have gained, I feel half the man I once was.'

Fundamentally, Ebony understood. Although Maynard had gained strength, speed and far greater sensory perception, he had, in turn, lost some of his humanity. Physical ageing was gone, as was his ability to show emotions: fear, pride, joy and sadness were trapped inside. Yet, although Maynard's passion had since abandoned him, Ebony could see his benevolence remained.

'I'm sure everything will fall into place soon, so don't lose heart,' Alim reassured.

A little farther into their journey, another question came to Ebony. 'Those beasts that attacked Wilheard—you and Sylvia called them suoido or suoidi, but Emmanuel does not mention them in his book. Have you fought with them before?'

'Suoidi, or suoido if there is only one, are something that Minch Emmanuel may never have encountered. My comrade Elgin Hosp and I discovered notes and sketches detailing many monstrosities in Fordon Latnemirt's chamber soon after he attacked the castle. Although I did not fight such creatures then, I have faced numerous in recent years.'

Maynard shifted the conversation. 'You mentioned in Sanct Everard that this Sylvia spoke of a curse. She recently raised the subject with me as well.

'Sylvia has spoken to you?' Ebony asked.

'Yes. Sylvia claims that the engravings on the Stone King's plinth are the curse, but I believe this to be a misconception. The statue is cursed, and anyone unfortunate enough to view it is deemed consequentially a threat by the spellbinder.'

Alim, who had been listening to Maynard, hummed with intrigue. 'Then, if I am not mistaken, the Pentominto—which is what the inscriptions are— were etched by someone who knew this Fordon character, and this someone carved these letterings as a precaution against any future conflict.'

'That is my assumption,' Maynard said, 'which is why we must locate the Stone King.'

'Incidentally, Alim,' Ebony said, 'Do you mind if I ask what happened to your grandfather?'

Alim knew what Ebony was thinking. 'He lived until a ripe old age and died of natural causes. Of course, he saw the Stone King, among other things, but if he faced the same troubles as everyone else, he never mentioned or warned against them.'

Ebony turned to Maynard again. 'Did you ever meet a Ted Larring?'

'It is possible, my lady. I have met and helped many people over the last 40 years but rarely ascertained names.'

Alim shrugged. 'Whatever the truth of the matter, I will think about it at a later date.'

'All right,' Ebony said.

A short time had passed when the trio reached the derelict bust of Godfrey Sanine.

Remnant Tales of Stilly:
Passion and Benevolence

'And here we are,' Alim said, pushing aside the low-hanging branches of a tree near the stone plinth.

Maynard peered up at the ravaged eyes of the sculpture. Even though he had seen the bust many times over the years, a sinking feeling always struck him. The stone was already in a sorry state, but Maynard knew what he had to do then would be the final insult to the king.

Maynard unsheathed his weapon and turned away from the statue. 'Pore over the plinth for anything you may have overlooked. Duplicate the Pentominto as best you can...' He paused for a moment. 'I recommend you do so with haste. We are no longer alone.'

Alim, shadowed by Ebony, jogged towards the Stone King and heaved, pushed and scrubbed everything they could away from the plinth, unveiling further carvings.

'There!' Alim exclaimed. 'We have found some--'

A suoido leapt over a bush several metres away and charged towards Ebony and Alim. Mercifully, it never had a chance to reach them.

Maynard skewered the suoido's neck, forcing the beast to crash to the floor. Two more replaced the fallen suoido, this time targeting the swordsman. Maynard brought his weapon up, slashing the first of the suoidi diagonally before bringing the blade back down on the other, killing both in quick succession.

Ebony could hardly keep up with Maynard as he took down each suoidi, the swordsman almost dancing as monster after monster came at him. No matter how many appeared, he remained unperturbed, outperforming every threat with frightening ferocity. Indeed, the resulting bloodshed was enough to turn her stomach.

'All right,' Alim said, stealing Ebony's focus. 'I think I have all of it. Unless you see anything I might have missed.'

Ebony looked at Alim's notes, back at the statue, and again at the notes. 'It looks all in place to me. Let's tell Maynard.'

The pair stood and looked towards the swordsman, ducking a limb as it flew their way.

'Maynard!' Alim shouted, cupping his hands round his mouth. 'We have all the details.'

Remnant Tales of Stilly:
Passion and Benevolence

'Then step away from the king!' Maynard called back.

As Ebony and Alim took refuge behind a line of trees, Maynard slew all the suoidi surrounding him with a horizontal swipe of his blade, save for one of the beasts, which he knocked back with a hefty kick. Dropping his sword, Maynard moved to the dazed suoido and dragged it to its feet. Taking hold of the creature by its underbelly, he heaved it into the air and tossed it with all his might towards the statue.

A loud crack sounded as the suoido struck the statue, the monster landing so hard that it died instantly. Maynard followed behind the suoido, using it to leap towards the stone before the corpse could disappear. Under the sheer power of the ensuing kick, the already damaged bust and plinth shattered, scattering everywhere.

Maynard straightened and recollected his sword. Then, as before the ambush, everything was calm.

'I don't think that could have got much more intense,' Alim said, trembling with a mixture of nervousness and excitement.

Maynard looked behind Alim and Ebony. 'Do not rest yet.'

Hearing a gurgling from behind them, Ebony and Alim turned their attention. Twigs snapped and flora flattened as a repugnant black substance seeped from the cracked ground, forcing anything in its way aside.

The fluid stank, forming a rancid taste in Ebony's throat. The smell was almost enough to make her retch, but the figure that emerged from the pool was what disturbed her the most: standing at over seven feet tall, clad in black armour that repelled all manner of colour and light, stood a faceless being, a gigantic sword with a serrated edge in hand.

Despite the lack of eyes, Ebony could feel the being glaring down at her. She shuddered as a cold hand touched her shoulder from behind. Maynard pulled in front, his own smaller sword tight in his grip. The humanoid, a tougher variant of redifass known as a Warrior, remained where it was and turned whatever gaze it had on the swordsman.

'Make haste for Wilheard town,' Maynard said softly, focusing solely on the redifass. 'Run as fast as you can... do not look back.'

Before Ebony could think about what was happening, Alim snatched her upper arm and whisked her away. 'Time to put your running abilities to the limit, dear girl!'

The sudden movement caused the redifass to give chase. Maynard responded by dashing towards it, barging the being to the floor. The redifass twisted as it dropped, allowing it to regain footing as soon as it hit the floor. Turning its attention towards Maynard, the redifass swung its sword perfectly horizontally, aiming for his neck. Maynard ducked the slash and leapt to one side as a nearby tree crashed down, felled by the humanoid's colossal sword.

The redifass resumed its pursuit of Ebony and Alim, leaving Maynard to catch up.

Although smaller than the redifass, Maynard was more than a match for his opponent. Indeed, being the faster and stronger of the two, Maynard easily outpaced the redifass, tackling the giant and mercilessly hurling it to the ground with an almighty thud. On its back, the redifass counted a thrusting attack, forcing Maynard to evade a similar stab. Regaining its balance once again, the redifass did not continue after the other two; instead, it focused solely on the swordsman, who was proving too much of a hindrance to ignore.

Ebony panted as she tailed Alim. He was as fast as ever, but this time, she was able to keep up with him. Everything around her was a blur, her attention centred on getting away and back to Wilheard. Would Maynard be all right? She wanted to tell Alim her concerns but could not get the words out between each heavy breath.

'I'm sure Maynard is fine,' Alim called back to Ebony as if reading her mind. 'I can't imagine that kind of brute would be too much of a challenge for him.'

Clock Tower came into view through the thinning trees, as did the roofs of other buildings. The two stopped a dozen metres away from the woodland's exit.

Exhausted, Ebony dropped to her knees and looked at Alim. He collared the sweat from his eyes and bent over, placing his hands on his thighs. He looked at Ebony briefly and then tilted his head to his left. 'It would seem that everything is coming alive. I bet you have never seen the town so active, dear girl.'

Ebony craned her neck to see. Standing a few feet from one another and guarding what appeared to be the forest border, she saw four heavily armoured men, each equipped with lances. Finding her feet, Ebony stepped closer. As she did so, more soldiers came into view. Men and women, all similarly outfitted in metal, formed a line and kept an eye out for anyone (or anything) that might emerge from within the thickets. As expected, Ebony and Alim were spotted as they approached the edge.

'You there!' called one guard with an intense voice. 'Advance and be recognised!'

Several nearby troops held their weapons down, pointing the spear tip where Ebony and Alim stood. The pair crept into view with their arms held in the air. The guard, who had initially spotted the two, squinted exaggeratedly as if he had never seen another person in his life. 'Are you denizens of Wilheard?'

'Yes,' Ebony answered. She nodded towards Alim. 'Actually, my friend here is visiting and--'

The guard interrupted. 'What, in all things holy, are you doing in the forest? Don't you know what's going on about town?'

'We are very much aware of what is going on,' Alim said with a hint of annoyance. 'I dare say a lot more than you.'

Taken aback by Alim's rebuttal, the soldier was, for a moment, lost for words. 'Don't you be giving me any of your backchat, son! Now—the pair of you come out here this instant!'

Ebony groaned. 'But we are waiting for--'

'What did I say about backchat?' the guard said, interrupting Ebony a second time. 'Come on out. I don't want to have to go in and get you, but I will if--'

A heavy sword slammed down in front of Ebony and Alim. The redifass had finally caught up with the pair, bursting from the surroundings and intent on finishing its hunt. The sword missed Ebony by three feet, causing her and the guard to tumble backwards as if blowing them over.

Redifass were not known to be particularly clumsy. Sacrificing speed and impulse for accuracy, the beings, if able to catch their target unawares, would invariably hit their mark. Not being aware of the redifass's location, neither Ebony nor Alim would have had a chance to dodge the looming attack. All the same, the humanoid missed, but this was not without reason.

Before apparently escaping Maynard, the redifass had suffered extensive wounds, most notably a long slash that reached along the length of its facial area. Further gashes and stab wounds riddled its body, including the broken shard of steel that had been Maynard's sword protruding from the punctured breast armour.

Before the redifass could rectify its mistakes, Maynard vaulted from the same direction as the giant and landed on its shoulders. He placed his hands on either side of the redifass's head and made a sharp twist, the sickening sound one could expect following suit.

Maynard rose almost ominously from the redifass and looked at Ebony and Alim. 'Apologies to you both—I was stricken by momentary recklessness. The redifass should never have reached you.' Maynard turned his attention to the soldier who had approached Ebony and Alim moments earlier. 'Is everything well?'

'Yes, thank you, all things considering,' Ebony answered, helped up again by Alim. 'In fact, these kind soldiers were verifying our wellbeing before letting us through.'

The guard, who was only just righting himself, nodded frantically. 'Th-that's right,' he stuttered. He stepped aside. 'Be s-safe.'

'Ta very much, old boy,' Alim replied, stifling a laugh. 'I am certain we will be just fine.'

Maynard collected the broken steel from the ground, now free of the dispersed redifass remains, and walked through the line of soldiers. 'Very well,' he said. 'I appreciate your concerns and efforts.'

With that, Maynard, Ebony and Alim walked back into town, leaving the line of soldiers to piece together what they had just witnessed.

'His confidence appears diminished.'

Captain Burley sighed as he peered through the misty glass of a small window. The congregating Wilheard army resembled insects from his vantage point in the castle.

'Are you referring to Fordon Latnemirt, sir?' Nolan asked as he rummaged through an assortment of decayed weaponry.

Oliath wheeled away from the window. 'Yes, and all very abruptly. Something has not gone to plan.'

Cordelia, watching her male counterpart as he threw aside useless weapons, harrumphed. 'That would explain the old man's sudden edginess. Still, Fordon remains a present danger.'

'Undoubtedly,' Oliath said. 'I am not suggesting Latnemirt is the same as how we found him, but something is amiss. It is as if the vigilante has done something to upset him. He keeps cursing the very name of Maynard, at least.'

There was a moment's silence.

'What are *your* plans, sir?' Cordelia asked her boss.

Oliath murmured and pinched the bridge of his nose. 'As it stands, we have little choice but to go along with what Latnemirt says, and since I cannot anticipate what that will be, all ideas seem pointless. If the two of you have any suggestions, I'm listening.'

Nolan and Cordelia kept quiet.

'Not to worry,' Oliath continued. 'It is not the first time we have been forced to think on our feet. When the time for action comes, we will know what to do.'

'Indeed you will, Captain Burley.'

All attention snapped towards the voice sounding from the top of a staircase. Fordon made his way down the steps, his hands clasped behind his back and a false smile fixed on his face. Oliath's heart felt as if it were thumping against his ribcage. How much had the old man heard?

Fordon spoke on. 'The time for my—or perhaps I should say *our*—plans to be acted upon is rapidly approaching. That insufferable sovereign knight has, it would seem, become aware of some of my resources.'

Fordon was speaking about the bust of King Godfrey in the eastern woodland, which Maynard had destroyed hours earlier, but the significance of his words held little meaning to Oliath.

'The ytyism spell I had placed on the stone king has been lying practically dormant. I owe a fraction of my current strength to that spell. Feeding from the energy that it gathered has benefited me greatly. Be that as it may, this is not much of a concern and does not truly worry me. If only I had had the power to destroy that bust at the time. Alas, the original spell was just too much for me to...'

Oliath frowned at the old man's lapse of speech.

The voice in Fordon's head spoke to him then: a gentle voice, silent for many years, that had recently become ever more garrulous.

Do you see the way he looks at you? He is trying to figure you out, the voice told Fordon. *They all are... they all think you are a fool. They think they know you...*

Fordon awoke from his musing, the same forced grin returning. 'Never mind—there is no use worrying about it all now. You see, Captain of the Guard, I have problems aplenty, and many people, as has always been the case, stand in my way. I can tell you now that I do not need more complications in this already complex matter.'

'Do you see me as a threat?' Oliath asked.

Fordon gave a humourless laugh. 'Of course I see you as a threat. You think you know me—that I will eventually let my guard down. You are a shrewd man, Captain, and for all your spying on me, you will have learned a lot. However, if you believe my frustration indicates lost resolve, I can assure you that you are mistaken.'

Oliath swallowed and shifted his gaze to the floor, lost for a suitable response. He could not remember the last time he felt this nervous—and to think this old man was the cause of that anxiety.

That put the fool in his place, the inner voice continued. *Is that fear in his eyes?*

Fordon snorted and turned away from the captain, walking towards the throne room. He beckoned Oliath to follow, who did, along with Nolan and Cordelia. 'Now you believe that it is I who poses a threat to you. I will not

312

deny that my heart is very much on my sleeve when it comes to my aspirations—it has been that way for most of my later life. As you will come to realise, I will not face confrontation lying down—not from the sovereign knight, not from Rosaleen, and not from you, Captain of the Guard, but that does not mean we are incapable of seeing eye-to-eye.'

Oliath cleared his throat so that he could at least utter a response. 'And what exactly are your aspirations?'

Fordon pushed open the grand doors of the throne room and stepped inside, linking his fingers behind his back once more. The clinking of shoes echoed throughout the hall, which Oliath noted had returned to splendour. Fordon led the three following him to the table that centred the room and gestured for them to sit down. Oliath sat directly opposite the older man, as always Nolan and Cordelia taking either side of their boss.

Gazing at Oliath, Fordon steepled his fingers and leant into his seat. A silence followed: a silence that seemed to last longer than it should.

He thinks he knows you, but he does not... he does not know you as you know him, the voice said. *Perhaps he could know. Perhaps you could make him understand.*

Fordon finally broke the hush. 'Despite what you might think, there is little you know about me. Although I was against it initially, I think it would be counterproductive to keep you in the dark.'

Oliath kept quiet. Unlike Fordon, his posture was rigid: sitting forward in his seat and leaning on the table.

'As I mentioned, Captain, I have been observing you—much more than you realise. However, do not concern yourself with that fact. During this time, I have come to understand how you work—what motivates you and even how you see the world. You harbour exceptional intelligence, and that is something I do not say lightly.' Fordon shifted forward. 'If you are to truly appreciate my intention, then I must explain them.'

'Why me?' Oliath asked. 'What makes you think I will see things your way?'

Fordon once again sat back in his chair. 'I cannot guarantee you will, but I know that you and I are not that different.'

Oliath wrinkled his nose.

'Don't look so indignant,' Fordon said. 'We both believe in what is best for the future.'

Oliath scoffed at the remark. 'I know exactly what I want, old man, and how I wish to realise it. Unlike you, however, I am not nearly as overt.'

The comeback made Fordon smile. 'If you say so, Captain.'

He thinks he knows you…

'Besides,' Oliath continued before Fordon had a chance to speak further. 'You say I know little about you, but that does not mean I know nothing.'

'Oh?' Fordon said, cocking an eyebrow. 'I did not mean to suggest such… pray tell, what is on your mind.'

Emboldened, Oliath smirked. 'I know you want control and will not stop until you get it.'

Fordon haughtily dismissed the suggestion with a flick of his wrist. 'Far too simplistic.'

'Furthermore,' Oliath went on. 'I know you were not born in this century—or the last, for that matter—and that goes for the vigilante, too. I can tell you are weary of the world by how you choose your words. However, instead of simply accepting how life is, you have the hubris to tell people they are wrong and say what is best for them.'

By now, Oliath had Fordon's complete attention, the mage's smile waning as the atmosphere became all the more serious.

Oliath talked further, settling back into his chair and finally feeling more in control. 'There is something else. Despite how noble you feel, your selfishness is almost palpable. Whilst you are happy for people to stand by your side, you have no qualms in despatching those who do not, and I will go as far as to say that you are happy to exploit the former to achieve what you ultimately desire. I admit that I cannot begin to understand *what* this desire truly is, but it is strong enough for you not to let it go and simply die peacefully.'

Once again, there was an awkward silence.

He thinks he knows you…he knows nothing.

'Your words are harsh, Captain Burley,' Fordon uttered, gently tugging on his beard. He turned his attention to the decorative table and scanned its spiritual design. Anjyls denied the will of livnam and the damned that was coming from all directions, desperately trying to scale a circular wall of mountains, in the centre of which, a pool of light that supposedly led to paradise.

Fordon slid his hands over the surface and looked back towards Oliath. 'Look at this design... magnificent, would you not agree? Despite having no actual experience when it comes to a spirit world, the sculptor has managed to create something so detailed and real, something that would have taken an inestimable amount of hours, in which many, even now, believe what they see to be the true depiction of the Naitsir faith. You do not strike me as a particularly pious man, Captain Burley, but I am confident that even one such as you can marvel at the beauty before you and appreciate the labour that went into its very design. Regardless, and no matter how ingenious something might be, that does not change the fact that it manifested from inside someone's head.'

Oliath folded his arms and shrugged. 'So I can presume you are not a believer of the Naitsir faith.'

'That is beside my point. You see, Captain, I am the creative sort as well. You claim I want control, but that is not true—far from it. I want to create a world different to what you see now. One that is without the unnecessary hardship and ignorance that is present. Of course, a world is no true world without life.'

'And how do you intend to achieve such a thing? Is your sorcery alone even capable of such grandeur?'

Fordon's smile returned. 'I am pleased you asked, and there is a reason why I mention religion. However, I suggest you abandon all beliefs you might hold, for they are lies and assumptions. The world and life as we know it was not created by a single, supreme god, but rather by a species, albeit one possessing a celestial essence that we, as humans, might perceive as godly.'

Oliath pinched his lips between his finger and thumb, contemplating what the mage said. 'So you are saying we are the product of alien life?'

This made Fordon chuckle. 'One could label them as much, or even a race from another dimension. They call themselves ytied.'

'Where is your proof that such a race exists?'

Remnant Tales of Stilly:
Passion and Benevolence

Fordon stood from his chair and walked from the table. 'Where do you think my powers originate?'

Oliath did not answer; he continued to ponder.

Fordon resumed talking. 'In truth, one need not believe in ytied to learn their ways. Yet, I can tell you that I have personally met one. One banished by her brothers and sisters. A fallen goddess, if you will.'

Oliath gazed at Fordon, following the old man's movements.

'Your current thought would be that of doubt, Captain Burley. Why should you believe me? You do not have to, for what I say will prove itself in time.'

'Say that I do believe you. With all that I have seen in recent days, I can give you the benefit of the doubt. Yet, that still does not explain how you hope to achieve anything.'

Fordon stood at the throne room's balcony entrance and peered at the blue sky. 'As I am now, I cannot, and you are right to question my current power. For me to be able to create a world like a ytied, I need to be as powerful as a ytied. Indeed, Rosaleen, the fallen goddess I met, promised me exactly that— for me to transcend humanity and become one like her—a brother. Alas, I was a fool to believe such words. It was all deception, merely to use me to do what she was too frightened to do herself.' Fordon lowered his voice. 'All because of Phyeroc...'

Oliath frowned. 'What is a phyeroc?'

'Complicated,' Fordon said as he turned his attention back to the table. He had not intended for Oliath to hear that last part. 'What is important is how I will punish Rosaleen. She betrayed my trust, but that will not cloud my judgment, and I will bring a better future. I will be more than Rosaleen could ever be.

'So you have been gathering strength over the centuries? Like from that statue you mentioned... the Stone King, was it?'

'Yes, the bust of Godfrey—the last king of Stilly. However, compared to the girl's power, such energy is insignificant.

'Girl?' Oliath said.

'Yes... the one with the sovereign knight you call a vigilante.'

'You mean Ebony Gibenn?'

'Ebony Gibenn,' Fordon repeated. 'Although she does not realise it, that girl has the necessary power for me to confront Rosaleen as an equal.

The only thing Oliath could offer, as could Nolan and Cordelia sitting beside him, was a look of astonishment.

'Indeed,' Fordon continued, once again playing with his beard, 'I failed to obtain similar energy from Evelyn centuries ago. I was careless at that time. I risked losing not only Evelyn's energy but mine own. The danger I face now is not much different, but then, nor is my purpose.'

'You see revenge as a purpose?'

He thinks he knows you... he knows nothing.

'Do not mock me, Captain. Granted, my desire to destroy Rosaleen is strong, but that is not my ultimate aspiration.'

No, Oliath thought, *it's all about those ytied.* 'So what does Evelyn, and more importantly Ebony, have to do with your ambition?'

'Admittedly, that is all about Phyeroc. I do not wish to delve too deeply into it all, but in essence, phyeroc means prophecy. Rosaleen believed Evelyn to be a danger to her existence, and she intended for me to be the princess'— as she was at the time—assassin. This, Rosaleen lied, was all she wanted, but she did not explain what she feared about Evelyn. However, I did not have to ask to discover her true intentions.

'Before her planned execution, after the murder of a sister and brother, Rosaleen fled to the human world, in doing so sacrificing some of the qualities that make her a ytied. During her escape, Rosaleen sustained horrific, albeit nonfatal, injuries. Daring not to pursue their forsaken sister into our world, ytiedinity simply created a prophecy—a fate that would eventually bring Rosaleen to justice. During her time in Stilly, she has sought to counter Phyeroc and use it against her siblings. Throughout history, ytied have specifically led people, albeit subliminally, to rise against Rosaleen. Of course, it is left for her to discover who these people will be.'

Oliath closed his eyes and leaned on the round table, pushing two fingers into his left temple. He was struggling to piece it all together. 'So Evelyn turned out to be one such person influenced by the ytied?'

'This is without a doubt.'

Oliath groaned. 'This is so complicated. It is enough to give me a headache.'

'You know not the half of it. In any case, Ebony Gibenn is the victim of an identical fate. The poor girl—I truly wish that I could leave her be. Alas, she is an unavoidable sacrifice.'

'Unavoidable?' Oliath repeated scornfully. 'Nothing you said changes the fact that this is for your own selfish gain, solely because you cannot accept how things are.'

'Enough!' Fordon roared. 'I do not need to justify myself to you, Burley, and if you can still claim ignorance after all that I have said, then I am merely wasting my breath. The world is corrupt, and that is all because of Rosaleen. She deserves nothing but an empty death, and I will be there to see her get just that. I can create a better world only once I have succeeded in this task.'

'You self-righteous fool!' Oliath said, letting out a sardonic laugh. 'I imagine you see yourself in favour of these ytied, put on this planet to defeat this Rosaleen you so hate.'

*How dare he say such things! That ignorant buffoon—he knows **nothing**!*

Conjuring his curved sword to hand, Fordon slammed it into the centre of the table, striking the pool of light and turning it black as the blade pierced through the ornate surface. This ended Oliath's laughter.

Fordon drew attention to the sapphire stone fixed into the hilt. 'Rosaleen also hoped for me to uncover something else while in Wilheard: Omnipotent, an orb with almost limitless capabilities that can create as well as destroy. Rosaleen ultimately designed Omnipotent as a vessel for energy. The more energy it gathers over time, the more lethal she can become once it is back in her grasp. Are you familiar with Stilly's royal history, Captain?'

'Vaguely,' Oliath replied.

'It was rumoured that Godfrey, the last king of Stilly, had hidden Omnipotent with his daughter Evelyn. Many took this literally, but it turned out to be within a statue of her image.'

Fordon was referring to the sculpture of Evelyn, located in Old Market Square. Oliath quickly surmised this. 'I know the one,' he said. 'It has a hand missing.'

'Yes. I believe that Ninapaige, one of Rosaleen's renegade creations, found the orb first. I will not waste time explaining what little knowledge I have on that imp, but I know she does not intend to return it to her mistress. I considered taking Omnipotent for myself to use it against Rosaleen, but this is a reckless thought that I have since abandoned, as she would have dominance over the orb and use it against me. As a result, I have produced my own Vessel. This sapphire—Ascendancy—I have fashioned to work similarly to Omnipotent. Once it holds enough energy... well, I am confident you understand what this would mean by now.'

'So what does this mean for me... and my team?'

Fordon's grin returned, more menacing than before. 'I have no interest in harming any of you, and to be frank, I have little interest in your underlings. You, on the other hand, Captain, despite revealing yourself as a disappointment, still hold enough promise. If need be, I suppose I can persuade you by other means.'

Oliath's boldness evaporated then, replaced by the same sinking feeling as before.

The sword was a masterpiece. Like no other Maynard had ever seen.

'No payment is needed,' Drah Leets said. 'This one is my pleasure.'

Maynard held the large blade in one hand, high enough so that he could examine its length in full. The two-toned weapon, gold and silver, was light for its size, a neat gap reaching along the centre of the steel from the hilt to where the colours joined into a point.

'It's a design I've been meaning to forge for a while now,' Leets told Maynard. 'Because of its size, it ain't meant to be used with the one hand, but you look like a chap who can wield it however you see fit.'

Maynard slapped the flat of the blade with his palm. 'It is solid,' he said. He traced his finger along the edge, drawing blood. 'It is also sharp. You have my compliments, smith.'

Ebony winced as Maynard deliberately cut his finger. 'I don't think you'll be able to wear that on your waist.'

'Yeah,' Leets agreed. 'It's a bit longer than your last weapon. I'm surprised you wore even that on your 'ip, but I recommend you strap this'n to your back. I've put together just the sheath, so you needn't worry about findin' somethin' suitable.'

Maynard placed the sword on the workbench while Leets fumbled about in the clutter of his shop. Ebony stepped closer to the table for a closer look at the weapon. 'It is a beautiful piece... for something so dangerous, anyway. How did you manage to make something so unique?'

'Well,' Leets said, pleased with the praise, 'I would love to say it's a secret talent o' mine, but it's funny that you mention it, actually, as I didn't do anything out of the ordinary when it comes to the forgin' process if you know what I mean.'

Ebony did not have a clue what the blacksmith was talking about or what was funny, but she nodded anyway.

'Like I said, it's a shape I've been meanin' to forge for a while now,' Leets continued. 'Because of the empty middle, it is lighter than your average greatsword but no less durable. What makes the sword so special is the material I used. You see, most of the steel were from the old blade, and that may 'ave looked like any ordinary sword, but it weren't—I can tell you that now. That sword were blessed. Trust me—I know a thing or two about that kind of stuff. That said, them colours are of my doin'—y'know, just to give it a bit of character.'

Eventually finding the scabbard, Leets placed it on the workbench beside the sword and grinned widely at the silent Maynard. 'Will you be wanting any armour while you're 'ere?'

'Perhaps leather of some description,' Maynard said. 'Nothing too heavy.'

'As you 'ave it, sir.'

'When you say blessed...?' Ebony said, prompting Leets to elaborate on what he had said a moment ago.

Remnant Tales of Stilly:
Passion and Benevolence

The smith stood straight, exaggeratedly looking from side to side as if to make sure no one else was listening, even though he knew his apprentices and work partners were away from the shop. 'Well,' he spoke with mock whispering, 'it's funny you mention it, 'cause I ain't talkin' about religion or nothin'. Nah, I actually 'ad another type of sword in the shop until a few days ago—a short curved blade with a blue jewel in its hilt. It's been in my family for generations—like the blacksmith trade. It were an interestin' blade, to say the least. Ascendancy, I think it's called—a strange name for a sword. I studied it quite a lot—it gave me the creeps, although I don't know why. But I do know it were a blessed sword... like your one.'

'Was it stolen?' Ebony asked.

'Well, I could've just misplaced it, but I usually find my stuff with a bit o' lookin', so I reckon it got stolen.'

'Do you know who might have taken it?' Ebony continued questioning.'

'Not really,' Leets said, shrugging his broad shoulders. 'Mind you, it's funny you say that, 'cause it went missin' round the time I were questioned by Oliath Burley and 'is lot. Can't imagine they would 'ave much interest in takin' such things, though.'

Maynard groaned. 'The thickset one working for the captain of the guard is particularly light-fingered. He goes by the name Rida Prory. However, I fear that he no longer has the blade.'

'Then who does?' Leets asked.

'The original owner—a man with the potential to cause great catastrophe and the reason for Wilheard's recent miseries.'

'I always knew it were a blessed sword. More cursed, I s'pose,' Leets said, his tone offhand. 'By the by, will you be namin' your sword?'

'I have never named a sword,' Maynard said bluntly, strapping the scabbard to his back.

'Can I, then?' Ebony said. 'How about... Ardruism?'

'That's a funny word—not one I've ever 'eard,' Leets said.

'It is a joining of two words, actually,' Ebony clarified. 'The gold part represents Ardour, the silver Altruism.'

Maynard sheathed the weapon with a shunt. 'If you so desire, my lady, then so it shall be named.'

Ebony smiled, pleased that the name was so readily accepted.

The swordsman turned to Leets and offered him a firm handshake. 'You have my appreciation, friend. I have little in the way of payment, but you are welcome to what I own.'

'No payment necessary, sir,' Leets insisted, repeating what he had said when Maynard and Ebony arrived. 'And don't worry about the sword I loaned ya. It's a small cost for what you will do for Wilheard using that new one.'

'Again, my gratitude,' Maynard said, turning and walking from the shop, followed closely by Ebony, who had discreetly left a silver stinnep coin on the workbench.

Staring through the hollow eyes of a blank-faced mask, Ninapaige peered over Wilheard from the high branches of a tree. From her vantage point, she could see everyone and everything, all the while remaining hidden.

Humans amused Ninapaige greatly: how each individual seemingly went about their life in a blithe and almost dim-witted way differentiated them from any other creature. Yet, despite this innocent façade, she was all too aware of human cruelty and how many had a habit of being beyond the pale. Ninapaige knew more of these types than she cared to think. Typically single-minded, disgruntled and damaged in nature, these persons could be a latent danger to all those unfortunate enough to be near them. Ninapaige was not one to concern herself with the actions of humans, but this was relative. When she felt a need to intrude, it invariably involved those more aware of the world than they probably should be.

Wilheard's current adversity was the result of one such human. It was a complex matter, and how much of it was predestined seemed beyond even Ninapaige's comprehension, but she at least knew nothing was set in stone. Indeed, Ninapaige believed she had a part to play, which was not a simple process. Throughout the past, she, like so many others, it would seem, had been searching for certain people. These people had an important destiny, albeit one that led down different paths, and Sylvia had been one such person. Ninapaige had guided the woman (known as Luanna when they first met), and now Sylvia could help guide Ebony. Luanna's suffering had been a cruel fate, yet she was only a minor part of a greater purpose.

For now, as far as she was concerned, Ninapaige had played her part. How she could theoretically handle the actions of Ebony, Maynard, Fordon, and any other human was irrelevant; in that respect, she felt little more than a pawn. All she had done in the grand scheme of things was lead people to an inevitable destiny. She had done so for centuries, irrespective of how such matters concluded.

Ninapaige removed the mask from her face, flipped it in the air, caught it, and put it back on. The ceramic now donned a contemplative expression: a sneering top lip with one raised eyebrow that creased the forehead.

Ninapaige gazed at Castle Stilly. Fordon Latnemirt was considerably more formidable in the ways of sorcery than most. His studying of Pentominto had even allowed him to create a vessel he was fully adept at exploiting. More was the pity that the man demonstrated a fundamental foolishness despite his intellect. He had even deluded himself into believing that his Ascendancy jewel could one day match Omnipotent, but this was inconsequential. What mattered was what he intended to do presently.

Rosaleen still held a firm control over Fordon, the extent to which the man was oblivious. Fordon's life energy was Rosaleen's to own; she had bestowed a great deal of this power, among other attributes, upon him. Centuries ago, Fordon became more powerful; his demise would have returned not only the energy Rosaleen had given him but also the energy he stole from others. Fordon had learned this truth before returning to Wilheard, but all that had happened, including his reactions, had been Rosaleen's intention. In his blind rage, his quest to become more powerful had only made the mage a better morsel for the forsaken ytied.

Intriguingly, things were a little different now: Fordon had found a way to hide energy from Rosaleen using his Ascendancy. In theory, this meant the life energy he collected (and if he kept it separate from Rosaleen's power) was his alone, and she would not gain anything. Could Fordon conjure enough energy to defeat Rosaleen? An improbability, even if he lived for millennia.

Incidentally, Ninapaige could sense the presence of another ancient vessel within Wilheard, something she knew Ebony possessed.

Then there was Maynard, or Sombie as Ninapaige liked to call him. With his newfound strength, he could defeat Fordon with the help of the girl and others. Yet, how could Ninapaige assist in their struggles? Challenging Fordon herself, even with her far superior knowledge in ytyism, was out of the question. Fordon was, in essence, Rosaleen's creation, and Rosaleen was Nianapaige's mistress; to attack Latnemirt directly would be an attack on her mistress, something she could not do.

Once again, Ninapaige tossed her mask into the air, the porcelain face showing a pert smile upon its return. She covered her face and went back to looking at the town. Was this sensation in her belly one of excitement? She could not deny it: things had become interesting, and that sent a shiver through her body. Uncertainty always had a way of causing nerves to flare, and although Ninapaige knew how things were likely to turn out, she could not predict how the erratic humans below would achieve this.

Never mind; humans are what they are. Ninapaige guessed she would have to continue her little game of shepherding, and although she refused to take part in the battle directly, she could still pass the power to make it so she did not need to. This would ensure things went more smoothly, and she already knew how to go about it.

Chapter 12

What would the future hold? This was the only question in Ebony's mind at that moment.

Atop a hill northeast of New Market Square, she clutched the lucky charm heart and peered over the crowded streets. The gathering of people had swelled by the hour, and following the increase in guards and soldiers alike, it was almost as if the whole town had emerged from their homes. Despite the will of authority figures, many of the townspeople had flooded the streets from New Market Square to the foot of Castle Way, and the din of uttering voices made it difficult to make much sense of what was going on. Although inconvenient, none of the soldiers and guards could deny that apprehension had brought the civilians out; of all those who wanted only to hide away, perhaps just as many had had enough of doing so.

Ebony's parents were also somewhere in town. In a fit of what she could describe only as enthusiasm, her father had rolled up his sleeves, tightened his belt and burst out of the cottage. *"Fixing the house can wait,"* he had declared. *"I'm off to help build stuff!"*

By this, Abraham meant he would help fix anything that might need repairing or knocking together, such as makeshift barricades and perhaps even weapons like wooden stakes that could be used for defence. Sylvia had followed Abraham's example; as a doctor, she too would put herself to good use in the coming hours.

Many others in town were doing what was within their means. Ebony pondered whether she could be doing something similarly constructive, but she felt compelled to stay near Maynard.

Placing her treasured crystal heart in a pouch, Ebony sighed inwardly and turned her attention to particular individuals in the crowd.

'If it comes to it, we'll help ya out,' Ebony overheard one man with a pinched face announce to an armoured soldier. 'We ain't about to just sit and do nothing.'

This evoked several grunts of approval from those surrounding the man. The soldier pursed his lips, doubting whether the man would follow through with the bravado. Regardless, he asked everyone to refrain from obstructing the army, something he had reiterated with fellow fighters as he made his way along the gathering.

Ebony switched her gaze towards Alim and then Maynard.

Sitting nearby Ebony, Alim tugged at his bottom lip as he scanned through a scroll with Pentominto on it. He was deep in thought, typically undisturbed by the noise and fuss around him. Over the past day, Alim studied the symbols copied from Godfrey's bust. Ebony was no closer to understanding the ancient language, but Alim claimed he now had a few tricks up his sleeve.

Maynard was fixated on the castle, his frame rigid and intimidating. Discounting his new sword, he had equipped himself with an array of weaponry, most notably a longbow he held in his right hand and a quiver packed with arrows fastened to his left hip. Ebony squinted at the castle, attempting to pinpoint where Maynard was looking.

'Will you be heading towards the throne room?' Ebony asked Maynard. 'Is that what you are looking at?'

Maynard did not meet Ebony's gaze; instead, he kept his eyes on the castle. 'Getting there is a priority, although I do not expect to find him.'

'You mean Fordon Latnemirt,' Ebony said. 'If you do not expect to find him in the throne room, why even go there? What do you expect to discover?'

Maynard, unperturbed by the inundation of questions, maintained his scrutiny of the castle, giving his customary moment of silence before answering. 'The chamber will seem the most obvious place to search for Latnemirt. With that in mind, I believe he will have laid a trap, and it is integral that I get to the location before the army. To do that, I will enter from the castle's exterior gatehouse and then proceed from the balcony.'

Ebony peered along the gatehouse wall. There were various footholds and protruding sections; small arrow slits and other hollows in the stone would provide a route for someone with a firm grip and substantial agility.

Finally, Maynard turned his attention away from the castle and towards Ebony. 'When the time for action comes, I will have no time to tarry. Leaving you and Mister Larring behind is inevitable, and you will be left to your own devices.'

Ebony gave a playful shrug. 'After all that we have been through, I believe that we are capable of looking after ourselves for a little while.'

Alim stood up. 'Don't worry, old boy,' he said, signifying that he had been listening the whole time. 'Ebony and I will likely stick behind the armed forces.'

Maynard nodded and turned back to the castle. 'Very well, but be sure to watch your backs. The both of you are more important than you might realise. Now... prepare yourself.'

Ebony's skin prickled as she looked towards the castle. A cluster of redifass rose from a pool of purple smoke in the moat. One after another, they stepped up from the water, surrounding the entire front of the castle to form several lines. A dozen suoidi also appeared from the purple mist, baring their teeth and snarling to make their frightening appearance even fiercer.

The hum of voices that had been filling the streets came to a stop as everyone became aware of what was happening. For a long moment, there was a silence; all eyes fixed towards the top of Castle Way. Wilheard's army remained steadfast in position until ordered to do otherwise. After a while, the smoke disappeared, but none of the creatures moved far from the moat.

Catching everyone by surprise, a deep, resonating voice ended the calm, unsettling many townspeople. The voice, introducing itself as Fordon Latnemirt, boomed from the sky like thunder, announcing an ultimatum. 'People of Wilheard,' Fordon said. 'Is every one of you truly blind to the corruption Stilly harbours? Can any of you claim that there is no need for change?'

Change. The use of that word made Ebony shudder. To think, only weeks ago, it had been almost a mantra: a simple desire blown out of any reasonable proportion. With the making of new friends and the reuniting of her mother came a danger that not one person would ever expect.

Fordon spoke of his plight and vision, of ytiedinity and ytyism and of Rosaleen. 'A great threat lay ahead, and only I, Fordon Latnemirt, have the knowledge to contest this danger. Alas, as I see you standing there now, it would seem hardly any of you will accept this reasoning. I realise what I say is no small asking, yet I can offer you a better world in which to live, one where people can live in peace. Invariably, such ambitions are unachievable without hardship, determination and sacrifice. To attain this, I insist on absolute compliance. If all follow me, the world could be a prosperous one. Naturally, the alternative would be that you deny me, but remember this— two days ago, every one of you witnessed with your own eyes of what I am capable. Such a state of affairs need not be repeated. I implore you… do not make me your enemy.'

Without hesitation, an overwhelming majority cried their disapproval. Wilheard's army shook their weapons above head and beat their shields on the ground while civilians bellowed and stomped their feet. The crowd was awash with fear, yet the resilience to repel what might be forced upon them was all the more palpable.

'A foolhardy decision,' emanated the sonorous voice once more. 'One I will rectify presently…'

No sooner had Fordon finished his discourse, the thrum of a longbow sounded, an arrow piercing through the air with terrifying speed and striking a suoido in the head with pinpoint accuracy. At over 200 yards from his target, Maynard calmly took another arrow from its hold and placed it against the string's nocking point. This time, he aimed for a redifass, again hitting the being's head, the arrow landing in the middle of its featureless face. Both monsters collapsed instantaneously.

The rest of the monsters loped down Castel Way. Seeing the redifass and suoidi approaching them, panic among the civilians ensued. Alim stepped farther away from everyone else, leading Ebony with him to avoid being dragged into the chaos.

Maynard loosed arrow after arrow, striking at least one monster with every projectile as the creatures descended the hill. This allowed the rest of the armed forces to prepare, with acting leaders captaining sets of troops and shouting for them to get ready. By the time the content of Maynard's quiver was spent, the army of Wilheard charged in the castle's direction to meet their opponent, roaring from the top of their lungs.

The odds of the battle were in Wilheard's favour: for every non-human, there were 10 soldiers. This made battling the redifass relatively straightforward, the monsters of whom struggled to keep track of the multiple targets. The suoidi, conversely, presented a different problem. Being of such heavy build, the creatures used their mass to rush or flatten the slighter humans, goring any soldier that did not recuperate quickly enough. To help counter this, Maynard targeted these monsters first. Dumping his longbow and unsheathing the greatsword from his back, he dashed toward Wilheard's army, doing so with such speed that his first victim did not see him coming.

Maynard struck a suoido as it lunged, its mouth wide open even when it came back down, the head now without a body. The next target had an even more gruesome demise; coming down with an axe-like slice, Ardruism struck its target's middle, severing the beast entirely.

Sharpshooters fired their Lunsser Pistols from the rear and sides of the leading battalion, faltering enemy attack. With all the different offence types, it did not take Maynard much effort to cut through and reach the drawbridge.

'Look at him go!' Exclaimed Alim, who was watching Maynard vault his way up the castle wall. 'He really is quite the athlete.'

'He is impressive,' Ebony agreed, although no longer surprised by his capabilities. 'But what are *we* going to do? Making our way through the crowd will prove awkward at best.'

Alim peered over the advancing troops and scratched his nose. 'True. And I'm sure we won't just be allowed to waltz on through'—he pointed out a line of guards keeping civilians at bay—'perhaps we can sneak round the side somehow when things have calmed down.'

This would take longer than hoped: as the pair planned a route round to the castle front, an explosion occurred at the gatehouse. Smashing its way out from the castle's courtyard, a new monster appeared. Large and robust, this additional threat was another redifass, a type known as Brute. Following the Brute, dozens of smaller redifass emerged from the obliterated gatehouse; these redifass were also different from the Skirmisher sort that Wilheard's army had so far fought. Taller, faster and with superior swords, Ebony recognised this type to be the same as the one Maynard had slain in the woodland: a Warrior.

The Warrior redifass charged towards their human opponents, leaving the Brute behind. Seemingly uninterested in fighting directly, the Brute turned its attention towards the drawbridge. Taking the bridge's chains, it wrenched the links from the remaining stone of the gatehouse, pulling the portcullis down with it. With the drawbridge free of its hold, the Brute lifted it from its position, snapping the wood and wrapping it in the mangled steel before tossing the heap towards Clock Tower. Stricken a third of the way up, the tower crumbled under its own weight and disappeared into a plume of dust, the bells whining as they went down with it.

Ebony gasped at what she witnessed, the sight shaking her very essence. She dreaded to think how many people could have fallen foul to the devastation.

'FIRE!' yelled a captain to the battalion's rear, his order followed by the bang of a cannon. Struck on its left breast, the Brute stumbled towards the moat, twisting from the blow.

'FIRE!' bellowed the same man, commanding soldiers in control of a separate cannon. The Brute doubled over as the ball hit its stomach, tumbling onto its knees with a thud.

'Together now, lads,' said the captain, waiting for the Brute to right itself. 'Steady… steady… FIRE!'

The two cannons blasted at once, both cannonballs striking the target near the centre of its chest. Once again, the Brute fell from the impact, tumbling backwards and into the moat.

Cheers erupted from the crowd below as the giant dropped for the last time, but the moment was bittersweet in light of Clock Tower's and the drawbridge's destruction.

'Tender spirits,' Alim muttered. 'What a mess this has become. What say we lend a hand, dear girl.'

'How do you mean?'

Alim pulled out a scrap of paper. 'I think I have this one sussed,' he said, prodding the Pentominto he had written on it. 'But I guess there is only one way to find out.'

Stepping from the throne room balcony and into the unexpectedly tidy hall to which it belonged, Maynard listened to the destruction outside. Judging from the noise, matters were intensifying quickly, but he could not turn back now. Indeed, by the time Clock Tower collapsed, he was deep in other problems.

Keeping to the side of the room, Maynard stepped sideways, Ardruism held firmly in both hands, ready to strike anything that might jump out in an ambush. At first, everything remained in place, but the swordsman knew he was not alone; something was there, and he could feel its eyes on him.

Seeing nothing on his level, Maynard shifted his attention upwards to spy a diamond-filled chandelier rocking back and forth. Clinging to the ceiling, mostly hidden in the shadow of an arched alcove, a large, lizard-esque creature disturbed the fixture with the swing of its tail. The plaster around the chandelier crumbled from the persistent rocking, stone fragments falling close to the swordsman's feet.

Maynard took a few steps back and then leapt to one side as the mass of diamonds came crashing. He steadied himself and looked back towards the creature, which remained obscured in darkness. A rumble like thunder echoed about the chamber as flames emitting from the behemoth's nostrils briefly illuminated it. Eventually, the creature stirred from the shadows. Exposing a slender frame, its spine flexed with a slithering motion as it crossed the uneven ceiling and then down the wall.

This creature, another product of Fordon's sorcery, was a daloug. Resembling a dragon, the daloug had a long body, neck and a whip-like tail. Its legs were short and bowed, and the toes were padded, allowing superior climbing. The head, similar to that of an alligator, was full of pointed teeth.

Maynard snatched a mirrored shield from one of the armoured suits encircling the room and dropped to one knee. As if on cue, the daloug took a deep breath and belched a column of fire, its flames smashing into the shield. So intense was the heat that Maynard could feel the metal warming. Once the daloug had exhaled all it could, Maynard tossed the shield towards its head and then dashed towards it. The dragon slid out the way of the projectile with the grace of a snake, successively dodging the following sword swipe. The daloug retaliated with an attack of its own, whipping its tail and then snapping its teeth, decimating the decorative table centring the chamber as Maynard jumped away.

For a while, the pair evaded one another, Ardruism failing to make any significant contact and the daloug managing only to destroy the throne room's contents. Despite Maynard out-manoeuvring his opponent, the daloug seemed to have the advantage. Sporadically spitting fire at Maynard, the dragon left its human opponent with little option than to keep on the move. Even with the increase of broken objects, which Maynard used to attack the daloug, he could not slow it.

Maynard needed to get closer and desperately searched the throne room for something to help him achieve this. The daloug had destroyed most of the armour and weapons, and although the shields were largely intact, taking one would provide little protection. Even if a shield could protect him against the fire, it would not save him from the tail or the dragon's bite. Still, he felt that he needed to hurry. During the battle against the daloug, Maynard had been unaware of the drawbridge's destruction, thus assumed Wilheard's infantry would reach his location at any moment. Be the soldiers a help or hindrance, he did not relish the thought of any avoidable injury.

Leaping over yet another lash of the dragon's tail, Maynard landed next to the remains of a broken armour suit. He flung a breastplate and ornamental sword in quick succession. As expected, the daloug dodged the former by slinking to one side, and the blade missed by a considerable margin. Fortunately, this had been the plan.

Along the ceiling length remained a few chandeliers similar to the one the daloug had dropped. Although not sharp enough to cut through anything substantial, the blade struck a supporting beam with enough force that the connected chain snapped.

The daloug spluttered a growl as the heap of metal and jewellery slammed on top of it, a spray of fire pouring from its mouth as its long neck slapped the marble floor. Before the daloug could figure out what happened, Maynard was over it; the last thing the dragon likely saw was the giant, two-bladed sword coming down on its head.

Close to Sanct Everard, a soldier grunted as she finished off a fallen redifass. Taking a step back as its remains dispersed, she rolled her neck and glanced up Castle Way. Worn out from all the fighting, she groaned upon spying a suoido galloping towards her.

'Watch out!' she shouted, forming a line with eight nearby soldiers.

As the soldier watched the beast get closer, she realised she was the immediate target. Doubtless, the beast's sheer weight would crush her to death, as well as the two standing next to her. Come what may, she would not let that happen without causing at least some damage.

Reaching a distance of three metres from the group, the suoido lunged. The troops braced for impact, raising their swords in unison before bringing their blades down again, swinging simultaneously on the soldier's call. The timing had been perfect, and the beast would have suffered a deadly blow. At least, that was what the soldier presumed; she had closed her eyes, not wanting to witness her own doom.

A few seconds had passed by the time the soldier reopened her eyelids, doing so one at a time. What she saw then bewildered her.

'No, that's not right,' Alim said, the row of soldiers looking towards him. 'It's not supposed to do that.'

The group looked back at the suoido, which was somehow suspended mid-leap. Although continuing to move towards the troops, it now travelled at a fraction of the speed.

'That's amazing,' Ebony said as she looked over Alim's shoulder. 'What did you do?'

'Thank you, I guess, but'—Alim shifted his glasses and looked back down at his notes—'this is a ytyism enchantment designed to immobilise living beings—or any moving object, for that matter. The monster is held to some degree, granted, but not stationary, as it should be.'

'It is still incredible, Alim,' Ebony reassured, patting him on his upper back. 'You shouldn't be so hard on yourself, old boy.'

This made Alim smile. 'If you say so... Sorry to have bothered you, folks—I'll get out your way.'

Remnant Tales of Stilly:
Passion and Benevolence

'No trouble at all,' the soldier said, shrugging before hacking the suoido with her companions. By the time it disappeared, the beast had still not even reached the ground.

Alim continued his spell casting from a distance, picking suoidi and redifass that appeared to be overwhelming soldiers. Uncertain as to whether he was friend or foe, Wilheard's soldiers regarded Alim with a mixture of confusion and fear. Despite their apprehension, they did not attack, but Ebony noticed that Alim was attracting less tolerant attention.

Redifass and suoidi, not engaged in combat, turned their attention towards Alim and Ebony. As if receiving a new order from their master, the monsters moved towards them.

As within the woodland, the pair ran. This time, Ebony sprang into action first, grabbing Alim's arm and pulling him towards the passages between buildings. Darting round corners and under arches of tight alleyways, they pulled away from the suoidi; the beasts struggled to manage the twists and turns of the streets, carelessly smashing into buildings and walls as they tried to keep pace. In contrast, the redifass had less trouble navigating the lack of space, keeping sight of their targets the whole time.

After a few minutes of running, Alim spotted a shop with a broken door. 'Head for that building!' he called to Ebony, pointing to the shop ahead.

Ebony entered the shop first, closely followed by Alim, who slammed what remained of the door behind him. Moments later, a redifass crashed headlong into the door, forcing it open but tumbling to the floor in the process. Alim, aided by Ebony, pulled a nearby cabinet on top of the fallen humanoid to keep it down. A second and third redifass entered the building shortly after. Redifass number two tripped over its fallen companion as it ran into the room, hitting the floor like a sack of potatoes. Redifass number three, seeing what happened to number two, slowed to a stop and stepped over the gathered heap. By then, Alim and Ebony had already escaped through another door to the back of the room, climbing out a window to the rear of the building. Regrettably, this led to an open road, which left them exposed again.

'Can't you sto... stop them?' Ebony panted to Alim as they continued to sprint. 'What about tha... that spell of yours?'

'I'm trying… dear girl,' Alim panted back. He mouthed a few of the words he had memorised, but it was no good: it was too awkward under duress.

Redifass number three eventually caught up with Ebony and Alim. Worse still, numerous others of its kind had found them, blocking what seemed to be all remaining escape routes.

This was not the end for Ebony and Alim, despite how it appeared, as someone else had been searching for the pair, and this someone had found them.

Looking back to where she had been running, Ebony noticed a sheet of light materialise. The translucent wall soared along the street, blowing apart her pursuers before passing harmlessly over her and Alim and continuing to eliminate what remained of the redifass. The light, its purpose supposedly done, vanished as quickly as it had emerged.

Ebony looked around for any signs of threat before turning to Alim. 'How did you do that?'

'I didn't,' he replied. 'At least I don't think I did—I can't imagine I would do something like that by accident.'

Ebony and Alim were not far from where Clock Tower had collapsed. The vicinity was deserted, and from her position, she could hear that distant fighting was ending. Cheers emanated from north of the town, closer to Castle Way, getting louder as the remaining beasts fell to their human opponents.

Wilheard was victorious.

Ebony sighed in relief. 'It seems the soldiers have won. Work can begin on finding a way into the castle now.'

'Agreed,' Alim said. 'Shall we press on, or do you need to catch your breath?'

'I'm all right, but there is no sense in rushing when the drawbridge is gone. While we wait for a makeshift crossing, perhaps we can reflect on what… just…'

Ebony shuddered as she felt a child-like hand slowly reach over her left shoulder. Before she could turn her head, a pair of arms wrapped about her neck, causing her to freeze in alarm.

'Do not worry, young human,' came a strangely familiar voice, whispering into her ear. 'I am not here to harm you.'

As if sensing Ebony's anxiety, Alim turned to face her, immediately seeing a flamboyant imp on the woman's back. 'Oi!' he called, pointing at the jester. 'Take your hands off her!'

'Not so fast, boy!' said Ninapaige, staring at Alim with piercing, violet eyes, 'Stand still, and you might learn something.'

Alim froze in a mid-running position.

Ninapaige cackled, kicking her little legs with joy into Ebony's back. 'I believe that is what you were trying to do, boy.'

Ebony winched as Ninapaige kicked at her, aggravating the bruising on her back. She faced forward, unspeaking and unable to turn her head.

Ninapaige turned her attention back to Ebony. 'By the way, I lay claim to that wall of light a moment ago. You are very welcome.'

The imp continued whispering, her voice childish in pitch. 'Do you know who I am, girl?'

Ebony swallowed before answering. 'I recognise your voice... somehow, as if from a dream. Sylvia told me... You are Ninapaige.'

The little woman chuckled as if to confirm that Ebony was correct. 'You know something?' she went on, keeping a tight hold on Ebony, 'I broke a little promise I had made myself—I said that I would not interfere in all this human conflict. Never mind... some promises are not worth keeping, especially if I am not obliged to keep them.'

'Sylvia told me about you,' Ebony said.

'Oh? All good, I hope.'

Ebony swallowed again, this time a little harder. 'From what I could gather, you are very powerful... and flippant.'

This caused Ninapaige to shrill with laughter. 'Some things were more flattering than others, then. Incidentally, I noticed that you referred to *her* as Sylvia.

'She prefers that.'

'Really?' Ninapaige said with genuine surprise. 'After all these years, she has only just taken to the name?' She harrumphed. 'Life still holds wonders after all. Still, perhaps you will learn to call her *mother* one day.'

'What do you want of me?' Ebony asked.

Ninapaige answered with another question. 'You do know why things are how they are, don't you? With Sylvia, I mean. I suspect not, but you will— you are an exceptionally smart girl. Isn't it funny how destiny can turn one's life upside down? Is this the *change* you so desperately wanted?'

Ninapaige brushed her fingers under Ebony's hair and hooked it behind her ear. 'Now that I get a closer look at you, I notice how much you resemble your mother. I remember her face well... You also look very much like someone else I once knew. I made a promise to that particular person a long time ago, and *that* is one promise I intend to keep. You, like Sylvia, are valuable to this world, more so than which Fordon Latnemirt, Sombie, or any living human truly comprehends. Sylvia and Luanna have done their part; now it is your turn. Put this energy in your stone heart.'

Ninapaige placed her hand on Ebony's head. A pleasant warmth spread from her scalp down to her neck. The sensation flowed down her back and along her arms to her fingertips, reaching her legs and eventually her toes.

Ebony was overcome with unexpected sleepiness; her eyelids grew heavy, her vision blurring.

She could feel the stone street on her back. Had she fallen?

So tired now.

Had she been laid down?

So tired... too tired.

'There he is,' Wiley said through gritted teeth. 'The fool...'

Dexter and Meddia looked where Wiley was pointing, spotting Rida down a moonlit corridor. Rida did not notice the other three in return, his attention drawn to something round a corner. Assuming there could be something dangerous, Wiley refrained from calling out and ensured Meddia did the same; she was the only one genuinely pleased to see the corpulent man.

The three had been searching for Rida a while now, which frustrated Wiley even more when the sounds of battle outside resonated through the castle halls.

Wiley leant his back against the wall closest to Rida, folded his arms and looked at the shorter man in silence. He waited a moment for Priory to explain why he had sneaked off.

Rida did not acknowledge his housemates, but he knew they were there.

'What are you playing at?' Wiley said in a harsh whisper when Rida continued to ignore him. 'Why did you not stay in the room?'

'Same as you lot, I guess,' Rida retorted, all the while keeping his attention on whatever it was round the corner. 'I'm guessin' you didn't come out jus' to look for me... Did ya?'

Wiley opened his mouth to argue, closing it again when no words came out. This was the first time Rida had dumfounded him.

Rida went on. 'I woz jus' lookin' about, that's all. I ain't hurtin' nobody. Anyway, I 'eard a noise comin' from the throne room, so thought I'd check it out.'

Dexter and Meddia stood just behind Rida, looking in the same direction. Wiley did not bother questioning further and instead joined them.

Maynard could see the *Other Four* standing at the far end of the hall, but he was more concerned with the man directly ahead of him.

Nolan gazed at Maynard for a long moment, taking the opportunity to study the sovereign knight properly for the first time. 'I suspect you are looking for that old man Fordon Latnemirt. Do you even know where to find him?'

'I have my ideas,' Maynard replied.

Nolan grunted. 'I have no doubt—you know him well. After all, you are an equally old man, so to speak.'

Maynard did not respond.

Nolan waved his arm dismissively. 'Frankly, I do not care to relate to what is happening between you and the sorcerer. In fact, despite his tedious anecdotes on what he has been through and what he intends to achieve, I find myself unable to think beyond you and your capabilities. Does this flatter you?'

'No. What I am is troubled, particularly by your frivolity on the situation.'

This made Nolan pucker his lips. He placed his hands on his hips and nodded. 'Your opinion of me cannot be helped, but you are wrong to assume that I do not respect the situation, especially when it involves Captain Burley. We both have our loyalties, and my devotion to him is unwavering... I would follow him into any forlorn battle if need be.'

'Is that how you view the current circumstances? Forlorn?'

Nolan kept silent, instead choosing to look out the window and at the moon.

'It need not turn out this way,' Maynard spoke on. 'You declare that we are bound by our loyalties. This may not be to the same people, but that does not make us enemies. The captain of the guard wants what is best for Wilheard, and in that, we are mutual allies, Shakeston.'

The mention of his name caused Nolan's hair to stand on end. 'You seem to know a lot about people. What else do you know about me?'

'I know that you, although intelligent, are rash at times—doggedly intent on doing what could be seen as highly unreasonable.

Nolan's face creased into a smile as he looked down from the moon and back towards Maynard.

'I also know you are hardly ever seen without your female counterpart. I suspect Lawford is nearby, and it is not just coincidence that we meet outside the Armoury.'

'Indeed not,' Nolan said, 'and if you can spare me your sanctimony for a little while, perhaps *we* can find out more about *you*. It would be a shame if Latnemirt were to kill you before I could see your strength in personal combat. I understand you have already been through a lot recently, but if you cannot defeat Lawford and me, then what use are you to Wilheard? Come, old-timer. Show us what you are capable of, and we will see if you can stand against greater confrontations.'

Nolan walked into the armoury and disappeared from view. Maynard paused a moment longer, gazing at the open doorway. A dull yellow light emitted from the room; everything inside was silent. He did not have time to waste, and playing this little game was not something for which he had much patience. Alas, in his way, the lieutenants stood, posing a distraction that needed addressing for the sake of the immediate future. If he were to ignore the two, they would surely pursue him: that was in their nature, and in the face of their usual honour, Maynard anticipated nothing but intemperate hostility.

Maynard rolled forward as he stepped into the artillery room, dodging a spiked club intended for his chest. The weapon whistled through the air, hurtling above him and through the doorway, thrown with so much power that it fractured the stone wall on the other side of the corridor. Cordelia had been the assailant, and she was reaching for another weapon. Maynard did not have time to confront her as Nolan forced him to twist out the way of a vertical sword slash, the blade of which cracked as it struck the floor. Maynard managed to unsheathe his sword after the second attack, sidestepping another of Cordelia's projectiles while defending himself from a second swing by Nolan. Maynard, reacting faster than the other man, had enough of an opening to force him back, shattering Nolan's weakened blade as it collided with the nearby wall. Before Maynard could follow through with a more significant blow, he turned his attention to Cordelia, who was once again primed for further assault. Maynard leant back to one side as Cordelia loosed an arrow for his heart. The projectile sliced through his clothing, piercing his skin and drawing blood. A second arrow, aimed for his neck, nicked his shoulder. Cordelia was now the most significant threat, and if Maynard wanted the upper hand, he needed to take her down first. Charging the woman, he forced her to discard the bow and withdraw a sword of her own. He feinted a swing for her neck and, as she raised her weapon in defence, kicked the side of her legs. This caused her to lose balance and drop to her knees with a pained grunt. Nolan naturally went to her aid, punching Maynard square in the ribs and forcing the sovereign knight to one side. The hit was brutal, as expected, but not enough to cause him to stumble. Maynard retaliated by fisting Nolan in the jaw, using just enough power to drop the lieutenant. Once again, this left Maynard only enough time to switch his attention back to his other opponent. Cordelia raised her sword in one last attempt to maim her enemy, but with Nolan temporarily down, Maynard could focus entirely on her. Disarming the woman with now relative ease, he placed his boot on her torso and pushed her away. She slammed into the wall behind her, the wind temporarily taken from her lungs. Maynard did not allow for recuperation, following through by throwing the woman overhead and into a rack of rusting weapons, causing the whole structure to collapse under her weight. Nolan snatched a nearby sword and stumbled to his feet, taking one last fruitless swipe. The weapon was no match for Ardruism; the greatsword cut the smaller weapon in two, rendering it useless. As with Cordelia, Maynard tossed Nolan aside onto the broken pile of weapons where his fellow lieutenant lay dazed.

Maynard resheathed Ardruism on his back and peered down at his fallen opponents.

Nolan rolled onto his side. 'Not bad for an old-timer.' He spat a globule of blood. 'You are as strong as people say.'

Cordelia dragged herself up and rested her back on the wall. 'We are not so conceited that we expected to be a match for you, and it is good to know you have the strength and determination to fight for what you believe is right.'

'Do you think this strength of yours is enough to fight Latnemirt?' Nolan said.

There was a brief silence before Maynard answered. 'I can only hope.'

'As can we,' Nolan went on. 'Captain Burley needs you. Our desire to outdo your efforts in recent weeks has landed us in more trouble than I like to admit. A warning, though, old-timer—the sorcerer is an ambitious man and dangerous in his convictions. We cannot explain where he gets his power, but he has it in abundance.'

'Will you be all right?' Maynard asked.

Cordelia choked a laugh. 'Don't congratulate yourself too much, vigilante. You didn't batter us that much.

Remnant Tales of Stilly:
Passion and Benevolence

'You undoubtedly noticed the four clowns standing outside'—Nolan nodded towards the corridor; the *Other Four* were now standing at the doorway—'they can help us. We will be with you shortly.'

Maynard did not question further. Following a single nod, he left.

'How are you feeling now, dear girl? Are you sure you are up for continuing?'

Ebony smiled thinly at Alim. 'I'm fine, thank you, Alim. Honest.'

Alim nodded and turned his attention back to the makeshift bridge Wilheard's guards were assembling, using giant beams originally intended for new housing. Ebony and Alim had since made their way up Castle Way and were now waiting to enter Castle Stilly. Although the army was keeping civilians at bay, none of the soldiers wanted to get in the pair's way.

Since their encounter with Ninapaige, Ebony and Alim had had little to say about what happened. According to Alim, Ebony had awakened within two minutes of losing consciousness, her head resting in his lap as he tried to stir her awake again. Ebony was unharmed; she had not fallen when Ninapaige attacked her (it was not really an attack, but Ebony did not know how else to describe the experience). Ninapaige, in Alim's words, had used magic to lower Ebony to the ground and vanished moments later, subsequently releasing the scholar from his immobility.

What troubled Ebony the most about the encounter was not knowing Ninapaige's purpose. Although more tense, she felt no different from how she had been before; she did not feel stronger or weaker, nor did she feel smarter or more confused.

Then there was what the imp had whispered: *"Sylvia and Luanna have done their part, and now it is your turn. Put this energy in your stone heart."*

Ebony told Alim this, but he had no suggestions for what it could mean. 'Stone heart? Despite how they sound, I'm sure something less harsh lies behind those words,' he had told her. 'Time will tell.'

'Well, I do have this.' Ebony reached into the pouch on her dress and pulled out her crystal heart. 'After all, stone can also refer to glass jewellery. This is a family heirloom of sorts.'

Alim frowned at the crystal but said nothing. If only Sylvia were there. She might just know what to make of it all.

Although Ebony's mother was not nearby, her father was. His voice woke Ebony from her daydreaming.

'That's right—place the beam about there.' Abraham said.

'Careful as ya lay it, boys and girls,' voiced the rugged tones belonging to Vincent Sawney. 'Lay it steady, like the man tells ya!'

The butcher was well suited for his role of Acting Captain of the Guard. He had taken to the position as if he had been away for a week rather than the few decades it had actually been.

'There we are!' Abraham said, brushing his hands together. 'Marching into the castle can now begin.'

Vincent acknowledged this by sending in a few lines of Wilheard soldiers, gaining the attention of fellow leaders to give the order for more to follow.

Ebony stood up and brushed her hands across her dress to rid it of any grit. Her movements gained Abraham's attention. 'It's pointless to try and stop you, so I won't bother. It's dangerous wherever you go, anyway,' he told his daughter. 'Can I at least ask that you do not wander off alone?'

'I have no intention of doing such a thing, Father, so don't fret. Alim will be with me, and from my experience, I seem to get through things just fine with him around.'

Ebony had not told her father about the encounter with Ninapaige, assuming it would worry him more. Besides, she still felt fine.

'I'll be sure to look after her, Mister Gibenn,' Alim added.

Abraham held out his hand for Alim to shake. This was the first time they had done so. 'I know you will. Make sure you come out safely, too.'

'Don-cha worry yourself, my good man,' Vincent said, over hearing the conversation. 'I'll be keepin' an eye on 'em both.'

I'm glad to hear that,' Abraham sighed. 'I have nothing else to say—my job here is done, so I'm off to find your... you know...'

Ebony gave a weak smile. 'Give her my best.'

Near a hundred Wilheard Soldiers lined the castle's gatehouse and southern courtyard walls, a dozen of which held lit torches. They awaited further instructions.

'So far, so good,' Alim uttered over Ebony's shoulder. 'I hope we can find Maynard soon, but I fear that will be easier said than done with all this greenery.'

Ebony hummed in agreement, looking at the overgrowth of foliage that appeared to cover a majority of the courtyard. The prospect of exploring the castle, walking wherever fancy took her, had always appealed to Ebony, but she cast the thought aside; the last thing she wanted now was to end up lost, especially if everywhere was in a similar state.

All was still, but this silence did little to calm nerves.

'Something is moving inside the trees, sir,' a soldier called to Vincent, pointing vaguely towards the thickets. 'I can't see anything, but I heard it coming from the--'

Before he could finish his sentence, a vine-like tail coiled about the man, snatching him into the forestry. The soldier let out a short-lived cry of surprise as he was pulled out of sight.

'Ready yourselves!' Vincent barked at the now uneasy troops. 'Come on, get your weapons up!' He turned his attention to Ebony and Alim as a female soldier was dragged away, this time by a giant hand. 'Best you stay out the way, lass—you too, mate. Stay behind one o' these pillars or somethin' and keep an eye on each other while I figure out what's goin' on.'

Without warning, the trees erupted into flames, forcing Vincent and the soldiers to shield their faces. As the mass of greenery burned away, the silhouette of a daloug rose up within the inferno, its eyes glowing in the fire's light. Flames flickered from the dragon's nostrils as it came more into view.

The fire spreading across the yard was intense, and the resulting smoke made visibility difficult. Fighting in such conditions seemed futile, and the only viable option was to retreat before the monster burnt them all alive.

Vincent commanded the force to withdraw. Noticing this, the daloug inhaled deeply and let out a tunnel of fire the length of the courtyard, intent on killing, or at least maiming, as many humans as possible.

Turning round from the courtyard exit, Ebony watched as the blaze rushed towards her like a tsunami. She instinctively held her arms up to shield her face, and to her surprise, it seemed to work. The fire crashed into the courtyard's front wall, bypassing the columns and spilling into the open guardhouse. As the flames died out, and to the daloug's confusion, none of its targets had been harmed. A glimmering blue coat of transparent, liquid-esque matter blanketed Ebony and all those near her.

Waking from momentary confusion, the daloug inhaled once more, ready for a second attempt at burning its victims.

The daloug's head snapped back violently as Ebony amassed the substance into a spherical, semi-solid matter and hurtled it into the dragon's open mouth, sending it halfway across the courtyard and into a burning tree. The impact was so considerable that the behemoth died instantly, felling the tree simultaneously.

Applause and cheers showered Ebony as the daloug's corpse dispersed into purple mist. Unfortunately for the soldiers, there was little time to celebrate; although the dragon was gone, the courtyard was still ablaze.

Wilheard's soldiers ran from the castle grounds in search of anything to carry water, soon returning with buckets given by helpful civilians. Acquiring water from the castle moat, the soldiers formed half a dozen lines and passed the filled buckets through the gatehouse and back into the courtyard.

'How did you do that?' Alim asked Ebony. The two were sitting just outside the castle and to the other side of the drawbridge.

'I don't know,' Ebony replied, watching soldiers run from the courtyard, only to re-join the end of a line with freshly filled buckets. 'It just happened. It seemed so natural—as if I've known how to do it all my life.'

Ebony grimaced then.

'Are you all right, dear girl?'

Ebony held out her left arm. Burns reached along her forearm and hand. 'I guess I didn't escape completely unharmed.'

Alim ripped the sleeve off his shirt and ran to the moat. He returned moments later, gingerly wrapping the water-soaked fabric about Ebony's arm. 'How does that feel? I'm not hurting you, am I?'

'Thank you, Alim. The burns don't seem too severe.'

'Good… that should suffice until we get you to a doctor.'

Ebony nodded. 'Yes, but not now. We have other matters to attend.'

The doctor's surgery was hectic, even with all the medical personnel on staff.

Sylvia collared the sweat from her brow. With the arrival of injured soldiers and civilians only just subsiding, this was the first time since the upheaval started that she had managed to catch her breath.

Sylvia stuck her head out her office window and yawned. Leaning on the windowsill, she tilted her head towards the castle. Smoke was billowing from within.

I hope Ebony is all right, Sylvia thought. Her daughter dominated much of her thinking, especially now that Abraham was back safe in the surgery and no longer a concern. Indeed, Abraham had insisted that Ebony was fine, having seen her not long ago. He had also mentioned Alim and Vincent were with her: friends new and old who would consider her wellbeing above their own, a consolation Sylvia had no reason to doubt.

Then there was Ninapaige… What was *she* up to?

The latch of Sylvia's office door clicked open, interrupting her ruminating. Abraham entered and gently closed the door again. He offered her a diffident smile and stood like a patient waiting for permission to sit. Ever since discovering Sylvia's true identity, Abraham had become cagey, uncertain what to say or think. Second-guessing how he felt had become near impossible. Was he sad, frustrated or relieved? Sylvia could not differentiate,

346

but if she could get him to open up, perhaps she would have a chance to address these feelings.

'Feel free to sit down, Abe.' Sylvia said, yawning a second time as she turned from the window.

Abraham eased himself into the wooden chair. 'I know how you feel,' he said, yawning as well. 'It will be nice to relax properly.'

Sylvia brought her chair next to Abraham and sat down, laying her head on his shoulder. 'I've been saying that for months. I don't remember the last time I felt able to truly unwind.'

A moment's silence ensued. Sylvia eventually interrupted it. 'A stinnep for your thoughts,' she whispered.

Abraham sniffed in amusement and put his arm round Sylvia's shoulders. 'I was just thinking how lucky I am to have you.'

Sylvia half-smiled, affectionately rubbing her cheek on Abraham's arm.

'I was also wondering why it took ten years for you to come back to me...'

The question took Sylvia aback, as if she had not expected someone to eventually ask. She stuttered, unsure what to say.

'You have told me a lot,' Abraham continued: 'curses, monsters, magic and a mysterious imp woman. It's a great deal to take in, and you know how slow I am when it comes to anything more complicated than dressing myself... But why so long?'

'I don't know what to tell you. It was not something I chose... I thought of returning all the time, but'—Sylvia pushed herself from Abraham and looked towards the floor—'Ninapaige said it was for the best. She told me I did not just look different in the mirror—I had to learn to be the woman I saw staring back at me. I had to forget Luanna—convince myself that woman is dead.'

That made Abraham's eyes water. The very thought still hurt him.

'I accepted Luanna had died, and I accepted my new life for ten long years, but I could never forget the life I had before, and I would never have wanted to forget. In the end, I took the opportunity to return home the moment I saw it. I had finally had enough of hiding and wanted only to face what may come. I told no one of my plans, not even Ninapaige.'

Abraham wiped his eyes and nose. 'This Ninapaige sounds a right miscreant!'

Sylvia tittered. 'Ninapaige can be offhand with her words, and she is without a doubt feisty, which is something that reflects her clown-like appearance, but she means well. Equally, Ninapaige is noticeably reticent and often keeps things from me. Whether this is to protect or because she does not feel a need to say anything is a mystery. I try not to think about it much these days... especially now that I'm back with the ones who matter to me most.'

Sylvia smiled plaintively as she dabbed Abraham's cheeks of the tears. 'I do not underestimate how you feel right now, Abe, and I understand how confusing and unfair it seems. When I was thrown into the deep all those years ago, my head felt as though it would explode. During that time, however, I have not only been able to come to terms with it but also somewhat figure out why things are the way they are. I am sure that you, too, will make sense of it all in time. Lucky for you, I am here to help make that process simpler.'

Abraham forced a smile and put his arm back round Sylvia, encouraging her to lean on him once again. 'Sylvia is a pretty name, at least.'

'I have Ninapaige to thank for that as well, and based on what I know, the name comes from a sad time. Despite appearances, Ninapaige is very old and has been wandering about for many years. On several occasions, she spoke about what she calls Phyeroc—a prophecy. She told me of certain people throughout history who are important. Do you remember the story of Queen Evelyn? She was the last ruler of Stilly and died without bearing children. Ninapaige said Evelyn had a special bloodline, but after the queen's death, she took it upon herself to search for other possible relations with Phyeroc. During this time, for whatever reason, she came across a little girl named Sylvia—a sweet child with abusive parents who were also her killers. Before Sylvia's death, and despite discovering that the girl was not related to Phyeroc as first thought, Ninapaige became very attached to the child, and the loss devastated her.'

'The parents were the girl's killers? What became of them?'

'Ninapaige said they got what they deserved, but did not delve into much detail. I didn't want to push her further.'

Abraham sighed. 'A wise decision, no doubt. That *is* a heart-breaking story.'

Sylvia linked her arms about Abraham's midriff.

'So if Ninapaige has spent all this time with you,' Abraham continued. 'Does that mean you are a part of this prophecy thing?'

Sylvia did not have a chance to answer the question.

Startled by a knock at the office door, a young man dressed in medical attire extended his head into the room. 'Are you busy, Doctor Enpee? There is another patient that needs examination.'

Sylvia stood and put her chair back in its usual place. 'Not at all—bring them in.'

Abraham pushed himself up from his own seat and walked towards the door. 'I'll leave you to it. I will see if I can make myself useful, but I doubt I'll go too far.'

'All right, Abe... we can talk about this again later,' Sylvia said, unsure if she could answer his question.

Ebony could not help but feel inward satisfaction. This newfound power was undoubtedly courtesy of Ninapaige.

'Are you feeling all right, Ebony?' Alim asked her for the tenth time.

'A little fatigued, but otherwise fine.'

Alim creased his face. 'This could be a result of the ytyism. I suggest you ease up a bit—lest you wear yourself out completely.'

Ebony acknowledged Alim's suggestion with a nod. She had been using ytyism at almost every given opportunity, and even though utilising the magic felt effortless enough, she still had no understanding of its power or what effect it might have on her body. Indeed, Ebony had essentially led the way from the courtyard. After helping to extinguish the flames, she went on to light rooms and hallways while removing strewn objects, regardless of how small they had been. She had also eased the burns on her arm and the aching in her back.

The use of ytyism had not been entirely self-indulgent. As Ebony, Alim, Vincent and a small group of soldiers progressed through the castle, they encountered half a dozen redifass. The humanoids had posed no threat, and she had turned them into ice or ash before blowing them apart. In one grisly instance, Ebony had inadvertently turned a redifass inside out. Either way, this removed the need for the soldiers following her to fight.

'You should take a little rest, lass,' Vincent had told Ebony, agreeing with Alim. 'In the meantime, perhaps I can figure out where we are.'

In the courtyard, the soldiers had split into three main groups. One set took the castle's eastern section, while the second took a more central route, leaving the remaining party to follow a westerly course. Ebony and Alim had been part of the latter team, which Vincent led. Encountering multiple paths during their exploration, Vincent split his party further until there were about half a dozen in each group.

Ebony's group passed through a dining room adjacent to a gutted kitchen and finally along the side of an overgrown garden below. At a guess, they were not far from the western towers.

Peering through the hollows of a glassless arch, Ebony spied what appeared to be a conservatory to the other end of the garden. 'We might be able to pass through there,' she suggested, pointing to the greenhouse. 'I imagine there is a set of stairs nearby.'

'We might as well, lass,' Vincent said huskily. 'Ain't anythin' better I can think to do.'

The group found a stairway and made their way down into the garden. Pushing and (in Vincent's case) hacking through the natural density, they reached the conservatory, which, to everyone's surprise, was full of fresh flowers.

Observing one particularly striking plant, Ebony leaned in to inhale its fragrance. 'Where could all these have come from?'

'It beats me,' Alim said, pulling stems away from a ramshackle door opposite where they had entered. The door opened with no resistance, revealing an even more impressive sight.

Alim gasped. 'Tender spirits! Come and take a look at this, dear girl.'

Alim stepped into another garden, Ebony following close behind. The area was filled with lush green grass, specially shaped trees and bushes, and hundreds of flowerbeds filled with multi-coloured flora, some so exotic that Ebony had never before seen the like. It was beautiful, especially with the early sunlight creeping over the curtain walls.

Regrettably, the group was afforded little time to take in the splendour; a sudden thud coming from the far end of the garden seized their attention.

The dilapidated iron door gave way on the third kick, slamming against the stone on the other side with an almighty clang.

Maynard took one last look up the three towers. If his assumptions were correct, Fordon Latnemirt would be in the second: Evelyn's Tower. Suavlant bolted his way up the coiled stairway of the lowest keep, stopping at the first door leading to the second tower. Unlike the one at the base, this door was pristine and unlocked. Keeping his back to the wall, Maynard eased the door open. Silence was all that greeted him, but he could sense that the Fordon was not far away; the stench of ytyism was too pungent for it to be otherwise.

Maynard found the entrance to Evelyn's chambers wide open as he stepped sideways up the passage. The faint sounds of movement emanated from within, getting louder as he approached. With his weapon waist high and tight in his grasp, Maynard peered into the chamber.

The circular keep was a remarkable sight, as if untouched by the ravages of time. Tinted silk curtains and drapes decorated the space, providing colour and warmth to an otherwise cold and lifeless stone room. A large bed covered with fur blankets and feather-stuffed cushions lay under the sole, open window west of the bedchamber, bathed in the morning light.

Fordon, who was to the west of the chamber with his back turned to the entrance, kept his attention fixed to a table before him. He had his hands clasped behind his back and stood with a calmness that suggested he did not realise Maynard was only mere metres away.

Remnant Tales of Stilly:
Passion and Benevolence

'Dawn is a beautiful thing, would you not agree?' Fordon said, speaking a bygone Stillian dialect. He extinguished the candle flame to his right with a sharp blow and then looked at Maynard via an elliptical mirror fixed to the wall above the table. 'It would be a shame to mar such splendour with violence.'

Maynard gazed at Fordon's reflection with stony silence.

Fordon turned from the desk and gave the younger man a passing glance as he walked towards the window. 'It's amusing, in a strange way, that even after all these centuries, we think and behave almost the same as we always have.'

'You are not the same man I once called a friend,' Maynard insisted.

He thinks he knows you… they all do, the inner voice told Fordon. *What could they possibly know?*

'Perhaps,' Fordon grunted, 'but I did say almost. I notice changes in you as well. You seem to have lost the passion you once had—your expression is dead, and you are confused as to why you even live. Tell me, Sovereign Knight… what do you fight for now?'

Maynard said nothing.

This silence caused Fordon to smirk. 'All the people for whom you once fought are long gone from this world. You are alone.'

'If your intent is to break me, the endeavour is wasted.'

'I suppose the changes are only superficial after all. You always were a tenacious man, Suvlant.' Fordon went on, turning his glance to Maynard. 'You are mistaken, however—I have no intention to break you. In fact, I have never hated you, nor have I truly hated anyone else in this kingdom. My animosity has only ever been directed at one individual.'

'Rosaleen,' Maynard uttered.

'Yes. You see me as a destructive force, but as I told you many years ago, she is the real enemy. I have always believed we could be allies, and it sincerely pains me that you no longer see me as a friend.'

'You slew the ones you called friends. You killed our king, you took my brother's life… you spilt their blood and even mine. You speak of betrayal, yet you remain unconcerned about your own perfidy.'

He hates you… he thinks he understands. Do not let him trick you… he could never understand.

Fordon dismissed the allegation, swiping the air with his arm. 'Do not presume to tell me how I feel! I did my utmost to amend your and everyone else's ignorance. Fighting was not a decision I took lightly, so how dare you, or anyone, judge me?'

'I judge you on what I have seen.' Maynard pointed at Fordon accusingly. 'You—and only you—chose this path, and *you* were the man who scorned any helping hands. I agree that we could have been allies—and in another time, we were just that, but the truer enemy of whom you speak has distorted any reason you once held. You know this—you knew it all those years ago, and Rosaleen uses you now more than ever. You are a danger, old friend, and I fear you will stoop to any depths to satisfy your hatred of that woman, even if it means sacrificing the innocent.'

He lies… he thinks he knows you… they all do. He thinks he understands. Do not let him trick you… he could never understand.

Fordon harrumphed. 'Your words—as noble as they are—hold little power for the means to sway me. I have not forgotten how Rosaleen corrupted me and even that I have become extreme in my actions. Yet, extreme actions are needed when facing extreme danger, and Rosaleen is the biggest of dangers—an outcast rejected even by her own kind. As long as she exists, more than just this world is in jeopardy.'

'You claim to recognise Rosaleen's menace, but have you ever considered her intentions?' Maynard said.

Fordon scowled at the question. 'What would you know of them?'

'Last we met… you stated that Rosaleen was searching for an object. You also mentioned that she feared Evelyn Sanine.'

Fordon took a moment to think. 'You are referring to Omnipotent, an orb she had lost upon exile and believed to be in Wilheard. She believed that Evelyn presented a risk, and after I had located Omnipotent, she would use it not only to regain strength but to counter Phyroc.'

'I remember much of what you said that day. In essence, you claimed to be just another puppet in Rosaleen's eyes, and you resented her for that.'

'Yes, and I am aware that the unrelenting hatred I feel for Rosaleen is somehow a divine joke on her part. On my return to Wilheard, I kept myself in solitude. I worked on healing myself using ytyism and created Ascendancy to amass further energy. Rosaleen wanted me to kill our princess, anticipating that with my death, all the energy she bestowed upon me would return to her along with Evelyn's life force.'

Fordon spoke on. 'Princess Evelyn, Minach Emmanuel... I wanted all the energy I could find, and in the unlikely event that I survived, I could use it against Rosaleen. A dangerous tactic, considering that my death would only serve to make her stronger, but it was a risk I was willing to take. I can see the disgust in your eyes, but sacrifices need to be made for the greater good.'

Maynard closed his eyes to hide his displeasure. 'I can see that you have not lost your resolve, and that you still cannot see how pointless this crusade is. You make the same mistakes that you made centuries ago. This is a convoluted game to Rosaleen, and you play right into her hands.'

He lies... do not let him trick you... he could never understand.

'If I am just the puppet you claim, Sovereign Knight, then all is beyond my control, including my decisions.'

Maynard looked Fordon directly in the eyes. 'Is that what you believe?'

'You know I do not believe it. I will not make the same mistakes as before, for I have long reconsidered my strategy. Rosaleen may be powerful enough to manipulate another's mind, even in her weakened state, but she does not have full control and is still mortal.'

Fordon walked back to the table. From there, he revealed Ascendancy. 'In the end, it all comes down to life energy, and I believe I *can* obtain enough to realise a better future. I lost Ascendancy centuries ago, but this was not merely recklessness but rather through design. Ascendancy has seen many wielders since then—some would have been meek, while others were ruthless. With every life taken by its blade, Ascendancy would claim the victims' vitality. I grew weaker as time passed, but I knew my patience would eventually bear fruit. I have always sensed Ascendancy's presence. She is my creation, after all, and I just needed to find her again.'

Maynard remained impassive. 'You have all that life essence in your possession, and it is something you would gamble? You surely underestimate Rosaleen. She would take it from you.'

Fordon's expression brightened then. 'That is the beauty of it! Rosaleen would not gain anything, even if I were to suffer defeat. As long as I keep the energy in Ascendancy, separate from her influence, she cannot take it. You see, Rosaleen's power is in me, and though I have tried, I cannot remove it. However, that does not mean I have to use it—all I must do is draw only from Ascendancy, not directly from my body.'

Maynard gazed at Fordon for a long moment. 'You are certain of this?'

Fordon sighed. 'I will not sit idly. I can stop Rosaleen—*we* can stop Rosaleen—and now that I have Ascendancy--'

'Your words are wasted,' Maynard interjected. 'I do not know this Rosaleen as you do, but even I can see this is futile. She all but owns you.'

He thinks he knows, the inner voice hissed. *He thinks he understands.*

Fordon brushed the suggestion aside. 'There is still Phyeroc... I just need to find superior energy. Admittedly, the vitality I have collected so far is trifling, and I have already drawn a significant amount of ytyism from Ascendancy. You understand that healing centuries of fatigue and creating an army does not come without great cost. '

'So from where do you mean to draw this superior energy? Evelyn Sanine is gone, her life force with her.'

Fordon laughed. 'My dear, Sovereign Knight, I know that you are not so obtuse that you have not figured it out. All we needed was to find the right people—those who pertain to Phyeroc and know ytyism.'

Maynard did not respond. His grip tightened on the hilt of his greatsword.

Fordon moved slowly to the front of the table. 'Do you honestly believe that with Evelyn's death, her bloodline ended? Have you been chasing after and protecting that girl without knowing why?'

'Evelyn bore no children,' Maynard insisted.

'So, for all your condescension, it would seem that you are not as enlightened as you would claim. I admit that such a rumour exists, but no one knows for sure, least of all you. Evelyn abandoned Wilheard. Ultimately, she was trying to escape destiny, and it is reasonable to assume that the young queen had succeeded—espousing a man and subsequently taking a new name. Her children would have enjoyed anonymity.'

'Even if you are to obtain such energy, do you believe it can raise you above humanity?'

Fordon's face contorted into a scowl. 'You still believe I want to transcend humanity?'

'Is that not what you said—that you would become a brother to the Ytied?'

'A crass assessment based on Rosaleen's lies. I merely believe I can create a better world, ridding it of the likes of Rosaleen. I would be *like* a brother.'

'It does not matter how you word it,' Maynard said, raising his weapon. 'Rosaleen will predict your every move and use it against you. You are only serving to invigorate her.'

'I have had quite enough of your lectures. I suspected my ideals would go unappreciated, as they always have. People like you will never understand. I can only do what I feel is right, and I will attempt it unaided if need be. Yet I ask you again, Sovereign Knight: what do you fight for now?'

'My purpose is clearer than ever, and I understand enough that you will only make the same mistakes forever. Innocent or not, Ascendancy has claimed many lives, as has that curse you placed on the Stone King, but I will not allow you to take any more, especially for a misplaced sense of righteousness. Ebony Gibenn's life is not yours to steal, and I will ensure you do not have it.'

Punish that fool! the inner voice finally demanded. *He hates you… he could never understand.*

The chamber darkened as Fordon raised his sword. Ascendancy glowed with an ominous light, sending a purple mist down his arm. 'So be it—deny me all you like. If you intend to hide the girl from me, then I will simply find her.'

Both men prepared for combat, but neither had a chance to make the first move. Ebony and Alim went up the tower as quickly as possible, leaping through the open doorway to Evelyn's chamber. Giving Ebony a cursory glance, Maynard returned his attention to Fordon.

'It seems the girl has saved me the trouble,' Fordon said in the same archaic dialect before switching to one Ebony could understand. 'With such likeness, surely I am not mistaken when I say that you are a descendant of Evelyn. Will you come to me of your own volition, or do I have to fight for you?'

Ebony did not respond with words. Swinging her arms upwards, she produced the same magic as in the courtyard and cast it at Fordon. With little time to react, Fordon clumsily deflected the blue missile to one side, sending it smashing into the chamber wall. The entire southern side of the chamber blew outwards with a loud explosion, sending the now obliterated bed and a mass of debris crashing to the ground below. A plume of dust consumed the area, forcing all inside to cover their faces.

'You share more than her comeliness, it seems, Fordon coughed. 'Evidently, you will prove to be just as troublesome.'

The blast had caused the stairway to cave in, leaving only one other way to exit the tower immediately. Waving his hands to clear the clouds away from his eyes, Fordon stumbled towards the new opening. He looked out for a second and turned again to the other three. 'A change of venue is needed. I am off to find a place with more space. I'll be waiting for you!'

Fordon leapt from the chamber and landed on a ledge three feet below. From there, he used a sloped support to reach the lower tower and the battlement walkway.

Maynard did not linger. With nary a word, he pursued Fordon.

'Ebony!' sounded Vincent's muffled voice, calling through the blockage on the stairway. 'Are you all right, lass?'

'I'm fine, Vincent,' Ebony replied with a cough. 'Alim and I are all right.'

'What happened? Vincent asked, only to retract the question. 'Don't bother answerin' that—it's good just to know you're unharmed. I'll try and find a way to clear this mess.'

Remnant Tales of Stilly:
Passion and Benevolence

Alim wiped the dust from his face and then used his shirt to clean his spectacles. 'What do we do now?'

Ebony brushed her fingers through over her head. She shrugged unhelpfully.

'Well, we need to think of something soon, dear girl.' He looked towards the giant hole. 'I guess we have little choice…'

'Are you insane?' Ebony protested from the farthest point away from the hole. 'You can't make me climb out there!'

Her knees trembled, causing her to lose balance. It had taken a lot of willpower to scale the tower, but at least she had not needed to see how high she was.

Alim linked his hands under Ebony's arms, forcing her to her feet. 'I understand your phobia, and I would never *force* you to do anything like this. Unfortunately, I fear we do not have the luxury of staying here. Who knows how long it will take to clear the way.'

'I could clear the rubble the same way I caused it,' Ebony said. 'How about that?'

'Would you want to risk it? What if the tower collapsed entirely?'

The prospect only caused Ebony's head to spin. 'What if I faint while we are climbing?'

'You've been up against worse things than this, dear girl… I won't leave your side, I promise. Look at it this way—it will be a momentous achievement if you do this, as not only will you be proud of yourself, but you will be able to go on to help Maynard. He needs you, Ebony. Wilheard needs you.'

That last part galvanised Ebony the most. She was so frightened; her stomach churned to the point she felt she could vomit. Yet if she did not find the courage, what would become of Wilheard?

With a tight grip on Alim's hand, Ebony extended her head through the hole and looked down, instantly bringing it back in. She squinted and took a deep breath.

'I can see the ledge,' Alim said, examining the route the two could take. 'It's roughly a metre down.'

'I saw it.' Ebony exhaled. 'Will you be going first?'

Remnant Tales of Stilly:
Passion and Benevolence

'Do you want me to?'

Ebony looked outside again. The ledge's width was generous enough (about two-and-a-half metres wide, Ebony supposed), suggesting the architects had intended for people to step onto it.

Alim went first, on Ebony's request, laying belly-down and lowering himself to the ledge. Shifting to the middle of the opening, he looked towards Ebony. 'Right, your turn. How do you want to do this?'

Ebony decided to mimic Alim. She dangled her legs over and pushed her toes into cracks and other spaces she found. With one hand tight on the broken wall, Alim put his other hand behind Ebony for aid, being sure not to touch her. Ebony found the ledge with little problem.

Alim turned so that his back was against the wall. Ebony stayed the way she was, unwilling to do the same.

'Now then... move like me and with small steps.' Alim stepped across the ledge sideways and with tidy movements, bringing his legs together before taking the next step. 'There is no rush.'

Ebony followed Alim's lead, shuffling behind him and not letting go of the wall until the pair reached the next obstacle: a slope extending to the neighbouring tower.

Although the connecting slope was nearly as wide as the towers, it was also relatively steep and a daunting six metres long.

'We could do this together if we sit in tandem,' Ebony suggested.

Alim studied the possibility. 'It's feasible. One of us might have to climb over the other, though.'

Ebony opted to be the one to sit in front, so Alim sat down on the ledge and held out his hand. Ebony took hold of Alim while holding the wall. She gingerly placed her right foot on the incline, and whilst finding some form of stability, she could not will herself to let go of the wall. Panic set in, and she brought her foot back to the ledge.

'It's no good. I-I can't do it.'

'That is quite all right, dear girl, don't worry. I tell you what—I'll shift forward a bit, and you sit behind me instead. That way, you can hold onto me. How about that?'

After a bit of thought, Ebony nodded.

'Righto, I'll just… move… a little…'

Before Alim could finish what he was saying, he slipped.

'Alim!' Ebony yelled as the scholar fell down the slope. She closed her eyes, her breathing quickening. What would she do now? Alim was surely doomed.

'I'm all right, Ebony,' Alim called after what seemed a lifetime.

Ebony opened her eyes and turned her head to find Alim. He was straightening his clothes and waving at her. She breathed a sigh of relief and eased herself away from the wall. 'Did you hurt yourself?'

'All well and no worse for wear, dear girl. Unfortunately, it seems there has been a slight change in plan. Are you ready to join me?'

Ebony wasted no time. With a sudden desire to get everything over and done with, she sat at the top of the slope and carefully eased herself forward, shifting her bottom across the stone ledge. As with Alim before her, Ebny slipped on the smooth surface, sliding downwards at speed. Ebony screamed as she descended, Alim snatching hold of her by the time she reached the lower tower.

Ebony held Alim for a long moment, her arms tight about him. He patted her back and chuckled nervously. 'That wasn't so bad, was it?'

Ebony responded with a similar giggle.

'Now,' Alim continued. 'If you can lighten your grip on me, we can continue.'

Ebony released Alim and composed herself. 'Sorry.'

'That is quite all right. Let's go.'

The pair shifted round to the other side of the lowest tower, by which point they were above part of the battlement. As with the other times, Alim offered to go first. The drop onto the walkway was approximately nine feet. Keeping his hands on the tower ledge, Alim dangled himself as low as possible before letting go. He landed with a thud.

'Oomph!'

Ebony looked down at Alim. He stood and once again straightened himself.

'Right… easy as you do it.'

Ebony sat on the very edge of the niche, held her breath and leapt. She fell directly on top of Alim, knocking him to the floor.

'Oomph!'

Ebony got up as quickly as possible. 'Are you all right?' she asked, pulling Alim off the floor.

'Marvellous,' he coughed. 'At least that is all over with.'

The two peered over the battlement and into the garden. Fighting had broken out once again as redifass filled the area. Fordon had summoned more Skirmishers during his escape. Ebony spied Vincent fighting against two redifass, pushing one away with brute strength before cutting down the other. He finished the first before it could right itself.

'We best not distract him,' Ebony said. 'Hopefully, Vincent won't be too confused when he doesn't find anyone in the tower. Let's get going.'

Fordon Latnemirt stumbled into the throne room, throwing the doors closed before dragging a nearby display case in front of them.

Oliath entered the hall from the balcony upon hearing the doors open. He had been watching the battle below, which had resumed with the summoning of more creatures. He glared at Fordon. 'Can you not see what your wilfulness has caused? Is this truly what you wanted?'

Fordon ignored Oliath and stumbled towards the balcony, leaving a trail of red. It felt like a knife was in his side. He would need to heal, but first, he wanted to get to his chamber.

'Look at the state of you,' Oliath went on, noticing Fordon's discomfort. 'Your ambitions will be your demise, and what would that prove? After all these centuries, can you still not see when it is enough? Be a man and admit defeat!'

That insolent clown! The voice in Fordon's head spoke. *He thinks he knows you… he thinks he is better than you.*

Walking on, Fordon scowled back at Oliath. 'Like you, Captain of the Guard? Like how you ended up in this castle because of a certain vigilante?

You are hardly in a position to lecture me when it comes to doggedness and restraint.'

'How dare you make such comparisons?' Oliath rebuked. 'I understand the trouble I have caused, and I fully accept and regret my behaviour, but it did not take the destruction of a town and people's lives to realise that.'

How dare you? How dare he! The inner voice continued. *He believes he understands your plight. This is not your fault.*

'I am tired of these condescending allocutions!' Fordon roared, causing a sharp pain to shoot through his abdomen. He faltered.

'This has gone far enough!' Oliath said, stepping into Fordon's path. 'I will not allow you to--'

Fordon thrust his hand towards Oliath's throat, cutting the younger man off before he could finish speaking. He lifted the captain into the air with unnatural strength. 'I have already told you, fool, that I will not tolerate anyone who stands in my way, but that does not mean I cannot make use of you.'

Released from Latnemirt's grip, Oliath dropped to the floor. Dragging himself towards the dais, the captain growled as dark energy forced itself from the pressure mark on his neck and into his mind. He pulled himself up into the middle throne, exhaling heavily as he sagged into it.

Fordon, continuing towards the balcony, said nothing more.

Droplets of blood dotted the walls and floors of the castle passages.

On his journey back to the throne room, Maynard stopped to pick up a marble anjyl spattered with red. *Ebony injured Fordon. What was that power she used? Where did she learn it?*

The questions preyed on his mind, and they needed answers. For now, however, they served only as a distraction.

'What are you looking at, old-timer?' Nolan asked Maynard, kneeling next to him.

Remnant Tales of Stilly:
Passion and Benevolence

A short time ago, Nolan, Cordelia and the *Other Four* again crossed paths with the sovereign knight. They, too, were on their way to the throne room, but instead of Fordon, they sought Oliath, who had made his way there a while ago.

Maynard handed the item to Nolan. Shakeston rubbed his thumb over the red markings. 'This is blood.'

'It is Latnemirt's,' Maynard said.

Nolan handed the anjyl to Cordelia, who rolled it over in her palm. 'You seem confident in that.'

Maynard stood up. 'I know he is hurt.'

'So you found the sorcerer,' said Nolan with heightened interest. 'And you managed to wound him?'

'No,' Maynard said curtly. He continued walking.

Puzzled by the answer, Nolan jumped to his feet and followed Maynard. 'But you did *find* Latnemirt, and I assume you know why he is hurt.'

Maynard did not respond.

Cordelia joined in. 'I will assume that Latemirt did not simply trip and fall. I would like to meet the one who managed to strike him. Does Wilheard's Army have a hidden gem?'

'Now you have got Cordelia interested,' Nolan went on. 'Why are you so tight-lipped about such a thing, old-timer?'

Maynard continued to ignore the lieutenants and pressed on.

Dexter and Wiley, who had been listening from several paces behind, whispered to one another.

'Did you hear that?' Dexter mouthed as Wiley looked at him. 'Who could it be?'

Wiley scrunched his lips. 'It could be a common soldier, but if it is someone the swordsman knows… well, that Ebony Gibenn character is often by his side.'

'You reckon it's her? How could she possibly have hurt Latnemirt?'

Wiley shrugged. 'It is just a thought—the best I can think of right now.'

A hand-shaped patch of blood centring the double doors of the throne room confirmed that Fordon had passed through, as did the obstruction on the other side. Cautiously, Maynard and Nolan pushed the heavy doors ajar, nudging the display case in the way. The two men peered through the opening.

From the farthest end, sunlight filled the open area, highlighting further blood dashes leading to the open balcony. The hall was the same as when Maynard had last seen it: ruined chunks of what was once a table; the shattered glass from fallen chandeliers; buckled armour and steel… all scattered and unmoved.

Beyond the carnage, Nolan could see someone sitting in the shadows on the other side of the chamber. 'Captain Burley. Is that you, sir?'

The group forced the doors open entirely and then edged into the hall.

Oliath, his body slumped on the centre throne, did not respond to his name.

Nolan and Cordelia exchanged a look of unease.

'Do you think he is…?' Cordelia said.

'No,' Wiley interjected. 'I can see movements. He seems to be breathing—and look at the fingers.'

The group looked at Oliath's hands. Sure enough, his fingers twitched.

'Sir,' Cordelia shouted. 'Are you hurt?'

Still, there was no reply.

The lieutenants paced towards their boss, leaving Maynard to stay behind with the others. By the time the pair was halfway closer, Oliath finally slurred something.

'Stay… from…'

Nolan and Cordelia, unaware Oliath had said anything, continued towards him.

'… away… me,' Oliath mumbled again.

'What has got into you, sir?' Nolan said, stepping up the dais.

'I said STAY AWAY FROM ME!'

Leaping from his seat, Oliath launched a fist into Nolan's chin, sending him back down the step.

'What are you doing?' Cordelia exclaimed, running towards Oliath to restrain him.

Oliath resisted Cordelia's arrest, pushing her away before throwing an identical punch to her jaw. The hit was so heavy that she tumbled off the podium, just as her male counterpart had done. She shook her head and looked with dizzy eyes at Nolan. He was unconscious.

'GET AWAY FROM ME!' Oliath yelled again, walking with menacing steps towards the warriors. 'I AM FILLED WITH RAGE!'

Standing over Nolan, Oliath lifted his foot above the floored man's head. Cordelia struggled onto her stomach and crawled over her companion. 'Don't do it!'

Oliath's boot hung over the two. 'I have no control over myself. I want to destroy... GET... AWAY... FROM ME!'

Oliath raised his leg as high as possible, ready to crush his loyal lieutenants. Yet, something took hold of him before he could bring it down again.

Maynard put one hand under Oliath's raised leg and the other hand under his arm. He launched the captain over the lieutenants, sending him crashing to the marble floor.

'You lot,' Maynard called to the *Other Four*. 'Help these two get out of the way!'

Dexter and Rida jogged to Nolan while Wiley and Meddia tended to Cordelia.

'Don't kill him, old-timer!' Cordelia said as Wiley and Meddia led her away. 'He is not himself.'

'I know,' Maynard muttered. He unclipped his scabbard and slid it across the floor towards the group.

Oliath rose from the floor, slow and ominous. His upper body bulged as he tightened his fists, the veins along his arms and neck protruding. Keeping hate-filled eyes trained on the sovereign knight, Oliath roared and charged at him.

Oliath swung his left fist at Maynard, forcing his opponent to defend with both arms. Maynard responded by thrusting his palm into Oliath's upper chest, temporarily causing the captain to drop to one knee. Oliath threw another left punch, this time successfully striking Maynard's hip before following through with a more powerful right-handed blow to the face. The hit knocked Maynard to one side, causing him to lose balance completely.

Remnant Tales of Stilly:
Passion and Benevolence

The might behind the punch was incredible: the hardest Maynard had ever endured. He regained his footing and readied himself for further attack.

Oliath hurtled towards Maynard and swung again with his left fist. As he had done before, Maynard guarded by holding up both arms, but this time, the attack had been a ruse. Instead of hitting him, Oliath grabbed his opponent's raised arm and yanked him closer. He head-butted Maynard twice, let go of him and then launched another right-handed blow to his face.

Blood trickled from Maynard's nose and mouth, dripping onto the floor. On his hands and knees with his back arched, he stared at the red pooling under him. Oliath was approaching again, his boots pounding the ground with every step. Maynard rolled sideways as Oliath's foot came down, evading the attack at the last moment and leaving the captain to stomp in the puddle of blood. Oliath scowled and took a step back. Maynard ran his hand under his nose and flicked the excess liquid away. His face, although bruised and throbbing with pain, remained impassive.

Oliath's strength was phenomenal, and as he pushed himself upright, Maynard concluded that he needed to take a more robust approach.

Oliath threw a barrage of punches. Maynard ducked and weaved every strike, not one of them making contact. The captain growled impatiently, adding kicks and attempted grabs to the onslaught, but to no avail. As Maynard anticipated, this enraged Oliath further but also led him to become desperate and clumsy.

With that, Maynard had his chance.

The sovereign knight twisted to Oliath's right, forcing his elbow into the muscular man's ribs. Oliath roared with pain and swung at his opponent. Maynard dodged back round to the front and kneed Oliath in the belly, then the face when the captain doubled over.

With his vision disorientated, Oliath made one last pitiful lunge for Maynard. This time, blocking the hit came all too easy for the sovereign knight, who unleashed his own succession of punches. One—a blow to the hip; two—the side of the face; three—under the chin.

Oliath plummeted backwards, propelled into the air by the finishing blow and ending up on the flat of his back.

'Ya killed 'im!' Rida shouted with dismay.

'He is merely unconscious,' said Nolan, having since stirred from his own blackout. 'Captain Burley can withstand more than the likes of that.'

Leaving Cordelia with Nolan, the *Other Four* rushed to Oliath's side.

Maynard peered down at the group momentarily before looking towards Nolan and Cordelia. 'All of you must take care—of yourselves and each other.'

Silence filled the hall then. Re-equipping his weapon, Maynard paced towards the throne room balcony, stopping when a small voice called out.

'You must take care, too,' Meddia said softly. Tearing a piece from her now ragged shirt, she jogged to Maynard and handed him the cloth.

Maynard dabbed his lip and nose before thanking the girl. Meddia smiled a toothy grin and skipped back to Wiley's side.

Maynard looked at the group one last time before disappearing from sight.

Maynard peered at the town below from over the parapet; the conflict between Wilheard's armed forces and Fordon's army raged on.

From the throne room, the blood led to the western end of the balcony, staining the steps reaching up to the tower that housed Fordon's chamber. Unlike the others, this tower was square, the room inside large, and, save for a scroll-full table to the far end, void of anything other than centuries of dust and dirt. As within Evelyn's chamber, Fordon stood over the bench, this time facing the entrance.

'Emmanuel also believed in Phyeroc,' Fordon said softly as Maynard entered his peripheral vision, 'as did your precious Evelyn, but I am certain you already knew this. Regrettably, I suspect that means nothing to you now.'

Fordon looked up from the table of scrolls and books to offer Maynard a troubled stare. He was visibly tired and looked ready to tumble at any moment. 'Emmanuel... Evelyn... they and others knew of the prophecy— followed it as a creed that dictated their very being and actions. Godfrey, on the other hand, believed adamantly in the Naitsir faith. He despised anything that challenged his spirituality—even going so far as to destroy opposing views. He was a good-natured man, but how would he have reacted if he had discovered his closest confidant lived a life of deceit?'

Fordon chuckled, but it was cheerless. He gazed at the cracks in the ceiling. 'And of his only begotten daughter. She acted behind his back, never intending to follow his principles. Do you think he would have been crushed to learn of these betrayals? You were one of the king's loyal sovereign knights—you knew of Emmanuel and Evelyn but did nothing to stop them. People call me a traitor, but what does that make the likes of you?'

Maynard refused to answer. Yet, if he had chosen to, would he have been able to find the words?

Fordon did not expect a response. Moving from behind the table, he stepped round to the side and brandished the now familiar, curved-bladed sword, the sapphire that was Ascendancy glowing from its hilt. 'I underestimated Emmanuel and Evelyn's power. At the time, I did not realise their involvement in ytyism predated mine, and despite not being in their circle, I shared their beliefs. We may not have had the same ambitions, but we all knew that the prophecy meant only one thing—to deny the forsaken ytied. Seeing as I am the only one of this little society still alive, I am left to fulfil this legacy.'

'Your words reek of complacency, and they always have. You are lying to yourself and trying to convince your conscience that your actions are justified. Nevertheless, deep down, not even you can overlook what you have done. Even after all this time, you fail to see your folly or the damage it has caused.' Maynard drew his sword and raised it against Fordon in what would be their last confrontation. 'I must stop you, old friend.'

The inner voice returned to Fordon then. *What would he know? He hates you… he blames you. This is not your fault… it is **her** fault.*

Fordon positioned himself in front of the table. He looked at the swordsman for a long moment before raising his own weapon, revealing his bloody injury. 'We do what we must and should never let the words of others falter us. Never stop fighting for what you believe in, Sovereign Knight… because I will not.'

Maynard made the first move. Rushing towards Fordon, he brought his greatsword down with a tremendous slash, slicing the table in half and launching its contents as the intended target danced to one side. Latnemirt retaliated by slashing at Maynard's neck, cutting at the air twice but missing both times. Maynard barged Fordon to widen the gap and attempted a horizontal swipe. Fordon leaned back to avoid the attack and then stabbed forward. The sovereign knight nudged away and responded with a kick that struck Fordon squarely in the chest, forcing him to the wall several feet away.

Maynard stepped back from the older man and moved to the room's centre, where he watched and waited.

Fordon wheezed as he clutched at his chest. The assault had hurt him a lot and worsened the untreated wound on his side. Using the wall as support, Fordon pushed himself up. Due to Ebony's ytyism spell, his power was ebbing; the energy he had gathered over the centuries was all but gone. He was a shell, his body no more useful than a carcass. How could he ever hope to match the sovereign knight in his current state?

The thoughts whirling about Fordon's head at that moment repulsed him. Yet, what else could he do? He had never wanted to use that cursed energy. Why would he? How could he use the power that had caused him so much pain, the very power that had twisted his mind and filled him with hate? That was supposed to be for *her*. He was supposed to use it to destroy *her* the same way *she* had destroyed him.

Maynard had been right all along. Fordon belonged to Rosaleen; if he used her energy, she would receive everything. Fordon would be Rosaleen's slave—her puppet. All his struggles will have been for nothing.

No, the voice in Fordon's head told him. *That is not true—it could **never** be true. This is just another obstacle. You have faced more significant obstacles before; indeed, you overcame every one of them. Use her power… use it to overcome this nuisance. You can always gather more energy… give Rosaleen the sovereign knight's vitality… take the girl's for Ascendancy. With her vitality, your dreams will come true. That will show them that **you** were right all along.*

Fordon dropped Ascendancy by his feet; moments later, a dull red light filled the room. His robes fluttered as tremendous waves of energy poured from his body. The force circulated Fordon's emaciated frame, imbuing him with a vigour that he had long thought abandoned him, sinking back into his flesh and coursing his veins.

The dark magic was so intense that Maynard instinctively shielded his eyes. Eventually, the force subsided, and with the room's atmosphere returning to normal, he lowered his arms. Fordon's body, no longer a wasted frame, was taut and swelled with muscle. He appeared so much younger that even a tinge of brown had returned to his long, grey beard. Injuries from previous clashes disappeared, as did the exhaustion that had creased his face.

The now corrupted Fordon rolled his neck and regarded Maynard with heightened malevolence. 'Now then... let's get this over with.'

Fordon sprinted towards Maynard and barged into him, sending the sovereign knight smashing into the eastern wall. Maynard felt the air come out of him as he hit the stone, the impact so hard that a crack formed. Before Maynard could slide back down to the floor, Fordon clutched his throat and forced his right arm against the wall, causing Ardruism to drop.

Dangling in the Fordon's grip, Maynard gazed into his eyes. The power that had dwelled deep within Latnemirt corrupted him entirely, attaching itself to his very being. This dark ytyism took hold of his self-control, destroying what little reason he had left and, in doing so, intensifying the hunger for his greatest desires.

'You had resisted Rosaleen's... hold on you all this time,' Maynard said, gasping for air. 'Now you simply let her in. Her necromancy will destroy you.'

The voice in Fordon's head fed words of encouragement. *He thinks he knows you... he knows nothing. He is trying to trick you.*

Fordon tightened his grip. 'My wellbeing is not your concern, Sovereign Knight. I fought this evil before, and I will do it again.'

Kill this pathetic man, the voice spoke on. *Tear him apart and claim his energy.*

Maynard forced his legs up and pushed his opponent away with all his might. Fordon released his grip and staggered back a few steps.

Fordon snorted. 'You are far more durable than I remember and still so strong. Nevertheless, how long can you hope to survive?'

Maynard lunged up from his knee and slammed both palms into Fordon's torso. Latnemirt recoiled, letting out a growl. Taking hold of Ardruism once more, Maynard swung the greatsword underarm, aiming to slice Fordon from below. Alas, Fordon was far too quick and effortlessly sidestepped the strike.

'Bravo, Sovereign Knight. There is fight in you yet!'

Fordon slammed his fist into Maynard's gut before he could attempt a second strike, causing the sovereign knight to tumble backwards. Lying out flat on the floor, Maynard felt broken and unable to move. Tilting his head to the left, he could see his sword; he stretched his arm to reach it. Fordon calmly walked up to the dazed man and stamped on his left arm, fracturing his wrist. Maynard shuddered from the pain but let out nary a whimper.

Fordon offered Maynard a pitying look. 'You tried your best, Sovereign Knight, but it seems fortune favours me.' Using ytyism, he summoned the arched blade back to hand. He struck the air with mock stabbing motions. 'It is a shame that we could not come to an amicable agreement—after all, we both only wished to make the world a better place. Perhaps the ytied now understand that I am the only one who can achieve this.'

Kill this pathetic man, the inner voice demanded. *Kill, kill, kill!*

Kneeling, Fordon lined the short sword to Maynard's chest and then raised it above head. He brought it back down on the sovereign knight's left breast, piercing through the leather armour and other clothing with ease.

Maynard lay as if nothing had happened, unable to produce enough strength to respond. He was tired, more so than he could ever remember. For nearly forty years, he had been restless, desperate to find the reason for his return. Now, within a heartbeat, all this vitality and longing drained from him. His eyes blurred, and his hearing muffled; the pain that had riddled his body moments ago faded away, leaving nothing but his thoughts: thoughts of regret, frustration and sorrow. He would die believing he had failed Wilheard, had failed his friends past and present and had failed his duty.

Stricken with a familiar, liquid-blue enchantment, Fordon twisted through the air and landed among the mass of scrolls spread across the ground. Ebony stood at the arched doorway with Alim right behind her. At first glance, with Maynard lying motionless, it seemed they were too late.

Remnant Tales of Stilly:
Passion and Benevolence

'Alim, see if Maynard is all right,' Ebony said. 'I will do my best to fend off Latnemirt.'

Fordon rose from the floor, his body bending like rubber. 'That is the second time you've struck me, girl. You—at the very least, the reincarnation of Evelyn Sanine—will not manage a third time.'

A trading of ytyism ensued then.

Alim made a direct line to Maynard and dragged him over to a shadowed corner. He dropped to his knees and examined the perishing man. Maynard's eyes were closed, and his chest, from which Fordon's sword protruded, was still.

Alim looked at the short sword. Fordon had sunk the blade all the way to the hilt. The severity of any internal injury was undoubtedly high, and extracting the weapon might exacerbate the damage. Contrariwise, a purple substance lined the wound, putrefying the immediate area of skin, and he wondered if leaving the sword in place would prove worse. Alim took hold of the hilt and heaved the sword out, a spurt of blood escaping with it. He tossed the blade aside, placed his hand over the gash and applied pressure.

The battle between Ebony and Fordon accelerated, the ferocity of their individual attacks growing grander and more destructive, causing the room to shake and the stone to crack and crumble. Although holding herself well against Fordon, Ebony's inexperience with ytyism was showing; whereas she relied on what came naturally, Fordon was more deliberate in his assault. He quashed every one of her attempts while encumbering her with his own magic.

Despite her apparent inferiority, Fordon was impressed.

'Superb,' Fordon laughed as he snuffed another ball of energy. 'Truly, your life energy will make a welcome addition to mine.'

Alim could see Fordon inching closer to Ebony. If only he could help her, or at the very least, help Maynard. The immobilising spell was unlikely to be of much use, even if he could muster it under such pressure.

A familiar, child-like voice spoke to Alim then, coming from what sounded like behind. 'Things are not going quite to plan, are they?'

Alim twisted his head round to see who was there. He squinted at the shadow, seeing no one.

Remnant Tales of Stilly:
Passion and Benevolence

'I will have to break my little promise once again, and likely not for the last time,' the voice continued, this time directly behind Alim's head. 'I cannot abide seeing you struggle, boy.'

Alim blinked, only to find Ninapaige kneeling beside him when his eyes opened. She gave him a pronounced wink and pressed a finger to her smirking lips. Taking Alim's arm, she positioned it so that his hand was above the stab wound on Maynard's chest and coaxed him to move it in circular motions. Using Alim as a conduit, Ninapaige passed a spell through him, quickly causing the gash to seal.

'The blade missed his heart,' Ninapaige said, moving Alim's hand so that it hovered over Maynard's shattered wrist. 'As insidious as it might seem, Latnemirt's poison alone will not kill Sombie. He is not as human as he once was, which should be obvious. A spell placed on him long ago has afforded him such immunities.'

Ninapaige jumped to her feet and leapt behind Alim. She placed her hands on his shoulders. 'As for you, boy... do you remember the Pentominto you took from the Stone King?'

Alim pulled a parchment from his belt and revealed it to Ninapaige. Without looking at it, she stepped next to Alim and placed her head beside his. 'I do not like to interfere too much in others' affairs—moreover, I cannot defy my mistress, nor do anything that could be construed as detrimental to her... at least not directly. Fortunately, there are always ways to circumvent this rule, and that is where you come in. Focus your thoughts on Fordon Latnemirt and repeat after me.'

Ninapaige whispered an unfamiliar dialect to Alim. He repeated the words, muttering them under his breath and triggering the Pentominto on the paper to glow.

'Perfect, child,' Ninapaige praised, 'and remember—whatever happens, focus your thoughts on Fordon Latnemirt.'

Alim felt a larger hand snatch at the scruff of his neck as soon as Ninapaige finished speaking. Alim jolted, startled by the sudden movement, but did not remove his gaze from Fordon.

Maynard's eyes snapped open. He released his grip on Alim and pushed himself to a sitting position.

Fordon stepped closer to Ebony, forcing her backwards and outside the doorway. She halted upon feeling the parapet of the staircase behind her, lowering her hands to prevent falling. Fordon seized the opportunity: pacing towards Ebony, he wrapped a bony hand under her chin and gently squeezed her cheeks, causing her body to numb.

Fordon tilted Ebony's head back, gazing directly into her eyes. 'I am impressed by your ytyism, girl, but I was ready for it this time.' He led her away from the ledge. 'Still, it seems these powers are too great for you to handle. Allow me to alleviate you of such burdens.'

Fordon's brow twitched as a sudden loss of control washed over him. With his fingers contracting, he lost his grip on Ebony and staggered backwards.

'What is this?' Fordon blurted, turning his attention to Alim. The scholar's eyes were fixed on him, his lips moving as he uttered a mantra.

Before Fordon had a chance to process what was happening, he growled as a sharp pain shot through his arm from the wrist. Maynard, who was back on his feet, threw him away from Ebony. Fordon absorbed the crash by rolling backwards before landing upright, just in time to see the sovereign knight dashing towards him.

Maynard's bade missed Fordon's face by an inch, lopping a clump of hair from his beard. Maynard left no room for retaliation, chasing Fordon about the empty space with unrelenting sword swipes, cutting the older man in several places ranging from his arms to his belly and one particularly close slash to the throat. Fordon, for a time, avoided serious injury, but with every dodge, he felt his body slowing and cramping.

Fordon fell to one knew with a grunt after Maynard kicked him in the calf. The sovereign knight followed the attack by slamming the pommel of his sword into Latnemirt's cheekbone. Fordon landed face down, blood and chipped teeth spurting from his mouth. Pushing himself up as quickly as possible, he turned to face Maynard again, who, holding Ardruism high, towered over him.

Fordon howled as his right arm fell to the floor, the limb severed at the elbow with a clean cut. Maynard raised Ardruism above head again, ready, at long last, to end this struggle, but Fordon was not about to give up just yet.

Remnant Tales of Stilly:
Passion and Benevolence

Using his remaining arm, he propelled Maynard away before regaining his balance.

Panting with angry breaths, Fordon turned his attention back to Ebony, electricity now emanating from his left palm. Weary from the battle, she sat on the floor, limp in Alim's arms. Upon Maynard's reanimation, Alim rushed to her; the incantation continued to slow Fordon for a while longer but soon faded when Alim ceased chanting. Fordon waved his hand clumsily and flicked the resulting electrical sphere at the pair.

Maynard convulsed as the magic struck him, the electricity forcing him to kneel. Fordon scoffed, managing a strained grin; the sovereign knight had reacted as expected.

Fordon limped over to the discarded short sword and picked it up. Holding it awkwardly in his left hand, he once again approached Maynard. 'I tried to give you a dignified death,' he said, staring at the sovereign knight as wisps of smoke emitted from his electricity-seared body. 'It was a sympathetic gesture on my part. I will not make that mistake again.'

They should pay for their insolence ... pay with their life, the voice said. *Kill them!*

Fordon stopped behind Maynard and pressed the blade to the side of his neck. He drew the sword back but stopped as he felt a sharp pang from behind. He looked down to see Ardruism protruding from his midriff.

The arched sword clanged as it hit the stone floor. Fordon placed his trembling hand round to his back, confirming that the greatsword had run him through. With his attention turned away from Ebony and Alim, he had not seen the pair take hold of Ardruism, nor had he anticipated they could lift the mighty blade, even between them.

Fordon staggered a few paces forward. Rising once more, Maynard pulled Ardruism from the older man. Fordon turned to face his assailants before looking directly into Maynard's eyes. In the space of a heartbeat, the sovereign knight impaled Latnemirt, plunging the greatsword through his abdomen.

Spluttering blood, Fordon heard the inner voice, present and talkative for so long, but for what would now be the last time. *They think they know you... but not even you know. They hated you... but not as much as you hated yourself. You are free now: free of torment, free of desire, free of hate… free from me. Perhaps in time, you will even be free of regret. Your service has been adequate… but my mistress has no further use for you.*

Drawing Ardruism from Fordon, Maynard carefully lowered him to the floor. In that moment, Fordon's body returned to its withered state, his strength and demeanour softening entirely.

'I guess the ytied were not behind me after all,' Fordon grimaced, showing bloodstained teeth. He gazed at Maynard with befuddlement and sadness. 'It was never meant to be.' Fordon held up his hand for Maynard to take. 'My desire to hurt you was so profound, but I could never understand why, and despite what I said, deep down, I had always hoped you would emancipate me from the incessant hate. We both know how blinded I was by it, but alone, I could do nothing. For all the pain I have caused, I do not deserve it, but allow me the temerity to ask that my death—and life—has not been a waste.'

Maynard tightened his grip on Fordon's hand. 'One man's hope is another man's bane. To protect loved ones is to deceive them. Misperception eventually begets understanding. One is not traitorous. One is not misbegotten… we must all fight for what we believe. I am sorry it came to this, old friend, and I will confront the one responsible for your misery.'

Fordon smiled one last time, this time with sincere happiness. 'All I ever wanted was to create a better world, never seeing that I did not have that right. May the ytied favour you for evermore.'

Ebony looked over Wilheard, the morning breeze tugging at her hair. Alim joined her and gazed at the horizon. The pair stood on the throne room balcony without speaking, appreciating a silence they thought might never come again. A sense of peace was in the air, but the two were not as alone as they had believed.

'Is Sombie up there moping?' Ninapaige said, breaking the calm. 'I cannot say I'm surprised. He is the unusual sort—equally sentimental and calm, as he is rash and aggressive.'

Ebony and Alim had left Maynard in the tower with Fordon's body. The sovereign knight was unresponsive, and despite (as expected) not showing any outward emotions, the devastation he felt for slaying an old friend was unmistakable.

Ninapaige was to the left of Ebony, sitting on the balcony's parapet with her back against the castle wall, her crossed legs perched in front. She was fiddling with something. 'They say that when a person dies, all the ytyism they created dies with them. That is, unless they pass their energy to another before death.'

Ninapage held up a gem, which Ebony did not immediately recognise. 'Hang on… is that…?

Now removed from the short sword's hilt, Ascendancy looked small and fragile. 'It's strange,' Ninapaige said, grinning at the sapphire. 'A part of him remains.'

'Does that mean Latnemirt could return?' Alim asked.

Ninapaige dropped the gem into her palm and closed her hand. 'Of flesh and bone? I would be surprised if he did. Although Latnemirt is gone, I still sense a tiny, beating force within. Perchance, he found a way of storing a fragment of his energy inside Ascendancy and thus away from my mistress. Alas, a majority of his power will return to her. That was inevitable, though it could have been much worse. With that in mind, I am sure, by now, you are beginning to understand life's hidden dangers.'

Ebony sighed but said nothing, too exhausted to think about future events. She swallowed as she looked at Ninapaige; this was the first time she had seen the impish woman properly.

'What will you do with Ascendancy?' Alim said, nodding to the Ninapaige's fist.

Ninapaige reopened her hand. It was empty. 'I will keep hold of it for now and out of sight of others. One never knows—it might actually be of use someday.'

Ninapaige, noticing the curiosity in Ebony's eyes, chuckled. 'Speaking of inherited energy, how have you found your new powers, girl?'

Ebony was unsure how to answer. What could she possibly say?

Ninapaige continued. 'You will have to keep it from now on, as it is not mine to own. Besides, I have carried it for centuries already, and I have grown tired of it.' The jester placed her hands behind her head and turned her attention to the sky. 'I hope her memories have not affected you too much.'

Ebony frowned. 'Memories?'

Ninapaige glanced at Ebony and then back to the sky. 'Just the powers? Perhaps time will see to that.'

'Who are you referring to?' Alim said, also frowning.

'Have you not figured it out, boy?'

'But why—how even—did you get hold of Evelyn's energy?'

Ninapaige chuckled again and stood up on the parapet. 'Fordon was mistaken about Ebony's heredity, but I was not about to correct such misunderstandings. Regardless, that is a subject for another time. For now, I bid you adieu.'

'Just one last thing,' Ebony exclaimed. 'If Fordon had killed me, he would have gained more than just my energy… I understand that, but what would he have been able to do if he had obtained Queen Evelyn's energy?'

No sooner had Ebony finished speaking, an eruption of cheers sounded from below, interrupting the tension.

Ninapaige smiled mischievously. 'I would not concern myself about such things if I were you, girl. If it is any consolation, though, it was never foretold.'

'Then why go through all the trouble?' Alim said curtly. 'Why did you bother showing up to help if everything is prophesied?'

Maintaining her grin, Ninapaige rolled her eyes. She pulled a mask with a peevish expression out from behind her back and put it over her face. 'Such matters are not as paradoxical as you might believe. Put it this way, boy— just because something is *said* to happen, that does not mean it *will* happen without a little persuasion, or even that it is inexorable. No prophecy, however divine, is truly set in stone. If it were, no one would seek to fulfil or challenge it. Some believe life is circular—in that it repeats itself. These same people, however, might believe that this circle can be broken and, in doing so, can create an alternate path.'

Alim placed his hands on his hips and looked to the horizon. 'But if this hypothetical circle is broken, would we not already know about it?'

'Perhaps... perhaps not... perhaps it just creates further circles: in one, said prophecy is achieved; in another, it is averted; and in another still, something incomprehensible happens.'

Alim shook his head. 'I will have to consider that theory further.'

Ninapaige burst out laughing. 'If it makes you feel better, boy, then go ahead, but perhaps save it for another time. I would prefer to lighten the mood, and by the sounds of it, I am not the only one ready for a happier frame of mind. If you don't hurry, the merriment will begin without you.' She turned to Ebony. 'As for you, girl, and like I said before, putting this newly-acquired energy in your stone heart might be wise. Fordon had the right idea with Ascendancy.'

Ninapaige turned her mask upside-down, its expression displaying laughter after she did so. 'By the way, girl, you did not answer me before. Was this *change* the sort you were looking for?'

Ebony offered Ninapaige a meek smile. That was the only response she could think to give.

Ninapaige leapt backwards off the ledge, disappearing from sight. Ebony stepped to where the jester had been and peered over, but all she could see was the moat below, its water undisturbed.

Alim put a hand on Ebony's shoulder. She turned round to see him smiling at her.

'You know, Ninapaige is right about one thing. Now is not the time for worry—we have done enough of that recently. Doubtless, many trials lie ahead, but we should now celebrate and relax.'

Ebony returned the smile and took Alim's hand in hers. 'Agreed. Perhaps not in that order, though. I really need a rest. Do you think we should disturb Maynard?'

'I'm sure he will join us when he is ready.'

Ebony yawned and led Alim away from the balcony. 'I expect you're right. He will probably want some time alone to gather his thoughts. Like all of us, I guess he still has much to learn.'

Ebony and Alim walked side-by-side back into the throne room. Vincent Sawney, as he had been since before the two went to confront Fordon, was there waiting. On Ebony's suggestion, he remained in the hall and spent the time tending to Oliath.

Oliath had recovered since Ebony last saw him, and whatever Latnemirt had done to him, the spell had since dispersed. Before she and Alim had stepped from the balcony, Oliath and the others had already made their way outside; from what Vincent told Ebony, they were sick of being stuck between the castle walls. Word of Fordon's defeat had not long reached the masses below, and she gathered that the cheers a short while ago were, at least partly, down to Oliath's emergence from the castle.

Vincent offered Ebony and Alim a crooked smile. 'I'm glad to see you in relatively good shape, lass... you too, mate.'

Ebony returned a weak smile.

'I presume all that bangin' and crashin' were down to you,' Vincent continued, looking at Ebony in particular. 'I still can't get my head round all that magic stuff, but the main thing is that you came out all right.'

'We made it in the end,' Ebony said. 'Just in time, I like to think.'

Alim nodded in agreement. 'You did amazingly, dear Ebony. You should be proud of everything you have achieved, including getting out of that tower.'

'True,' Vincent said. He had watched as Ebony and Alim ascended the outside of Evelyn's tower after a Wilheard soldier noticed them. Vincent had been in the middle of a battle at the time, but it did not take long for him to catch up with the pair. 'That was incredibly brave of you two, and I can tell you now that I wouldn't 'ave done that.'

Remnant Tales of Stilly:
Passion and Benevolence

Ebony chucked. 'I am just glad you didn't dig through the rubble only to find nothing on the other side.'

Vincent grunted amusement at the comment. He folded his arms and looked around the throne room. 'Talking of rubble, this place is a mess. Whatever went on in that tower just now has probably caused significant structural damage. I wouldn't recommend we hang about here if you understand my reasoning.' He paused a moment and looked towards the balcony. 'Come to think of it, where is the other one?'

'Maynard is likely where we left him,' Ebony said flatly, tiredness evident in her voice. 'I am sure he can care for himself, so there is no need to worry.'

'Maynard, eh?' Vincent murmured. That was the first time he had heard the vigilante's name, but he supposed he would hear it more from now on. 'In any case, if you are sure about that, I suggest we get moving.'

'I suppose people will be wondering what has become of us,' Alim said, patting himself down and checking his pockets. He reached into a pouch and gingerly removed the damaged remains of his smoking pipe. He looked at the snapped stem and sighed. 'And I'm sure they will be relieved to see us in one piece.'

Ebony smiled and linked her arms round Alim's. 'I guess we should be grateful nothing more serious is broken.'

'Right you are,' Alim groaned, walking by Ebony's side and following behind Vincent.

The trio made their way through the shadowed corridors of the castle and down the stone steps that eventually led to the courtyard.

Stepping out into the opening, Ebony shielded her eyes from the morning sun and made her way over the makeshift drawbridge.

'Ebony!' the familiar voice of Hazel Dolb called, standing behind a line of guards keeping civilians away from the castle. She was hopping up and down and waving. As Ebony approached, Hazel leapt to embrace her friend. 'I have been keeping an eye out for you. Tender spirits, you sure took your time! I'm glad you are safe, Ebs.'

'I am glad you are safe as well,' Ebony said, hugging Hazel back.

Hazel released Ebony and turned her attention to Alim. She gave him a squeeze. 'You too, Scruffy. I'm pleased to see you safe.'

Alim wrapped his arms about Hazel as best he could, his grip light in comparison. He did not know what to make of that nickname.

With her hands on her hips, Hazel stepped away a few paces. 'I won't bother asking what you got up to in there. There will be plenty of time for all that later. It looks like almost everyone made it out all right, but where is... whats-his-face--'

'Maynard?' Alim interjected. He looked towards the castle's front tower. 'He is alive, but if he is not still in the castle, then...' He shrugged.

Ebony shifted the conversation. 'How about you and everyone else?'

'I have a few scrapes and bruises, and I'm in need of a clean, but otherwise, I'm all right, m'dear. My parents are fine and at the farm with Colossus, who is on the mend from the other day. We are lucky compared to other people.'

Ebony looked down Castle Way and peered over Wilheard. New Market Square, where most of the battling had occurred, was a particular state. Stalls and similar wooden structures, which had only days earlier been a familiar sight, now lay scattered over the cobbled streets, revealing damaged homes, shops and other buildings. The absence of Clock Tower was, unsurprisingly, most noticeable: from Wilheard's tallest structure to a sorrowful mass of rubble in seconds.

Ebony, along with Alim and Hazel, made her way down castle way. 'Have you seen my parents... I mean, my father and Sylvia recently?' she asked Hazel, catching what she was saying a moment too late.

'Well, Sylvia is doubtless still in the surgery, but I saw your pop not long after all the fighting stopped,' Hazel replied, not seeming to have noticed Ebony's lapse of speech. 'I told him I would watch out for you, but it shouldn't come as a surprise that he will still be worried and is probably not far away.'

After passing through a few streets towards the surgery, Ebony found her father. He spun round after hearing his daughter's voice and jogged to her.

'Thank goodness you are all right,' Abraham said, lifting Ebony off the ground with a hug even tighter than Hazel's. He placed his daughter back on her feet and brushed the unkempt hair from her face. 'Are you all right? Are you hurt in any way? Do you need any help?'

'I am well,' Ebony chuckled, hugging her father again, 'all the better seeing you are safe and sound.'

Abraham gave Hazel a quick cuddle and then looked at Alim. Stepping towards the younger man, Abraham looked him straight in the eyes and offered his right hand to shake; his expression was firm, as was his grip, but both softened a short time later. Grinning widely, Abraham pulled Alim in for a hug and gave him a hearty slap on the back. 'I am happy to see you make it out all right as well. Thank you for bringing my Ebony back safely.'

For a moment, Alim remained silent, winded by the embrace. 'It was my pleasure,' he said eventually. 'In truth, it was in my interest to stay by her side—dear Ebony, here, is phenomenal.'

This made Abraham laugh. 'That is one way of describing her. After all, she has put up with me for years!'

This laughter gained the attention of several bystanders, including that of Basil Wolleb. He approached the group, as did Benjamin Oswin, who had been with him the whole time.

Basil forced a smile barely visible under his white beard, but he could not hide the bags under his eyes, which Ebony noticed he was struggling to keep open.

'Ms Ebony Gibenn, if I am not mistaken,' the mayor said as he approached the group. He stopped an arm's length away and looked at Alim. 'Forgive me, but I have forgotten your name, Mister…?'

'Larring,' Alim replied, also giving his first name.

'Very well. I will remember that.'

'I will remember, at the very least,' Benjamin smiled, introducing himself to the group. 'I am Mayor Wolleb's assistant.'

Basil harrumphed at the remark, although he felt no real offence. 'I am sure we will all get to know one another well enough in the near future, Benjamin. In the meantime—and if you folks do not mind—I would simply like a chat.'

'How can we help you?' Ebony asked.

Basil looked from side to side as if to make sure no one was listening and then leant closer to Ebony and Alim. 'I hope you do not mind my saying so, but I have seen the two of you quite a lot the past few days, albeit from a distance. You seem to have been very busy, as has that swordsman... I have no desire to pry into private affairs, but if you could fill me in on anything that might be in my—and Wilheard's—interest, I would welcome it.'

Ebony sighed. 'There is a lot to say, and I am not sure if I can easily find the right words, but I do know that the one behind Wilheard's attack has been... dealt with, for want of a better term.'

'You mean that Fordon Latnemirt?' Benjamin said, recalling the disembodied voice before the battle. 'It seemed to come from the sky.'

Ebony nodded.

'I see,' Basil said, taking a deep breath and looking to the middle distance. He exhaled sharply. 'And what of the vigilante?'

'I wouldn't expect him to emerge from the front of the castle if I were you,' Alim said. 'I am sure you know as well as we do that he is not much of a conversationalist.'

'Everyone needs to come to teams with what has happened, in their own time and way,' Ebony added. 'Maynard is no different. He will find you when he is ready to talk.'

'Maynard,' Basil repeated. 'It is nice to know his name finally. Calling him a vigilante was getting tiresome.'

There was a moment of silence, which Ebony broke. 'Are we in trouble?'

Basil forced another smile and shook his head. 'In truth, it is difficult to know what actions to take, which I am sure you can appreciate, but I am not about to go round interrogating people.'

This time, Ebony forced a smile. She bowed her head. 'I do not know if we can be of much help, but I—and I am sure Alim too—will be happy to do so however possible.'

'You have my gratitude,' Basil said. He gave a drawn-out sigh and looked around.

Many people were merry: cheering, laughing, and simply shouting joyfully.

'Do the celebrations upset you?' Ebony asked Basil, noticing deep creases on his brow.

'People are entitled to celebrate, but I must say I am not feeling any elation. Not everyone made it through the battle, and my thoughts are with those who lost someone.'

'Revelry is at the back of my mind, too,' Benjamin asserted. 'It is difficult to make sense of the destruction Wilheard has suffered, and of course, any deaths are hard to take. How something like this could happen in this small town… Then there is the matter of those beasts, the sorcery and more. I want to—or rather *need* to—understand how such things can exist.'

'Some will know enough to help the rest of us.' Ebony reached into a pocket and removed a familiar heart-shaped object. She briefly studied the crystal in her palm and smiled wryly; it really had been her lucky charm. 'I believe I know someone who can do just that.'

This comment earned Ebony a frown from the entire group, except for her father, whose expression showed comprehension.

Basil studied Ebony's face for a moment before clasping his hands behind his back and taking a step back. 'As I said, I am sure we will all get to know each other well enough in the near future. Take care of yourselves,' he said as he walked away, followed by Benjamin.

As the mayor and his assistant walked from view, Hazel turned her attention back to Ebony. 'Who is this mystery person you spoke of, Ebs?'

'That is a good question,' Ebony said. 'She is a doctor and a mother, but she is much more than what she appears, and I am sure she will explain what that all means in due time.'

Ebony grinned then, more widely than she had in some time. 'I think I have had my fill of change for now, but when I think of all the good that has come from it—learning of a world I did not even know existed and finding people old and new—then it is a change I am glad I experienced.'

Remnant Tales of Stilly:
Passion and Benevolence

Epilogue

Summer was at its end, and a chill had replaced the forest's humidity.

Maynard was alone with his thoughts in the darkness of the trees, away from human companionship and only Lithe for company. As he often did, the sovereign knight had told no one where he was heading but said he would not be long away.

Lithe vaulted a collapsed sarsen wall and came to a sudden halt. Patting its flank, Maynard dismounted the shire, walked the west of the spring, and under willow trees until coming to a dead end. At the end of this passage, below his feet, was an empty tomb filled with nothing more than stone and soil. The grave had no tombstone, but words were etched into a nearby cliffside.

Maynard lowered himself to his knees and inspected the carvings afore him. With his hand, he traced the marks stretching the length of the rocky surface. His fingers were too large to fit in the grooves, but Maynard knew that he had been the one to scratch them all the same. He pushed the thought from his mind and instead considered the inscriptions. He had read the archaic wording many times, but with old onuses put to rest, perhaps now the message would make for better understanding:

Maynard Suavlant.

Sleep, Sovereign Knight of Stilly, but not so deeply.

One man's hope is another man's bane.
To protect loved ones is to deceive them.
Misperception eventually begets understanding.
One is **not** traitorous; one is **not** misbegotten.

May your passion and benevolence absolve us from what we impose upon you.

'Are you still at a loss, Sombie?' asked a child-like voice.

386

Remnant Tales of Stilly:
Passion and Benevolence

Maynard, unstartled, stood and looked up into the trees. There, he spied a flamboyant figure, a porcelain mask with a playful smile pressed to the being's face. Maynard had felt the woman's presence before reaching the spring but had waited for her to approach him. Although this was their first encounter, Maynard knew who she was.

Ninapaige gazed at the sovereign knight for a long moment. 'You needn't feel alone anymore,' she said, speaking in the language of yore. 'You have gained much in the way of camaraderie, and I see they are all doing well, thanks in part to your efforts.'

Indeed, almost everyone had managed to return to some sort of normality in spite of all that had happened. Some continued to grieve for the dead, and others opted to support those who mourned. Most others wanted to mend the damage caused during the fighting and (for the sake of their sanity) put the summer behind them. Few were ignorant enough to want to forget what had happened entirely, even if that were a possibility: Wilheard's people will eventually erect memorials and monuments, observing annual commemorations henceforth.

'My success is a reflection of their efforts,' Maynard said. 'Additionally, I am indebted to you, as is the one you call Sylvia.'

Ninapaige laughed and lay on her belly, resting her head in her palms. 'Is she now? It is wonderful knowing that my efforts have not been in vain. Yet, we digress. Are you still at a loss?'

Maynard did not answer. He looked away from the imp.

Ninapaige rolled onto her back so that Maynard appeared upside down. 'There is much ahead that needs your attention, Sombie, but perhaps not in Wilheard.'

The jester re-righted herself and removed her mask. 'I notice that several individuals in the town have taken an interest in the ways of ytyism, besides Sylvia, the girl, and that scholar boy. I know you have been watching these people and can tell you do not expect any trouble to arise.' Ninapaige simpered at Maynard. 'I am thrilled you do not consider me a threat, either.'

That final part caused the hairs on Maynard's neck to stand on end. She was burrowing into his consciousness.

Ninapaige harrumphed upon noticing Maynard's agitation. 'If you want my advice, and I know you do, then take your new friends and head east to Thane. There, you will find a familiar red-haired man who will be pleased to see your face. Unlike you, he has not long been back in this world, and although he hides it, he is just as troubled as you are. There is no point hanging round here, and when it comes to ytyism, there are greater dangers further afield.'

Maynard remained silent.

'Do not look so alarmed,' Ninapaige said. 'As I stated a moment ago, you are far from alone, and you need not think you are.'

Maynard turned away from Ninapaige then. 'I will do as suggested,' he said, walking away. 'Thank you, little one.'

Ninapaige laughed. 'We will meet again, Sombie.'

Remnant Tales of Stilly:
Passion and Benevolence

Appendix

Stilly Historical Notes.

Castle Stilly & Sanine Lineage.
(Archives of Stilly: Volume one)

Like many stone keep castles, the decidedly ostentatious Castle Stilly (often mistakenly named Castle of Wilheard because of its location) was built as robustly as possible to withstand the inevitable attacks it would suffer throughout history. The castle's curtain walls are made from gneiss stone, taken from the rocky mountains of Adelaide. The thickness and height of the walls measure 15 feet wide and up to 40 feet tall, respectively. The castle's four towers, also of gneissic design, range from 60 to 180 feet. The shortest towers to the southeast of the castle served as the main outlook point of Wilheard; the three towers on the west side served as keeps and housed the royal chambers.

The castle exterior is complete with a moat, a wooden drawbridge, a gatehouse that also serves as a barbican, an iron portcullis and walkway battlements.

Work on Castle Stilly began in 1299SN and was completed an impressive twenty-two years later in 1321SN. It accommodated five generations of royals from King Theodore Sanine (1278-1360SN) to Queen Evelyn Sanine (1440- ?SN), the latter abandoning the castle at the age of twenty-eight. Evelyn Sanine's succeeding lineage (if any) and year of death are unknown.

First Generation.

King Theodore Sanine (1278SN-1360SN). **Queen Mikki Sanine** (1285SN-1375SN).

Arcane genius Theodore Sanine's ambitions showed at an early age. Although envisaging many great ideas throughout his life, it is unanimously agreed upon that the uniquely designed Castle Stilly is his queerest and by far his most ambitious innovation.

Remnant Tales of Stilly:
Passion and Benevolence

Although not unexpected in the light of his eccentricity, Theodore Sanine's choice to have Castle Stilly built on the northern cliffs of Wilheard was greatly criticised at the time of construction. The development proceeded nonetheless, and his proposals were followed precisely. Credit to Theodore's intellect, the castle remains standing centuries later.

Theodore Sanine married his queen in 1220SN. Not much is known of Mikki Sanine in the way of her preliminary family tree, including her maiden name. Although Mikki Sanine is said to have been strict, she was never considered cruel. Three years into marriage, and one year after castle completion, Queen Mikki gave birth to their daughter Teri and two years later their son Paul.

After the passing of Theodore, Mikki abdicated heirship of the throne to Teri.

Second Generation.

Queen Teri [Olvewhort] Sanine (1323SN-1379SN). **King Ithel Olvewhort.** (1328SN-1379SN). **Prince Olann Olvewhort.** (1347SN-1375SN). **Prince Paul Sanine.** 1325SN-1390SN

Queen Teri married in 1246SN to the wealthy Ithel Olvewhort, having fallen in love with his generosity. In 1247SN, Queen Teri gave birth to her only son Olann.

Because of her stringent upbringing, Queen Teri was a remarkably well-organised and courteous woman but considerably more indulgent than her mother Mikki, and although her rule over Stilly mirrored that of her parents, the raising of her child Prince Olann did not. This submissive attitude towards her son was primarily her biggest flaw, and Prince Olann was known to take advantage of his mother's docility. Although an intelligent man in his own right, Prince Olann was particularly belligerent. Because of this, Prince Olann never became the heir to the throne and lost his life at the age of twenty-five after taking part in a petty dispute. His death came the same year as his grandmother's.

In 1379SN, King Ithel died after a short illness, believed to be Acute Bronchitis. Never recuperating from the death of her son four years earlier and with the sudden death of her husband, Queen Teri committed suicide soon after by plunging from one of the castle's walkway battlements.

Third Generation.

King Doran Sanine (1355SN-1444SN). **Queen Charmion Sanine.** (1362SN-1448SN).

After the sad life and death of Queen Teri Sanine, who had no further children or grandchildren as heirs, the throne by default passed to her younger brother Prince Paul Sanine. After the death of his sister Queen Teri, the infirm Prince Paul had no desire to take heir. Left despondent by his sibling's suicide, along with the rumours that he saw the throne as cursed, Prince Paul handed power directly to his own son Doron: the official third heir to the throne. Granted the throne during his late twenties, the new King Doron vowed to continue the type of rule Teri had been known for. Yet, over the years, the apprehensive young king invariably worried whether his ruling was best for the kingdom of Stilly. This behaviour gave impressions of weak-mindedness, with the people of Stilly assuming the king was vulnerable to manipulation. Such negativity often ended unfounded, however; although worrisome, King Doron was not a fool, and he saw through all those who sought to deceive him, enforcing his power in a way that showed he was anything but weak. Certainly, it could be said that Doron was resolute in his decisions, even in the face of an outcry. One such instance was his matrimony to Charmion, a beautiful woman of peasant birth whom he married several years into his reign. Charmion mirrored King Doron's personality in many ways.

Although there were objections towards Doran and Charmion's marriage for a time, most cynics came to respect the matrimony.

Fourth Generation.

King Godfrey Sanine (1400SN-1466SN). **Queen Verity [Pothelm] Sanine** (1406SN-1467). **Princess Clover Sanine** (1404SN-Unknown.)

Remnant Tales of Stilly:
Passion and Benevolence

Soon after their marriage, Queen Charmion conceived and gave birth to future king Godfrey, four years later having their second child Princess Clover. Neither child seemed to mirror their parents in later life.

When aged in his late sixties, Doron handed the responsibilities of the throne over to his son Godfrey. Upon renouncing the throne, Doron famously stated: *"I have had this emotional encumber for most my life; these royal shackles will subjugate me no more"*.

By the time King Godfrey took to the throne, he was already married to Queen Verity. Verity was in the early stages of pregnancy and gave birth to their only daughter Evelyn just shy of nine months later. Overall, both King Godfrey and Queen Verity were considered reputable rulers.

A pious man, King Godfrey developed close relations with the clergy throughout his time of rule and had a very close friendship with the minach of the time, Emmanuel Grellic. During his life, King Godfrey was also believed to be secretive, accused by town folk and even other royal members of hiding mysterious possessions. Although such accusations never became known, it was rumoured that one of his secrets was a supposedly unique but dangerous ornament, which he was said to be monopolising. This was partially true; although Godfrey possessed such an object, he did not want it or desire anyone else to own it. This object's origins (and apparent otherworldly power) set a deep fear in King Godfrey; not only could it be dangerous in the wrong hands, but its existence contradicted his spiritual beliefs. Allegedly, Godfrey had it hidden with his daughter.

Although the above is conjecture and unsubstantiated rumours, what is known is that a renegade assassinated King Godfrey, Stilly's final king, bringing about what is now referred to as the Fall of Sovereignty. Queen Verity died of pneumonia one year after King Godfrey.

Clover was a wild card, with many seeing her as boyish. Although the princess was not next in line for the throne, this was never a concern for her. Like her great grandfather, Prince Paul, Clover was uninterested in becoming queen and was apathetic towards the royal atmosphere. As soon as Princess Clover reached the age of sixteen, she left Wilheard in favour of the more tranquil province of Adelaide. Princess Clover is not detailed after her departure, except for the rumours that she bore children.

Fifth Generation.

Queen Evelyn Sanine (1440SN-Unknown). Abandoned throne in 1468SN. Possible spouse or children unknown.

Queen Evelyn Sanine came to the throne soon after the death of her father, yet abandoned Wilheard in 1468SN, one year after the passing of her mother Queen Verity. Location after abandonment and reasons for the act (notwithstanding the conspiracies mentioned above) remain unknown, although it is strongly believed she, along with Minach Emmanuel and a select few, fled to Thane before departing elsewhere in Stilly.

Evidence of spouse, children and further knowledge is indefinite.

Printed in Great Britain
by Amazon

50146133R00218